Must Love Hellhounds

The *New York Times* Bestseller

New York Times Bestselling Authors

Charlaine Harris
Nalini Singh
Ilona Andrews
Meljean Brook

Four Tales of Devilish Dogs

BERKLEY

$7.99 U.S.
$9.99 CAN

S EAN

Praise for the authors of

Must Love Hellhounds

#1 *New York Times* Bestselling Author

CHARLAINE HARRIS

"[Has] the sure touch of a master." —*Crescent Blues*

"Harris weaves storytelling magic." —Lynn Hightower

New York Times Bestselling Author

NALINI SINGH

"Paranormal romance at its best." —*Publishers Weekly*

"Nalini Singh continues to dazzle and ensnare new readers." —*A Romance Review*

New York Times Bestselling Author

ILONA ANDREWS

"Andrews . . . demonstrates her mastery at balancing dark humor, clever mystery, and supernatural jeopardy. Andrews is the total package!" —*Romantic Times*

"Andrews's edgy series stands apart from similar fantasies . . . owing to its complex world building and skilled characterizations." —*Library Journal*

New York Times Bestselling Author

MELJEAN BROOK

"A fascinating series." —Nalini Singh

"Brook . . . creates fantastic, death-defying love . . . extremely erotic . . . with a paranormal twist." —*Fresh Fiction*

MUST LOVE
Hellhounds

Charlaine Harris
Nalini Singh
Ilona Andrews
Meljean Brook

THE BERKLEY PUBLISHING GROUP
Published by the Penguin Group
Penguin Group (USA) Inc.
375 Hudson Street, New York, New York 10014, USA
Penguin Group (Canada), 90 Eglinton Avenue East, Suite 700, Toronto, Ontario M4P 2Y3, Canada
(a division of Pearson Penguin Canada Inc.)
Penguin Books Ltd., 80 Strand, London WC2R 0RL, England
Penguin Group Ireland, 25 St. Stephen's Green, Dublin 2, Ireland (a division of Penguin Books Ltd.)
Penguin Group (Australia), 250 Camberwell Road, Camberwell, Victoria 3124, Australia
(a division of Pearson Australia Group Pty. Ltd.)
Penguin Books India Pvt. Ltd., 11 Community Centre, Panchsheel Park, New Delhi—110 017, India
Penguin Group (NZ), 67 Apollo Drive, Rosedale, North Shore 0632, New Zealand
(a division of Pearson New Zealand Ltd.)
Penguin Books (South Africa) (Pty.) Ltd., 24 Sturdee Avenue, Rosebank, Johannesburg 2196,
South Africa

Penguin Books Ltd., Registered Offices: 80 Strand, London WC2R 0RL, England

MUST LOVE HELLHOUNDS

A Berkley Book / published by arrangement with the authors

PRINTING HISTORY
Berkley trade paperback edition / September 2009
Berkley mass-market edition / September 2010

Cover art by Don Sipley. Cover design by George Long.
Interior text design by Kristin del Rosario.

For information, address: The Berkley Publishing Group,
a division of Penguin Group (USA) Inc.,
375 Hudson Street, New York, New York 10014.

ISBN: 978-0-425-23633-8

BERKLEY®
Berkley Books are published by The Berkley Publishing Group,
a division of Penguin Group (USA) Inc.,
375 Hudson Street, New York, New York 10014.
BERKLEY® is a registered trademark of Penguin Group (USA) Inc.
The "B" design is a trademark of Penguin Group (USA) Inc.

PRINTED IN THE UNITED STATES OF AMERICA

10 9 8 7 6 5 4 3 2 1

Contents

The Britlingens Go to Hell

Charlaine Harris

Batanya and Clovache were cleaning their armor in one of the courtyards of the Britlingen Collective, which sits atop a hill in the ancient city of Spauling. It was a fine summer day, and they sat on benches that they'd positioned to catch the sun.

"I'm as pale as a pooka belly," Clovache said.

"Not quite," Batanya said, after looking at Clovache rather seriously. Batanya was the older of the two; she was twenty-eight to Clovache's twenty-four. Batanya was pale, too, since she spent most of her time in armor of one kind or another, but that didn't bother Batanya.

"Oh, thank you. *Not quite*," Clovache said, imitating Batanya's husky voice. It was a pretty bad imitation. Batanya smiled. She and Clovache had worked together for five years, and there wasn't much they didn't know about each other. They had both done most of their growing up within the Collective walls.

"You are a bit like a pooka, though. Your hair is the same color as the back fur, and you like the night life better than the daylight. But I'm sure you wouldn't taste as good deep-fried."

Clovache stretched out a foot to kick Batanya, very lightly. "We'll go out to eat later," she said. "How about Pooka Palace?"

Batanya nodded. "Unless Trovis is there. If he's in the place, I'm leaving."

The two women worked in a friendly silence for a few minutes. They were polishing what they called their "liquid armor," the most popular single item of body defense in the Britlingen's huge collection. Liquid armor wasn't really liquid. It resembled a wet suit more than anything, but it was considerably easier to don. There was a keypad the size of a credit card on the chest. It allowed for communication with anyone else wearing a similar suit, and it had a personal sequence programmed into it that allowed only one wearer to use the armor. The material would toughen when the sequence was pressed in, to allow the wearer to be almost invulnerable; without this procedure, the armor was ineffective. The protocol had been added to prevent the armor from being stolen. Before the code had been added, a few Britlingens had been murdered for their armor. It was used in cooler weather. The two women had already cleaned their summer-weight gear.

Batanya had turned her suit inside out and was cleaning the inner surface with a pleasant-scented solvent from a large green pot. Clovache was using the all-purpose cleaner on the hardened pieces that could be strapped on over the liquid armor.

Clovache threw a finished piece down on the towel she'd spread on the ground and picked up another one. "Hard drill this morning," she observed.

"Trovis was not in a good mood," Batanya said.

"And why would that be?" Clovache asked, trying to sound innocent.

Batanya flushed a little, causing the scar that ran across her right cheek to stand out. Clovache had heard people tease Batanya about the scar, but they only did it once.

"He tried to jump me in the bathroom last night. I had to give him an elbow to the gut. Trovis is making a fool of himself."

Clovache agreed. "If he's trying to show you who's boss, he *is* a fool," she said. "And if he keeps it up, I shall go to Flechette and put it to her that Trovis should be removed from his command."

"That would make Trovis crazy, which is a good thing," Batanya said. "But it would make us look weak."

Clovache looked startled, but after a moment, she nodded. "I understand. We should be able to eat whatever Trovis puts on the table." She tested the strength of a strap. "If worse comes to worst, perhaps he'll have an accident."

"Hush your mouth," Batanya said, genuinely shocked. "After all—"

"Britlingens don't kill Britlingens," Clovache said dutifully. "We leave that to the rest of the world."

That was the first lesson a novice learned when he or she came to the fortress.

"There are exceptions," Clovache said stubbornly as she gathered up her armor. "And his obsession with you provides one."

"Not for you to say." Batanya stood, the sheet containing all her paraphernalia draped over one shoulder. "I'll meet you at the gate in a couple of hours?"

"Surely," her junior said.

Later that same afternoon, the two bodyguards strolled down to the Pooka Palace. Batanya grumbled about the narrow streets and their ancient cobblestones, which made it very impractical to keep a hovercraft at the castle. This was a source of grief to Batanya, who loved to drive fast.

Pooka Palace had opened its outside section in honor of the balmy weather. The place was full of familiar faces from the Collective. Though Britlingens had the run of the city, they tended to linger close to the hilltop castle. Naturally, the shops that clustered in the winding old streets around the base of the hill were mostly dedicated to serving the bodyguards and assassins who lived in the ancient castle. There were a lot of storefronts that advertised repair services, either of armor or of arms. There were magic shops filled with arcane items the witches of the Collective might need or want. There were dark-fronted shops filled with bits of machinery that the mechs found intriguing. There were at least a score of bars and restaurants, but Pooka Palace was Clovache's favorite.

Waiting at a fairly clean table was a friend of theirs named Geit, a broad-shouldered and genial man who could swing a sword with enough force to take off a head with one lop. He was an assassin; though Clovache and Batanya were in the bodyguard division, they didn't discriminate in their friendships as some did.

Geit had already ordered baskets of fried pooka and fish, and they'd just toasted with three tankards of ale when they saw a child from the castle approaching, wearing the red vest of a messenger. Though walking quickly, the boy was also playing with a conjuring ball; it was clearly a cheap one, but the ball was still charged with enough magic to keep it in the air for a few seconds each time he tossed it up. The child interrupted his play to scan the faces at the tables. He spotted them and trotted over.

"Lady Warrior, excuse me," said the child, bowing. "Are you Senior Batanya?"

"I am, squirt," Batanya said. She drained her mug of ale. "Who needs what?"

"Commander Trovis has, ah, requested that you and your junior come up to the fortress immediately, to the Hall of Contracts."

Geit whistled. "But you just got back from a job. Why would Trovis send you out again?"

"After the last one, I'd hoped we'd rest longer," Batanya said. "Getting out of that hotel was no fun, especially carrying a client who would burn up in sunlight. Well, we must go, Geit. Have a drink on us." After hastily finishing their baskets of food (a Britlingen never passes up a chance to eat), she paid the bar tab and looked away as Clovache gave Geit a quick kiss on the cheek. The two women followed the child back up the winding streets to the gate of the Collective. The guards on duty recognized them and nodded to indicate they could reenter without the usual search.

The Hall of Contracts was conveniently close to the witches' and mechs' wing, since witchcraft (enhanced by science) provided the transportation to at least fifty percent of the missions. In fact, Batanya couldn't remember the last time she'd gone overland to a job.

The hall itself didn't look important. It was a just a large room, one wall of which was decorated with some indifferent paintings. This was called the Wall of Shame; the art hung there depicted employees of the Collective who had screwed up in some notable way. (The Britlingen instruction model was heavily weighted toward learning by the mistakes of one's predecessors.) Aside from the paintings and some benches, there was only a table with a few chairs, a large lightsource, and some writing instruments.

Trovis was leaning back in one of the wooden chairs, his feet propped on the table. This was inappropriate behavior for the Hall of Contracts, for these contracts were the lifeblood of the Collective. Signing each contract was an important moment. Not only was this the main source of income for the Collective, but each contract might bring about the death of the Britlingens charged with fulfilling it.

"His promotion's gone to his head," Clovache muttered. "He wouldn't have dared behave so a halfyear ago."

The child scampered off once he'd gotten his tip, and Batanya and Clovache advanced to the table. One of the senior commanders, Flechette, entered from a side door, and since she had a staff in her hands, she used it to sweep Trovis's legs to the side, neatly knocking him out of his chair.

"Respect for the room," she said harshly, as Trovis scrambled to right himself. The two bodyguards kept their faces absolutely blank, which took a lot of effort. Flechette paid no attention to the lower-ranked Trovis's shock and anger, but threw herself into one of the chairs. Despite Flechette's apparent age—she looked at least sixty, which few Britlingens attained—she moved like a much younger woman. "You've summoned us," Flechette said. "What have you, Sergeant?"

Trovis collected himself. If he'd had a weapon, perhaps he would have drawn on his superior, but he'd come to the hall unarmed—an unusual circumstance for a Britlingen, even as poor a Britlingen as Trovis. "This customer has come in person," he said, biting off his words. He gestured toward a man standing at the rear of the hall, apparently examining one of the paintings—the one of Johanson the Fool, Batanya noted. She was trying to avoid meeting Trovis's eyes.

"What happened to this fellow?" asked a light voice, and the stranger turned to look at them inquiringly. He was a couple of inches taller than Batanya, who was of medium height for a woman. The stranger was lightly built, and fair, and wearing clothes that signaled he was from the city-state of Pardua, which lay about two hours' drive from Spauling. Batanya had visited there on business several times. In Pardua, poor vision was corrected by brilliantly colored and decorated goggles, and the stranger wore a striking pair: a shrieking blue, spotted with artificial purple stones. They made him look remarkably silly.

Since no one else spoke, Batanya said, "Johanson the Fool walked his client into an ambush. When it was over, he and his client were as full of darts as a pincushion has pins."

"I don't know what a pincushion is, but I take your meaning," the stranger said. He cast another look at the grisly picture. "I am here to hire two Britlingens as bodyguards. I don't want to end up like Johanson's client." He shuddered elaborately.

"Very well," said Flechette. "You understand, clients don't actually show up at the Collective very often. Usually the contract is negotiated on the witchweb."

"Is that right? I'm sorry I broke with proper procedure." The blond dandy minced over to the table. "I happened to be in Spauling and thought I'd come directly to the source. See what I was getting, in other words."

"You would be getting Clovache and her senior, Batanya," Trovis said, smiling broadly. "After he described the job, Commander Flechette, I knew they would be perfect."

"Why?" Flechette said. She had little use for Trovis, and she'd never hidden her opinion. After Batanya and Trovis had both been out of commission following a previous set-to, Flechette had begun watching the man like a hawk.

"They protected their last client under circumstances that no one foresaw," Trovis said, his voice silky. "Who could not be impressed by their performance? I am sure they can handle this."

Flechette eyed Trovis before turning her attention to the client. "What is your goal, stranger? And your name, incidentally."

"I'm so sorry! My name is Crick. And I need to retrieve something of mine that I lost in a rather dangerous place."

Bodyguards go into tense situations all the time (especially ones of Batanya and Clovache's caliber), so it wasn't the word "dangerous" that bothered Batanya: it was the bullshit detector shrilling in her brain. She looked at Clovache, who nodded grimly. Crick was not telling all the truth, certainly; and he was not the silly, rather effeminate Parduan he portrayed himself to be. The oblivious Trovis wouldn't have spotted the excellent muscle tone in the slender body. The bodyguards had. But clients lied all the time, didn't they? Batanya shrugged: what could you do? Clovache nodded again: nothing.

Trovis and Flechette went over the basic contract with the Parduan. It covered the price of transference by witchweb to the site the client chose. It covered the directive of the mission—to get Crick and his property back in one piece. It contained the standard insurance clause, so the treatment of any injuries the bodyguards sustained would be paid for by the client.

Batanya and Clovache paid attention, because that was part of the deal. All bodyguards had to be aware of what they'd agreed to do, and what they hadn't. Though the two had stood in the Hall of Contracts dozens of times and listened to exactly the same discussion, this preparation was as much part of the work as getting their weapons ready. No deniability on this job.

At last the prolonged contract session was over. Since Crick was a first-time customer of the Britlingen Collective, it had taken a bit longer than usual. Batanya noticed that Crick had asked some very shrewd questions.

"Will you sign?" Flechette asked formally, when Crick declared himself satisfied.

Crick picked up the pen and signed the contract.

"The client has agreed. Will you sign, senior?" Flechette asked Batanya. She sighed, but she picked up the pen and scribbled her name.

"You, junior?" Clovache followed suit.

"Now what?" Crick asked brightly.

"We withdraw, you give your bodyguards your place of destination, and they fetch the appropriate gear. They meet you here, then you go to the witchwing through that door. The witches and the mechs take over the transportation." Trovis was bored now, and showing it. He hadn't found an excuse to provoke anyone into a fight, the client had the money and had paid the asking price, and furthermore Trovis had arranged to rid himself of his most irritating subordinates for at least a few days—possibly permanently. There was nothing more to be wrung from the situation. He took the earliest opportunity to slip out of the room, if a rather solid man six feet tall can "slip" anywhere.

"Where's he slinking off to?" Clovache muttered.

"Some quiet spot where he can think of some other way to make me miserable," Batanya answered, and then was sorry she'd spoken. She hoped Flechette hadn't heard. Going over the head of one's superior officer to complain to a higher rank was not admired among the members of the Britlingen Collective.

But Flechette seemed intent on observing the courtesies required by her position as commander: she wished the client a successful journey, clapped Clovache on the shoulder and shook Batanya's hand, and advised them to eat before they left . . . her standard farewell. Then she drew herself up, gave the Britlingen salute, and said, "What is the law?"

"The client's word," Batanya said smartly. Clovache was a beat behind her.

Crick was watching, his eyes intent behind the ridiculous goggles. When Flechette had left, the two bodyguards drew closer to him.

"What temperature should we pack for?" Clovache asked. "What kind of fighting?"

Crick had been listening while the contract was explained, but nonetheless he asked, "You can't tell anyone what I say; is that right?"

Batanya nodded. Clovache just looked resigned.

"To Hell," Crick said. "We're going to Hell."

After a long moment of silence, Clovache said, "We'll need our summer armor, then."

"What happened was this," Crick said, suddenly chatty. He'd taken a seat at the table, and Clovache and Batanya followed suit. "I obtained a certain item from the King of Hell, and I misplaced it when I had to leave. I definitely didn't enjoy my stay with the king, and I'm afraid my abrupt departure may have angered him. As you may have deduced, I need to avoid Lucifer. I very much need to avoid him. I must get in and out of Hell as quietly as possible. Since I can't look in every direction at once, I hired you two to help me watch."

"So you're a thief." Batanya was entering a list of things she needed to take, using her wrist communicator. She glanced up long enough to make sure he was listening.

"Ah, yes. But a thief with a cause," Crick added brightly.

"Don't care," Batanya said. "No matter what you are, no

matter what your cause or motivation, we'll do what we've been hired to do." She looked him square in the eyes.

"Then we're all fine," Crick said, in his most foolish voice. One of the castle cats wandered in and leaped into his lap. He stroked its long orange fur. Batanya eyed it indifferently. She'd never been one for pets, though cats were at least preferable to dogs.

Anything was preferable to dogs.

"How long do you expect we'll be gone?" Clovache asked Crick.

"If we're not back in two weeks, we're not coming back," Crick said with a pleasant smile. "That would be my best evaluation."

Batanya remembered that Clovache had tickets to a concert in a week's time.

"Can you turn those tickets in?" Batanya asked. She ran her fingers through her short, inky hair.

"Nonrefundable," Clovache said gloomily. "Oh, well." She rose to her feet. "Senior," she said, her voice formal, "I ask leave to go prepare."

"I'll be there in a minute myself," Batanya said. "Go ahead." She eyed their client narrowly. As soon as Clovache had gone, Batanya said, "I know there's much you're not telling us. No client ever tells us the whole story. You always lie. But if there's some word you could speak that would help us prepare to guard you, now is the time to speak that word."

Crick looked down at the table for a long moment. The cat jumped out of his lap and left by a window. "Nothing," he said. "There's nothing else I can tell you now that will be of any assistance."

"All right then," she said grimly. "You've got two of Britlingen's best protecting you, Crick. I hope you appreciate that."

"I am paying well for the service," he said. His voice was cool.

Batanya might have told him that no amount of money could make up for the loss of their lives, but that wouldn't have been true. The Britlingen Collective had put a price on that, and Crick had paid it.

"I'll return shortly," she said, and rose to her feet. "The witches and mechs will be ready by then, too." She saw, with a grim satisfaction, that the mention of the witches made Crick shiver. Witches gave everyone the creeps.

Standing in the middle of her little room, Batanya hauled her backpack from the footlocker. She checked her wrist communicator. It showed her the list she'd made—not in written words, but in symbols. Some of the weapons she often carried would be useless in Hell. Any fray would take place suddenly and at close quarters, almost certainly, so taking some of the missile-firing guns would be useless, as would any of the weapons relying on sun power. Hell was underground in a vast network of intersecting tunnels.

"Batanya," called Clovache, whose room was across the hall. "What about crossbows?" The wrist crossbows were incredibly powerful and ranked at the top of Clovache's list of favorite devices.

"Do they kill demons?" Batanya called back. "I don't think so. I think we should take the . . ." What *did* kill a demon? The bespelled throwing stars, of course. "The throwing stars," she called. Steel? Silver? What else would be useful?

She went over all the armaments in her head as she pulled on her summer armor, which was a very lightweight, porous fabric spun by spiderlike creatures from Moraeus. The summer version was like wearing chain mail all over, though it had the texture and appearance of cloth. It was even more expensive and harder to find than liquid armor. The Britlingen company store sold it at what they said was cost—but Batanya had had to save for two years to purchase it. She'd loaned Clovache the money to buy her own summer armor during Clovache's first year as Batanya's junior. "Damn Collective," Batanya muttered as she put the few extra things she'd need into the prepared waterproof backpack that all Britlingens carried on their travels. It was always stocked with a few microthin clean garments, compressed cooked food that could be eaten on the run, a pill or two that provided bursts of energy and had to be used judiciously, some bandages and antibiotics, and a bottle of water. To forestall other kinds of emergencies, all the Britlingens, male and female, were injected with birth control drugs on a monthly basis. Those who skipped this injection were listed in bright red chalk on a big board in the entrance hall.

"Got your list?" she asked from Clovache's doorway. "Oh, have you checked your pocket?" Batanya had already touched her tongue to the artificial pouch in her right cheek, and she nodded when Clovache's right hand flew to her left armpit. Clovache nodded in confirmation and then burrowed back into her closet.

"Yes, I just need to write Geit a note." Clovache's voice was muffled. She was probably searching for some paper and a pen, items Clovache didn't need too often.

"Are you and Geit knocking armor?"

"Yes. He's very vigorous."

Smiling, Batanya shook her head, though Clovache couldn't see her. "You'd do better to keep Geit as a friend," she said. "But I guess it's too late for that."

Her junior reemerged. "He will be. I always stay friends with my lovers. It's my gift." Clovache's light brown hair stuck up in spikes all over her head. She hadn't pulled on the armor's hood yet. It was her least favorite piece of protection. Batanya was none too fond of it either, though her own close-clipped curly black hair lay so close to her skull she might as well have been wearing the hood already.

Together, checking and rechecking their equipment, the two bodyguards went down the list. Traveling very light made careful preparation even more crucial. The older warrior noticed that Clovache had slipped the frame of her wrist crossbow into the special compartment on the outside of the pack, and she kept her mouth shut. If it made Clovache feel stronger, the slight extra weight was worth it.

At last the two decided they were ready, and they walked out of the dormitory. Neither Batanya nor Clovache bothered to lock their doors behind them. Theft was a rare occurrence in the castle. It was punishable by death. Of course, unlocked doors made elaborate practical jokes very easy to stage. Batanya touched the scar on her cheek.

Their employer was waiting in the Hall of Contracts, just as he'd been bid. Batanya gave the Parduan a sharp nod to indicate they were ready to go. Crick stood, brushed the wrinkles out of his outer tunic, and said, "I suppose now we meet the witches and the mechs?"

"Yes," Clovache said. "No way around it, Crick."

He looked startled for a brief moment. "It shows, then."

Batanya snorted.

"That would be a yes, I take it. Well, well. Where do we go?"

"This door." It was heavy Moraeus wood and banded with metal. There were runes and other symbols from several magical systems incised in the stone all around the door and carved into the door itself. If the Britlingen Collective were destroyed at that moment, Batanya reckoned the Hall of Witchcraft and all within it would remain standing.

She knocked on the door, the pattern of a bodyguard, four evenly spaced knocks. After a moment, it swung open, and the three walked through, falling into the pattern they would assume for the journey: Batanya in front, her eyes moving from side to side, Crick following, and then Clovache, whose task was to keep her face forward but her ears behind—a tricky thing to do, but that was the traditional job of the junior.

The door swung shut behind them, and they were faced with a veiled man in white robes. His glistening silver hair trailed almost to the floor.

Fucking witches, Batanya thought. *Always posing.*

"We come for transportation," she said, though of course the witch already knew that. But she had to adhere to the ritual. The witches and the mechs went nuts if the rituals weren't followed.

"We're ready," said the witch, who appeared to be smiling behind the veil. "So few want to be sent to Hell. We've enjoyed the preparations." That was an unexpected bit of sharing; Clovache was almost inclined to think not too badly of him, when the witch added, "Of course, we've never gotten to bring anyone back."

"Which room?" Batanya asked, her voice quite level.

He inclined his head toward the doorway behind him and turned to glide into the huge room ahead of them. He moved with an eerie smoothness. Batanya and Clovache had wondered between themselves if the witches practiced moving like that. They had entertained the whole bar at the Pooka Palace one night by acting out the Floating Walk 101 class. Batanya turned to exchange a weak grin with Clovache. That had been a very good night.

In the middle of the room was a shallow basin raised on a plinth, and in the basin was a smoky fire. A group of seven witches stood in a casual circle around the basin, and they all seemed prepared with small vials of herbs or chemicals, and a number of focus items. The children taken in by the Collective came in handy for the witches' rituals, too. At the side of each witch was a boy or girl of ages ranging from fourteen to five. Each child held a cloudy globe.

In the corner of the room, a lone mech was seated on a stool before a vast and complex machine. Batanya saw her client's shoulders jump a little. The Parduan was wound pretty tight, and she hoped he didn't come unsprung. What would she do if he withdrew a weapon from his clothing and tried to kill the witches? Hmmm, that was a poser. The client's wish was law, right? But the witches were under the protection of the Collective; in fact, they were an essential part of the Collective's operation. The scenario presented a neat problem to debate over many tankards of ale when they returned . . . if they returned.

Batanya turned to the client and pointed to a little set of steps that led to a platform over the basin. "Up," she said, and went up herself ahead of him. The three crowded onto the small platform, and the two bodyguards put their arms around Crick, which made him jump yet again. "A Crick sandwich," he muttered foolishly, and over his shoulder Clovache rolled her eyes at Batanya, who sighed.

Then the witches began their chanting, their drawing of runes in the air, and their tossing of herbs on the fire, and the smoke began to rise, and the mech in the corner began his mysterious button punching on the machine, and then . . .

They were in Hell.

Of course, it was hot in the tunnel. The smell was most unpleasant. Hell had been named from the stories from Earth, and its atmosphere was not the only similarity that had spawned the comparison. Life on the surface above Hell was almost impossible because of the pools of gases that dotted the landscape. The beings that still lived above-ground were savage and very foreign. Down below, where the being named Lucifer ruled, was where almost all Hell's life was conducted. Its curved tunnels were notoriously dangerous and difficult to navigate.

Crick had a map, which he whipped out of a pocket in his tunic. The map was made from a very flexible material, and he held the unfolded surface wide open to peer at it, angling the face of the map toward the arched roof. That was where the tunnel's lightsource originated, though Clovache couldn't identify the devices that issued the light, or how those devices were powered. They'd found themselves in a main passage; Clovache noticed that other branch tunnel mouths within view were much darker and smaller. For the moment, the three were alone, but there was a clear sound of footsteps from the west. It was the work of a moment for Batanya to drag Crick backward into one of the dark tunnels, though the rock floor was so inexplicably slick that she almost landed on her back. Clovache leaped after her and skidded so hard she almost hit the wall. Crick still had his map spread in his hands, and he squawked, but it was through Batanya's fingers.

The two Britlingens pressed their client up against the stone wall of the tunnel, their bodies between the opening and Crick. Crick was very quiet now, having grasped the situation, and Batanya thought it safe to remove her hand. She eased a throwing star out of its sheath and held it at the ready.

Two demons walked past the mouth. They were perhaps five feet tall, red and bumpy, and though they had two arms and two legs, that was the end of their resemblance to humans. They did have cloven hooves and tails, and sharp pointed ears, but they were hairless and their genitals were barbed, whether they were male or female. Batanya saw Crick's eyes lock onto the crucial area, and she shared his wince. No matter how many times you had seen the demons strut their stuff, it was awful to imagine that "stuff" in operation.

The demons passed out of view without detecting their presence.

All three of them exhaled with relief, and Batanya put the star away.

"Let's just stay here for a moment," she whispered. "Tell us what your plan is." When Batanya made a suggestion in that particular voice, even if she had to whisper it, wise people listened, and Crick was at least that wise.

"All right," Crick said, just as quietly. He extracted something from one of his pockets—his garment seemed to have a hundred of them—and pressed a button. It was a tiny lightsource, probably battery powered, and he turned so that his body was between the light and the mouth of their tunnel. He handed the map to Batanya. Clovache squatted right beside him to add her body to the screen, and they all peered down at the map.

It was detailed, showing tunnel after tunnel, chamber after chamber. "How'd you get this?" Clovache said, her voice hushed and respectful. This was a valuable item.

"You don't want to know," Crick said, his tenor voice cheerful. "You really don't." His long, thin finger moved over the markings on the map for a moment, and then he said, "Here we are." There was a pulsing star at the spot he indicated.

"Too bad the other critters don't show up the way we do," Batanya muttered. "But at least we have a frame of reference."

"I couldn't afford the kind that shows all life-forms," Crick said apologetically.

"What, you actually paid for this?" Clovache's eyebrows were raised skeptically. She clearly thought he'd stolen it.

"Well, no. I mean I couldn't afford the jail time. The better ones were locked up tighter, and I was in a hurry," he said, without the slightest trace of shame.

"What is this object of yours that you 'left behind' the last time you visited this place?" Batanya said.

"It's a conjuring ball."

"But those are everywhere, you can buy one in any shop."

"Not like this one. It's for real."

The two Britlingens stared at their client. Conjuring balls, full of tiny machinery and spells and capable of performing very innocuous bits of magic like lighting candles or drying plates, were hugely popular gifts for children. Even a cheap one could entertain a child for hours until the magic ran down, and the more expensive models were almost as good as giving someone a pet. They might last two or three years, and could do quite a variety of tasks and tricks. But everyone knew that the balls were not permanent sources of magic. Sooner or later, they'd exhaust their power.

"You're telling us this conjuring ball is eternal?" Clovache said, her voice almost a growl.

"Yes." Crick looked rather proud.

"Did you make it?"

"No, of course not. I stole it on commission."

"You mean you stole it from the Lord of Hell because someone had asked you to get it?"

Crick nodded, looking pleased with her acumen.

"Who?" Batanya had a creeping feeling along her arms. This was getting worse and worse. "Who commissioned the theft?"

"Belshazzar."

"And you went back to Pardua without the ball? Having taken his money?"

"Taken it and spent it," Crick said, his foolish face looking rather downcast.

"We are so fucked," Clovache said.

There was a moment of silence while they all considered the truth of this. Belshazzar, a warlord of Pardua, was actually a glorified gangster. (Perhaps all warlords are.) Belshazzar was ruthless, drastic, and notoriously indirect in his punishments. He would enjoy amputating your hand if you stole from him, but he enjoyed even more kidnapping your mother, say, and forcing you to watch as he amputated *her* hand. Then yours.

"Hey, we're Britlingens," Batanya said bracingly. "Not only are we made of tough stuff, but we can hardly be blamed for what our client has done. Britlingens are hired hands, not the responsible parties."

"True," Clovache said. "Our Collective would intervene, if they had any notion of where we were. Trovis wouldn't pay ransom for us, but Flechette might. I'm not so very partial to my left hand, anyway. And maybe we can buy some time by persuading Belshazzar to kill Crick here, first."

"Thanks, bodyguards-sworn-to-protect-me," said Crick, somewhat coldly, "but let's leave the discussion of my possible demise for later. Right now, we've got a conjuring ball to retrieve."

"Did you hide it or was it captured?" Batanya asked.

"I hid it," Crick said. "I seized a moment of solitude."

"Where?"

He peered at the map. "Here," he said, and indicated a tunnel to the north of the one where they crouched. There was a fair amount of walking in between.

"If you had given the witches this map, they could have landed us right there," Clovache muttered.

"Yes, but then we would have landed in the barracks. So that seemed like a poor choice to me."

"You hid the ball in the barracks of the soldiers of the King of Hell?"

He shrugged. "It was where I was."

"How'd . . . No. Let's focus. Unless you have a better idea, we'll work our way closer and see what our chances are." It was obvious from Batanya's tone that she considered those chances slim to nil. "Lucky for you I don't have children, Crick, or I'd be cursing you in their names."

"Oh my goodness, that's hard to believe," Crick said blandly. "That you don't have children, I mean. What could the men of Spauling be thinking of?"

"Slitting your throat, most likely," Batanya said. "I know that's crossed *my* mind."

"What is the law?" Crick didn't sound at all worried.

"The client's word," Clovache said, but Batanya could tell it hurt her to say it.

"Let's get moving. Stop the jawing." Batanya wanted to correct Clovache's attitude. That was her job.

"This place gives me the creeps," Clovache muttered, by way of apology. "This is a very bad mission."

In a few seconds, Clovache's dark outlook was validated. Just as they were edging forward to take a gander out the mouth of their tunnel, they heard something moving in the darkness behind them.

It was something that was dragging itself along.

"It's a slug," Crick said urgently. "We must move now or be stuck to the tunnel walls in a coat of slug goo. Or we'll be absorbed."

They hadn't the faintest idea what Crick was talking about, but he'd been there before and they hadn't. Also, the smell that preceded the dragging sound was strong enough to make even the hardened bodyguards gag. Batanya checked to make sure the passage was clear, and the three darted out into the main tunnel, turning left; Batanya figured that was north. They left the dragging noise and the awful smell behind them, so evidently the slugs didn't move very swiftly. But after a few minutes, Batanya heard footsteps coming at a fast clip. At her hand gesture, the three leaped into a very small side tunnel, much narrower than the one that had been their first refuge.

This tunnel turned out to be occupied by three soldiers doing the nasty, and in this instance that was no euphemism. Since they were from different species, this was an unattractive and complicated undertaking. Before Crick's involuntary sound of disgust had cleared his throat, before Clovache had quite figured out how they'd all hooked up, Batanya had silenced the soldiers permanently with her short sword.

It was hard to say in the dim lighting that was only a step above darkness, but Batanya, cleaning her sword on the trousers of one deceased soldier, felt Crick might even look a bit green.

"Thank you," he said, after a moment.

"Don't mention it," she said.

They crouched in the gloom with the corpses, Clovache glancing at the bodies from time to time in curiosity. "Have you ever seen that?" she asked Batanya, pointing to the conjunction of a greenish brown snake-headed humanoid creature and a wolfwoman. Batanya shook her head. "This job is always an education," she said.

After a few minutes, it seemed apparent no one had heard the muted groans and gurgles of the dying soldiers; or perhaps if any passerby had, the noises had been perceived as arising from their activity. At any rate, no one came to investigate.

Batanya knew it was only a matter of time before they came face-to-face with someone who would challenge them. The traffic in the tunnel made it obvious that they were getting closer to the hub of Hell's activities. Several times various beings passed the mouth of their little hidey-hole, and each time the three held their breath until the footsteps had passed (if the creatures had feet). One of the slugs oozed by, and Clovache and Batanya got to observe firsthand how the creatures undulated through the tunnels, the slime oozing from their underbellies and sides to grease their passage. This slime hardened within seconds. Now Clovache understood why the floor of the tunnel was so smooth and even; the passage of the slugs, the largest of which was perhaps ten feet long and as big around as a medium barrel, had led to a gradual buildup of the substance. There was a coating on the bottom half of the walls, too, but it wasn't as thick and glassy as the layer on the floor.

"If we'd known, we could have brought metal cleats," Batanya said practically. "Perhaps *someone* should have told us."

Crick was wise enough to keep his response to himself. He just grinned at Batanya in a foolish way. "There'll be less traffic at nighttime," he whispered. "We'll have to wait it out."

Some hours passed, and the activity in the tunnels died down. The three spent the passing time trying to ignore the smell of both the heaped bodies and the dark area beyond them at the end of the tunnel, perhaps five yards farther. The area had evidently been used as a latrine in the recent past, and though the functional amenity was handy, it was also unpleasant to be around for any length of time—and all they had was lengthy time. Very lengthy. The two Britlingens dozed, ate a couple of energy bars, gave Crick another, and drank sparingly. Presumably there were underground springs somewhere; almost all living beings needed fluid. But they hadn't seen one, and the map showed only the tunnels.

"At least we haven't seen any animals," Clovache said in a bright whisper. "I wonder how they supply themselves with meat?"

"There are pens of cows and other edible creatures, kept pretty far distant from the rest of Lucifer's palace," Crick said. "Why are you glad we haven't seen animals?"

"They might bark," Clovache said quickly. In the dim light that pervaded the tunnels, which varied quite a bit from one tunnel to the next, she looked as if she wished she hadn't spoken.

Crick looked curious, which was probably his natural

condition. "You wanted to avoid dogs in particular?" he said. "Why?"

There was an awful moment of silence.

"Because this large scar on my face was caused by a dog. I got it on my first mission," Batanya said, with no inflection at all. "We were protecting a guy who bred attack dogs. His breeding and training methods were famous. A rival of his, as a *practical joke*, bribed one of our clients' kennel boys to feed the dogs an irritant that acted on their nervous system."

"How did that turn out?"

Batanya shrugged and looked away.

"Not very well," Clovache said. "I hadn't finished training. A man named Damon was Batanya's junior. This alleged practical joke cost him his life."

"Did your client live?" Crick asked Batanya directly.

She met his eyes. "Yes," she said. "He lived, though he lost a leg and one hand. Damon died after four hours. I got the scar."

That was end of all conversation for a long time.

Batanya gradually became convinced that it was night. It was hard to tell with no change in the light, but it felt like night to her. She gave Clovache a hand signal. After a quick check of all their accoutrements, the bodyguards prepared to move. According to the legend on Crick's handy-dandy map, they were about a mile from their objective as a crow flies, if a crow would be demented enough to navigate the tunnels of Hell.

Clovache glared at the map, which in some ways was a godsend, in other ways completely useless. Fumbling their way ignorantly would have been nearly suicidal, but the map would have been so much more valuable if it had shown the rooms that must be lying somewhere. Presumably, in this huge underground empire, there was a throne room for the king, a refectory of some kind, a prison, an audience chamber, and so on. As it was, they knew where they had to go in order to retrieve Crick's left-behind treasure, but they had no idea what they might encounter on the way there.

"It's not like we ever knew what to expect anyway," Clovache said to Batanya, who nodded. They'd been partners long enough to have abbreviated conversations.

As if her words had been a self-fulfilling prophecy, they rounded the next bend to find two armed guards blocking the way.

"We heard you coming a mile away," said the one who was least humanoid. He was a not a demon. In fact, Batanya had no idea what his origin was. He was quadrupedal, gray, and clothed in a material like cobwebs. He had a device in his hand that looked like the frame for a tennis racket. With a dexterous motion, he swung the thing toward them, and a large-weave net flowed out of the frame to land over Batanya and Crick, who was right behind her.

Clovache fled, rightly figuring that someone needed to stay free. To the hoots and jeers of the two guards, Batanya unsheathed her short sword and began sweeping the blade from side to side. To her vast irritation, the strands of the net stuck to the sword and moved with it. The net was so elastic that it didn't provide enough resistance to be severed.

"Shit!" she said. From the corner of her eye she saw that Crick had adapted and was working with his dagger. He was having better luck with his smaller blade than she was with her sword, so she pulled out her own knife and began cutting. The second guard, a human who looked quite a bit like Trovis, had drawn some kind of handgun, a hazardous decision in a rock tunnel. Since a ricochet was just as likely to wound her or her client as it was to hit the one who deserved it, Batanya threw her dagger through a rent she'd just made in the net and killed the Trovis-like human, who gurgled dramatically before he crumpled to the floor of the tunnel. There was a certain flash of satisfaction in the moment.

The net-thrower seemed startled that things weren't going his way, and he wasn't keeping the net mended quickly enough to contain Crick and Batanya. Crick was working very quickly, which was good, since Batanya had been forced to return to using her sword. She'd changed her technique to the more effective one of stabbing through the net in short jabs, rather than trying to sweep a large cut through the strands.

Batanya was startled to see something long and dark slide past her on the tunnel floor. By the time she realized it was Clovache, the other woman was on her feet and plunging her neotaser into the mass of the net-throwing thing's body. A good jolt of electricity will interrupt almost any being's thought processes, and it had a dramatic effect on their gray enemy. All four legs shot out and began skidding around on the slippery surface of the tunnel. The effect was weirdly like dancing, but when Clovache delivered another jolt, it became evident that the creature was in its death throes. It collapsed in a spidery heap, twitched a couple of times, and lay still.

"That was brilliant," Batanya said, trying not to pant.

"I took a running start, threw myself down, and away I went. It was just like sliding over ice." Clovache looked rather pleased at the compliment. "Especially at the sides of the floor where no one walks."

Crick was staring at them wild-eyed while Batanya cut the remnants of the tattered net away from their limbs.

"You all right?" Clovache asked him, clapping him on the shoulder by way of encouragement.

"Yes," Crick said. He took off the idiotic goggles. He had quite sharp blue eyes underneath them. Without the sparkly distraction, his face was bony and agreeable and intelligent. "I want to say right now, you two are worth every penny I paid."

"Say that after you get back alive," Batanya advised him, as Clovache deposited the neotaser into the pocket designed for it. After the slide across the slug slick, her summer armor was a little grubby, but completely intact. Clovache's hood had come off in the fracas, and she tugged it back over her matted hair. ("If you have an iota of vanity, this is not the job for you," the sergeant who'd recruited her from her home village had said. Clovache, like all the young recruits, had lied.)

"We have to get out of here fast," Batanya said, and without another word, they all stepped over the bodies and hurried down the tunnel. With a glance at the map, Crick indicated a dark opening to the side, again to the left, and they ducked into it, none too soon. Howling, another gray quadrupedal creature loped across the spot they'd just vacated.

Batanya wondered if the gray creatures had some kind of mind-link. Perhaps the dead one had sent some kind of signal when he was wounded.

After a long moment, they heard an eerie wailing. The second soldier had found his dead buddy. This was going to draw all kinds of attention to the area, and the faster they relocated, the better.

Batanya made the punching gesture with her fist that meant "move out," and they hurried away from the wailing. This time they were going west, following Crick's gestures. This tunnel was particularly slick, and they had to pick their way very carefully to avoid landing on their asses. The unpitted glassiness of the slugs' hardened secretions argued that this passage was not much traveled by the minions of Lucifer; that was the good part. It also argued that the slugs used it a lot. That, of course, was the bad part. Batanya had a momentary image of being beneath one of the slugs as it moved with its slow, sure, rippling motion. She could feel the goo clogging her nose and mouth until she couldn't breathe. She would harden to the floor after the slug had passed.

Then she shook herself vigorously. Letting one's imagination take over was an indulgence that sapped the energy of a warrior. She glanced over her shoulder at Crick, who was shuddering. Maybe he'd had the same mental image.

From behind him, Clovache hissed, "Hurry up!"

Their luck held for ten frantic minutes. Then they heard the dragging sound of an approaching slug, and there was no handy escape hatch. In fact, there was not an intersecting tunnel opening as far as the eye could see. If there was one around the next bend, they simply couldn't count on reaching it before they met the oncoming slug.

"Back," Batanya ordered. Abruptly, they were hurrying as fast retracing their steps as they had been going forward. The first tunnel mouth they spotted also contained an approaching slug; it was so close to issuing forth into their main tunnel that its antennae were waving in their direction. They kept on going, hearing the relentless progress of the larger creature behind them, until they spotted another opening, a much smaller one.

It was like a baby tunnel, but it represented safety at that moment, and they dove into it with all haste. They had to crawl in on their knees. At least it was extensive enough to hold all three of them.

"The slugs don't seem to be sentient," Batanya said, keeping her voice low. "That is, I don't think they're smart enough to be working for the King of Hell. I think the slugs made the tunnels."

Crick said, "Lucifer adapted the idea from the slugs. When the surface planet was growing uninhabitable, he began exploring down here; or at least, he sent his creatures and hirelings down here. Many of them died because they underestimated the sheer power of the slugs. The nasty things don't think much, but they've got very strong instincts, and they can attack with surprising speed when they're angry."

This was a flood of information. "What makes them angry?" Clovache asked.

"Anything blocking their way," Crick said.

"What do they eat?"

"Anything blocking their way." Crick looked apologetic. "They seem to take nutrients from the soil. But when they run over someone, they generally pause on top of them, and suck up everything they can."

That was *much* worse than Batanya's mental image, and she felt quite sick for just a moment. "Then we'd better not get under them," she said, in the toughest voice she could manage. "Why don't Lucifer's warriors clear them out of the tunnels? Surely they're the ones in the greatest danger?"

"Lucifer needs the slugs too much," Crick explained. "They do most of the digging for him. Of course, he can't really direct where the slug tunnels go, but they add to his palace for free. At the same time, the slugs stabilize the tunnels with their secretions. He only has to shore up the occasional roof. Plus, the slugs are good at patrolling the existing passageways. If he loses the odd fighter, he doesn't really care."

"You know a lot about this." In the dim light, Batanya couldn't read their client's expression, but she had the impression he flinched.

"Yes," he said. "I was a prisoner here for quite some time. Lucifer enjoys talking."

"This is information it might have been good to have before," Batanya said. "Not so much about your imprisonment, though that's interesting, of course." Batanya could be polite when she chose. "This stuff about the slugs . . . We needed to know that before now."

"Why don't you tell us something else we might need to know?" Clovache suggested. "Just in the interest of keeping you alive." Another slug was coming. They could hear the distinctive dragging sound, inhale the noisome smell. They were stuck here for a few minutes.

"Belshazzar heard from an informant that the conjuring ball was in the private cabinet of the King of Hell," Crick said. "It was a commission steal. I was hired by Belshazzar partly because I'm good, partly because I owed him a lot of money anyway. But I did succeed in getting the ball, though it was in the darkest corner of the darkest cabinet in Lucifer's apartment . . ."

"Less with the colorful and more with the facts," Batanya said firmly.

Crick was a bit disconcerted to be knocked out of his storytelling groove, but he nodded obligingly. "Actually, it was in a special room off the king's bedroom. His, ah, toy room, so to speak. Belshazzar was pretty sure I'd get to see that room when Lucifer found out I was actually one of the last of the Harwell Clan."

Batanya's eyes widened. Clovache looked bewildered.

"What does that mean?" she asked.

"It means our client here has special physical attractions."

Clovache looked him over, couldn't see it. She liked her men big and burly. "Like what?"

When Crick just shrugged, Clovache looked at her lieutenant. "What?" she asked.

Batanya said, "Crick here has two penises."

"Get out of town," Clovache said. "Really?" She sounded both admiring and intrigued.

Crick nodded, trying to look modest. "There are few of us left. We don't tend to be model citizens, according to the rules of other societies, so the Harwell Clan has been decimated in the last decade."

"Is there *anyone* who doesn't want to hurt you?" Clovache asked.

"Sure. You two."

"I'm not so sure about that," Batanya muttered. She pulled her hood down and ran her fingers through her short black hair. "Okay, so how'd you get the conjuring ball into the barracks?"

"They didn't know I had it," Crick said. "When I decided it was time to take my leave of the king—his demands got rather tiresome—I ran away, taking the conjuring ball with me. When it was obvious I was going to be captured, I concealed it."

"Where?" Batanya asked bluntly.

"Ah, in the only available place."

"And they didn't search you thoroughly?" Batanya was professionally astonished. "It wouldn't get by us."

Crick half-bowed to them. "I have no doubt," he said politely. "However, they thought I might have stolen one of Lucifer's big pieces of jewelry or some of his coins, which could not be concealed in the same manner, and they didn't think of checking me to see if I'd made off with anything else of value. I, ah, couldn't tolerate the concealment anymore, so in a moment when no one else was in the room, I hid the ball. They'd parked me in a room in the barracks while the sergeant needed them to beat another prisoner, and that gave me ten minutes locked by myself in a room without a window. I took advantage of the opportunity."

"So you want us to take you back into the barracks, find the room where you were held, extract the conjuring ball, and get you out again alive. To return you to Spauling. Where you have to seek sanctuary because Belshazzar wants to kill you. Or perhaps you want to send the ball to Belshazzar in the hopes that he'll honor his original contract with you. And King Lucifer wants you back in his playroom."

"I suppose all that's true," Crick said. For the first time, when he tried to sound cheerful, he failed.

"Belshazzar is angry because of your tardiness and your loss of the ball, and Lucifer is angry because you ran away before he'd finished playing with you."

"That's a fair summary," Crick admitted.

"How'd you get the fee for the witches at the Collective? I'm just curious," Clovache said. "It's not my business. But I know they don't extend credit." Batanya's shoulders heaved with silent laughter at the idea.

"Ah, well, I may have lifted a few things from the houses of various nobles in Spauling."

"A few things? Must have been more like a cartload, to have afforded us."

"You'll be interested to know I got a price break as long as I specified the two guards I wanted to hire."

Both the women became very serious instantly. "Trovis," hissed Batanya.

"He really has a big hate against you," Crick said. "When he heard where I needed to go, he jiggered around the duty roster so that your names came up."

Batanya and Clovache looked at each other. "When we get back," Clovache said, "we'll take care of him. This has gone on long enough."

"Why does he hold such a grudge?" Crick asked. The two turned as one to stare at him. "Oh, ladies, come on! We're in this together. If I make it back alone, I'll kill him for you."

"Good enough," Clovache said. "My esteemed senior, here, turned him down so forcefully she broke his arm."

Crick whistled silently. "I take it a plain refusal wouldn't suffice?"

"He wouldn't take no for an answer," Batanya said. "He was waiting in my room when I came home one night. I tried being tactful, which doesn't come easily to me. I tried being firm. I tried being rude. He persisted. The time came to try force."

"He broke her nose," Clovache said to Crick. "He broke her collarbone. But she broke a major bone of his, so she won."

"He cried," Batanya said, her lips curving in a slight smile. "But enough of happy reminiscences. We've hunkered here long enough. Time to be on the move."

This time Crick had to brace himself a bit before he stepped out into the larger tunnel. Batanya thought she knew what had made him run before he was ready, during his earlier stay with the king. Maybe he'd lost his nerve, maybe he'd lost his ability to handle the physical tastes of Lucifer, but Batanya was willing to bet he'd lost his tolerance for the tunnels.

She couldn't deny that she shared a bit of that feeling. In fact, Hell was awful. She took a deep breath of the thick stinking air, and the closed-in feeling began to lay a blanket over her normal brisk spirit. The indirect light wasn't bright enough to really illuminate the way; it was better than nothing, but its dull consistency added to the gloomy atmosphere. They'd moved out again, but their pace was too slow. Batanya felt that their energy was being sapped by the place.

Batanya realized their mission had to be completed at what speed they could summon. They needed to get out of the tunnels and back home before they grew too tense—or too depressed—to cope. She'd never encountered such a set of circumstances.

"You remember our last mission?" she said suddenly to Clovache.

Clovache was visibly surprised at Batanya's question. "Of course."

"That was a very bad situation. The building exploding, our client being completely defenseless and unable to walk. Yet I never despaired, and I never thought we wouldn't get out of it."

"Senior, do you have a fever?"

"The tunnels are getting to me and Crick, here. You don't seem to be as bothered by them. You may have to take over the lead."

"I don't mind them. Just say the word, senior."

"Thanks, junior. I'll let you know."

Batanya turned and began to lead the way again. Crick kept possession of the map, using whispers or a pointing finger to give directions. They kept to smaller tunnels so they'd be less likely to meet up with Hell's denizens. The downside to this stratagem was that when they did meet up with a creature, there was no side tunnel to help them dodge the attack, which came instantly. During an incredibly long journey that seemed to last at least six hours, but actually lasted perhaps two, the Britlingens killed at least ten of Hell's odder creatures. Only by the narrowest of margins, the three avoided the slow but inexorable progress of two slugs. Batanya's fingers began to tremble, and she knew the time was approaching when she'd have to hand over leadership to her junior.

But before she had to cede her position, they were captured.

It happened very quickly. They were caught in the worst possible situation, in a long stretch where there weren't any hidey-holes to duck into. Also, the tunnel was gently curved, so the oncoming enemy was hidden from them until there was no possibility of escape. No change in sound announced their coming. These soldiers were like large dust bunnies. They progressed by rolling silently down the slick floors. At first, Batanya was inclined to laugh, but Crick's expression told her that they were in big trouble. "Run!" he said hoarsely. "Run!" They reversed, but Batanya, who was now in the rear, was overcome within seconds.

It was like being sucked up in a vacuum cleaner, Batanya thought, as she gagged and choked on the dust and bits of hair and trash that made up the creature's body. It managed to get strands twisted around her wrists and to lift her off the floor so she had no traction. She began to kick out and throw her body from side to side, but somehow the dust bunny surrounded her with strands and particles of debris that restrained her efficiently.

"Clovache!" she called. "You?"

"Held fast," came a muffled voice. "Crick?"

There was only a choked series of coughs to indicate Crick's position.

The ball began rolling down the tunnel, Batanya inside. She rapidly became so dizzy that her priority changed from escaping the creature to not throwing up.

The heat increased as her encompassing, nebulous captor rolled through the passages. Finally, the sense of constriction eased. The wretchedly sick Batanya felt that they'd arrived in a large open space. Then movement blessedly ceased, and all the threads and bits of debris that had snared her simply unknitted. "Oh, shit," she said, a second before she landed on a stone floor that had never known the passage of a slug.

The impact knocked her breathless for a minute, but the second she could inhale she was on her feet with her short sword drawn. The dustball that had held her rolled away, and for the first time she saw Lucifer's great hall. It had a high vaulted ceiling and was randomly dotted with stone pillars. There was a throne carved out of the stone; it had been created when the rest of the hall was mined, and it stood in dark splendor by itself in the middle of the vast space. The handsome gentleman standing on its bottom step was wearing a three-piece suit and a neck scarf decorated with a huge ruby stickpin. He was blond. He was smiling.

"I always thought Lucifer would have black hair," Clovache whispered, as she got up on one knee. She was a yard away, and she had given in to the impulse to vomit. Crick? Batanya looked around for their client, and she found him on the floor behind her. She positioned herself in front of his prone form and got ready to fight.

"Brave but foolish," said the blond man. "Look." He pointed behind her, and very cautiously Batanya turned her head. Just in the edges of the light that hung over Lucifer's head was a host of creatures—demons, more of the quadrupeds, wolfmen, snakemen, dust bunnies, humans. There were at least two hundred of them, and they were all armed in one way or another.

"Well, shit," Batanya said for the second time. She nudged Crick with her heel. "Shall I die in your defense?" she asked. Crick groaned, rolled on his side away from her, and puked, considerately aiming away from her boots. Clovache staggered upright and with fingers that were shaking so hard they were almost useless, she attached her wrist crossbow to her left arm, the bow cocked and at the ready and the arrows neatly lined up in their strap. Batanya had never been prouder of her junior.

"Surely he doesn't want you to," Lucifer said. "You two are so . . . formidable. The great thief Crick wouldn't want to condemn two brave warriors to death unnecessarily?"

"No," Crick moaned. "No, don't do it."

"That's good, Crick! Now they can provide entertainment for my troops," Lucifer said, smiling angelically.

"The Collective would frown on that," Batanya said.

Lucifer's smile dimmed a little. He strolled over to the little cluster of shaken outer-worlders. His nose didn't wrinkle when he got within smelling distance, so Batanya figured his olfactory sense must have been damaged by his long sojourn in the fetid air of Hell. "The Britlingen Collective," he said, only the faintest trace of a question in his voice. The two women nodded in unison. Lucifer made a face; a disappointed face, Batanya decided.

"I have no wish to fight the Collective," Lucifer said. He brightened. "On the other hand, who'd know?"

"If we don't come back, everyone would know," Batanya said. "Our souls belong to the Collective. You're aware of our death clause?"

Everyone who'd heard of the Britlingens had heard of the death clause. When a Britlingen died, his or her soul appeared in the recording hall, reenacting that death. The reenactment was recorded for posterity. The recordings were required viewing during the course of instruction.

"Perhaps some of my people could keep you just at the brink," Lucifer suggested. "They're quite talented at that."

"They'll die out of sheer pigheadedness," Crick said, his voice raspy. "Lu, what the hell?"

Lucifer was close enough now for Batanya to see every detail. He was formed like a man, and was extremely handsome; his short blond hair was more golden and thicker than Crick's, but it was smoothed back in the same way. Lucifer was also thin and well-muscled like Crick, but he made no pretense at foolishness. Even a sick bodyguard could register the avidity in his eyes when he looked at the recaptured Harwellian.

Clovache stood on Crick's far side, her back to Batanya's. There was a long moment of tension while they waited to hear what Lucifer would say.

"Oh, all right," Lucifer said. He sounded both gleeful and a little sulky, as if he'd gotten what he wanted but it could have been a little better.

"All right what?" Batanya said, not relaxing in the least. A wolfman was snarling at her from three yards away, and she was keeping her eyes on him. He was close enough to a canine to give her the creeps. She was ready to sweep the sword across his throat, given half a chance. She could feel Clovache trembling at her back. The trip through the tunnels had taken its toll on the junior Britlingen.

"We'll make a deal," Lucifer told them. He took a step closer. "Stand down, and your client only has to stay for a week with me. Fight, and he stays the rest of his life."

"Why are you willing to make such a deal?" Batanya said, after examining the idea briefly. "Kill us both, and you have him forever anyway."

"True. But you're right, I don't want to get in bad odor with the Collective," Lucifer said. "I'll hold you all for a week, enjoy the delights of Crick . . . then you can all three return to the Collective, more or less unmolested. Besides, when I was taking inventory a few days ago, I found that an item is missing from my collection of wonderful things. I'd like to ask Crick a few questions about that, while we're having fun. But I swear he'll live, especially if he talks quickly."

Batanya's leg was touching Clovache's, and she could feel Clovache's leg begin to shake a bit harder.

She didn't believe Lucifer, of course, but she couldn't think of any counteroffer that would give them an advantage. The wolfman advanced an inch or two, his lips drawing back from his fangs. Another one of the four-legged creatures with a net eased a little closer on her left.

"What is the law?" Batanya said quietly.

"The client's word," Clovache whispered. There was a moment of silence.

"I accept your offer," Crick said to Lucifer. His voice was devoid of any inflection.

"Oh, that's good then," Lucifer said. He beamed at the three. "Ladies, you can stand down. I have a lovely jail just waiting for you, and you can enjoy it all by yourself. I won't permit any company. Crick, for you I have something else entirely." The host of creatures circling them began yowling and laughing, or making whatever noise passed for it.

Batanya turned to help Crick up, and their eyes met squarely.

"He won't keep to his word," Crick said very close to her ear.

"What shall we do?" Batanya said. "We can fight to the death. I will kill you now, if you would prefer that to him." She jerked her head toward the advancing Lucifer.

"No," Crick said. "That part's bad, but not fatal. I can get through it and even enjoy some of it. He won't let me go, though. Something will happen to me, or you. We have to get out with the conjuring ball. I might as well die here if I don't get out with it. It's in Barrack Three, on top of the first cabinet on the right."

Batanya said, "All right," having no idea what she could do with the knowledge. "I'll ask to speak to you in a couple of days."

Crick patted her on the shoulder, turned to nod at Clovache, whose face was streaming with sweat, and then bowed to Lucifer.

"Marl, take them to the cells," Lucifer instructed the wolfman, and draped his arm across Crick's shoulders to lead Crick away.

Batanya heard him say, "Love, I've gotten some new toys since you were here last," and then the wolfman snarled at her. When he could see he had her attention, he jerked his shaggy head northward. The two Britlingens surrendered their weapons to two quadrupedal net-throwers, then trudged off, following the wolfman's lead. The crowd of Lucifer's hirelings surrounded them, but aside from an occasional poke or prod or gobbet of spit didn't offer them harm. Batanya didn't like being spit on, but then again, no one had ever died of it, unless you counted the acid-spitting lizards she'd encountered on a previous job. She cast an uneasy look through the crowd and didn't spot any.

"Well," she said to Clovache, "We've been in worse spots."

"Right," Clovache said, with some effort. Batanya could tell Clovache's stomach was still acting up. "This is an evening at the Pooka Palace compared to some of the places we've been."

Batanya almost smiled, to the astonishment of the crowd.

* * *

Jail in Hell was about what you'd expect. They passed through the guardroom, with weapons hung on the walls that even Batanya had never seen, and many that she had. The weapons ranged from full-tech guns to your basic swords and spears and clubs. The guards were your basic hostile and contemptuous louts. A snakeman flicked his forked tongue out to touch Clovache's cheek as she passed him, and he laughed in a hissing kind of way at her expression of disgust. The wolfman growled, "Keep your tongue to yourself, Sha," and Sha snapped to attention, or at least as close to that as a curved spine like his could manage.

Clovache and Batanya had to strip under all eyes, because they couldn't remain in their armor; they had expected that, but it wasn't pleasant, of course. They donned the drawstring pants and shapeless tunics they were given, along with pairs of thick socks with padded soles. Then Marl, who appeared to be the shift captain, unlocked a heavy door with a peephole in the middle, and held it open for the prisoners to pass through.

The cells were rough-floored, having been hewn out of the rock instead of being created by the tunneling slugs, and the dimensions were roomy since occasionally they had to house creatures much larger than humans. Batanya assessed hers in one quick look. There was a latrine in one corner, which was quite an odd shape since all species don't poop the same way, and there was a cot, twice as wide as Batanya's bed in Spauling, to accommodate a variety of creatures. Clovache's cell was right by hers, and there were bars from floor to ceiling in between, spaced a little less than the breadth of a hand apart. In the same manner, the front of the cells were also barred from floor to ceiling, so the prisoners were always in view of their fellow prisoners and whoever happened to be in the jail block. There were only six cells. The first cell on each side was empty. The last one on the left became Batanya's, and the one next to it, Clovache's.

The two cells directly across from theirs were also occupied by humans. Opposite Batanya, a young man was sitting on his cot. He jumped up eagerly while the guards were locking up Batanya. He was wearing the same prisoners' outfit, but on him it looked good.

The youth was slender, ethereally lovely, and very pleased to have some company. "People who can talk to me!" he said in a melodic voice. "Am I not beautiful? Do I not deserve to be admired?"

Since Batanya was busy pulling down the tunic and tightening the drawstring on the pants, she didn't answer immediately. When she'd gotten herself arranged and the guards were occupied with Clovache, she turned to give him an examination. "Oh, yes, you're pretty as a picture," she said politely. "Why are you here instead of in Lucifer's bed?" If Lucifer was hooked on men, she couldn't imagine him turning down such a choice morsel. The rich chestnut of the youth's hair, his wide green eyes, his smooth-as-silk tan skin . . . Well, it was enough to make your mouth water, if you'd been in any mood for fun and games. Batanya wasn't.

"Oh, I was for a while," he said. Even his voice was pleasant; just deep enough to be masculine, formed by a smiling mouth. "He was so incredibly lucky to have me! I shone in his bed like a star in the night sky! Not that I've seen the night sky in many ages. But I do remember it," he added wistfully. He pulled his own tunic off over his head and doffed his trousers in a second graceful gesture. "Do you notice how lovely my ass is? Is not my cock perfect? And my legs—so straight, so well formed."

The guards hardly gave the prisoner a glance as they exited. Presumably they'd seen the show before. Batanya was pleased to see that Clovache was regarding the young man with interest. He rotated slowly so that both newcomers could get a comprehensive look at his assets.

"Yes, very nice," Batanya said, which was not nearly enough for the youth.

"You can't have seen anything like me before," he said to Clovache, coaxingly.

"That's for damn sure," she agreed, cocking an eyebrow.

"Yes, one of kind," he said proudly. He couldn't seem to speak of himself any other way. "It's simply inexplicable that Lucifer could prefer anyone else to me. Though some of the things he liked to do hurt me and bruised my fair flesh," he added, looking a little sad. "However," he said, brightening, "the blue tint did look fascinating against my normal skin tone."

The two Britlingens tried hard not to look at each other.

"You can put your clothes back on," Batanya said. "You're certainly very attractive, but we have more urgent things to think of. What is your name, handsome?"

"Narcissus," he said. "Isn't that beautiful?"

"Yes," Clovache said, with every appearance of sincerity. "We've heard of you." She turned to Batanya and winked. Batanya was relieved her junior was feeling well enough to react to the young man.

"Oh, my fame has spread even to . . . wherever it is you come from?" This idea made him very cheerful. He picked up a small mirror and began examining his own face in it.

"I guess the guards let him have a mirror so he'd shut up," Batanya muttered. Narcissus, totally involved in his reflection, didn't seem to notice his fellow prisoners anymore.

"Excuse me," called the woman across from Clovache.

The two Britlingens went to the front of their cells. "Can I help you?" Clovache asked. It was a ridiculous question, but it would start the conversational ball rolling.

"Can you tell me what year it is?" the woman asked.

"That depends on what dimension you inhabit," Batanya said. "And what planet you live on."

The woman sighed. She appeared to be in her forties. She had short brownish hair, straight white teeth with a marked gap in front, and a pleasant face. "I hear things like that here all the time, and I'm not sure what to make of it," she said. She was wearing tailored pants and a blouse with funny dots down the front. Batanya realized, after a moment's study, that these round objects were the means of holding the shirt closed. Buttons, that was what they were called. There was a heavy jacket with big lapels and a hat and goggles hanging on a peg on the wall, the only place in the cell to hang possessions.

"You're not wearing the prison outfit," Clovache said. "Why is that?"

"I don't know. I landed on an island in the Pacific, after the longest flight I've ever had." The handsome woman looked momentarily confused. "I don't know exactly where we were when our plane began to falter. And my navigator didn't survive the landing." She was silent for a long moment. "When I got out of the plane, I was stumbling around, and I went between two palm trees, and suddenly I was here. I was caught right away by some of those spidery things, and they brought me down to show me to the handsome gentleman. Is his name really Lucifer? Have I gone to Hell?"

"You landed on Hell. Now we're below the surface, of course. What country are you from?" There was something oddly out of place about this woman.

"I'm from the United States of America," she said. "I'm an aviatrix."

Clovache looked over at Batanya, who shrugged. "I don't know what that is," she said.

"I fly airplanes," the woman said with simple pride.

"I'm afraid you're not on Earth any longer," Batanya said. "At least . . . you're not in the same dimension as Earth. We were just there a few weeks ago."

"I figured that I couldn't be back home. And I am surely not in the Pacific." The woman sat on the cot, as if her knees had simply given out. "I don't know how long . . . What year is it? I left in 1937."

"The year here wouldn't be the same as the year it was when you left," Clovache said. "We are Britlingens."

The woman's face stayed blank.

Batanya said, "You seem to have been caught up in some event, or some magic, unknown to us."

The woman took a deep, shuddering breath. "What year was it when you were last on Earth?" she asked, as if not quite certain she wanted to know the answer.

"Ah . . . well past your time," Clovache said. She glanced across Narcissus's cell to Batanya. "After 2000, anyway, though I'm not sure I ever noticed what year it was." She shrugged. "We knew we weren't going to be there long."

"It was in the 2000s," Batanya agreed.

"I can't understand this," the woman said quietly. "I must be insane."

"What's your name?" Batanya asked. Maybe a change of topic would break the woman's black mood.

"Amelia Earhart." She glanced from Batanya to Clovache as if, despite everything, she thought they might recognize her name. She and Narcissus had that in common, anyway.

When Amelia saw that the two Britlingens hadn't heard of her, she shrugged. Then her whole posture stiffened as the prisoners all heard a sound approaching the big door that was supposed to seal off the cells, though the guards had left it open. It was a sort of scratchy, snuffly sound. "Ah, the dogs," Amelia said. "It must be almost dinnertime."

"Dogs?" Batanya said hoarsely, at almost the same moment that Clovache said, "What kind of dogs?"

"They're large," Narcissus said. He was taking a break from staring at his reflection. He was polishing his mirror with the hem of his tunic.

"Large!" Amelia laughed, the first normal sound they'd heard in this place. "They're giants!"

Two huge black hounds came through the doorway and began sniffing down the corridor. They had short, shining fur, pointed ears, and long, thin tails. Their mouths were open and their long pink tongues were lolling out, providing a sharp color contrast to their sharp white fangs and their glowing red eyes.

Batanya pressed herself as far back in her cell as she could go, unless she could gouge a niche in the stone wall. She managed to say, "Do they let the dogs come into the cells?" Dogs! It would be dogs! Why couldn't the prison level be guarded by hydras, or gargoyles? Anything besides dogs.

"No," Narcissus said. The dogs swung their heads toward him and took a tentative step closer to the bars of his cell. With a complete disregard for the long, sharp teeth and the demonic eyes, Narcissus moved to the front of the cell and stretched his hand between the bars. The fearsome beasts took a big sniff, and the one nearer Narcissus let the young man scratch his head.

The three women stared at this, and Narcissus smiled. "Even dogs are attracted to me," he said happily. "But you know, I love them, too."

Batanya shuddered when she thought of some of the things she'd seen in her travels. She hoped the bars remained in place, for Narcissus's sake. "Attracted" could translate in many ways.

After a moment, the hounds seemed to lose interest in Narcissus and resumed their prowl down the corridor. The red eyes fixed on each prisoner in turn, and a growl began rumbling through their chests as they came to Batanya's cell. Her face was set in the clenched expression of someone completely determined not to show what she was feeling, but she was pale and sweating.

"Just stay back from the bars," Clovache said, keeping her voice smooth and calm with a huge effort. "They can't get you. They're just reacting to your . . ." Clovache couldn't bring herself to say the word in connection to her senior.

Batanya understood her, though, and she said it herself. "Yes, they smell my fear." She hated this, hated herself for feeling it. Hated having a weakness. *You're a warrior,* she told herself. *That was years ago. You're too old to feel this, now.*

Both the hounds thrust their heads against the bars of her cell, and they began to bay. It was like nothing she'd ever heard. It took every ounce of grit she had to keep her knees stiff. Two human guards came rushing down the corridor to check out the hounds' agitation. The hounds were by now so excited that they wheeled and leaped toward the guards, who were completely taken by surprise. Both men were armed with a form of gun, but before the stocky man on the left could draw his from its holster, the nearest hound had leaped upon him and taken out his neck with one huge bite. The guard's head, its expression still startled, rolled grotesquely across the floor, coming to stop at Amelia Earhart's cell. The other man was faster and steadier. He was ready to fire before the second hound was on him. His finger tightened on the trigger and the first bullet thudded into the beast leaping for him. The hound landed short, whimpering, and its decapitating buddy swung his head toward the attacking guard and growled.

But the tall, brawny fellow was not going to back down. "I'll shoot you down!" he screamed, and the dogs seemed to think better about attacking someone as aggressive as they were. The one that had been shot was healing already. A gout of black blood spattered on the stone was the only reminder of the wound.

"They're not going to die," Batanya said. She and Clovache noticed at the same moment that the black blood on the stone was beginning to hiss, and a cloud of smoke was rising from the place where it had lain. When the smoke dispersed, there was a miniature crater in the floor of the corridor.

"God almighty," said Amelia Earhart.

Narcissus crooned to the dog, "Did the nasty man want to shoot you?" and the hound that had been shot snuffled the hand that Narcissus extended through the bars. Even the guard watched incredulously.

The hound licked Narcissus's hand.

Clovache's mouth fell open and they all waited to see what would happen. But Narcissus didn't scream and fall on the ground in pain. He stood regarding the huge beast with self-centered benevolence, and the huge tongue, long and thin and somehow obscene, slathered the beautiful pale hands with dog spit. Only the blood was corrosive.

"Hmmm." Batanya was calmer now. She was ashamed of her display of fear, and she'd begun thinking. The hounds padded off the way they'd come, the guard watching them cautiously and keeping his gun drawn. Only when they'd left the room and he'd watched them exit the guardroom beyond did he squat down to get a grip on his former colleague's ankles. He tugged. Leaving an unpleasant swath of body fluids in its wake, the corpse began moving. Finally, it vanished from sight. After a moment or two, the guard came back for the head. He didn't speak to the prisoners, and the prisoners didn't say a word.

After he was gone, Clovache said, "I'm guessing the guards are chosen among the unpopular and the incompetent."

Narcissus smiled. "Yes, the guards don't last long. For a while, I got special concessions when I told them that since the dogs liked me, they'd be less likely to attack the ones who gave me things that made me happy. That worked for while; I got the mirror, and some extra food, and even a hairbrush. But then the bigger hound got angry with the female guard, one of those insectlike ones, and snapped off her foreleg. I didn't get any extras after that."

"How'd she walk without the foreleg?" Clovache asked.

"Not very well. In fact, I had to laugh," Narcissus said.

Batanya looked at him. He was quite heartless, she decided, unless the pity and sympathy were directed at him. But he wasn't useless.

"How often do the hellhounds come around?" she asked Amelia.

"Twice a day, at least that's what they did yesterday," Amelia said briskly. "I think this is morning, and this was their first visit. Do you know what time it is?"

Batanya shrugged. "I lost track."

"I guess they're let loose for regular patrols. Or maybe they're controlled some other way. I haven't seen a handler. They get to do what they want, as you saw."

Batanya sat on her bed and began to think. At least she and Clovache were side by side. There was no point in counting on any help from Narcissus. At any moment, his mirror could distract him, and his only concern was himself. At any moment, he could decide that his own comfort and pleasure were better served by inaction than action. But Amelia seemed plucky.

Perhaps Narcissus, a mythological character known even in Spauling's literature, could be considered timeless. Maybe he was even immortal. But Amelia Earhart, according to her own testimony, was a complete human, tied to a specific time line in Earth's history. Somehow, she'd time-traveled successfully, a fact that the magicians and technicians who powered the Britlingen Collective would find extremely interesting. Not that they had any business tampering with time; in fact, the possibility gave Batanya deep misgivings. But returning with Amelia, if that was possible, would make up for having let their client Crick get captured. Plus, Amelia seemed like a sensible woman, and she didn't seem to have any idea of how to return to her own time and place in the world, whatever that might have been.

"Listen, Amelia, Clovache," Batanya said. She didn't like that Narcissus could overhear, but she had no option. She had no writing materials, and she wasn't telepathic, and she didn't know sign language. *When I get back,* she thought, *I'll ask the teachers to put sign language on the curriculum.* She smiled. It was extremely unlikely they'd live to do that, but she could tell her survival sense had decreed that she should plan on it.

Amelia and Clovache both came to the front of their cages.

"How long do we have before they feed us?" Batanya asked Amelia.

Amelia pondered. "They should be by with something pretty soon," she said. "The feeding's not exactly regular, but we do get three meals a day. It's pretty much the same food no matter what the time of day is: not really breakfast, dinner, supper."

Batanya said, "We have to get out of here. Sooner or later, Lucifer will get tired of Crick, or he'll forget he doesn't want to alienate the Collective—we'll explain that to you later, Amelia—and he'll have us killed, or we'll meet an 'accident.' You'll notice he's pretty careless with his soldiers."

"I'm listening," Amelia said. "What about sissy-boy, here?" She nodded toward Narcissus's cage. A glance told Batanya that the beautiful youth was busy brushing his chestnut hair.

"He's all for himself," Batanya said. "The best we can hope is that he doesn't get in our way." Narcissus, still sans clothing, began examining his body, pore by pore, as far as Batanya could tell. He lifted his genitals, gave them a good scan, and then dropped his package as casually as if it'd been a bunch of wilted flowers.

"What's your plan?" Clovache said.

"Here it is." It didn't take long to explain.

In a little while, two guards (the one who'd escaped the hellhounds, and Sha) brought in a cart with four large bowls. The pass-through hatches for the bowls were at the bottom of the bars in the door, and each bowl was shoved through with very little care for whether it slopped over or not. A bucket of water followed it. This must have been intended for both washing and drinking, since there was a dipper hanging from the side of the bucket. Sha, the snakeman, still found Clovache attractive and showed his admiration openly.

"Show me what you've got, little one," he hissed to Clovache, who looked a little anxious. Sha had a spear, and a dagger thrust through his belt. Lucifer had ordered the guards not to go into the cells, but Sha might disobey.

"He can't let you out, and he can't go in," Amelia said. "He doesn't have the key on his belt." Batanya could tell by the relaxation in her shoulders that Clovache was relieved, though her face remained stony as he continued to tell her what he'd like to do with her.

"Who does have the key?" Batanya said to Amelia. She didn't want Clovache to think she was worried. "The other guard doesn't have it either."

"I think the commander of the guard has it at all times, at least as far as I've been able to see. That would be the wolfy one called Marl."

Clovache grew tired of Sha's suggestive remarks and told him to fuck off. Batanya laughed, but she noticed that Amelia looked quite shocked. "I'm sorry," Batanya called. "We are rough soldiers, and our language is sometimes just as rough."

Amelia's face cleared, and she managed to smile back at Batanya.

"Did you notice how that guard couldn't take his eyes off me?" Narcissus asked, and the three women sighed in unison.

Batanya hunkered down to examine the contents of her supper bowl. She had a very rudimentary Plan A, and she turned it over in her head while she ate.

There was no Plan B.

Like good Britlingens, Batanya and Clovache consumed everything in their bowls. Batanya wasn't sure what the meal was—some kind of noodle and some meat, though what the creature had originally been was anybody's guess—but it wasn't spoiled. She sniffed very carefully for poison, and asked Amelia how she'd felt after the other meals she'd eaten.

"Fine," Amelia said, astonished.

At last Clovache took a mouthful to see if the food was drugged, since that was the job of a junior. The Britlingens waited for a few minutes.

"I feel fine," Clovache said, and without further ado they dug in. There was a hunk of bread in the bowl, too, and it was fairly good. No vegetables; she guessed those would have been hard to produce underground. Not a healthy meal, but it would supply the energy they'd need.

"Save a bit of meat," Batanya said.

After they'd eaten and rested, the two Britlingens exercised. Amelia and Narcissus were interested, Amelia because she was obviously a normally active woman and because she was bored, and Narcissus because he thought exercise might improve his body. Amelia showed them how to do "jumping jacks," which amused Batanya. They ran in place, lunged, squatted, punched at the air in jabs (Amelia called that "shadow boxing"), and completed a hundred push-ups (at least, Clovache and Batanya completed a hundred). After a few more exercises, they all took a nap, for lack of anything better to do. The guards didn't reappear for at least four hours, and then when they opened the door at the end of the corridor, it was to push the cart through again, so it was time for lunch . . . or maybe supper. Possibly breakfast?

Batanya was ashamed that she'd lost track of how many hours they'd moved through the tunnels before they'd been captured. They'd left Spauling in the middle of the afternoon, though that didn't necessarily mean they'd arrived in Hell at the same time of day. And, really, did it make a difference? Some of the denizens of Hell were sure to be awake around the clock.

When she heard the click of the hounds' claws on the stone floor, Batanya got ready, though her hands were not steady and sweat was already trickling down her back.

"I fucking hate dogs," she whispered, but Clovache heard her.

"Have you reached in your pocket?" Clovache asked.

"Your outfits don't have pockets," Amelia said.

"We brought our own," Batanya told her.

After a particularly successful mission, their client had given Clovache and Batanya a sizable bonus. Clovache had wanted to take a trip to Pardua and go to the famous male whorehouse there to see the dancing, but Batanya had persuaded her to visit a special medical technician instead. Batanya had a false wall in one cheek, prepared with careful and expensive surgery. In that secret thin pocket, she'd stowed a small flat blade. It was sharp enough and long enough to open a vein, whether her own or someone else's, but it was strictly an emergency option.

The time had come to use it.

Clovache had a similar false pouch on the underside of her arm, high up near the pit. A *very* thorough search would have uncovered her pocket, and possibly Batanya's, but they hadn't been searched very thoroughly, proof of the fact that the worst soldiers got prison guard duty in Hell. Clovache stepped to the front of her cell at the moment Batanya did.

"Narcissus," Clovache said. The young man stopped examining his fingernails and looked at her. "Don't be upset," she said steadily. "I promise you they'll heal."

"Good luck," Amelia said, very quietly, as the hounds entered the jail corridor. Their massive black heads swung from side to side, as if they were considering who would taste best. Their red eyes glowed like burning coals.

The Britlingens held out the bits of meat they'd saved, for the hounds' inspection. They were standing as close together as they could get at the juncture of their cells. Noses twitching, the two beasts approached cautiously. Clovache's hand was just within the bars, and the hound sniffing at her meat shoved his head closer. It was much too broad to fit between the bars, but his nose extended inside the cell. While Clovache's left hand fed the hound, her right hand slid between the bars to grip the broad studded collar, and then her tiny blade scored the hound's skin at the neck. A gush of blood told her she'd struck the best spot, and that blood sprayed on the bars of the cell as the hound reared back, baying and shrieking.

The blood also spattered on Clovache's hands.

Batanya's hound turned slightly to leap against the bars at the juncture of the cells in an attempt to get at Clovache, and as he reared with his chest and stomach exposed, Batanya's bladed hand darted out to rake the hound's skin. She'd had the presence of mind to pull off her tunic and hold it to the dog, too, which was a good thing, since she didn't get an arterial spray. Pulling the soaked tunic back through, she immediately rubbed the bloody cloth over the metal of the bars. She stuffed the tunic down at the bottom of the bars, so the blood remaining in the cloth might do some good. This left her standing bare-chested, but she pulled the blanket from her bed and draped it around her shoulders. She hoped they wouldn't notice the absence of her tunic.

A group of guards rushed in to investigate the dogs'

commotion, and it took everything the Britlingens had to look stunned. Though Narcissus had flinched when the dogs were hurt, he was silent, at least for the moment. Amelia provided a great distraction by screaming up a storm, and since the guards looked at her and the hounds first, Batanya and Clovache had the chance to slide their thin blades into places that might escape inspection. Batanya's went into the thick padding of her socks, and Clovache's into a tiny crevice in the stone floor of her cell.

"Hands in the water!" Batanya said hoarsely, and Clovache immersed her hands in her water bucket. Batanya hoped it was quick enough to save Clovache's skin.

"They attacked each other!" Amelia told the guards. The American woman was not a great actress, but she did look very excited. They believed her.

"I've never seen them turn on each other," Sha hissed, but he didn't seem inclined to ask more questions. After all, the prisoners were in their cells, and unarmed.

Though the hounds were still whining, their wounds were healing fast. Narcissus called them to him and stroked their huge heads while they whimpered. Narcissus had kept silent for so long that Batanya was hopeful he wouldn't blurt out some information. He was watching all the action with an expression that sat oddly on his face.

"He's thinking about something besides himself," Clovache muttered to Batanya, who was standing as close as she could get, because she wanted a look at Clovache's hands. "That can't be good." Tears were running down Clovache's face. That meant the water immersion hadn't completely worked.

"Steady," she said, and Narcissus moved to the corner of his cell to look at the bars on Batanya's. Batanya followed the direction of his gaze. The bars were beginning to smoke; just a little, easy to miss in the murky atmosphere, but still . . . Their eyes met. *Come on, beautiful,* she thought. *Give me this. I'll admire you till the pookas return to their burrows, if you'll just give me this.* She tried to smile winsomely, but it was too much of an effort. She gave him a good, hard stare. She was much better at that.

"What are you doing, bitch?" screamed Sha. Clovache whirled to face him, her fingers scattering drops of water. The skin of her hands was blistered, and Clovache clasped them behind her after a quick downward glance.

"Washing my hands, since the hounds slobbered all over them," Clovache said. "What did you feed them, razor blades? Why'd they bite each other?" Sha glared at her, suspicion written all over his scaled face, and a third guard, one of the dustballs, rolled around in an unbelieving manner.

The steam coming off the bars was slowly increasing in density, and any moment the guards would notice. If sheer force of will could have moved them, they would have shot back outside the doors. The hounds, casting malevolent looks at Batanya and Clovache, skulked out into the guardroom. The guards, after a few more threats and a lot more curses, followed. The doors slammed shut just in time, because the smoke was beginning to really pour off the bars that had been touched with hound blood.

"Let me see your hands," Batanya said, and Clovache held them out. There were bright red blisters covering the palms of Clovache's hands. They looked so painful that even Narcissus winced in sympathy. (He felt better after he looked down at his own white, unsullied hands.)

Clovache shrugged. "Worth it, if we get out. Will they come back in if we make a lot of noise?" she asked Narcissus.

"No," said the beautiful youth after a moment's thought. "Others scream and plead all the time. And they only came in before because the hounds were howling, and the hounds are favorites of Lucifer's. An ogre beat his heads against the bars for an hour before they came to check, two weeks ago." He looked at the Britlingens expectantly.

"You were so clever to keep silent when the hounds were in here," Batanya said hastily. "I was so proud of you. I don't know how we'd accomplish this without your help."

Satisfied temporarily, Narcissus gave her a lovely smile and fetched his hairbrush.

The smoke roiled and thickened, and the air got even worse. After perhaps five minutes, the smoke began to dissipate, though the thick atmosphere made it hard to see what damage had been done. Batanya positioned herself carefully and swung the heavy water bucket at what she figured was the weakest point. She got as close as she could to examine the weak spot. She hadn't caused any visible damage, but the impact of the metal-rimmed bucket against the bars hadn't felt as violent as she'd expected. Heartened, Batanya swung the bucket again, putting all the strength of her upper body into the movement. The bars bent outward, and a few flakes fell off the fast-corroding metal. She swung again, and the metal bent outward. Clovache had grasped her own bucket in her damaged hands and began the same procedure on the bars of her own cell. That didn't go as swiftly, because smearing the blood on a wide section had produced better results than a more intense application in a few spots. With a roar of sheer focus, Batanya swung the bucket for a tenth time, and a section of the bars broke off, creating an aperture large enough to allow her to climb out. Amelia cheered, Narcissus gaped, and Clovache sagged against her cot with relief. The next instant, she was back to swinging her bucket. While Batanya ran to hide behind the door, Clovache began to yell in time with her attacks on the bars.

Narcissus had told them the guards were slow to react to prisoner noise, and it took a few minutes before the combination of Clovache's piercing screams and the banging of the bucket roused them to come check. The first one through the door was the snakeman, Sha, and Batanya was on his back instantly, slicing the side of his neck with her tiny blade. His blood was not red, more of a deep purple, and it didn't spray, but welled sluggishly from the gash. But he crumpled to the floor, scaled hands clutching at the wound as if to keep his blood inside. Batanya leaped over him to attack the dustball. It didn't seem to have a mortal spot to wound, at least to human eyes, but Batanya swung her arm as if there were a sword in it instead of an inch-and-a-half blade, and the startled dustball rolled farther into the corridor, bringing it closer to Amelia's cell. Amelia thrust her arms through the bars and brought them together, as she would as if she had caught an assailant's neck. Batanya had wondered if Amelia's arms would cut through the dustball, but the aviatrix seemed to be compressing an area. The dustball reacted in an agitated fashion, so at least it was seriously frightened at being held like that. Compression was the key to defeating the creature.

Clovache, halfway out of her own cell, climbed back in to get her blanket from the cot.

"Stand away," she yelled to Batanya, who obeyed instantly. Clovache tossed the blanket over the creature, and then she and Batanya threw themselves on it. The dustball began to deflate as they pressed it against the bars of Amelia's cell, and when the two Britlingens dug their feet in and pushed harder, the escaping air achieved a moaning sound. The smell was even more unpleasant than the other smells in the jail, and Amelia looked really queasy.

After a silent struggle that seemed to go on for hours, the dustball was squashed flat. When the Britlingens cautiously released their pressure, a large lump of hair, trash, and dust fell to the stone floor. Clovache threw the blanket on top of it, in case it could pump itself back up, and she dragged the snakeman's ghastly body on top of that, while Batanya divested Sha of his dagger.

"What's happening?" Marl called from the guardroom. The door had swung shut behind Sha and the dustball, so he didn't have a good view, and he wasn't at the peephole—too cautious, maybe.

"Help! Help! He's killing me!" Clovache screamed. Furious that Sha was interfering with a valuable prisoner, Marl threw open the door and rushed into the prison wing, sword drawn. Batanya tripped him and stabbed him through the neck with Sha's dagger. Within seconds, they'd gotten the keys off his belt and Batanya was unlocking Amelia's cell.

The tall woman didn't waste any time getting out, and the four former prisoners clustered together for a minute.

"Amelia, Narcissus, I don't know what you want to do, but Clovache and I have to rescue our client," Batanya said. "Does either of you have any knowledge of where Lucifer's chambers are?"

"I do," Narcissus said. "I spent hours there, entrancing and entertaining him." He made a ludicrous attempt to look modest.

"Will you take us there?" Batanya asked. There was no time for finesse. They were in the middle of hostile territory.

"We want to keep you with us as long as we can," Clovache said more diplomatically, "and if you can't help us, we have to be on our way."

"Since you ask so nicely," Narcissus said, casting a cold look in Batanya's direction, "I will lead you there."

There was no question that Amelia wanted to go. She was pale with anxiety, and choking on the suffocating miasma of the jail. The four ex-prisoners crept to the open door. The air in the guard chamber outside was remarkably stinky, but it was a big improvement nonetheless.

For a few seconds they just breathed.

The great thing about the guardroom was the weapons hanging on the walls. Batanya felt much more like herself with a gun in one hand and a sword in the other. Clovache spotted their armor, and seized it with a yip of delight. She was about to shimmy into it when Batanya stopped her. "It's too Britlingen," Batanya said. "We need to be guards." The two pulled on the green pants and tunics that the guards wore. Clovache reluctantly bundled the two suits into a backpack. She would have felt much better with it on her body, but Batanya knew Clovache could see the sense of her decision. To compensate, Clovache armed herself to the teeth with two guns, a short spear, and a dagger.

"We're going to pretend we have you two in custody," Batanya explained to Amelia and Narcissus, who had pulled on his clothes. "If we herd you ahead of us, that's a good way for Narcissus to guide us to our client without it being obvious we don't know the way." Amelia nodded. She was so anxious to leave the jail that she couldn't form words.

The Britlingens held their new weapons at businesslike attitudes. When Batanya glanced down at the gun she held, she found she had no idea what would happen when she fired it, or even if she had it pointing in the right direction. Narcissus stepped ahead of them, casting a look over his shoulder to make sure they'd all noticed his beautiful butt. They smiled at him reassuringly and nodded to show encouragement and admiration. He led them to the right into the large trunk corridor they'd traversed to get there.

When they passed another group of Lucifer's soldiers, Batanya gripped the gun so hard she thought it might bend, but no one questioned them. One woman whistled after Narcissus, which pleased him no end, though he seemed equally happy when a snakeman pinched his left lower cheek.

"When you get through with him, pass him along," hissed the snakeman.

"Lucifer wants him," Batanya said, shrugging.

Because of the uniform tunics they'd donned in the prison area, they went a long way without challenge. The two Britlingens looked very different without the hoods of their summer armor, and they were certainly sufficiently tough to pass as guards. As they moved through the tunnels, the traffic increased and the tunnels themselves became wider and decorated with paintings and lamps. These bits of civilization gradually increased in frequency and splendor, until they found themselves in the audience hall where they'd first seen Lucifer. Narcissus led them across this, though they were going much more slowly now because of the groups of servants or soldiers who were also crossing the large space. Hell sure was busy. Lucifer wasn't in the great hall, to Batanya's relief. She wanted to reclaim Crick when there weren't scores of Lucifer's minions around.

After they'd freed their client, all they'd have to do was fight through all these savage creatures to get to the surface, or at least find some quiet and undisturbed spot so the

Britlingens could trigger their beacon and their party could be returned to the castle in Spauling.

That was all they had to do.

Batanya quelled a moment of despair. Britlingens never gave up. There was a client to save. She thought of her picture going up on the Wall of Shame, and her lip curled in distaste.

They were brought up short just at that moment by the four guards barring the two magnificent doors. Narcissus's dead halt meant this was Lucifer's personal suite.

Talk their way in, or just start killing? If a troop of soldiers hadn't appeared just at that moment marching by on some other business, Batanya might have found out how well her new sword worked. But there were at least twelve soldiers, and two of them were the quadruped net-throwers. Batanya had formed a strong disinclination to tangle with them again, if she could help it. Clovache glanced at her senior, a question in her face, and Batanya nodded.

Clovache said, "Lucifer wants these two," jerking her head to indicate Amelia and Narcissus.

"He didn't say anything to us," the guard with the fanciest uniform said. She was a huge woman with golden skin and golden eyes. Narcissus fluttered his eyelashes at her, and she choked back a surprised laugh. "I'm Ginever, day captain," she said.

"I'm Clovache, prison guard. The Master apparently told Marl, who ordered us to bring them," Clovache said.

Ginever looked surprised, as if Lucifer talking directly to Marl was unlikely. It probably was, considering Marl had been a lowly prison guard overseer.

"Let me just ask," she said. "He's got his shiny toy back, and he doesn't like to be disturbed when he's playing."

Batanya felt an unexpected wave of pity for Crick. The Harwell Clan was nearly extinct because of its members' unusual physical attribute. Being gifted had its price. When Batanya had the time to be curious, she promised herself she'd learn the clan's history.

"This one is wanted to join in the fun," Clovache said, pointing to Narcissus. "You can see the attraction."

"Oh, yes," said the golden woman, smiling. "Oh, yes. He's been here often enough before. Well, I must check." She knocked on the left door, a quick set of three raps. Her ear to its surface, she waited. She must have heard some sound of assent, because she drew back to open the door. Batanya exhaled a silent sigh of relief.

"In, prisoners, move your feet!" she said, as curtly as a real prison guard. Ginever was no fool and certainly had a full complement of arms as well as three comrades, and the sooner they were out from under her eyes, the better.

Clovache led the way, followed by Narcissus and Amelia Earhart, with Batanya prodding from behind with the sword.

Lucifer, a flogger in his hand, was standing by a pillar. Crick was bound to the pillar, his back exposed and striped with blood. Batanya gulped, resisting the nausea that rose in her throat. Lucifer was staring at them, trying to figure out their presence, and in the split second before he could decipher their intent, Batanya leaped at him with the sword.

She got him, right through the stomach, but not before he managed to swing the flogger. It raked Batanya's back without enough force to draw blood through her clothing, but enough to make her dig in the sword for all she was worth.

Lucifer's beautiful face was twisted with anger. Despite the blade in his guts, he said, "I'll kill you for this, if I live."

"Oh, of course you'll live," Clovache said. Narcissus was looking at Lucifer hungrily, as if seeing someone else lovely was enough to excite his libido. Amelia was throwing up into a pot on the floor. Crick looked at them as if they were all as beautiful as Narcissus. But what he said was, "Get me out of this."

"The key?" Batanya said. Lucifer sneered at her. Batanya pulled a dagger from her belt. "You don't need both those pretty blue eyes," she said. "Which one do you want the most?"

"On the table by the bed," Lucifer said. Clovache ran to fetch it, and Batanya risked a glance to check on Narcissus and Amelia. Suddenly Lucifer bellowed at the top of his lungs, and in quick response there was pounding at the door. Ginever called, "Master? Master?"

"Kill them all!" Lucifer yelled, and the door began to bow inward.

"Find an exit," Batanya told Amelia, who'd finished being sick. "There's sure to be one." Amelia nodded, braced herself visibly, and began scanning the walls of the huge room. It was a very busy boudoir. It contained an enormous bed, many hangings, lots of torture paraphernalia and knickknacks, and a roaring fire; about what you'd expect of the personal apartment of the King of Hell.

"Here," Amelia called. She'd pulled aside a wall hanging depicting—well, it was as complicated as the threesome of soldiers they'd seen in the tunnels—and sure enough, there was a door.

"It doesn't lead to the surface," Lucifer said. "You're all going to die. But not before I have some fun with each of you, I hope."

"You already had fun with me," Narcissus said plaintively. "Surely you haven't forgotten *me*?"

"Just kill him right now," Lucifer advised Batanya, and for a second she was tempted. But there were other things to do, and besides, she had a jumbled feeling that killing Narcissus would be like breaking an ancient porcelain vase. He wasn't very useful, but he was beautiful.

Lucifer's wound was healing, as she'd expected, and he wouldn't be on the floor for long. The pounding at the door had accelerated, and there wasn't time to do more than wrap one of Crick's chains around the no-longer-bleeding lord and lock it with one of Crick's locks. Clovache had Crick moving and had picked up one of Lucifer's tunics and pulled it roughly over their client's head. Crick himself bent with obvious pain to pull on some shoes, and then they were tumbling out the door Amelia had found.

Batanya hadn't been sure Narcissus would follow, he'd

seemed so intent on forcing a compliment from his former lover—or torturer; but the beautiful youth trailed after them, though he didn't seem nearly anxious or urgent enough to suit her.

The door had to be blocked behind them. There was nothing in the dusty passage to help them do this, and the door didn't lock on this side.

Clovache said a few choice things, and Crick said, "Stand back." His voice was shaky but clear, and Batanya was grateful that he was well enough to remain on top of their perilous situation. Crick muttered a few words under his breath and pressed his hand in a curious gesture toward the door.

"It will hold them for a few minutes," he said, and they hurried away. "That's pretty much all the magic I have, so don't expect more," he added, getting the words out with an obvious effort. The passage was stone-floored like the rest of the underground palace, but it had been made strictly by men. The roof was braced, and there was no slug slime on the floor and walls.

"Do you know where this leads?" Batanya asked Narcissus.

"I didn't even know it was here," he said. "I never tried to escape from Lucifer before." Of course not.

It would have been wonderful to have Crick's map, but there was no telling where it had gone after Crick had been stripped. It wasn't like they had a lot of choices to make; the passage had so far not branched off.

"We're going northwest," Crick said, when they paused to get their breath. By now, the back of Lucifer's tunic was striped with Crick's blood. His face looked even bonier than it had before. Batanya admired his fortitude. "That's the direction of the guards' barracks."

"You're still determined to retrieve the conjuring ball," Batanya said with resignation.

"I might as well go back into that room and let him kill me there if I don't return with the ball. I held out telling him where it was. I can't come back to get it."

"Crap." Batanya wanted to pat him or choke him, she wasn't sure which.

"What is the law?" Clovache said sullenly.

"The client's word," Batanya said, with resignation.

They started out again, trying to move faster. Amelia was uncomplaining, but she was panting heavily, and she stumbled from time to time. Narcissus was in better shape, but he was not as keen as the rest were on getting out of Hell. Crick kept pace gamely, but he didn't object when Batanya put her arm under his shoulder to help him along.

The passage did branch off, finally, though the dust on the floor would surely indicate which way they'd taken. There was no help for it. They barged on straight ahead, since according to Crick that was still the best way to the barracks. The passage had led them slightly uphill, Batanya had noticed, and ahead of them they saw extra light coming from a grate in the floor.

The small group paused, and Clovache whispered into Narcissus's ear, "You must keep silent." They crept forward as quietly as they could, and Batanya felt Amelia's arm quiver with the effort the older woman was making to calm her ragged breathing.

When they got very close to the grate, Batanya leaned Crick up against the wall and stepped silently up to it by herself.

She was looking down into one of the soldiers' mess rooms. There were about twenty various creatures sitting around a table eating bread and meat, and drinking—those that had mouths—from bowls. They were all talking (or growling, or hooting), and when there was a loud alarm, at first they ignored it. Suddenly a large snakeman bounded into the room, and he bellowed (as much as his throat would permit him), "To arms! Lucifer has been attacked!" Whether from devotion or fear or professional pride, the collection of soldiers cleared out of the mess hall in double quick time.

"Shit," Batanya said, and Crick tried to smile.

"I agree," he said. "But at the same time, this is the last

place they'd expect us to come, and if they're clearing out, this is our best chance to retrieve the ball."

"Which way?" Batanya said, having no argument to make with that.

"Forward," he said, trying to put some energy in his voice.

So on they hurried. Two more grates were passed, Crick taking a careful look down each one, and at the third one he said, "This is it."

Batanya's shoulders wanted to sag with relief, but she kept herself braced and ready for action. She had an awful feeling she could hear the sound of pursuit coming up the passage; it was some way distant, but their pursuers would catch up quickly since they were all fit. So she wouldn't think about what would happen after that, she squatted down to remove the grate, which wasn't secured in any way; why would it be? Before she could speak, Crick grasped the rim and lowered himself down to the bed that was almost squarely beneath the grate. He gasped in sudden pain and dropped heavily, and the bed broke. Crick ended up on the floor, curled in a ball. In a flash, Batanya lowered herself through the opening and dropped a lot more gracefully.

"You idiot," she said as she helped Crick to rise. "Where is it?" He pointed to some cabinets lined up against the wall, obviously intended to hold the soldiers' effects.

"On top," he said. "On top of the first cabinet to the right." This proved to be a narrow cabinet with three lines scratched on it. Batanya opened the cabinet, stood on the lowest shelf, and heaved herself up. Sure enough, back against the wall where it would be out of sight, there was the conjuring ball, hastily concealed by Crick months before. It was wrapped in a rag that had been used to wipe it clean. Remembering where Crick had kept it concealed, Batanya was grateful. She grabbed the ball and leaped down, bounding over to Crick in almost the same moment. He took it and tossed it up to Clovache. Batanya gripped Crick around the hips and lifted. Clovache and Amelia reached down and seized Crick's upstretched hands, and together they bundled the thief up into the passage again. Once he was out of the way, Batanya made a good leap to seize the lip of the opening herself, and with the help of the two women she managed to join the others, just as the door of the room below opened with a crash.

"Now," she said to Clovache. "Now!"

Clovache pressed a lump behind her ear where the beacon was implanted. Then she pressed it again. Batanya reached behind her own ear and pressed hers three times. Five people to transport.

Nothing happened.

"Fuck," Batanya said. "Can the ball get us out of here?"

"I don't know how to get it to . . ." Crick began, and then the sounds of pursuit became immediate. Batanya swung around to face the oncoming horde, and Clovache picked up her short spear and hurled it at the lead figure, one of the snakemen. He fell and the others stumbled around him, but it was only a matter of seconds before they were overwhelmed. Crick dropped the conjuring ball, and Amelia retrieved it automatically. "I want to go back," she said, almost weeping.

Pop!

There was confused swirl of colors and sounds, the impression of a high wind, and they were standing under a brilliant sun on what appeared to be a small island. The sea surged all around; there was no other land in sight. There were a few palm trees, and Batanya heard a bird scream. A wrecked airplane was crumpled on the beach before them, a dead man lying next to it. Amelia's face was a study in shock, and Batanya was sure her own face matched it. Clovache, thinking very quickly, seized the conjuring ball from Amelia's hand, and said, "To the beacon."

Pop!

The sounds and colors again, the dizzying whirling feeling, and then they all arrived on the platform in the hall of the magicians and mechs.

There was quite a crowd in there; and it took Batanya a

long second to realize she didn't need to kill them. Clovache actually took a swipe with her short sword, which made her commander leap back smartly.

"Hold!" Flechette bellowed. "Hold, you fool!"

After a moment of reorientation, Batanya understood she didn't need to stand in front of Crick any longer, and she stepped aside. Crick was doubled over, gasping in pain. Amelia stared around her, so stunned it would be hard to pick one emotion from another as they crossed her face. After a moment's evaluation, Narcissus trotted down the few stairs to the handsomest person he could see, a young mech woman. Though he was grimy and wearing his prison tunic, she looked at him as if she'd seen the face of a god, which Batanya supposed was not too very far from the truth. Narcissus held out his hand, and the mech had a hard job to decide whether to shake it or kneel to kiss it. She settled for holding it and basking in the smile Narcissus bestowed. "Do you like dogs?" he asked her.

Batanya and Clovache helped Crick down to the floor. Crick said, "For a bit, there, we didn't know if you would get us out in time." He made an effort to sound casual. That was exactly what Batanya had been thinking, but she hadn't wanted say it out loud (especially in front of her junior).

"This asshole almost prevented us from extracting you," Flechette said, and for the first time Batanya noticed that Flechette was gripping Trovis by the arm. "He tried to persuade the magicians and mechs that you'd sent a false signal, that the minions of Hell would home in on the beacon if they acted on it."

"I didn't believe him," said the young mech woman, with a shy smile. "I called Flechette to overrule him."

"Can I execute Trovis?" Clovache asked. "He has tried to have us done in more times than I can count, and all because Batanya wouldn't lie with him and broke his arm making him back off."

"Ah," said Flechette. "Perhaps we shouldn't kill him . . . but he must be punished."

Clovache still had the conjuring ball. Though Trovis

made an effort to dodge and to twist out of Flechette's grip, Clovache ran her arm around Trovis's neck, looked down at the ball, said, "Go back!" *Pop!* She and Flechette and Trovis were staring at a vast green sea, scraggly palm trees, a wrecked airplane, and a dead man.

"Drop Trovis's arm," she told Flechette, who did, at least partly from surprise at getting an order from a junior. Clovache took a step back from the gaping Trovis herself, gripped Flechette's shoulder, concentrated on the ball, said, "Back to the hall," and *Pop!* They were back in the magicians' hall.

Minus Trovis.

"Brilliant," said Batanya.

When she'd collected herself, Flechette said, "This is just. No one will dispute it."

Trials had never really caught on at the Britlingen Collective.

"Who—and what—have you brought with you?" asked the tall, veiled magician who had ushered them in on the day they'd departed. Every magician and mech in the room, even Narcissus's new admirer, was electrified with excitement at Clovache's demonstration.

"This is Amelia Earhart," Batanya said, taking care to pronounce the name correctly. "She is a . . . She can operate a flying machine, and she left home, which was America, on Earth, in July of 1937."

"A time traveler," exclaimed the magician. His eyes, above the veil, were almost glowing with interest. "And that is surely Lucifer's conjuring ball."

"It's the island. That one tiny island," Batanya said. "That's the key. Amelia landed on it by accident, and then as she explored the island, she found herself in Hell. The island is a portal of some kind. Once Amelia had come through, she could pass back, with the help of the conjuring ball. She took Clovache and the rest of us through. Then our homing spell finally worked, and we returned through the portal to land here. So the conjuring ball can take you through the portal, if you're with someone who's passed through it once." Batanya couldn't decide if her theory was complete nonsense or not. The magicians and mechs could study their magical hearts out and tell her their findings.

In the meantime, she would have happy daydreams of Trovis on a deserted Pacific island in 1937 in the middle of nowhere.

"If this proves to be true, you have experienced amazing magic," the veiled magician told Amelia, who looked heartened by the greeting.

"Well, thank you very much, sir," she said. "I'll try to make myself useful. I don't guess you can send me home? Not to the island." She shuddered. "But to America? In my own time?"

"Not at this moment," said another magician, "but maybe we can work on it with your help."

"Sure," Amelia said.

"Crick," Flechette said, "we will take you to the medical rooms. Was your mission achieved?"

"Yes," he said. He was glad of the two men who came to help him down the steps, but he turned to look back at Clovache and Batanya. "And I was very satisfied with the service."

A week later, Batanya and Clovache had returned to their favorite courtyard to spar with each other. First they used weapons, then they wrestled. They were sweaty and limber and pleased with themselves when they were through, and though Batanya pointed out a few mistakes her junior had made, they sprawled on the grass in the sunlight in good harmony.

"How is Geit?" Batanya asked.

"Glad to see me again, and very vigorous in telling me so," Clovache said, smiling to herself. "Did I hear someone knocking on your door at night?"

"Unexpectedly, yes." Batanya grinned, which made her scar more obvious. But who cared?

"Do tell?"

"Our client," Batanya said.

"Oh, my honor! Then you've experienced . . ."

"Oh, yes," Batanya said, her voice rich with satisfaction.

"I didn't get a very good look in Lucifer's chamber," Clovache said, "being in imminent danger and so forth. How is he all . . . arranged?"

"Very satisfactorily," Crick said, dropping onto the ground beside Batanya.

"How are you today, Harwell Clansman?" she asked.

"Very well, Britlingen." He smiled down at her. "But I have to go to Pardua to give Belshazzar his conjuring ball, now that I'm well enough to travel."

"Will you be there long?"

"Depends on how much Belshazzar believes me."

"What, do you need a sworn statement?" Clovache said. "We were there, we saw the conjuring ball, we saw you retrieve it, and in fact we came within a breath or two of losing our lives for it. Though it turned out to be quite handy, if you can concentrate. That's all I did, you know, concentrate on where I wanted to go."

"Ah, but am I taking Belshazzar the same conjuring ball that we retrieved?" Crick said. "That's what he'll wonder."

Clovache gaped at him. "And why would you not?" she demanded. "Oh. Oh, it's very valuable. But he commissioned you to steal it!"

"And what am I?"

"A thief," Batanya said, without opening her eyes. "Dear Crick, you are a thief." Her hardened hand slipped into his bony one.

After that, they all enjoyed the blue sky and the floating clouds, the light breeze that stirred their hair. Perhaps they were all thinking about how excited the magicians and the mechs had been when they'd seen the conjuring ball; how they'd peppered Crick with questions, most of which he couldn't answer, about the ball's properties and history and operation; how they'd disappeared with it for a few days, taking Amelia with them, to "make sure it still worked."

"Be careful along the road, and come back when you

can," Clovache said, when she got up to take her gear into the castle.

"Oh, I will," Crick said. He lay back in the green grass, smiling gently at Batanya. "I'm thinking of taking an apartment down the hill, in Spauling."

"Really?" Batanya said. "That's very interesting." She was on her feet. "Invite me to the housewarming, will you?"

"You'll be the only guest."

Angels' Judgment

A GUILD HUNTER NOVELLA

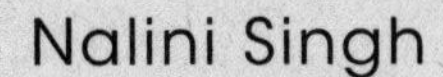

Nalini Singh

Cadre of Ten

The Cadre of Ten, the archangels who ruled the world in all the ways that mattered, met in an ancient keep deep in the Scottish Highlands. No one—human or vampire—would dare trespass on angelic territory, but even had they felt the need to give in to the suicidal urge, it would have proved impossible. The keep had been built by angels, wings a prerequisite for access.

Technology could've negated that advantage, but immortals didn't survive eons by being left behind. The air above and around the keep was strictly controlled, both by a complex intrusion detection system and by units of highly trained angels. Today's security had turned the sky into a cascade of wings—it wasn't often that the ten most powerful beings in the world met in one place.

"Where is Uram?" Raphael asked, glancing at the incomplete semicircle of chairs.

Michaela was the one who answered. "He had a situation in his territory that required immediate attention." Her lips curved as she spoke, and she was beautiful, perhaps the most beautiful woman who had ever lived . . . if you didn't look beneath the surface.

"She makes Uram her puppet." It was a murmur so low that Raphael knew it had been meant for him alone.

Glancing at Lijuan, he shook his head. "He's too powerful. She might control his cock, but nothing else."

Lijuan smiled, and it was a smile that held nothing of humanity. The oldest of the archangels had long passed the age where she could even pretend at being mortal. Now, when Raphael looked at her, he saw only a strange darkness, a whisper of worlds beyond either mortal or immortal ken.

"And are we not important?" A pointed question from Neha, the archangel who ruled India and its surrounds.

"Leave it, Neha," Elijah said in that calm way of his. "We all know of Uram's arrogance. If he chooses not to be here, then he forfeits the right to question our decisions."

That soothed the Queen of Poisons. Astaad and Titus seemed not to care either way, but Charisemnon wasn't so easily appeased. "He spits on the Cadre," the archangel said, his aristocratic face drawn in sharply angry lines. "He may as well renounce his membership."

"Don't be stupid, Chari," Michaela said, and the way she did it, the tone, made it clear she'd once had him in her bed. "An archangel doesn't get invited to join the Cadre. We become Cadre when we become archangels."

"She's right." Favashi spoke for the first time. The quietest of the archangels, she held sway over Persia, and was so good at remaining unnoticed that her enemies forgot about her. Which was why she ruled as they lay in their graves.

"Enough," Raphael said. "We're here for a reason. Let's get to it so we can return to our respective territories."

"Where is the mortal?" Neha asked.

"Waiting outside. Illium flew him up from the lowlands." Raphael didn't ask Illium to bring their visitor inside. "We're here because Simon, the mortal, is growing old. The American chapter of the Guild will need a new director within the next year."

"So let them choose one." Astaad shrugged. "What does it matter to us as long as they do their job?"

That job happened to be a critical one. Angels might Make vampires, but it was the Guild Hunters who ensured those vampires obeyed their hundred-year Contract. Humans signed the Contract easily enough, hungry for immortality. However, fulfilling the terms was another matter—a great many of the newly Made had changes of heart after a few paltry years of service.

And the angels, despite the myths created around their immortal beauty, were not agents of some heavenly entity. They were rulers and businessmen, practical and merciless. They did not like losing their investments. Hence, the Guild and its hunters.

"It matters," Michaela said in a biting tone, "because the American and European branches of the Guild are the most powerful. If the next director can't do his job, we face a rebellion."

Raphael found her choice of words interesting. It betrayed something about the vampires under her tender care that they'd seize any chance of escape.

"I grow tired of this." Titus stirred his muscular bulk, his skin gleaming blue-black. "Bring in the human and let us hear him."

Agreeing, Raphael touched Illium's mind. *Send Simon in.*

The doors opened on the heels of his command and a tall man with the sinewy muscles of a street fighter or foot soldier walked in. His hair was white, his skin wrinkled, but his eyes, they sparkled bright blue. Illium pulled the doors shut the instant Simon cleared them, cloaking the room in lush privacy once more.

The retiring Guild Director met Raphael's eyes and nodded once. "I am honored to be in the presence of the Cadre. It's not a thing I ever thought to experience."

Unsaid was the fact that most humans who came into contact with the Cadre ended up dead.

"Be seated." Favashi waved to a chair placed at the open end of the semicircle.

The old warrior settled himself without any fuss, but Raphael had seen Simon in his prime. He knew the Guild Director was feeling the kiss of age. And yet, he was no old man, never would be. He was a man to be respected. Once, Raphael might've called such a man a friend, but that time had passed a thousand years ago. He'd learned too well that mortal lives blinked out with firefly quickness.

"You wish to retire your position?" Neha asked with regal elegance. She was one of the few who continued to keep a court—the Queen of Poisons might kill you, but you'd admire her refined grace even as you took your last agonizing breath.

Simon remained coolly composed under her regard. Being Guild Director for forty years had given him a confidence he hadn't had as the young man Raphael had first seen take the reins. "I must," he now said. "My hunters are happy for me to stay on, but a good director needs always consider the health of the Guild as a whole. That health flows from the top—the leader must be eminently capable of undertaking an active hunt if necessary." A rueful smile. "I'm strong and I'm skilled, but I'm no longer as fast, or as willing to dance with death."

"Honest words." Titus nodded approvingly. He was most at ease among warriors and their kin—for though he might rule with brutal strength, he was as blunt as the hard line of his jaw. "It's a strong general who can give up the reins of power."

Simon acknowledged the compliment with a slight nod. "I'll always be a hunter, and as is custom, I'll remain available to the new director till my death. However, I have every faith in her ability to lead the Guild."

"Her?" Charisemnon snorted. "A female?"

Michaela raised an eyebrow. "My respect for the Guild has suddenly increased a hundredfold."

Simon didn't allow himself to get drawn into the dialogue. "Sara Haziz is the best possible person to take my place for a number of reasons."

Astaad settled his wings. "Tell us."

"With respect," Simon said quietly, "that is no concern of the Cadre's."

It was Titus who reacted first. "You think to defy us?"

"The Guild has always been neutral for a reason." Simon's spine remained unbending. "Our job is to retrieve vampires who break their Contracts. But through the ages, we've often found ourselves in the middle of wars between angels. We survive only because we *are* seen as neutral. If the Cadre takes too much of an interest, we lose that protection."

"Pretty words," Neha said.

Simon met her gaze. "That makes them no less true."

"Is she capable?" Elijah asked. "This, we must know. If the American Guild falls, the ripple effect could be catastrophic."

Vampires would go utterly free, Raphael thought. Some would slip softly into an ordinary life. But others, others would murder and kill. Because at heart, they were predators. Not so different from angels when all was said and done.

"Sara is more than capable," Simon said. "She also has the loyalty of her fellow hunters—I've had a significant number of them come up to me this past year and suggest her name as a possible successor."

"This Sara is your best hunter?" Astaad asked.

Simon shook his head. "But the best will never make a good director. She is hunter-born."

Raphael made a note to find out her name. Unlike normal members of the Guild, the hunter-born came out of the womb with the ability to scent vampires. They were the best trackers in the world, the most relentless—bloodhounds tuned to one particular scent. "And Sara?" he asked. "Will she accept?"

Simon took a moment to think. "I have not a single doubt that Sara will make the right decision."

Chapter One

Sara wasn't used to feeling sorry for vampires. Her job, after all, was to bag, tag, and transport them back to their masters, the angels. She was no fan of indentured servitude but it wasn't as if the angels hid the price of immortality. Anyone who wanted to get Made had to serve the angels for a hundred years. Nonnegotiable.

You didn't want to bow and scrape for a century, you didn't sign the Contract. Simple. Running out on the Contract after the angels delivered their part of the bargain? That just made you a welsher. And nobody liked a welsher.

However, this guy had worse problems than being returned home to a pissed-off angel. "Can you talk?"

The vampire clamped a hand over his almost-decapitated neck and looked at her as if she were insane.

"Yeah, sorry." She wondered how the hell he was still alive. Vampires weren't true immortals—they could be killed by both humans and others of their kind. Cutting off the head was the most foolproof method, but the majority of people didn't go that way—it wasn't as if the vamps were going to stand still for it. Shooting out the heart worked, so long as you then cut off the head while they were down. Or fire. That did the job.

But Sara was a tracker. Her job was to retrieve, not kill. "You need blood?"

The vampire looked hopeful.

"Suck it in," she said. "You're not dead. Means you're a strong one. You'll last till I can get you home."

"Dhooooo."

Ignoring the gurgled rejection, she crouched down to slide an arm around his back so she could drag him to his feet. She was only five feet three, and he was considerably taller. But she wasn't bleeding out from her neck, and she worked out seven days a week. Grunting as she got him up, she began to walk him to the car. He resisted.

"Need a hand?" A deep, quiet voice, aged whiskey and smoldering embers.

She didn't know that voice. Neither did she know the body that moved out of the shadows. Six feet plus of solid, muscled male. Heavy across the shoulders, thick in the thighs, but with the liquid grace of a trained fighter. One she wouldn't want to be up against in a fight. And she'd taken down vampires twice her size. "Yeah," she said. "Just help me get him to the car. It's parked at the curb."

The stranger all but picked up the vampire—who was starting to make vaguely understandable sounds—and dumped him in the backseat. "Control chip?"

She pulled her crossbow off her back and aimed it at the vamp. The poor guy scrambled back, pulling his feet completely into the vehicle. Rolling her eyes, she returned the crossbow to its previous position and withdrew a necklet from its spot hooked into the waistband of her black jeans, under her T-shirt. Reaching in, she paused. "Don't try anything funny or I'll shoot you for real."

Slumping, the vampire let her clamp the circle of metal around his rapidly healing neck. The science behind the device's effect on vampiric biology was complex, but the results clear—the vampire was now constrained from acting without a direct order from Sara. Helpful didn't begin to describe the control chip because even this injured, the vamp could probably rip off her head in two seconds flat.

Sara liked her head, thank you very much.

Crawling back out, she shut the door and looked up at the other hunter—and there was no doubt in her mind as to his vocation. "Sara." She thrust out a hand.

He took it, but didn't speak for a long time. She couldn't bring herself to protest—something in those dark, dark green eyes held her in place. Power, she thought, there was an incredible sense of power in him. Then he spoke, and the decadent whiskey of his voice almost blinded her to his actual words.

"I'm Deacon. You're much smaller than your reputation suggests."

She wrenched back her hand. "Thanks. And don't offer to help next time."

Most men would've walked off, egos dented. Deacon simply stood there, watching her with those intense eyes. "It wasn't a criticism."

Why the hell was she still here? "I have to deliver Rodney to his master."

"You have a rep." He stepped closer, his eyes drifting to the strap that bisected her body. "You and your crossbow."

Was that amusement she saw on that oh-so-serious face? "Don't knock it until you've tried it. My bolts are made to carry the same properties as the necklets—it keeps me out of harm's way until the target's safely chipped, and given their ability to heal, it hardly hurts."

"Yet you had a necklet."

She took off the crossbow. "Move." This close, all she could see was Deacon, his chest a mile wide. Maybe she was a little affected, but hey, she had a pulse. He was sexy as hell. That changed nothing. She was a hunter. And he might be Guild, but he was also an unknown. "My best friend loves them." She didn't get why, but then, Ellie didn't get the crossbow, so they were even. However, Sara had promised to try the things, since Ellie had tried the crossbow on her last hunt. "I asked you to move."

He finally shifted back a few inches. Enough that she could pull open the passenger door and drop the crossbow inside it. Rodney was almost completely healed, but he'd gotten blood all over the interior of the rental car. *Damn.* The Guild would cover the expenses, but she didn't particularly want to ride around in that mess. "I have to deliver the package."

"Let's talk to him first."

She closed the passenger door. "And why would we do that?"

"Aren't you curious about who cut him?" He had ridiculously long lashes, she thought. Dark and silky and completely unfair on a man.

"Probably some vampire hate group." She frowned. "Morons. Never occurs to them that they're attacking someone's husband, father, or brother."

He kept staring at her. "What?" She rubbed at her face, glad her dark skin tone hid her stupidly hot reaction to this stranger.

"They told me you had brown skin, brown eyes, black hair."

That sounded about right. "Who's 'they'?"

"I'll tell you after we talk to the vampire."

"Carrot and stick?" She narrowed her eyes. "I'm not a rabbit."

His lips curved up a little at the corners. "For the sake of camaraderie." Reaching into his battered leather jacket, he pulled out his Guild ID.

Curious enough not to cut off her nose to spite her face, she jerked her head toward the car. "I'll go into the front seat, take off the necklet." Unfortunately—or fortunately, depending on your point of view—vampires couldn't speak while chipped. "You get into the back and make sure he doesn't—"

"I won't fit in the car."

She took him in. It was all she could do not to ask him to strip naked so she could lick him from head to toe. "Okay," she said, stuffing her suddenly energetic hormones back into storage. "New plan. I'll get him to lower the window, and you put your arm around his neck while we talk."

And that was what they did. Rodney was more than happy to chat once Sara introduced herself.

"You like to shoot people." He made it sound as if she was a maniac. "With a bow and arrow!"

"You're behind the times—I switched to a crossbow last year." It was faster, but she kinda missed her specially designed bow. Maybe she'd go back to it. "And it doesn't even hurt."

"Says you."

She blinked. "How old are you?"

"I just turned three." Vampires counted their age from the time of their Making.

Sara shook her head. "And you tried to run? Why the fuck would you do something so stupid?" His sire, Mr. Lacarre, was way past mad.

"I don't know." He shrugged. "Sounded like a good idea at the time."

Clearly, they weren't dealing with the sharpest knife in the drawer. "Oooookay." Her eyes met Deacon's. Not a ripple in their night-shadow green depths, but she could've sworn he was holding back laughter. Biting off her own smile, she returned her attention to Rodney. "Simple question."

"Oh, good." The vampire grinned, showing both fangs, something the old ones never did. "I don't like hard things."

"Who cut you, Rod?"

He swallowed and blinked rapidly. "Nobody."

"So you tried to decapitate yourself?"

"Yeah." He nodded, which meant Deacon was holding on very lightly. Not that it mattered. Sara had her crossbow as insurance.

"Rodney." She put all the menace she was capable of in that single word. "Don't lie to me."

He blinked again and—oh my God—he was going to cry. Now she felt like a bully. "Come on, Rod. Why are you scared?"

"Because."

"Because . . ." She thought about what would scare a vampire that bad. "Was it an *angel*?" If it had been his sire, she couldn't do anything about it except report the bastard to the Vampire Protection Authority. However, it was also possible the attack had been orchestrated by one of Lacarre's enemies, in which case the angel would take care of it himself.

"No." Rodney sounded shocked enough to be telling the truth. "Of course not. The angels Make us. They don't kill us."

And the boy was living in la-la land. "So who else scares you that bad?" She caught Deacon's eyes again at that moment and found her answer in their no longer amused depths. "A hunter." Or someone Rodney had mistaken for a hunter. Because real hunters didn't kill vampires.

Rodney started sniffling. "Please don't hurt me. I didn't do anything."

"Hey." Sara reached out and, ignoring his flinch, patted him on the shoulder. "I'm interested in collecting my retrieval fee. I only get half if you're dead, so it doesn't make sense for me to kill you."

Rodney looked at her with hope a shiny gem in his eyes. "Really?"

"Yep."

"What about—" Lowering his voice, he pointed at the arm around his neck.

Deacon spoke for the first time. "I'm her boyfriend. I do what she says."

She stared at him, but Rodney apparently found the claim highly reassuring. "Yeah, you're the boss," he said to Sara. "I can tell. My Mindy, she likes to be the boss, too. She told me I should run away and you know, we could go on like a cruise."

Sara pressed a her finger over his lips. "Focus, Rodney. Tell me about the hunter who cut you."

"He said all you hunters hate vampires." Rodney's voice got very small. "I didn't know that. I know it's your job to track us, but I didn't think you hated us."

"We don't." Sara wanted to pat him on the head. Jesus. "He was just being mean."

"You think so?"

"I know so. What else did he say?"

"That vampires were the scum of the earth, and that the angels were being polluted by our presence." He made a face. "I don't know how that could be true since the angels Make us."

Sara was so surprised by the sudden burst of sense that it took her a second to process it. "Yeah, that's right. So he was lying. He say anything else?"

"No, he just got out his sword—"

Sword?

"—and tried to cut off my head." He sat back, recital finished.

"What did he look like?" Deacon asked.

Rodney jumped, as if he'd forgotten the danger at his back. "I couldn't see. He was wearing a black mask, and black everything. But he was tall. And strong."

That included half the hunters in the Guild. Sara tried to get more out of Rodney, but it was a bust. Neckleting him again, she drove to Lacarre's, very aware of Deacon following on a big monster of a bike. He remained outside the gates while she went in to deliver Rodney.

Rodney's master was waiting for him in the sitting area of his palatial home. "Go," he ordered.

Sara removed the necklet and put it on the table for Lacarre to return to the Guild as Rodney shuffled off like a penitent schoolboy. Snapping his cream-colored wings shut in anger, the angel picked up an envelope from the table. "A receipt confirming payment. I sent it through as soon as you called to say you had Rodney."

Checking it quickly, she slid it into a pocket. "Thank you."

"Ms. Haziz," he said, scowling, "I'll be frank with you. I never expected Rodney to attempt an escape. I'm not sure how to punish him."

Sara wasn't used to talking to angels for longer than it

took to get the assignment. In most cases, she didn't even see them then—they were way too important to consort with mere mortals. That's what vampires were for. "You know a Mindy?"

Lacarre stilled. "Yes. She's one of my most senior vampires."

"Jealous type?"

"Hmm, I see." A nod. "I've been spending extra time with Rodney—he's a child and I'm afraid he'll get eaten up if I don't teach him some skills."

Sara wasn't even going to ask how Rodney had gotten through the Candidate selection process. So many people wanted to be Made that it was anything but a slam dunk. "He's no mastermind," she said. "I think if you punish him too harshly, he'll break."

Mr. Lacarre nodded. "Very well, Guild Hunter. Thank you." It was a dismissal.

Leaving Rodney with a master who was still irritated, albeit no longer furious, felt vaguely wrong. But the vampire had chosen his future when he asked to be Made. Now he'd be somebody's slave for the next ninety-seven years. As she walked out, her path crossed with that of a slender redhead. The woman was dressed in a daring scarlet suit that molded to her body like second skin. It made a statement.

She would've kept going but the redhead stopped her. "You brought Rodney back."

Mindy. "It's my job."

The older vampire—much older from the sheer ease with which she faked humanity—all but gritted her teeth. "I didn't expect him to survive this long—he can barely tie his shoelaces."

"How did he get Made?" Sara asked, unable to swallow her curiosity any longer.

Mindy waved a hand. "He was fine bef—" She belatedly seemed to realize who she was talking to. "Good-bye, Guild Hunter."

"Bye." Interesting, Sara thought. Everyone knew—even if the knowledge had never actually been confirmed—that a tiny percentage of Candidates went insane after the transformation. This was the first time she'd seen an example of someone who'd been diminished instead.

Deacon wasn't around when she got back into the rental car, but he'd found her again by the time she reached her hotel. She parked in the underground garage and got out to see him bringing that monster motorcycle to a stop beside her. "How did you get past security?"

He took off his helmet, unzipped his jacket, and swung off the bike. Gorgeous male muscle. Oh, so touchable. Something very tight in her stomach wound even tighter. Dear God, but the man was sex on legs.

Chapter Two

Taking a deep breath to wash away the rush of raw hunger, she headed for the elevators, weapons bag in hand. Experience told her management would get a little testy if she walked in wearing her crossbow. "So? Security?"

"It sucks."

That was her estimation, too. "It was the most convenient location for this hunt."

Being stuck in an elevator with the man was an exercise in frustration. His smell; soap and skin, heated up from within to create something uniquely Deacon—pure male with an edge of steel—wrapped around her like an aphrodisiac. Since she couldn't not breathe, she was overdosing on it by the time the elevator kicked them out on the third floor. "Stay here." She held up a hand. "I need to check your credentials."

He leaned his back up against the wall opposite her door. "Say hi to Simon from me."

Keeping an eye on him, she swiped her keycard and entered the room. It was fairly basic—a double bed beside a small chest of drawers, a table with just enough room for the hotel phone and maybe a laptop, a couple of chairs. Really, everything she needed while on a hunt. The call to Simon's cell phone from her own went through without problems.

"Deacon," she said the instant he picked up. "Who is he and why is he here?"

"Give me a description."

She did. "So?"

"Yes, that's Deacon. He's on a job and it's something I want you on as well—I assume you've completed the retrieval for Lacarre?"

"Yeah." Intrigued by what he *wasn't* saying, she put a hand on her hip. "What's the job, and does it have anything to do with vampires getting their heads lopped off?"

"Deacon will explain. We need to sort this out fast."

"Will do." She paused. "Simon. The other thing . . ."

"It's all right, Sara. The decision doesn't have to be made today. Or even tomorrow."

But Sara knew it did have to be made. "After this job. I'll give you an answer."

"I'll wait for it." A pause. "Sara, Deacon's extremely dangerous. Be careful."

"I'm pretty dangerous, too." Hanging up after a few more words, she went to the door and pulled it open. The man in question was standing on the doorstep. Her eyes drifted down to the duffel that had materialized at his feet. "Whoa. You're not staying here."

"I have a lot to tell you. I'll crash on the floor."

Her streak of curiosity was a pain in the ass sometimes. "Yeah, you will." Waving him in, she locked the door. "So, let me guess—we have to find and neutralize this psychopath pretending to be a hunter." There'd been five murders in the past week and a half that she knew about. All vamps. All killed by decapitation.

Deacon dropped his bag on the floor beside hers and shrugged off his jacket to reveal a rough navy shirt that threw his eyes into even brighter relief. "I'm not so sure he's pretending. I've been on his trail since the day after the second murder, and all signs point to a hunter."

"I don't believe you," she said, remaining by the door, arms crossed.

Putting his jacket over the back of a chair, he pulled it out and grabbed a seat before bending down to unlace his boots. "Doesn't mean it's not the truth."

"Hunters don't go around killing innocent people." It wasn't what they were, what they did. There was honor in being a hunter. "We make sure vampires don't get killed more often than they already do." Legend had it that before the formation of the Guild, vampires who dared try an escape were simply executed upon discovery.

Having removed both boots and socks, Deacon stretched out his legs and tipped his chair back against the table, eyes intent. "Bill James."

It was a punch to the gut, a fucking knife to the heart. "How do you know about that?" Nobody but the three hunters who'd gone after him—and Simon, of course—knew about Bill. To the others, he'd died a hero, been given a full Guild funeral.

Deacon continued to watch her with absolute, unwavering focus, a calm that made her wonder if the man ever let go. "My name is Deacon, but most people know me as the Slayer."

She stared. He wasn't joking. Fuck.

Pushing off the door, she walked very quietly to the bed and sat down on the edge. "I thought they made you up. Like the bogeyman."

"The Guild recruits and trains some of the deadliest men and women in the world. We need a bogeyman."

She shook her head. "Ellie's never going to believe I met the Slayer." It was a joke, the name. Taken off a television show. "The Guild really has a hunter whose job it is to hunt our own?"

"Only when necessary." He didn't speak again until she raised her head. "And you know it sometimes *is* necessary."

"Bill was an aberration," she said. "Something snapped in him." The other hunter had taken to killing children, savaging them with an inhumanity that made her gorge rise even now.

"Hunting our own is a rare thing," Deacon acknowledged. "But it happens. That's why there's always a Slayer in the Guild."

"Why didn't you track Bill?" Because it was Elena who'd had to kill the older hunter. Sara had been determined to do the gut-wrenching task—Bill was her friend, but he'd been Ellie's mentor. But Bill had attacked her with a tire iron in an ambush none of them had seen coming. She'd been unconscious before she hit the ground. And her best friend had had to knife her mentor to death.

He looked at me as if I'd betrayed him, Ellie had said afterward, her face splattered with Bill's lifeblood. *I know he had to die, but I can't stop thinking that he was right. His blood was so hot.*

"Sheer bad luck," Deacon said, dragging her back to the present. "The situation went critical so fast that I couldn't get back in time—I was on the other side of the world." He didn't move, a predator at rest.

"Hunting?"

"Business," he said to her surprise. "The Slayer's rarely called for. I'm a weapons maker by vocation."

"Deacon? Wait a minute." Pulling her bag across, she unzipped it and grabbed her crossbow. The familiar, stylized *D* stared up at her from the bottom of the stock. "This is your work?"

A small nod. "I make tools for hunters."

"You're the best there is." This crossbow had cost her a mint. As had the bow she adored. "And you slay in your spare time? Nice." Shaking her head, she put the crossbow back into the bag. "How come I've never heard of you personally?"

"It's not a good idea to be friends with the people you might one day have to kill."

"A lonely life." She hadn't meant to be so blunt, but she couldn't imagine that kind of an existence. She was no social butterfly—not yet, anyway—but she had a core group of friends who kept her sane and balanced.

"Slayers are chosen from the loners." Raising his hands, he undid the first few buttons of his shirt. "Do you want the shower first?"

She wanted to lick her lips, that's what she wanted to do. The man's skin stretched golden and strong over that muscular physique, and she could see dark curls of hair in the open triangle of his shirt. Her body tightened . . . expectant, ready.

Cold shower time.

"Thanks," she said, getting up. "I'll make it quick."

Deacon just nodded as she grabbed her gear and hauled ass. The Slayer was delicious, no question about it, but she wasn't in the market for a lover. Not when she was about to make the biggest decision of her life. A decision that might make her existence even lonelier than Deacon's.

Male hunters were macho idiots—and she meant that in the best way—as a rule. Playing second fiddle didn't come easily. And it didn't get much more second fiddle than being the Guild Director's man.

Deacon finally unclenched the hand he'd fisted the instant he sat down in the chair. Sara Haziz was not the woman he'd been led to expect. Simon had some explaining to do.

"Brown skin, brown eyes, black hair, my ass," he muttered under his breath. The woman was an erotic fantasy come to life. Small, curvy, perfect. Gleaming coffee-and-cream skin, hair that probably fell to her waist when released from that tight braid, and brown eyes so big they saw right through him.

This was not the woman Simon had described as his "sensible successor." That made her sound about as interesting as shoe leather. It didn't even hint at the power beneath the surface, the strength in that backbone. He'd met her only a couple of hours ago, and already he knew she could bust balls with the best of them.

The woman would make a perfect Guild Director.

Which meant he should keep his hands, and his thoughts, to himself. No sucking on sexy Sara's neck. Or other parts of her body. The office of Guild Director was a necessarily public one. Deacon didn't do public.

"But she's not director yet." He tapped a finger on one jean-covered thigh, his eye on the bed.

He wanted Sara. And he didn't want lightly. But seducing her wasn't on the agenda.

"Keep her safe. She won't accept a bodyguard, but you can accomplish the same thing by keeping her with you on the hunt."

"I work alone."

Simon's face was granite. "Tough. She's one of my best hunters—she won't slow you down."

"If she's one of the best, why does she need babysitting?"

"Because the Cadre knows she's my chosen successor. I wouldn't put it past certain archangels to 'test' her."

Deacon raised an eyebrow. "Were you tested?"

"They almost killed me." Blunt words. "It's tough to win against five old vamps on your own. I survived only because I happened to be with my wife at the time. Two pissed-off hunters against five vamps is much better odds."

So here he sat, listening to water cascade in the bathroom as he fantasized about kissing a slow path down Sara's body. It wasn't doing anything to lessen his arousal. And if she walked out to find him hard as fucking stone, he knew damn well he'd be spending the night in the corridor outside.

That, he couldn't chance—he had to keep her in sight. Simon had been very clear about that. If the archangels planned to test her, they'd do it when they thought her vulnerable. So he'd make sure she never was. Shoving a hand through his hair, he got up and checked the room. It was fairly secure. No outside windows—claustrophobic but safe, no entrances or exits aside from the door—which he jammed shut with a special tool of his own making, and no vents large enough for anything to get through.

By the time Sara exited the shower wrapped in a fluffy hotel robe, rubbing at her hair with a matching towel, he was confident enough of her safety to go have his own shower. A freezing one. "Christ." He gritted his teeth and bore the onslaught. Pleasing his cock wasn't as important as ensuring that the Guild went on.

He'd asked Simon about that. Why would the archangels potentially sabotage an organization that made their lives a hell of a lot easier?

"It's a game," Simon had said. "They need us, but they'll never allow us to forget that they're the more powerful. Attacking me, attacking Sara, isn't about stopping the Guild—it's about reminding us the Cadre is watching."

Sara heard the water come on and quickly finished drying her hair before picking up her cell. She had no idea what time zone Ellie was in, but her best friend answered after a single ring.

"Sara," she said, "do you know what a skill it is to wrap three-feet-tall porcelain vases so they don't break in transit? And I did it! These gorgeous babies don't have a scratch on them. Genius, thy name is Elena."

"Do I even ask?"

"They were a gift." Ellie sounded delighted. "They'll look perfect in my living room. Or maybe one in the bedroom, one in the living room."

Ellie's preoccupation with her décor struck a familiar chord in Sara. Hunters made nests. It was a response to the fact that they spent so much time on the road, and in the gutter. Sara was worse than most—she loved her parents but they were feckless hippies at best. She'd gone to ten different schools by the time she was seven. A solid, stable home was as necessary to her as breathing. "Can't wait to see them."

"You sound funny."

"I met the Slayer."

A pause. "No shit." The whistle was a long one. "Scary?"

"Oh yeah. Built like a tank." If Deacon ever came after her, she'd have to make sure he never got within punching distance. A single hit with one of those big fists and her neck would snap. "Ellie, there's a hunter going around killing vampires."

"Fuck." Elena's voice changed, became darker. "You're hunting him?"

"Yeah."

"I'm in New York, landed a few hours ago. I can be on the next flight."

Sara was already shaking her head. "I don't know what's going on yet."

"You can't go after him alone."

"I'm not. Deacon's with me."

"The Slayer?" Her relief was open. "Good. Look, Sara, I'm hearing things."

"What?"

"All of us know you've got Simon's position anytime you want. But I had a conversation with a high-level vamp on the plane home and he knew your name."

Simon had warned her of this. "The Cadre takes an interest in the next Guild Director."

Elena's silence was long. "I know you can't run and hide from this, so I'll just say—be damn careful. The archangels aren't anything close to human. I wouldn't want to be within ten feet of one."

"I don't think any of them will bother to personally check me out—probably send some of their vampires to have a look." And she knew how to handle vampires.

"Lucky you have the Slayer with you. Serious manpower when you need it." A faint pinging sound came over the line. "Gotta go. I think the takeout's arrived."

Hanging up, Sara stared at the phone. Yes, it was lucky, wasn't it, that Deacon had shown himself to her when he spent most of his time in the shadows. And how very *convenient* that she'd been posted on a hunt to the very city where the serial killings were taking place. Eyes narrowed, she waited.

Chapter Three

Deacon walked out a couple of minutes later, dressed in nothing but a pair of jeans. Her hormones danced. Damn near did the foxtrot. She refused to join in. "Simon sent you."

To his credit, he didn't bother to deny it. "Two birds. One stone." Grabbing a fresh T-shirt from his duffel, he pulled it over his head. "You know it's the right decision."

The fact that he sounded so coolly logical made her want to shoot him with the crossbow just to make a point. "The Guild Director can't be seen as weak."

"She also can't be seen as stupid." Intractable will in those midnight-forest eyes.

Putting down the cell she'd been squeezing half to death, she dug out a brush and began to pull it through her hair. "Tell me about the killer. Is there any chance it could be an impostor?"

He didn't say anything for several seconds, as if not trusting her sudden capitulation. "Yes. But as of right now, I have three possibles—all hunters. We'll visit them one by one."

"Tonight?"

A small nod. "I figure we give it four hours, enough time for the killer to relax his guard."

"Why didn't you follow him after he hit Rodney?"

"There was no visible trail."

She snorted. "And your job is to babysit me."

"Babysitting you isn't what I want to do." Quiet, intense words, stroking over her skin like living velvet. "But since taking you to bed is out of bounds, I'm stuck with babysitting."

Heat exploded across her skin, a raw, dark fire. "What makes you think I'd let you within a foot of me?" Her voice held the rough edge of desire, but it could as easily have been anger.

"What makes you think I'd ask nice?"

"Try anything and I'll cheerfully gut you with your own knife."

Deacon smiled. And it turned him from sexy to devastating. "This'll be fun."

But four hours of fitful sleep later, she was in no mood to play. Pulling on her gear before joining Deacon in the corridor, she adjusted her crossbow and set her jaw. "I don't like the fact that we're hunting one of our own."

Silence.

She glanced at him as they began to walk down to the garage, and saw nothing. No expression. No emotion. No mercy. In that moment, he was the Slayer. "How many have you had to kill?"

"Five."

She blew out a breath at the single precise word, and opened the door to the stairs. No point in making hotel security crazy by being caught on the elevator cameras armed to the teeth. "Why you?"

"It has to be someone."

She understood all about that. "I never wanted to be Guild Director."

"That's why you were chosen—you'll do what the director is meant to do."

"As opposed to?"

He exited first, and she knew it was a gesture of protection. Annoying, but on the scale of annoyances, minor.

"You know about Paris. They had that director a few years ago who politicked himself into the position. Almost got all his hunters killed, he was so busy grandstanding."

Sara nodded and headed to the bike, their chosen method of transport tonight. "I always wondered how that could've happened." Hunters were a tough, forthright lot as a whole. Slick made them suspicious.

"Some people say he struck a deal with a powerful cabal of vampires, that they influenced the vote."

Very old vampires were rumored to have mind-control abilities, and one of Sara's more important qualifications for the position of Guild Director was that she had a natural immunity to *all* vampiric abilities. Like Ellie and the other hunter-born, she'd always been meant for the Guild. "I'm surprised he's still alive."

"Don't be so sure—he hasn't been seen since he was deposed." Handing her a spare helmet, he watched as she put it on, then settled his own. "Can you hear me?"

She nodded, realizing the helmets were miked. "Where're we going first?"

"Timothy Lee. He's shorter than Rodney described, but Rod was traumatized. We can't trust his recollection."

She was about to reply when she suddenly *knew* they were no longer alone in the garage. Already straddling the bike behind Deacon, she looked across to the door they'd used to exit the stairs and saw a vampire. She had no need to ask if Deacon had made him, too—the Slayer had gone motionless the same instant she had.

Meeting the vampire's gaze, she felt the hairs on the back of her neck rise. He was an old one, his power so potent it thickened the air until she could barely breathe. When he didn't say anything, she decided to remain silent, too.

Deacon started the bike and backed out of the space. "Watch him," he said into the mike.

As he turned the motorcycle, she twisted her head to keep the vamp in sight.

The tall, dark-haired male didn't so much as blink as they drove out of the garage.

"Games," she muttered. "They're letting me know I'm being watched."

"Testing your strength."

"You know, I can see their point—can you imagine what would happen to the world if any of the major chapters had a weak director?"

"Paris," Deacon said again.

She nodded, though he couldn't see her. "What was his name—Jarvis?"

"Jervois."

"Right." Jervois's weakness had led to a disorganized European Guild. Vampires had taken immediate advantage. Most had simply escaped, planning to lose themselves into the world. But a few . . . "Several vamps gave in to bloodlust. The news reports said the streets ran with blood."

"They weren't far wrong. Paris lost ten percent of its population within a month."

Put in such finite terms, the horror of it was chilling. "Why didn't the angels step in?" In her native New York, Raphael ran the show, and as far as Sara knew, no bloodlust-ridden vampire had ever set foot in the city. Since that was statistically impossible, obviously Raphael had taken care of any problems with such flawless efficiency no one had heard so much as a murmur.

"Word is"—Deacon's voice turned cold—"Michaela decided the humans needed a lesson in humility."

Michaela was one of the more visible archangels, a stunning beauty who enjoyed attention enough to pose for the human media on occasion. "I think that one," Sara said, "would be happy to push us all back to a time where she'd be looked upon as a goddess."

"There are a lot of people even now who see the angels as God's messengers."

"What about you?"

"Another species," he said. "Maybe they're what we'll become sometime in the next million years."

It was an interesting hypothesis. Sara didn't know what she thought. Angels had been around since the earliest cave paintings. There were as many explanations for their existence as there were stars in the sky. And if the angels knew the truth, they weren't telling. "So, why Timothy Lee?"

"He's been in the city during every one of the murders, he's capable of doing the job—"

"We're all capable."

"Yes. So that wouldn't matter as much, but Timothy's a very dedicated hunter. He sees it not as a job, but as a calling."

"Is he hunter-born?" Having been best friends with Ellie for so many years, she knew that for those born with the ability to scent-track vampires, entering the Guild *was* less a choice than a compulsion.

"No. But he worships the hunter-born."

"Not healthy, but not psychopathic either."

Deacon nodded. "That's why he's one of three. The other two have their own little idiosyncrasies but all hunters are strange to some degree."

"You've met Ashwini, haven't you?"

She heard him choke. "'Met' isn't quite the right word. She shot me the first time we came into contact."

"Sounds about right." She grinned, but it didn't last long. "If it is one of these three, you'll execute him?"

"Yes."

"No police?"

"I'm authorized to do this. The law will never become involved." A pause. "They're glad we police ourselves. Hunters who turn bad have a way of upping the body count."

"Like vampires."

He didn't say anything, but she felt his agreement in the tense stillness of his body. Eerily quiet, the night seemed to discourage further conversation, and they rode in silence until Deacon pulled over to the side of a still, dark street. "We'll go on foot from here."

Stowing her helmet alongside his, she followed him as he led her down the street and to a chain-link fence. She frowned. "This looks like a junkyard."

"It is."

Okay, that was truly odd. Hunters almost never lived in crappy places. They were paid very well for sticking their necks out chasing vampires who might just tear those necks off. "To each his own."

"He has a hellhound."

She thought she'd heard wrong. "Did you say hellhound?" Visions of red eyes pulsing in a miasma of sulfur danced through her head. Then the pitchforks started circling.

"Big, black thing, probably bite your hand off if you look at it wrong. Timothy calls it Lucifer's Girl." He took something from his pocket. "Tranquilizer dart." Then he was gone, and if she hadn't seen it, she'd never have guessed he could move that fast.

She stayed with him, both of them scrambling over the chain link to land with hunter silence on the other side. There was no bark, nothing to alert them they'd become prey—Lucifer's Girl came out of the darkness like a raging whirlwind. Sara ducked instinctively, and the dog's body jumped over hers . . . to meet the clearly rapid-acting tranquilizer in Deacon's hand. Instead of allowing the dog to fall, Deacon caught its muscled weight and lowered it gently to the ground.

"You like her," Sara said, incredulous.

Deacon stroked the dog's heaving sides. "What's not to like? She's loyal, and she's strong. If I have to execute Timothy, she'll miss her master."

"You'd adopt her, wouldn't you?" She shook her head. "There go your chances of ever again getting a girl."

He raised his head, looking at her in that intent way of his. "Not a fan?"

"She's got nine-inch fangs." Only a slight exaggeration.

"A woman would have to love you an incredible amount to put up with that kind of competition." She jerked her head toward the building on the other side of the mountain of scrap metal and God knew what else. "Yes?"

"Let's go. Tranq will keep Lucy out for a while."

Lucy?

They took their time finding a path through the junk, checking for booby traps in the process. When they finally reached the tumbledown shack that Timothy called home, it was to discover the place empty. A little breaking and entering later, they were inside, but saw nothing even close to a smoking gun. The fact that Tim wasn't home meant nothing—hunters kept irregular hours as a rule.

She watched as Deacon took something from his pocket and placed it on the bottoms of all the shoes he could locate. "Transmitters," he told her. "Battery life of about two days. So if there's a kill in that period, and he wears a pair I've tagged, I'll be able to trace his movements."

"Who's next on the list?"

He told her after they scaled the chain link—petting Lucy along the way, and waiting long enough to ensure that she was coming out of the tranq okay. "Next is Shah Mayur. Loner, does the job but doesn't seem to have any contact with other hunters."

"Like someone else I know."

Deacon ignored the comment as they straddled his bike and took off.

Grinning, she pressed herself to the heat of his back. "What put Shah on your radar?"

"He's had five complaints filed against him by the VPA."

The Vampire Protection Authority had been set up to stop cruelty and prejudice against vamps. They never won court cases—it was extremely hard to make a vampire look the victim when you had pictures of their blood-soaked kills—but they could kick up a serious stink. "What for?"

"Excessive violence against a vampire during retrieval."

"Hmm." She thought about that. "Why don't you sound more excited?"

"Because all five complaints came from the same vamp."

Her own burgeoning excitement deflated. "Probably someone with an ax to grind."

"Yeah, but we have to check him out."

Shah Mayur lived in a much more ordinary home—in terms of its attractiveness to hunters. His apartment occupied the entire third floor of a freestanding town house.

Sara frowned. "Getting in's going to be a problem." Deacon had already told her there was no internal access, so they couldn't break in downstairs—and the ladder that Shah used to get up and down was currently pulled up. That didn't mean he was home. According to Deacon's intel, it could be raised or lowered by remote. Shah wasn't a trusting sort. But he was also supposed to be on a flight to Washington as of an hour ago. "Any ideas?"

Deacon was staring up at the back wall when she turned to him. "Can you climb that?"

She followed his gaze to what looked like some kind of a water pipe, a reasonably substantial one. "Yeah." The request surprised her. "I thought you were babysitting me."

"We're probably under surveillance," he told her, voice matter-of-fact. "I can't defang you completely."

"That implies you could." She shot him a sweet smile laced with bite. "We have to consider something else—if we are being watched, then the angels and high-level vamps have to know what we're up to. I'm not going to deliver a hunter into their hands." Angelic vengeance could be soul-destroyingly brutal.

Deacon looked into her face, unblinking. "That's why we have to get to him first. We'll deliver death with mercy."

Giving a nod, she accepted the transmitters he held out and ran to the pipe. She was light enough—and more importantly, had enough muscle—that it was fairly simple to pull herself up. When she reached the window ledge, she found it an easy, wide perch. So close, it was tempting to push up the window and go in, but she took her time checking everything out.

Just as well, as it turned out.

Shah had rigged a garrote across the opening, at the exact height to cut anyone coming in. From the faint glitter, she guessed it was covered with crushed glass. Gruesome, but home security wasn't a crime. Double-checking for any electrical wires that might be connected to an alarm, she glanced down at Deacon and signaled her intention to enter.

He nodded once and signaled back. *Two minutes.*

Pushing up the window, she stepped in with care, avoiding the lethal stroke of the garrote by bending low. She found herself in what looked like the living room. It was dark. But not dark enough to hide the man sitting silently in the armchair.

Chapter Four

"I expected Deacon," he said in a silky soft tone.

"Shah Mayur, I presume."

"Sara Haziz." A lilt of surprise. "Since when are you a Slayer?"

"Call it a sideline." She noted the gun in his lap. "You're prepared."

"Didn't want my head lopped off before I had a chance to explain that I'm not a homicidal killer." This time, the tone was wry.

She liked him. Didn't mean he wasn't a murderer. "So if I leave?"

"I'm not going to shoot you. Tell Deacon I'll meet you both outside." A pause. "And Sara, it's not good form for the future Guild Director to be breaking and entering."

"Why does everyone act like it's a done deal?" she muttered and backed out, keeping an eye on his hands the whole time. If necessary, she could jump—it would break a few bones, but it wouldn't kill her. Not like a bullet would.

Whether Shah replied, she didn't hear. It was far easier

to go down the pipe than it had been to come up. "He's heading down to talk."

Deacon's face went very quiet. Dangerous. "He's not supposed to be here."

"He knew you were coming. And he knows your name."

That made him go even more still. Sara found herself fascinated. Did Deacon ever let himself go? Or was he this contained even in the most intimate of situations? It was tempting to kiss him and find out, but with the way he drew her, she knew she wouldn't stop at a kiss.

The whisper of Shah's ladder sliding to the ground was a welcome distraction. She waited as the other hunter descended, his gun nowhere in sight. Of course, that simply meant he was good at hiding his weaponry. Elena would approve, Sara thought. Her best friend usually had spikes secreted in her hair, and knives strapped to her thighs. That was just for starters.

"Hello, Deacon." Shah turned out to be tall, dark, and very handsome, with shining black hair that swept his shoulders.

"I'm impressed." Deacon subtly angled himself so he protected Sara.

She stopped herself from rolling her eyes and used the chance to retrieve her own gun from the small of her back. Then she moved out of Deacon's night-shadow so she'd have a clear line of sight.

"Spying's my thing. I work intel for the Guild."

The Guild had an intel division? Sara wondered how many more secrets she'd learn as Guild Director. It was temptation indeed for a woman as curious as her. But was she willing to give up everything she was, give up the possibility of a family, children? Yes, there were men who'd be more than happy to sleep with the Guild Director, but they weren't the kind of men she'd touch with a barge pole.

No, Deacon was her type. Cool, controlled, strong. And about as likely to sleep with the woman who'd effectively be his boss—if she accepted the directorship—as he was to start spouting jokes. Reining in her wandering thoughts, she met Shah's gaze. "And we're just supposed to believe you?"

Shah shrugged, giving her a secretive smile. "Or I could tell you all about the time you and Elena decided to try out the stripper pole at Maxie's."

How the fuck had he learned about that? She scowled. "If you work intel, why didn't Simon clear you?"

"Deacon runs his ops independently." He shrugged. "I could've played hard to get, but I figure you two are a good bet when it comes to keeping secrets. The future director and the Slayer. Who're you going to tell?"

Deacon suddenly had his hand around Shah's neck, a knife to his abdomen. "Take off your shirt."

Shah blinked, hiding his surprise behind charm. "Didn't know you swung that way."

Deacon pushed the knife a little.

"Fine." Unbuttoning the shirt with rapid fingers, Shah shrugged it off.

"Sara, check his body for marks of a struggle. One of the vamps put up a hell of a fight."

Sara did a close inspection, but all she saw was smooth, unblemished skin. "He's clean."

Shah rubbed at his throat when Deacon let him go. "You could've asked nice."

"And you could've stabbed him in the heart." Sara snorted. "Drop the act. You're about as helpless as a piranha."

"Can't blame a boy for trying." He smiled, revealing dimples he no doubt used as a tool. "If you want my take, I'd put my money on Tim. Have you seen that dog of his? Probably made a deal with the devil and got that as insurance. Now the thing's possessed him."

Sara shook her head, noting the gleam of amusement in his eyes. "I don't think you should throw stones—I saw the teddy bear on your couch."

Interesting. A suave, sophisticated spy could go bright red under cinnamon-dusted skin. "It's my nephew's. And if you don't need to manhandle me anymore, I'd like to go to sleep." With that, he turned and left.

"He didn't hit on you." It was a quiet statement.

She pursed her lips. "And you felt the need to point that out, why?"

"Shah doesn't have any close hunter friends, but he's popular with the ladies. He hits on anything with breasts, but petite dark-haired women are especially his type."

"Thank you for crushing my self-esteem under your boot." Restraining the urge to kick him, she grabbed her helmet and thrust it on.

Deacon took his seat, putting on his own helmet before starting the engine. They were ten minutes from Shah's home and cutting through a deserted parking lot when Deacon came to a halt. "Fight or run?"

She'd seen the vampires in the shadows. How many? Five, no, seven. Seven against two. "Run." Stupidity wasn't what had kept her alive this long.

It was only as Deacon was peeling out of the lot that she realized he'd left the choice up to her. It was . . . unexpected.

Their third stop of the night was a gay bar. Sara stared up at the bar's name. "Inferno." She turned to the silent man by her side. "Is it me or are we seeing a trend here?"

A quirk of his lips. It was sexier than a full-fledged smile from any other man. "I'm leading you into sin."

She couldn't help it. She laughed. "Obviously, suspect number three is gay. Right?"

"Marco Giardes." He nodded up. "Lives above the bar."

"Huh?"

"Owns the place. Bought it with an inheritance."

Sara shrugged. "Doesn't bother me. Bother you?"

A bit of red stained his cheeks. Her mouth fell open. "What?"

He blew out a breath. "You'll see."

"We're going in?"

"Yeah. He doesn't know about me—unless he's another

spy. We're just two hunters who heard about his place and decided to drop in."

Since hunters were known to do things like that to support each other, it was a perfectly believable cover. And despite the fact that it was close to four a.m., the bar was jumping. "Weapons?"

"No problem for hunters."

"Then let's go."

They flashed their Guild IDs and got waved in by the heavily muscled bouncer . . . who gave Deacon a thorough going-over. Sara bit the insides of her cheeks when the big, tough Slayer shifted a little behind her.

The instant they entered the main floor, conversation stopped, then restarted in a huge rush. She was welcomed with smiles—there were several other women in the crowd—but the attention was most definitely on Deacon. So when he put his hand on her hip and pulled her up against him, she didn't protest. "Poor baby," she murmured. "They really like you."

"It's not funny." She'd never *heard* a blush before.

A beautiful male with the slinky body of a catwalk model strolled over. "What a shame," he murmured, noting their body language. "I hope you're taking good care of him."

Sara patted Deacon's hand where it curved over her hip. "The best."

"Will you let him dance with us?"

Sara could feel Deacon's horror in the absolute frozen lines of his body. It was tempting to tease, but . . . "He's not much of a dancer."

Giving another mournful sigh, the blond walked away. Unable to keep it in any longer, Sara turned and buried her face in Deacon's chest as her body shook with laughter. His arms came around her, his lips at her ear. "We're going to a *girl* bar on our next date."

That simply made her laugh harder. Tears leaked out of her eyes. By the time she got it out of her system, the scent of Deacon was well and truly in her lungs. The man smelled delicious. A little bit of heat, a little bit of sweat, a whole lot of dangerous. Perfect.

Hands flat on that gorgeous chest of his, she looked up. "I guess they know a manly man when they see one."

His lashes, long and beautiful, shaded his eyes, but she saw the glint in them. "What about you?"

Her answer was interrupted by a discreet cough. She turned to find a man who could only be another hunter. His stance was easy in the way of someone who knew how to move in a fight, his eyes watchful . . . and at the moment, amused. "Welcome. I don't believe we've met before."

"Sara." She stuck out her hand. "This is Deacon."

"Sara Haziz?" The hunter's smile turned dazzling. "I'm so delighted to meet you. I've heard of you, of course. Please, come in." He glanced over his shoulder. "Pierre, prep a table." Returning his attention to them, he gave a short nod. "I'm Marco. With the Guild but not for long."

"Oh?"

He smiled again, displaying a row of gleaming white teeth. "I decided this bar is my true love after all."

Not many hunters retired. But it wasn't completely unheard of. "You won't miss the thrill of the hunt?"

"It's a young man's game. I'm in my late thirties now, but don't tell."

Deacon finally broke his silence. "Your bar's doing well—we heard about it on the hunter grapevine."

"Some of my best customers are hunters," Marco said, genuine pleasure in his voice. "They bring their girlfriends, mates, don't blink an eye. I'm very glad to have been a part of that fraternity. Please, come. The drinks are on me." With that, he turned and led them to a table on the edge of the dance floor.

They all took a seat and drinks were ordered. Sara noticed that Deacon barely touched his—whiskey, of course—and neither did Marco. She took a sip of her cocktail and made a true sound of pleasure. "This is sinfully good."

"Yes, the bar's becoming quite well-known for its cocktails."

She smiled and they chitchated for several minutes. "Does this place have a ladies' room?"

Marco grinned. "Of course. I can show you."

"No, just point me in the right direction." She leaned in close and whispered, "I need you to stay here and protect Deacon."

Marco's eyes twinkled. "The big ones want to pit themselves against him, and the pretty ones want to take him home and give him a whip."

Deacon's face remained expressionless, but his green eyes held a distinct warning. Laughing, she got into the act and stroked his cheek as she left. His stubble made her fingertips want to go exploring, but she strolled to the bathroom instead, getting several approving looks from the crowd.

It wasn't her fault she got distracted by a conversation with another hunter and ended up at a door that didn't lead to the toilets. Unfortunately, it was locked solid and coded with a touchpad. Hiding her disappointment, she made a point of asking for bathroom directions again and went in to use the facilities before returning to the table.

"Get lost?" Deacon asked before Marco could.

"Yeah." She laughed. "Someone dragged me off to ask if you really were as hard as you looked."

Deacon flushed. "Keep going."

She knew it was another warning. But the byplay had the effect of disarming any suspicions Marco might've had. He laughed and said a few more words before getting up to go mingle.

Deacon didn't look particularly happy, but waited to speak until they were on the bike heading back to the hotel. "You didn't make it to his apartment."

"No need." She grinned. "He crosses his leg like guys do."

Silence.

She took pity on him. "You know, one ankle over the knee, encroaching on other people's space."

"You got a transmitter on his shoe."

"When I asked to go to the bathroom." She felt exceedingly smug about that. "And that's not even the best part—he was wearing solid hunter boots." Increasing the odds that he'd use the same footwear if he decided to go out killing.

"My guess—the killer's not going to move tonight. Not after Rodney."

"Won't he be frustrated by the fact that he failed?"

"Possible, but this guy's not stupid. He does his homework, strikes only when he knows his prey will be vulnerable."

"If you had more people, you could put watches on both Tim and Marco, and if necessary, Shah."

"Ever tried following a hunter who doesn't want to be followed?"

"Point taken."

She thought of the three they'd visited. "Did you ask Simon to run background checks?"

"Might already have come through."

He was right. He pulled out and turned on a PDA that looked as tough as he was as soon as they got back to the hotel—all three reports were waiting in his e-mail.

"Pretty standard stuff," Sara said, as she lay flat on her back on the bed with the PDA in her hands. "Timothy had a hunt go bad, hasn't been seen in public since, but we know he's alive. Shah really is a spy. Doesn't mean he isn't a killer."

"Gut instinct?"

"That if Shah was going to kill, he'd do it in a way no one would ever trace back to him." She looked at the last page. "Marco is a solid hunter with a stable personal life—he's playing happy families with a vampire, so he clearly likes them."

"You ever been tempted?" The bed dipped as Deacon braced a knee on the bottom edge and looked down at her.

Chapter Five

Her mouth went dry. "Tempted?"

"To take up with a vamp?"

Oh. "Sure, they're gorgeous." But not *real*, not like Deacon. "Don't tell me you don't agree."

"The whole bloodsucking thing's kind of a turnoff."

"Yeah, that trips me up, too. I don't want my partner thinking of me as a midnight snack." She switched off the PDA and laid it carefully on the small chest of drawers beside the bed. "Have you ever had a vamp feed on you?"

A shake of the head, his eyes lingering on her lips. "You?"

"Emergency feed," she said, suddenly hot in the T-shirt and jeans that had been fine moments before. "The guy was so badly off, I had to do something."

"Hurt?" Those night-shadow green eyes were drifting over the rise of her breasts, the dip of her stomach.

She breathed deep, saw him suck in his own breath at the movement of her chest. "Not as much as you'd expect. They have something in their saliva that takes the edge off." Stretching out her legs, she raised her arms above her head. "And you know they can make it feel good if they want."

He didn't answer, his attention very much on her body as she relaxed from the stretch. Then he moved onto the bed, bracing himself above her using his forearms. "Yes?"

A simple question—one that made her pause and think. Hunters weren't prudes, but Sara had never had a one-night stand. It simply wasn't in her. Yet she'd wanted Deacon from the instant she'd seen him. And from the arousal he was making no effort to hide, she knew full well he wanted her, too.

But they weren't just two hunters who'd met on the road. "Are you going to get all weird after?"

"Define 'weird.'" He settled himself more firmly against her.

She bit back a moan. The man was hot, hard, and more than ready. "I need you to follow orders if I become director." Her former lovers wouldn't hesitate, because she hadn't been a candidate for the critically important position then. But now she was very much a candidate. "Are you going to expect special treatment?"

"I'm not in bed with the future director. I'm in bed with Sara."

"That's good enough for me."

It was tempting to rush, but she stroked her hands into his hair and tugged. The kiss was a punch to the system. Making a sound of sheer pleasure, she wrapped her arms around his neck, her legs around his waist. The man was big, solid all over. A wall of flesh and bone and muscle contained by granite will. She wanted to rub against him until she purred.

He bit her lower lip. She gasped in a breath and then it was happening again, the wild rush of sensation, the near-unbearable pleasure, the need to taste him deep. When the kiss broke this time, she nuzzled at his throat, kissing her way along the taut tendons of his neck. He smelled so damn good.

He tugged her back for another kiss, and somewhere in between, she realized his hand was on her bare back, under her T-shirt. She wanted more. Breaking the kiss, she let go of him and tugged at her T-shirt. Deacon rose off her enough that she could pull it over her head and off.

"Green?" He traced the scalloped lace of her bra with a single, teasing finger.

She began to unbutton his shirt even as he unhooked her bra. "It's my favorite color."

"Lucky for me." The last word was a groan as she flattened her hands on his chest. "Damn lucky."

"Off," she ordered.

Grunting, he rose to a kneeling position and slid off her bra before getting rid of the shirt. But he didn't come back down straight away. Instead, he reached out to close one big hand over her breast. She cried out at the unexpectedly bold touch, her eyes clashing with his. Deep green, but no longer calm or unaffected.

It made the last of her inhibitions fall away, and when he bent his head to her breast, she thrust her hands into his hair and held on for the ride. The Slayer knew what he was doing. There were no hesitant caresses, no requests for more permission. He'd asked once, and she'd acquiesced. Now he took every advantage. Truth to tell, it was beyond erotic being with a man so sure of himself in bed. So sure . . . and so utterly involved. Now she knew the answer to her question—when Deacon lost control, he *lost* control.

God, could he get any sexier?

She wrapped her legs around his waist and kissed him wet and deep and open. "I think you should take off your pants."

Nuzzling his way down her neck to her pulse point, he reached down to hers instead. But rather than opening the jeans, he slid his hand under the waistband to cup her with bold familiarity. She arched into him, wanting more. "No teasing."

A nip at the soft flesh of her breast. Shuddering, she thrust her hands into his hair and tugged. "Don't you talk in bed?"

His response was to kiss his way down her breastbone, before sitting back up. Withdrawing his hand with obvious reluctance, he undid her jeans and pulled them off, along with her panties. A still, darkly sensual moment as he simply looked at her. Her body arched in silent invitation. Taking it, he bent down until his lips touched her ear . . . and whispered such wicked promises, such decadent requests, she thought she'd melt from the inside out.

"Okay, stop talking." It was too much sensory input, too much pleasure. "Right now."

He smiled and sat up, his gaze never leaving her face. The intimacy was blinding. Then one big hand spread on her thigh, thumb stroking the insanely sensitive inner surface. She cried out in the back of her throat . . . and twisted out of his hold to sit up on her knees.

A flicker of surprise, followed by a smile, slow and sure. "Fast and sleek, and pretty." He bent to run his lips along her neck as she pulled out his belt and threw it to the floor, then started on the buttons of his fly. "Mmm." A sound of pure male appreciation.

Pushing his pants down just enough, she closed her hands around him. His big frame shook. *"Sara."* And then he was pressing her onto her back, tugging off her hands and sliding into her in one solid push.

Her entire body arched up off the bed. Wow, she thought, seconds before her sanity fractured, Deacon was built exactly in proportion.

Body tingling from the aftereffects of the best orgasm of her life, Sara stared at the hotel ceiling. "I knew we had chemistry, but that was unnatural."

The arm across her waist squeezed a little. "I live to please."

Sexy, uninhibited as hell when you got past the control,

and he had a sense of humor. "I don't suppose you're in the market for a long-term relationship?"

She'd expected shocked silence, but he answered straight away. "I wouldn't make a very good lover for the director."

"Don't like the spotlight, do you." It wasn't a question, because she knew the answer. And part of her wished she didn't. Because she liked Deacon, more than liked him. Each time he revealed some new facet of his personality, she found it complemented hers on the deepest level. There was promise here. And it wasn't just about sex. "Don't you ever get lonely?"

"Being alone's never been a problem for me." His fingers played over the curve of her hip. "You're going to accept, aren't you?"

"Yes." She'd always known it would come to this. "The Guild is important. It needs to have someone at the reins who cares enough to make sure it remains strong, that hunters are protected from vampires and angels both."

"What about the hunting?"

She stroked her hand along his forearm. "I'll miss it. But . . . not as much as some. My best friend, Ellie, she'd go stir-crazy within a week."

"Elena Deveraux? Hunter-born?"

"You've met her?" She turned to him. Face relaxed with pleasure, hair all mussed, and green eyes lazy, he looked like a big cat sprawled beside her. A big, dangerous cat.

"Heard about her," he said. "They call her the best."

"She is." Sara was damn proud of Ellie, considered her more sister than friend. "I worry about her."

"You worry about all hunters."

And it was true. She did. "I guess I was meant to be director." Her sense of responsibility was part of who she was. She could no more walk away and leave the Guild in weaker hands than she could force Deacon to change his lifestyle to accommodate hers. "How did you end up the Slayer?"

"The Guild keeps an eye on possibles. I was approached by the last Slayer and offered the position."

He'd accepted, Sara knew, for the same reason she would.

"Someone has to do the job." But it was also a calling of sorts—she knew she'd love being director, that it would challenge and excite her in ways normal hunting couldn't hope to match.

"And that someone might as well be the best."

She smiled and shifted to face him fully, his hand on her hip, her own under her head. "Have you ever met an archangel?" The tiny hairs on her arms rose at the very idea.

"No. But you probably will."

She gave in to the shivers. "I hope it's not for a long, long time." Angels she could deal with, but archangels were a whole different story. They simply didn't think like human beings in any way, shape, or form.

Deacon's lips curved. "I think you'll handle it when the time comes." Reaching out, he brushed her hair off her face.

The tenderness of the gesture did her in. Again, she felt that promise. That tug that this could be so much more. "Right now I just want to handle you." And she did.

An hour later, and despite her lack of sleep, she couldn't turn off, too revved up by pleasure. Deacon could do amazing things with his tongue, she thought, happily buzzed. Maybe the endorphins lit up the right areas of her brain because she sat bolt upright and leaned over to pick up the PDA.

"What?" Deacon asked, one arm heavy around her waist.

She turned it on and checked. "Argh, it's not here." Returning the PDA to its previous position, she slumped back onto the bed.

"What?"

"A picture of Marco's boyfriend." She made a sound of frustration. "Look, we've been looking at this like it's some hate-crime thing, but what if it's a normal crazy who's using that to throw us off the scent?"

Deacon pushed his hair off his face and raised an eyebrow. "Explain 'normal crazy.'"

"Maybe the boyfriend dumped Marco. Maybe Marco

went batshit. And now maybe he's out cutting up vampires who look like his beloved."

Deacon frowned. "The victims don't fit a type—they've been blond, dark-haired, black, white."

She blew out a breath. "It seemed like a good idea."

"It might still be a good idea." His hand went quiet on her skin. "No physical similarities, but they were all known to fraternize with humans more than usual."

"That tracks," she said, feeling herself on the edge of understanding. "I found Rodney through his human friends. He can't let go."

"Two of the victims had human lovers."

"Not a biggie," she said. "Human-vampire pairings are fairly common, especially with the younger vamps."

"Yeah, but it's a distinct pattern when you put it together with the other stuff." Pushing off the sheet, he got out of bed.

Lord have mercy.

She stared unashamedly as he went to his jacket and grabbed a small black device. "This thing tracks the transmitters via GPS. I set it to beep if any of them moved, but just in case . . . No, they're all where we put them. The transmitters anyway."

"I'm worried about Tim," she murmured, wondering whether Deacon would mind if she used her teeth on that firm, muscled flesh of his. "No one's seen him for days. If he's not the killer . . ."

"Yeah. But someone's feeding Lucy—else she'd have been weaker."

"Point." She pulled the sheet over her head. "I can't think with you naked. Get dressed."

The chuckle was rich, unexpected, and so damn gorgeous, she almost jumped him again.

"*Now.* That's an order from the future Guild Director."

"Whose naked toes I want to bite."

She curled said toes and continued to grin. "Hurry up."

Still chuckling, he seemed to be obeying. "How about a quick shower? We're sweaty."

"That shower is tiny." But she lowered the sheet.

His expression dared her.

She was such a sucker, she thought, getting up and sauntering off. But she got the last word . . . by driving him certifiably crazy while he was trapped in that steamy glass enclosure.

Chapter Six

It was seven a.m. when they set out again—sleepless, but amped up on happy hormones, as Sara liked to think of them, and armed to the teeth. It was obvious the vampires shadowing her were building up to something—no reason to give them an easy target.

The streets were still winter-dark when they rode out, the fog curling over the houses like a whispered caress. Even the junkyard looked dreamy and somehow softer in the muted light.

"Let's take the front route today," she suggested. "I'll say I'm here to check up on him on orders from Simon."

Deacon nodded and pulled the bike to a stop in front of the padlocked gate. "Lucy should be here any moment."

But though they waited, Deacon's favorite hellhound didn't appear. A bad feeling bloomed in the pit of Sara's stomach. "Wait." Getting off, she picked the lock and waved Deacon through. It was tempting to leave the gate open for an easy exit, but she didn't want Lucy escaping and terrorizing the neighborhood—and maybe getting terrorized herself if she couldn't find her way back home.

Gate locked, she got back on the bike and they roared their way to Tim's house/shack—or as close as they could get considering the random piles of junk. There was a light on inside. "He's home." Taking off her helmet, she hooked it on one handlebar, while Deacon did the same with his on the other.

"I don't like this." The Slayer's words were calm, his eyes intent as they made their way through a gap in the junk to emerge into a relatively open space near Tim's home. "Something's wrong."

Her instincts agreed. "Let's do a circle of the house, make sure things are—" She saw them then. The vampires. Crouched on wrecked cars, lounging between towers of metal, leaning against the side of Tim's shack.

She knew there'd be no running this time. "We need to get inside the house." It was the only defensible position. Her crossbow was already in her hands.

"They'll be ready for that." Deacon's back met hers as they stood facing in opposite directions.

"Unless Tim's barricaded himself inside."

Deacon said nothing, but she knew what he was doing. *Listening.* If Tim was alive and inside the house, he'd let them know. But it was Lucy they heard, a sudden set of sharp barks and then nothing. The vampire closest to Sara swore loud enough that the sound carried. "Damn devil dog ate half my leg."

It was such an ordinary thing to say, but she knew he was in no way ordinary. Not only did he carry centuries of experience in his eyes, he moved like a man who knew how to use every shift to his advantage. But there were no weapons in his hands. The archangels were nothing if not fair. Of course, their concept of fair meant two hunters—possibly three—against what looked like fifteen vamps.

"Somebody upped the stakes," she murmured under her breath.

"I don't recognize any of them, even the old one. Means they belong to someone other than Raphael."

She'd been thinking the same. "Good to know my own

archangel isn't trying to kill me." She aimed the crossbow at the leader of the group. "Guess it's time for target practice."

The vampire smiled, polished and smooth. "I want but a sip, milady." A voice that held echoes of gallantry and cruelty. "They say the Guild Director tastes sweet indeed."

Since she doubted very much that Simon would've allowed anyone to munch on him, she took that with a grain of salt. "You so hard up for blood then?" She moved a little toward the house. Deacon moved with her.

The vampires kept their distance . . . for now.

"You wound me, *petite guerrière*."

Little warrior? Sara almost shot him on principle. "You want to be chipped?"

"Lies, sweet lies." He waved a finger. "You're only allowed chip-embedded weapons on a hunt. If you use illegal copies on me, you can't be Guild Director."

Damn. She hadn't expected the bluff to work, but his response meant he was smart. Smart plus old was not a good combination in a vampiric opponent. "I really will shoot you if you get any closer—and if I put a bolt through your heart, it'll leave you helpless."

The vampire spread his hands. "Alas, I have my orders. My master does not see how a human female could run a guild of warriors."

"There are female archangels." She felt Deacon's body tense, ready itself for battle.

"Ah, but you're not an archangel." And then he *moved*.

So did Sara and Deacon. It was as if they'd been doing this for years. Shooting the crossbow as she ran sideways, she skewered the lead vamp in the shoulder—she'd been aiming for his head, damn it—and reloaded superfast using Deacon's patented technology. Hunters loved his weapons for a reason. She'd shot five more bolts by the time they were blocked in again. But now they were within a three-second run of the house.

Deacon had stayed back to back with her the entire time, accommodating her smaller stride with an ease that told her exactly how good he was at combat. From the sounds she'd heard, he was using some kind of a gun but not anything that shot bullets. The vamps were too close for her to risk a check, but she didn't think he'd been injured anywhere.

"Enough playing?" she asked the vampire who seemed to be the mouthpiece of the entire group.

The handsome man had already removed the bolt and now tossed it at her feet. "That was rather unladylike."

"Well, you weren't exactly gentlemanly in attacking me." She could feel the edge of sunrise in the distance. Too bad the vamps wouldn't crumble to dust at the first touch of the sun's rays. Only in the movies were things so convenient. Some vampires did suffer from light sensitivity, but she bet every single one in this bunch was capable of walking around under noon-light itself.

"Ah," the vampire said. "That is so. But you have a knight to protect you."

"I don't need a knight," she said, knowing full well this was about more than physical strength alone. "I'm not a queen to hide behind my troops. I'm a general."

The vampire's expression grew strangely quiet. "Then I will stop being a gentleman."

This time, she couldn't reload fast enough. Dropping the crossbow, she started to fight with knives, nicking him in the throat, catching a second vampire with a kick to the gut. Behind her, Deacon was taking out vamps left, right, and center. But they were severely outnumbered. This was in no way a fair fight.

Whoever had orchestrated this wanted Sara to die. Why? She slashed a line across one vampire's neck, and the blood that hit her was hot and fresh and nauseating. The vampire staggered back, hand clamped over his throat. She kept fighting, kicking and breaking knees. Something burned into her shoulder, and she stabbed a knife through the ear of the vamp who'd decided to turn her into a breakfast buffet.

Howling, the attacker fell away. Deacon growled then, and she'd never heard a more chilling sound. He took out three more coming at her, holding off two others on his own side as she grabbed the gun she'd tucked into her lower back. "Ready!" she yelled, and started firing to cover his reloading.

They were closer to the house. But not close enough. If Tim was in there, he was either injured, dead, or didn't give a shit. Else he'd have been shooting as well. Which meant it was time for drastic measures. Simon had been very clear in his instructions.

"We walk a precarious line. The angels need us. But if we prove too powerful, they'll cheerfully wipe us from existence. Hurt the vampires they send after you, but try not to kill. Because if you do, you become a threat, not an asset."

Problem was, the vampires were healing from the nonfatal wounds only to continue their relentless—and openly deadly—assault. "Deacon?"

"Yes." Agreement.

Even as her hand moved to retrieve the miniature flamethrower strapped to her thigh, a knife hit the vampire in front of her, severing his carotid artery. As he choked on his own blood and fell away from the attack, another knife lodged in the eye of the vampire she'd hit with her first bolt.

Neither knife was Sara's.

Then the shooting started.

Knives from the left. Gunshots from the right.

And a clear pathway to the house. It had been the best choice at the start, a place from where they could make a stand. But now the odds had changed. "You thinking what I'm thinking?"

"Fight."

Smiling, she palmed a second gun from a shoulder holster and began firing two-handed.

Five minutes later, they had their backs to the house and the vampires were bloody and broken; caught between their guns and whoever was throwing knives—and other things—from the vicinity of the fence.

The head vamp raised his hands, palms out. "I yield."

There was a collective groan from the other vampires—all still alive—as they collapsed onto the ground. Sara couldn't believe it. "You think I'm just going to let that go?"

The vamp smiled. "Politics is a most unkind mistress."

"Should I expect any other visits from you?"

"No. The test has been passed." He blinked, his injured eye healing at a phenomenal rate. "And the archangels have little interest in the inner workings of the Guild."

"So the whole trying-to-kill-me thing? What was that?"

"It had to be done." Shrugging, he turned to his troops. "It's time to go."

Another five minutes and there wasn't a single vampire to be seen in the cool dawn light of a winter morning. Sara finally lowered her weapons and glanced at Deacon. He was bloody, his jacket torn in several places, but it was the look in his eyes that rocked her to the core. He was pissed. "Goddamn it, Sara. I don't like you being hurt." And then he kissed her.

It was hot and wild and amazing . . . until Lucy began howling. And someone coughed.

Sara tore away from the kiss, gun raised—to see a tall woman with long white blonde hair pulled into a ponytail, her eyes frankly curious and her body plastered with knives. "So," Ellie said, with a huge smile, "you and the Slayer, huh? I like." She looked Deacon up and down, and whistled. "Best Friend Seal of Approval bestowed. With gold foil edging, even."

Grinning, Sara went to hug her. Elena shook her head. "I love you, Sara, but you're all bloody with vampire."

"Ugh." Sara looked down at her soaked clothing. "I thought I told you to stay away."

"Would you have done that?" Ellie raised an eyebrow. "Exactly."

Giving up, Sara threw up her hands. "We need to check on Tim—the hunter inside." She turned to Deacon. "Think we should send Ellie in? We wouldn't want to get blood all over Tim's floor."

Deacon's eyes gleamed. "Good idea."

Elena glanced from one to the other. "Do I have 'sucker' written on my forehead? I don't think so. I know all about Timothy's demon fiend of a sidekick."

Despite his words, Deacon was already at the door. "Tim?"

"I'm okay," came the groaning answer as Lucy went into a barking frenzy. "Luce, girl, down." A few growls but the dog quieted.

"Cover me," Deacon said and opened the door.

Sara was ready to shoot Lucy—to disable, not kill—but "the damn devil-eyed dog" was sitting attentively by the sprawled form of her master, grinning as if she wasn't just waiting for a chance to bite off their faces. Tim had a gun in hand, a nasty bruise on the side of his face . . . and smelled like a distillery.

"Jesus, Tim," Ellie muttered, waving a hand in front of her hunter-sensitive nose. "What, you took a beer bath?"

Tim winced. "Shh."

"You've been on a bender?" Sara blew out an angry breath. "We thought you were dead." Or a serial killer.

"Hey," he muttered, "I got conscious long enough to shoot them, didn't I? And I'm allowed to go on a bender after I find a vampire torn to pieces by a hate group—they even cut off his fingers one by one. How fucking noble."

Sara had had one of those cases, too. She'd baked non-stop for five days after. Her neighbors loved her. "Who's been feeding Lucy?"

"Me, of course." He gave her an indignant look. "As if I'd leave my baby without food." He kissed that mangy black head. "She knows where her stash is. And I leave fresh water all over the place."

"Tim," Sara pushed, "this is important. Can you prove where you've been the past few days?"

He gave her an oddly clear look. "Hiding in a corner of Sal's All-Night-All-the-Time bar. Matchbook's on the table."

Deacon called the number and confirmed Tim's story. Happy at the news, but cognizant of the implications, Sara rubbed her face. "Ellie, can you make sure Tim detoxes and gets that bruise taken care of? Deacon and I have something to handle."

"I'm fine," Tim murmured and tried to stand. Only to fall flat on his butt. "Or maybe not."

Elena nodded. "No sweat. You need a hand?"

It was Deacon who answered. "Stay close. If we need backup, we'll call."

"Gotcha." Pulling "yummy" faces behind Deacon's back as he walked out to make another call, Ellie gave Sara the thumbs-up.

It was impossible not to smile, but that smile was gone by the time she reached the bike and Deacon. "It has to be Marco. And if not, we're in deep shit." Because that meant they had an unknown crazy out there.

"I just checked with Simon. Shah left the city two hours ago, so if there's another killing . . ." He shook his head. "We can't wait for that. It's time to play hardball with Marco."

"You think you can break him?"

Deacon's face was a grim mask. "Yeah."

It should've scared her. It didn't. Because she knew how to play hardball, too. "Let's do it." Getting on the bike, she took the helmet he held out. "After this is over, I want a shower in a really big bathroom."

"I'll get us the penthouse."

"What makes you think you'll be sharing it with me?"

"I live in hope."

Oh, she definitely wanted to keep him, she thought, as they closed the gate behind themselves and headed out. Maybe there was a way to make it work? But she knew there wasn't. She could hardly see Deacon in a tux at some "do." And the Guild Director had to play politics. Nobody liked a powerful presence like the Guild in the city, but that wariness could be turned into respect and even welcome by a little subtle maneuvering.

A long time ago, the Guild had chosen the veil of secrecy. The end result had been a spate of Guild-burnings that had razed many a chapter building to the ground, killing a devastating number of hunters in the process. No one wanted a repeat of that.

Suddenly conscious that Deacon had dramatically reduced his speed, she twisted to peer around one muscular arm. "Oh, no fucking way." Pulling off her helmet, she stood on the back of the bike, using Deacon's shoulder for balance. "You yielded," she told the vampire standing in the middle of the road. "This time, we'll be aiming to kill."

Chapter Seven

"Milady, you misunderstand me." A serious expression. "I have need of the Guild's services."

Sara really didn't feel like helping someone who'd tried to separate her head from her body not that long ago, but hunters existed for a reason. "Someone run out on a Contract?"

"No. One of your hunters has taken one of us captive. If you would please organize a rescue, we'd be most grateful."

She squeezed Deacon's shoulder. No way was this a coincidence. As she sat back down, Deacon maneuvered the bike to the side of the road. "Talk," they both ordered at the same time.

"Silas," the vampire said, shifting to stand on the sidewalk beside them, "had a relationship with the hunter. Unbeknownst to anyone, they went their separate ways two weeks ago."

Around the time the killings started.

"The hunter's name is Marco Giardes." The vampire spread his hands. "I have no idea of what happened between the two of them. But I received a message from Silas a few minutes ago stating that Marco was holding him captive in the basement of his home."

Sara wondered if Marco had guessed at her and Deacon's true motives after all. Something had to have triggered this. "Did he say how long he'd been there?"

"Silas walked into the hunter's bar an hour ago with his new inamorato." He snorted. "He is young, thinks being a vampire makes him invincible." A meaningful rub at the shoulder she'd wounded.

"Damn vampire wanted to rub Marco's face in his new affair." Sara almost felt sorry for Marco. Almost. Because if everything this vampire was saying was right, then Marco had gone out and killed five other men, none of whom had done anything to him. Not to mention how he'd terrified Rodney. "Do you have any other information?"

"Silas's new lover is no more." A shrug. "Silas got the message out before Marco realized he had a second cell phone. I've received no messages since, so the hunter has likely remedied that."

Deacon stared at the vamp. "If you know where he is, why aren't you mounting a rescue? You have a big enough group."

A long pause. The vampire looked up, then down, lowered his voice. "Raphael was *not* pleased when he found out about the attack on Sara. We are not his people. He has forbidden us from doing anything in his territory except that which relates to our departure—even feeding." A long, shuddering sigh. "We're to leave on the first plane out of the country."

"Silas is a tourist?" Sara asked, rapidly thinking through her options.

"Marco met him during a hunt. Silas came to be with him." Another glance upward. "We would appeal to our archangel for help, but he doesn't particularly care for Silas."

Sara didn't trust the vampire an inch, but she had a feeling he was telling the truth about Marco and Silas. There was a layer of concern in his voice that betrayed an obvious affection for the younger vampire. That wasn't as weird as it sounded. Vampires had once been human, after all—it took a long time for the echoes to fade entirely.

"Fine." She put her helmet back on. "I guess it's time for the Guild to ride to the rescue."

Deacon started the engine in silence and they headed off, leaving the vampire standing at the curb. "I think he was straight with us," she said. "You?"

"It fits with what we know." His voice was an intimate darkness in her ear. "Looks as if Raphael likes you."

"I've never met him. Or even talked to him on the phone." She drew in a deep breath. "I don't think it has anything to do with me."

"No?"

"No." She knew exactly where humans ranked in the scheme of things as far as archangels were concerned. Somewhere below ants. "It's the fact that some other archangel tried to horn in on his territory. He's pissed." And when an archangel got pissed, things got brutal. "Did you hear what he did to that vampire in Times Square?"

A slow nod from Deacon. "Broke every bone in his body and left him there. As a warning. He was alive throughout, the poor bastard."

"So you see why I don't *ever* want Raphael to take an interest in my welfare."

Deacon didn't say anything, but they both knew that as Guild Director, she'd have a much higher chance of attracting Raphael's attention than an ordinary hunter. But still, how many times did an archangel contact any human directly? Sara had never heard of it. They ran everything from their towers.

Manhattan's Archangel Tower dwarfed everything in the entire state. Sara had often sat in Ellie's way-too-expensive apartment and watched the angels flying in and out. Their feet, she thought, likely never touched the earth. "You know, I think Ellie's got a higher chance of meeting an archangel than I do."

"Why?"

"Just a feeling." A prickling across the back of her neck, a kiss of the "eye" her great-grandmother claimed to possess. "Think we should call her for backup?"

"If Marco's in there alone, we can take him. Let's check things out first—I don't want to panic him." A pause. "Though it sounds like Silas is no prize."

"Yeah. But Marco hurt Rodney, who's about as dangerous as your average rabbit." She hoped his master hadn't been too hard on him. And that Mindy the Bitch had gotten her head torn off.

"We're here." He pulled over and parked. "The bar should be closed."

Stowing the helmets, they headed to the bar . . . only to come to an abrupt halt when a little old lady on her way down from farther along the street stared at them and backed away very fast. Sara looked at Deacon, really looked. Big, sexy, loaded up with weapons . . . and stained rust red. "Oops."

He smiled, slow and with a glint that said he was thinking about getting naked. With her. "We better wrap this up before the police arrive and all hell breaks loose."

Nodding, she shoved aside the thought of soaping up his delicious body and picked up the pace. "How're we getting into the basement?"

Deacon raised an eyebrow. "We ask."

"Wha— Oh, that'll work. Two hunters, needing sanctuary and somewhere to clean up. I'm good with that."

The door to the bar was locked shut, all the neon turned off. Deacon went to knock, but Sara grabbed his hand and pointed to the intercom hidden discreetly to the side. Pushing the button, she waited.

"Yes?" Marco's voice. Sounding tired, but not the least bit aggressive.

"Marco, it's Sara and Deacon. We need a place to clean up."

"I can see that." The door clicked open. "Come on through."

They went in. Sara waited until the door had closed behind them to whisper, "Is it just me or does he sound way too normal?"

Deacon was frowning as well. "Either he's one hell of a good actor or something else is up."

Marco stuck his head out the door that led up to his apartment. He whistled when he saw them. "Must've been some fight. The bathroom's big enough for two." A sharp grin that tried to hide exhaustion and failed.

Again, nothing weird about that if he hadn't yet had a chance to go to bed.

Then she saw the mess that was the bar itself. Bottles shattered, blood on the floor, what looked like bullet holes in the walls. A second later, Marco stepped out from behind the door, and it became apparent he was sporting the beginnings of a serious black eye. "Do I dare ask?" She raised an eyebrow.

Marco thrust a hand through his hair. "Come on up and we'll talk."

"Now would be better," Deacon said, unmoving.

The bar owner looked from one to the other and said, "Shit." Sounding like his heart had just broken into a million pieces, he sat down on the last step, head in his hands. "He set me up. The bastard set me up."

Sara was starting to get a headache. She'd come in here expecting to rescue a hurt vampire from an unhinged hunter, and found a shattered lover. "How about we take this from the top?" she suggested, staying out of attack range in case Marco actually was that good an actor. "Where's Silas?"

"Locked in the basement." Marco's eyes were bleak when he glanced at them. "I needed time to get my shit together before I called the Guild."

"And the man who was with him?"

Marco nodded at the bar. "Silas came up behind him and . . ." He stared at his hands. "I couldn't believe it. But the blood, God, so much blood."

Leaving Deacon to keep an eye on him, she pulled herself up onto the gleaming wooden surface and looked down. A vampire's bright blue eyes stared up at her. She sucked in a breath. If she hadn't been able to see that his head was no longer attached to his body, she'd have thought him alive. "Dead," she confirmed to Deacon. "The question is, how did he get that way?"

"Silas," Marco repeated dully. "He came in here, strutting like a damn peacock. I should've left him outside but I—" He swallowed, hand fisted, pain apparent in every taut tendon. "I thought maybe he'd come to apologize. I didn't see the kid till after."

"Apologize?" Sara had the sinking feeling they'd all been drawn into one seriously bad lover's tiff.

"For cheating on me." Marco finally looked her full in the face. "Here I was, being a putz. I gave my notice at the Guild, set up this place, all because he said he hated knowing I was putting my life on the line with every hunt. I even asked Simon to talk to some of the senior angels, see if we could maybe get the rest of Silas's Contract transferred to an angel in the States so we wouldn't have to keep going back and forth."

"Here." Sara grabbed a dented but still whole bottle of water and threw it at him. "Breathe."

"I can't." He chugged the entire bottle, then threw it aside. "He was just using me. Wanted out of his Contract—his angel doesn't like him. I could've swallowed that. Hell on the ego, but I'd have swallowed it. I *loved* him. But the whole time we were together, he was with . . . who the fuck knows. More than one guy."

"Marco, that doesn't make sense." Sara folded her arms. "Why would he set you up if he was the one cheating?"

"'Cause I dumped him." And in that moment, Sara saw the hunter Marco was. Hard, lethal, certainly very good at his job. "I told him to get out and stay out."

"Which meant he lost any chance of getting his Contract transferred." Deacon didn't move from his position by the door. "It sounds good. But all the evidence points to a hunter."

"He took my stuff. My weapons, clothes, one of the ceremonial swords I collect." Marco ground his teeth together.

"I feel so fucking stupid. I knew he didn't handle rejection well, but I never thought he'd go around killing people just to get back at me."

Sara glanced at Deacon. He shook his head in a slight negative. She agreed. Marco was very, very believable. But it was his word against this Silas's. If they backed him, the vampires would take it badly—unless they had proof. In which case, Silas would disappear to face angelic justice. Hunters could kill, but only in exigent circumstances, or when they had an execution warrant. It made more sense for angels to deliver any necessary punishment—they were faster, stronger, and far more cruel than the vampires they Made.

"Security cameras," she asked Marco. "Did you record the fight?"

"No." Self-disgust marred the handsome lines of his face. "I turned them off when I realized it was him—didn't want anyone seeing how much of a fool I'd been. At least I wasn't stupid enough to leave my gun behind. Shot grazed his head, knocked him out."

That explained how Marco had gotten the vamp into the basement. "We need to talk to Silas." Sara stepped forward, expecting an argument.

Marco got up. "I'll take you—let's see what the bastard has to say."

Letting him go on ahead, they followed with weapons drawn. Silas was pounding on the door by the time they got there.

"Help me!" More pounding. "Help! I can hear you!"

"Quiet." Deacon's voice cut through the pounding like a knife.

Sara took the lead. "How'd you end up locked in the basement?"

They got pretty much the same story as from Marco . . . but with the roles reversed. By the time it was over, Sara's headache had turned into a thumping monster. How in hell were they going to fix this? The wrong move and a lot more blood would spill.

She looked to Deacon. "Got handcuffs?"

He handed her a thin plastic pair. "They'll hold." Marco lifted up his hands without question when she turned. Clicking the cuffs shut, she led him back upstairs, stashing him on the stairway that led up to his apartment . . . after blindfolding him and tying his feet together, then redoing the cuffs to lock him to the railing. Hunters were extremely resourceful when it came to survival.

"I won't run," Marco told her, a broken kind of pain in his voice that hurt her.

"For what it's worth," she said, "I believe you." If she was going to be Guild Director, she had to learn to judge her people. "But we need proof."

"He's smart. Part of his charm."

Silas hadn't sounded particularly charming to Sara, but then, she wasn't in love with him. Patting Marco on the shoulder, she walked out, pulling the door shut behind her. "Rodney," she said to Deacon.

"That's what I thought."

"But even if he can tell their voices apart, how seriously is anyone going to take him?" She pulled out her cell phone. Hesitated.

"It's a start."

As she waited for the phone to be answered, she found her eyes locked with Deacon's. "I'm going to have to deal with messes like this all the time as director."

A nod. "And you'll care enough to find out the truth." Bridging the distance between them, he touched her cheek. "We're lucky to have you."

The phone was picked up on the other end. "Yes?"

Sara dropped her head against Deacon's chest at the sound of that voice. "Mindy, I need to speak to your master."

"I got punished because you tattled."

Chapter Eight

Sara didn't have time to engage in a pissing contest. "You should've been more careful."

"Damn straight," Mindy said. "I'm four hundred years old and I can't get rid of the twerp. Not your fault. Hold on."

Surprised, and glad something was going right, she took a deep breath as Lacarre's cultured voice came on the line. "Hunter." A demand for why she was calling, and permission to speak, all in one word.

She explained. "If we could borrow Rodney for a few minutes, it might help clear things up."

"Since the victims included two of my own, I'd be very interested in learning the identity of the perpetrator. We'll be there shortly."

Closing the phone, she hugged Deacon. "Think anyone would notice if I chucked it all in and ran screaming for the hills?"

Warm, strong hands rubbing over her back. "They might send the Slayer after you."

"No flirting. Not now."

"Later, then." He didn't stop the back rub. "I think this officially equals the oddest case of my career."

"You and me both. I don't know why I'm always surprised when vampires act as weird as ordinary humans. It's not like they gain the wisdom of the ages with the transformation." His heart beat strong and steady under her cheek. Solid. Calming. A woman could get used to that kind of an anchor.

They stood in silence for a long time, until Sara's heart beat in rhythm with his. "Did you ever consider another career?" she asked in a low, private whisper, realizing she knew nothing of his past. It didn't matter. It was the man he was today who fascinated her. "Aside from the Guild?"

"No." A single word that held a wealth of history.

She didn't push. "Me, either. I met my first hunter while I was living on a commune—don't even ask—when I was ten. She was so smart and tough and practical. It was love at first sight."

His chuckle sounded a little raw. "I saw mine after a bloodlust-crazed vampire destroyed our entire neighborhood. The hunter found me standing over the vampire, chopping his head off with a meat cleaver."

She squeezed him tight. "How old were you?"

"Eight."

"It's a wonder you're not a psycho vampire-killer yourself."

Somehow, it was the right thing to say. He laughed softly and all but folded himself around her, kissing her temple with a tenderness that shattered her remaining defenses like so much glass. "I decided I'd rather be one of the good guys. I don't like tracking and executing my fellow hunters—every kill hurts like a bitch."

And that, Sara suddenly knew, was why the last Slayer had chosen Deacon as his successor. The Slayer had to love the Guild with all his heart and soul. Every decision had to be made with the wrenching power of that love—Deacon would never execute a hunter without absolute, undeniable evidence. Otherwise, Marco would've been dead days ago.

Lifting up her head, she kissed his throat. "How do you feel about carrying on a secret affair with the Guild Director?" She couldn't let him go. Not without a fight.

"I prefer the world know full well I consider a woman mine." An uncompromising answer. "Secrets just come back to bite you in the ass."

There went that possibility. Before she could come up with another, the front door vibrated under the force of an imperious knock. Lacarre had arrived. "Showtime." Pulling away from Deacon, she walked over and let in both Lacarre and his entourage—Mindy, Rodney, and unexpectedly, the vampire who'd originally asked for their help. "Please come in." She raised an eyebrow at the one who didn't belong.

"We found him loitering," Mindy said, waving a hand with insouciance that told them she couldn't care less. "Lacarre decided he might be of help."

The foreign vampire didn't look especially pleased to have been dragged inside, but nobody said no to an angel.

"Where are the two men?" Lacarre asked, keeping his wings several inches off the floor so they wouldn't drag on the sticky mess of glass, blood, and alcohol that coated the varnished surface.

"One's behind there." She nodded at the closed door that led up to Marco's apartment. "And the other's in the basement."

Mindy stroked a hand down Deacon's arm. "Do they look like this one?" It was a sultry invitation.

Deacon said nothing, just watched her with eyes gone so cold, even Sara felt the chill. Deacon did scary really, really well. Mindy dropped her hand as if it had been singed and returned to Lacarre's side quick-fast. Rodney was already cowering behind the angel's wings.

"You'd make a good vampire," the angel said to Deacon. "I might actually trust the city wouldn't fall apart if I left you in charge."

"I prefer hunting."

The angel nodded. "Pity. Rodney, you know what you have to do?"

Rodney bobbed his head so fast, it was as if it were on springs. "Yes, Master." He looked childishly eager to please.

"Come on." Keeping her voice gentle, Sara held out her hand. "I didn't hurt you last time, did I?"

Rodney took a moment to think about that before coming over to close his fingers around her own. "They won't be able to get me, will they?"

"No." She patted his arm with her free hand. "All I want you to do is listen to their voices and tell me which one sounds like the man who hurt you."

They went to Marco first, Lacarre and Mindy following. It made the hairs on the back of her neck rise to have a powerful angel and his bloodthirsty vampire floozy behind her—she was able to bear it only because Deacon was bringing up the rear, with Silas's friend in front of him. "Marco." She banged on the door. "I want you to threaten to cut off Rodney's head."

Rodney shot her a wide-eyed look. She whispered, "It's just pretend."

Marco began yelling a second later. Eyes wide, Rodney skittered away from the door and Sara *felt* her stomach fall. "Is it him?" she asked, after Marco went quiet.

Rodney was shivering. "No, but he's scary."

Lacarre wasn't fond of the basement idea, but he came down with them. And when Silas refused to do as ordered, the angel whispered, "Or would you rather *I* come in for a private . . . talk?" Silky sweet, dark as chocolate, and sharp as a stiletto sliding between your ribs.

If Sara had ever had any delusions about trying to become a vampire, they would've died a quick death then and there. She never wanted to be under the control of anyone who could put that much cruelty, that much pain, into a single sentence.

Chastened, Silas made a wooden threat. About as scary

as a teddy bear. Sara was about to order him to do it with more feeling when Rodney turned around and tried to run back up the stairs. Deacon caught him. "Shh."

To Sara's surprise, the vampire clung to him as a child would to its father. "It was him. He's the bad man."

Lacarre stared at the back of Rodney's head, then at Sara. "Bring this Silas upstairs. I will hear from the hunter as to what happened."

Sara had her crossbow at the ready, but it proved unnecessary. Tall, dark, and striking Silas, his clothes torn and bloody, followed them meek as a lamb. Leaving him in front of Lacarre and Mindy—with the foreign vamp skulking in the background—she released Marco and walked with him to the others.

Silas glared at his ex-lover. "You kill and put the blame on me."

Marco ignored him, staring straight ahead as he recited what Sara believed to be the truth. Around the time that he got to his rejection of Silas, the out-of-town vampire gasped and said, "I believed you!"

"Be quiet!" Silas screamed.

Lacarre raised an eyebrow. "No. Continue."

"He has done this before," the foreign vampire said. "Three decades ago, when a human he'd been romancing left him for another vampire, he killed four of our own kind."

Sara met his eye. "Were they men with strong ties to humanity?"

"Yes." A trembling answer. "He told me the bloodlust had gotten hold of him. He was young . . . I protected him." The clearly shaken vampire took a deep breath and turned his back on his former friend. "I no longer do."

Silas screamed and jumped up as if to attack, but Deacon brought him down with a single chop to the throat. The vamp went down like a tree. Marco flinched but didn't turn even then.

"As I said," Lacarre murmured, "it's a great pity you don't wish to be Made. If you ever change your mind, let me know."

Deacon's smile was faint. "No offense, but I like being my own master."

"I'd tempt you with beauties like Mindy, but it seems you've made your choice." He walked over to Silas's unconscious body. "The Guild has the right to demand restitution and proffer punishment. What is your will?" A question aimed solely at Sara. As if she were already director.

Sara glanced at Marco, saw the struggle on his face and knew there could be only one answer. "Mercy," she said. "Execute him with mercy." For they all knew that Silas wouldn't be allowed to live. "No torture, no pain."

Lacarre shook his head. "So human."

She knew it wasn't a compliment. "It's a flaw I can live with." She never wanted to become anything close to what Lacarre was—so cold, even when he looked at her with such apparent interest.

"So be it." Walking over to Silas, he bent and gathered the vampire in his arms with effortless strength. "It will be done as you asked."

As he walked away, Mindy and the others trailing behind the wide sweep of his cream-colored wings, Sara saw Deacon put a hand on Marco's shoulder. A single squeeze. Words whispered so low that she couldn't hear what was said. But when Deacon moved back to her side, Marco no longer looked like he was dying a slow, painful death. Oh, he was hurting plenty, but there was also a glimmer of stubborn will, the kind that made humans into hunters.

He turned to Sara. "I'm withdrawing my resignation from the Guild. I thought . . . I hoped, but I can't stay here anymore."

"I'll make sure Simon knows."

"Not necessary, is it, Sara?" he said quietly. "So long as you do."

Sara said good-bye to Deacon outside the hotel six hours later. He had his gear and she had hers. Ellie was waiting for her in a clean rental car, ready to start the drive to New York. One last road trip before she became bogged down in the myriad responsibilities that came with running one of the most powerful and influential chapters of the Guild.

"The next year's going to be brutal," she said to Deacon as he sat sideways on his bike, his legs stretched out in front of him, and his arms folded. "Just as well you said no—I probably couldn't carry on a secret affair even if I tried." She should've laughed then, but she couldn't find any laughter inside her.

He didn't do anything sappy. He was Deacon. He stood, put his hand behind her neck, and kissed the breath out of her. Then he kissed her again. "I have some things to do. And you have a directorship waiting for you."

She nodded, the whiskey and midnight taste of him in her mouth. "Yeah."

"You better go. Ellie's waiting."

Squeezing him tight once more, she turned and walked away. He was right to do it this way. Whatever they had, the sweet, shining promise she could still see hovering on the horizon, it deserved to be left whole, instead of being crushed under the weight of unmet expectations.

"Drive," she said to Ellie the instant the door closed behind her.

Ellie took one look at her and didn't say a word. In fact, neither of them spoke until they'd crossed the state line. Then Ellie glanced over and said, "I liked him."

The unadorned remark splintered every one of Sara's defenses.

Dropping her head into her hands, she cried. Ellie pulled over to the side of the wide-open road and held her while she sobbed. Her best friend didn't insult either of them by spouting bullshit platitudes. Instead, she said, "You know, Deacon didn't strike me as the kind of man who lets go of things that matter."

Sara smiled, knowing her face was a blotchy mess. "Can you see him in a tux?" Her stomach tightened at the idea.

"Let me get the visual. Okay, I have it." Elena sighed. "Oh, baby, I could lick him up in a tux."

"Hey. Mine." It was a growl.

Ellie grinned. "I have a pulse. He's hot."

"You're an idiot." One who'd made her smile, if only for an instant. "I can just picture him shaking hands and playing Guild politics. Not."

"So?" Ellie shrugged. "The Guild Director has to do all that stuff. Who says her lover has to be anything but a big, scary, silent son of a bitch?"

It was tempting to agree, to hold on to hope, but Sara shook her head. "I have to be realistic. The man's a complete loner. It's why he's the Slayer." Dragging in a shaky breath, she sat back up and said, "Take us to New York. I have a job to do."

Strong words, but her fingers found their way into a pocket, skating over the tiny serrated sawblade hidden within. It was Deacon's. The man had some really interesting weapons—like a gun that fired these spinning circular babies instead of bullets. It was what he'd been using out in Tim's junkyard. That made her wonder how Lucy was doing.

A tiny smile tugged at her lips—who knew her favorite memory of Deacon would be of him cuddling a vicious hellhound of a dog?

Chapter Nine

Two months later, Sara stared at her reflection—the woman who looked back at her appeared both poised and quintessentially elegant in a strapless black sheath. Her hair had been styled in a sophisticated bun at the back of her head, her new bangs swept to the side with an elegance she'd never have been able to achieve in the field, and her face made up with skill that highlighted her cheekbones, brought out her eyes. "I feel like a fraud."

Simon chuckled and walked to stand behind her. "But you look precisely what you are—a powerful, beautiful woman." His eyes dropped to her necklace. "Good choice."

It was that shiny serrated blade. Deacon's blade. She'd had it strung on a silver chain. "Thanks."

"Some of the people you meet tonight will try to sneer at you. There are a few who see hunters as nothing more than jumped-up hired help."

"Oh, like Mrs. Abernathy?" she said, tone dry as she named the society matron whose party she was about to attend. "She asked me if I'd like some help with 'appropriate clothing, dear.'"

"Exactly." Simon squeezed her shoulders. "Here's some advice—anytime one of those 'blue bloods' tries to bring you down, remember that you deal with angels every day. Most of them would pee their pants at the thought."

She choked. "Simon!"

"It's true." He shrugged. "And someday, you might even deal with a member of the Cadre. No matter how important they think they are, most humans will never come within touching distance of an archangel."

"I'd probably pee my pants then, too," she muttered.

"No, you won't." Unexpectedly serious words. "As for the upper-crust vampires, remember, we hunt them. Not the other way around."

Sara nodded and blew out a breath. "I wish we didn't have to do this crap."

"Angels might scare us, but hunters scare most other people—including a lot of vampires. Reassure them. Convince them we're civilized."

"What a con." She grinned.

Simon grinned back, but it wasn't his face she wanted to see beside hers in the mirror. "Okay, I'm ready." This was her first solo outing as Guild-Director-in-training. The transition would be complete by year's end.

"Go get 'em."

The party didn't bore her silly. It was the last sign—had she needed one—that she was the right person for the job. Ellie would've shot at least five people by now. Sara smiled and parried another nosy question while soaking up the relentless flow of gossip. It was all intelligence. Hunters needed to know a lot of things—like who a vampire might run to, or which individuals might sympathize with the angels to the extent of going vigilante.

Of course, to all outward appearances, she was simply mingling—just another well-dressed female among dozens of others. Mrs. Abernathy had beamed at her when she arrived. "Probably surprised I didn't turn up in blood-soaked leathers," she muttered into her champagne flute during a moment's respite on the balcony.

"Would've worked for me."

The smile that cracked her face was surely idiotic, but she didn't turn. "Is it the leathers you like or the body in them?"

"You got me." Warm breath against her nape, hands on her hips. "But I could get used to this dress."

"Hey, eyes up." She put the champagne flute on the waist-high wall that surrounded the balcony. "No scoping the cleavage."

"Can't help it." He turned her with a stroking caress.

And the air rushed out of her.

"Oh, man." She leaned back and twirled a finger.

Of course Deacon didn't give her a fashion show. He flicked at her sideswept bangs instead. "I like it."

"Ransom said it makes me look like I have raccoon eyes."

"Ransom has hair like a girl."

She grinned. "That's what I said." Throwing her arms around his neck, she kissed him with wild abandon, and it felt way beyond good. So she did it again. "The debutantes are going to wet their panties over you."

He looked horrified.

"Don't worry." She pressed a kiss to his jaw. "I'll scare them away."

Deacon caused such a stir she thought they might have a Chanel No. 5–scented stampede in the ballroom. She also thought it'd make him turn and run. That he'd come . . . well, hell, it had stolen her heart right out of her chest. But she didn't expect him to stand at her side with quiet focus, as if the attention didn't even register.

A few of the men tried to use his presence to ignore her—male chauvinist pigs—but Deacon deflected the ball back at her so smoothly, the others never knew what hit them. Sexy, dangerous, smart, *and* he knew how to deal with dunderheads without making a scene. She was so keeping him. And stabbing a knife into the heart of any debutante/trophy-wife-wannabe who came within sniffing distance.

"I expect," he whispered in her ear during a rare minute of privacy, "large amounts of sexual favors for being this good."

Her lips twitched. "Done."

And she was. Done over thoroughly.

By the time they reached the apartment, she was burning up for him. They didn't make it to the bed the first time. Her pretty, slinky dress ended up in shreds at her feet as Deacon took her against the door, his mouth fused with hers. She came with a hard rush that had her clutching at his white dress shirt with desperate hands.

The second time was slower, sweeter.

Afterward, they lay side by side, face to face. It was an indescribably intimate way to be, and she hardly dared speak for fear of breaking the moment. "There goes your secret identity. As of tomorrow, you're going to be in gossip columns from here to Timbuktu."

He nipped at her upper lip. "I bought the tux."

She blinked. "You bought the tux." Bubbles of happiness burst into life inside her, rich and golden. "More cost-effective than renting one if you plan to use it a lot."

"That's what the guy at the store said." Shifting closer, he stroked his hand over the sweep of her back, his skin a little rough and all perfect. "But . . ."

"No buts." She kissed him. "I'm too happy right now."

A smile against her lips. "This 'but' you have to deal with, Ms. Guild Director." Light words. Serious tone.

She met his gaze. "What is it?"

"I have to resign as the Slayer."

"Oh. Yes, of course." As of tonight, he was too well-known, and more importantly, by staying with her, he'd get to know too many hunters . . . make too many friends. "We'll find a replacem—"

"That's what I was doing. I have a candidate for you."

Nodding, Sara stroked her fingers over the square line of

his jaw. "I can't be your boss." It was a solemn realization. "I need to be your lover."

Deacon reached out to draw a circle around the spot where her necklace had rested before he'd taken it off. "I figured I'd go totally independent with the weapons."

"That works." The tightness in her chest eased. "Kind of seems one-sided though. You're giving up everything."

"I get you." A simple statement that meant more than she could ever articulate.

She swallowed the knot of emotion in her throat. "I talked to Tim a week ago."

Deacon frowned. "Tim?"

"Lucy's pregnant."

The frown turned into a slow, spreading smile. "Really?"

"Yes, really." She threw a leg over his and snuggled close. "He's going to keep one of the pups for me. I was going to call it Deacon."

He started laughing, and it was infectious. She buried her face in his neck and gave in.

The puppy was black as pitch, with big brown eyes and feet so big he promised to become a monster like his mom. Since it would've been a little confusing to have two Deacons in the house, they decided to call him Slayer.

Magic Mourns

Ilona Andrews

I sat in a small, drab office, one of many in the Atlanta chapter of the Order of Knights of Merciful Aid, and pretended to be Kate Daniels. Kate's phone didn't ring very often, so I didn't have to pretend very hard.

Unfortunately, when it did ring, like right now, the person on the other end was rarely interested in a facsimile. They wanted the real thing.

"Order of Knights of Merciful Aid, Andrea Nash speaking."

A female voice on the other end murmured hesitantly. "You're not Kate."

"No, I'm not. She's on medical leave. But I'm filling in for her."

"I'll just wait until she comes back."

I said good-bye to the disconnect signal, hung up, and petted my SIG-Sauer P226s lying on Kate's desk. At least my guns still liked me.

The real Kate Daniels, my best friend and partner in butt-kicking, was on medical leave. And I intended to do my best to let her stay on medical leave, at least until her wounds stopped bleeding.

The magic wave fell. The mysterious orange and yellow glyphs on the floor of Kate's office faded. On the wall, the charged air inside twisted glass tubes of a feylantern turned dark, while the ugly warts of electric lights in the hallway ceiling ignited with soft light. Inside my skin, the secret me stretched, yawned, and curled up for a nap, with her claws securely tucked away.

We lived in an uncertain world: magic flooded us in waves, screwed things up, and vanished. Nobody could predict when it came and went. One always had to be prepared. Sometimes though, no matter how prepared you were, the magic left something behind that you simply couldn't handle, and then you called the police, and if they couldn't help, you called the Order. The Order would send a knight, someone like me, who would help you with your magic problems. At least, that's how it was supposed to work.

Very few people could have expertise in both tech and magic. Kate chose magic. I chose tech. Give me a firearm and silver bullets over swords and sorcery any day.

The phone rang again. "Order of Knights of Merciful Aid, Andrea—"

"Can I speak to Kate?" An older male voice tinted with country accent.

"I'm filling in for her. What do you need?"

"Can you take a message for her? Tell 'er this is Teddy Jo callin' down from Joshua Junkyards. She knows me. Tell her I was drivin' on through Buzzard, and I saw one of them fellers she hangs out with, the shapeshifters, run like hell through the Scratches. Right below me. There was a big dog chasin' him."

"How big was the dog?"

Teddy Jo mulled it over. "I'd say as big as a house. A one-story. Maybe a bit bigger. Not as big as one of them colonials, you understand. A regular-person house."

"Would you say the shapeshifter was in distress?"

"Hell yeah, he was in distress. His tail was on fire."

"He ran like his tail was on fire?"

"No, his tail was on fire. Like a big, furry candle on his ass."

Bingo. Green five, shapeshifter in dire distress. "Got it."

"Well, you tell Kate I said hello and not to be a stranger and all that."

He hung up.

I grabbed my gun belt and sent a focused thought in the direction of Maxine, the Order's secretary. I had no telepathic abilities whatsoever, but she was strong enough to pick up a thought if I concentrated hard enough. *"Maxine, I have a green five in progress. I'm responding."*

"You have fun, dear. I hope you get to kill something," Maxine's voice said in my head. *"By the way, do you recall that nice young man whose calls you aren't taking?"*

Raphael. He wasn't exactly the type of man a woman would forget. *"What about him?"*

"He usually calls for you twice a day, at ten and at two. He hasn't phoned today. At all."

I killed a twinge of disappointment. *"Perhaps he got the message."*

"Could be. Just thought you would like to be aware."

"Thanks." Raphael was trouble. And I had enough trouble as it was.

I picked up my favorite pair of P226s and ducked into the armory, where I kept my assortment of guns. As big as a house, huh? I took my Weatherby Mark V rifle off the rack, petting the hand-laminated fiberglass-and-Kevlar stock. A classic. When you absolutely have to have a job done correctly, use the best tool for it. There was only one weapon with more stopping power in the armory. Referred to as Big Unit by male knights, and Boom Baby by me, it sat in a glass case all by itself. Boom Baby ate Silver Hawks: .50 armor-piercing, incendiary, explosive, silver-load cartridges. To get Boom Baby out of its case, I'd have to show a lot of probable cause. That was fine with me. The Weatherby would more than do the job.

I grabbed .416 Remington Magnum cartridges and headed out the door, before somebody decided to stop me.

In our age, a woman could have a gasoline car, which worked only during tech, or a vehicle that ran on charged water, which worked only during magic. My Jeep was Order issue and equipped with an electric engine and a magic one, so it functioned during both tech and magic. Unfortunately, it didn't function very well.

The engine started on the fourth try. I hopped in and steered out of the parking lot, joining a steady stream of riders and carts heading west. Mine was the only hoof-free transport on the street. The rest consisted of horses, mules, donkeys, and oxen.

The city lay in ruins. Heaps of dusty rubble and small mountains of broken glass marked the locations of once stately office buildings, ground to dust by magic's relentless jaws. Atlanta grew around them. New apartment buildings, built by hand rather than machine, sprouted atop the carcasses of the old ones. Stone and wood bridges spanned the gaping drops of crumbled overpasses. Small stalls and open markets replaced Wal-Mart and Kroger. The old Atlanta might have fallen like the trunk of a great tree struck by lightning, but its roots were too strong to die.

I liked the city. I wasn't born here, nor did I come to Atlanta by choice, but now the city was my territory. I had walked its streets, sampled its scents, and listened to it breathe. Atlanta wasn't sure about me. It tried to kill me every now and then, but I was confident we'd come to an understanding eventually.

Forty minutes later I turned off the main road on James Jackson Parkway and followed it around the bend to Buzzard's Highway. When magic was up, it flooded deep in this part of the city. Tall trees flanked the road, huge pines and dogwoods, still green despite the impending October. A twisted metal sign slid by: the white letters spelling out SOUTH COBB DRIVE, all but covered by BUZZARD scrawled in black paint. Pale wind chimes, made of turkey vulture skulls and string, hung from the tree limbs overshadowing the road. A cheerful welcome. Not quite sure what they were trying to tell me. My goodness, could it be some sort of a warning?

My Jeep slid onto an old bridge over the Chattahoochee River. The old maps claimed that heading north would bring me into Smyrna and turning southwest would deliver me to Mableton, but neither any longer existed.

I crossed the bridge and pulled over to the side of the road. A vast network of ravines lay before me. Narrow, twisted, some a hundred yards deep, although most were shallow, they tangled together and veered apart, like tunnels of a giant dirt-eating termite. Here and there remnants of the old buildings perched, halfway down the slopes, flanked by sickly brush. A highway cut through the ravines, running atop the cliff tops, interrupted with wooden patches of bridges. Above it all, black-winged vultures glided on the aerial currents.

The locals called it the Scratches, because from above the place looked like a giant buzzard had scratched in the dirt. The Scratches came into being after the very first flare, when the magic returned to the world in a three-day wave of disasters and death. With every magic wave, the ravines grew a little deeper.

Far to the south, the Scratches united into a gorge that eventually became Honeycomb Gap, another hellish magic spot. The highway itself served as the favorite drag-racing spot for idiot juvenile delinquents. Somewhere in this mess of soil and air was my green five, the shapeshifter in distress. Hopefully still alive and nursing a singed tail.

Atlanta housed one of the largest shapeshifter societies in the country. The Pack, as it was known, counted over fifteen hundred members, subdivided into seven clans according to their animal forms. An alpha couple ruled each clan. The fourteen alphas made Pack Council, presided over by Curran, the Beast Lord of Atlanta. Curran wielded unbelievable power and ultimate authority. He was the Alpha.

To understand the Pack, one had to understand the shapeshifters. Caught on the crossroads between animal and human, they could give in to either one. Those who surrendered to the animal side began the catastrophic descent into delirium. They reveled in perversion and cruelty and gorged themselves on human flesh, raping and murdering until people like me put them down like rabid dogs. They were called loups, and they were killed as soon as they were discovered.

To remain human, a shapeshifter had to live his life according to a very strict mental regimen detailed in the Code, a book of rules, which praised discipline, loyalty, obedience, and restraint. A shapeshifter knew no higher calling than to serve the Pack, and Curran and his Council took the idea of service a step further. All shapeshifters underwent martial arts training, both as individuals and in squads. All learned to channel their aggression, to handle being shot with silver bullets, to use weapons and firearms. Coupled with their numbers, their strict discipline, and their high degree of organization, having the Pack in the city was like living next to a thousand and a half highly skilled professional killers with enhanced senses, preternatural strength, and power of regeneration.

The Order found the Pack's presence very troubling. The shapeshifters didn't trust the Order, and rightfully so—the knights viewed each shapeshifter as a monster waiting to happen. So far Kate was the only agent of the Order who had managed to earn their trust, and they preferred to deal exclusively through her. Getting a shapeshifter out of a bind would go a long way toward improving my standing with both organizations. At least on paper.

I put the parking brake on and walked upwind from the Jeep. Hard to smell anything with the exhaust fumes searing the inside of my nose. Teddy Jo had probably exaggerated the dog's size—eyewitnesses usually did—but even if it was as large as a "regular-person house," finding it in the labyrinth of the ravines would prove tricky. The highway didn't just run straight. It veered and split into smaller roads, half of which led nowhere; the other half ended up rejoining Buzzard.

I crouched on the edge of the ravine and let the air currents tell me a story. A touch of sickeningly sweet rot of decomposing flesh and the odd, slightly oily stink of vultures eating it. Twin musk of two feral cats enjoying a bit of competitive spraying over each other's marks. A harsh bitterness of a distant skunk. The scent of burning matches.

I paused. Sulfur dioxide. Quite a bit of it, too. It was the only scent that didn't fit the usual odors of animal life. I returned to the Jeep and followed the matches north. There were times when my secret self came in handy.

The stench of burning sulfur grew stronger. A low growl rolled through the ravine below, dissolving into heavy wet panting, followed by a frustrated layered yelp, as if several dogs had whined in unison.

I guided the Jeep along the edge of the ravine and peered down. Nothing. No giant dogs, just a shallow twenty-five-foot gap with a bit of scarce shrubs and trash at the bottom. A broken rusted fridge. The remains of a couch. Multicolored dirt-stained rags. A house had apparently thrown up down the slope and now perched in a ruined heap on the edge, where the ravine veered left.

An excited snarl rumbled through the Scratches, the deep primeval sound of an enormous beast giving chase. The hairs on the back of my neck rose. I stood on the brakes, swiped the Weatherby from the seat, and jumped out, taking position on the edge.

A shaggy shape exploded from around the bend of the ravine. Saffron-colored with a sprinkling of dark spots on its sloped back, the animal flew over the refuse, the muscles of its powerful forequarters pumping hard. A bouda. Shit.

The werehyena saw me. A cackle of trilling terrified laughter exploded from its muzzle.

Please don't be Raphael. Please don't be Raphael. Please . . .

The bouda veered toward me, changing in midleap. Its body snapped, twisting like a broken doll. Bones thrust out of the flesh, muscles sliding up the new powerful limbs, a carved chest, and a humanoid torso. The beast's jaws exploded, growing disproportionately large, its face flattened into a grotesque semblance of human, its forepaws stretched into hands that could enclose my entire head. A bouda in a warrior form, a monster halfway between hyena and man. For a shapeshifter, to assume this form was a victory, to make it proportional was an achievement, and to speak in one was an art.

The werehyena's jaws gaped open, displaying three-inch fangs. A bloodcurdling scream ripped from him. "Drive away, Andrea! Drive!"

Raphael. Damn it.

"Don't panic." I sighted the bend through the scope. "I have it under control." A thing that sent a bouda in warrior form running, especially one as crazy and lethal as Raphael, had to be treated with respect. Fortunately, the Weatherby delivered respect in a Magnum cartridge. It would stop a rhino at full gallop. It sure as hell would handle an oversized dog.

The ground shook as if from blows of a giant hammer. The refuse on the ravine's floor jumped in place.

A colossal thing burst from around the bend, nearly level with the ravine's wall. Blood-red and massive, it slid on the trash and crashed into the curve. The impact shook the slope. The remnants of a house quaked and slid down in a shower of bricks, bouncing from the creature's three canine heads.

A twenty-foot-tall three-headed dog. Whoa. This was quite possibly the coolest thing I'd ever seen through the scope of a rifle.

The dog shook, flinging rubble from his fur. Thick, deep-chested, built like an Italian mastiff, it gripped the ground with four massive paws and charged after Raphael. Behind it a long whiplike tail lashed, the barb on its end shaped like a snake's head. The mouths of its three heads hung open, displaying gleaming fangs longer than my forearm. Three forked serpentine tongues hung out as it thundered to us, flinging foam from between the horrid teeth. The drops of drool, each big enough to fill a bucket, ignited in midair.

It was built too thickly. The bullet might not penetrate.

However, I didn't need to kill it. I just had to delay it long enough for the knucklehead to reach me. I sighted the muzzle of the center head. The nose shot would deliver maximum pain.

"Run, damn you!" Raphael howled, scrambling up the slope toward me.

"There's no need to scream." Excitement buoyed me, the ancient thrill of a hunter sighting his prey. The beast's dark nose danced in my scope.

Steady. Aim. Breathe. You have time.

A triple snarl ripped from three huge maws.

Gently, slowly, I squeezed the trigger.

The Weatherby spat thunder. The recoil punched me in the shoulder.

The dog's middle head jerked. The Weatherby's magazine held two rounds and one in the chamber. I sighted and fired again. The middle head drooped. The beast yowled and spun in pain. Perfect. The Weatherby wins again.

In a desperate leap, Raphael launched himself up the slope toward me. I caught his arm and hauled him up. We dashed to the Jeep. I hopped into the driver's seat, Raphael landed in the passenger's, and I floored the gas pedal.

A howl of pure frustration shook the highway. In the rearview mirror the dog sailed out of the ravine as if it had wings and landed on the road behind us.

"Faster!" Raphael snarled.

I drove, squeezing every last drop out of the Jeep's old engine. We hurtled down the highway at a breakneck speed. The dog gave chase with a triumphant howl that shook the ground beneath the car wheels. It closed the space between us in three great bounds and bent down over the car, its mouths opened wide. The foul, corrosive breath washed over me. Raphael jumped up and snarled back, his hackles up. Burning drool hit the backseat, singeing the upholstery in an acrid stench of melted synthetics.

I swerved, taking a sudden turn onto a wooden bridge and almost sending the Jeep off the edge into a gap. Monstrous teeth snapped a foot from the backseat.

The dog snarled. In the rearview mirror I saw its muscles bunch as it gathered itself for a leap. Before me, Buzzard's Highway ran straight and narrow, ravines on both sides. Nowhere to go. *That's it, we're done.*

Inside me, an animal raked at my flesh, trying to spill out of my skin. I clenched my teeth and stayed human.

The dog jumped. Its huge body flew toward us and then jerked back, as if an invisible leash had snapped, reaching its full length. The giant canine fell, its paws waving clumsily in the air. In the rearview mirror I saw it rise. Its bark rang through the Scratches. The dog barked again, whined, and jumped back into the ravine.

I slowed to a speed that would let me make a turn without sending us to a fiery death in the gap below. "You! Explain!"

In the seat next to me Raphael shuddered. Fur melted into smooth human skin, stretched taut over a heartbreakingly beautiful body. Coal-black hair spilled from his head to his shoulders. He looked at me with smoldering blue eyes, smiled, and passed out.

"Raphael?"

Out cold. With magic down, changing shape took a lot of effort and combined with the strain of that run, Lyc-V, the shapeshifter virus, had shut him down for a rest.

I growled under my breath. Of course, he could've stayed conscious had he not changed into a human. But he knew that if he shifted shape, he would pass out on the seat next to me, nude, and I would be forced to stare at him until he slept it off. He had done it on purpose. The werehyena Casanova strikes again. I was getting really tired of his ridiculous pursuit.

Ten minutes later I pulled into an abandoned Shell station and parked under the concrete roof shielding the pumps.

I hugged my rifle and listened. No snarls. No growling. We were in the clear.

My heart hammered. I tasted a bitter patina on my tongue and squeezed my eyes shut. A delayed reaction to stress, nothing more.

Inside, my secret self danced and screamed in frustration. I chained it. Control. In the end it was all about control. I had learned to impose my will over my body in childhood—it was that or death—and years of mental conditioning in the Order's Academy had reinforced my hold.

Breathe. Another breath.

Calm.

Gradually the bestial part of me settled down. *That's it. Relax. Good.*

All shapeshifters struggled with their inner beast. Unfortunately, I wasn't an ordinary shapeshifter. My problems were a lot more complicated. And the presence of Raphael only aggravated them.

Raphael sprawled next to me, snoring slightly. Until he awoke, speculating on why a giant three-headed dog with burning drool had chased after him would be pointless.

Look at him. Napping without a care in the world, confident I would be watching him. And I was. I had met handsome men in my life, some born with classically perfect features and the physique of Michelangelo's *David.* Raphael was not one of these men, and yet he left them all in the dust.

He had his good qualities: the bronze skin, the masculine jaw, the wide sensuous mouth. But his face was too narrow. His nose was too long. And yet when he looked at women with those dark blue eyes, they lost all common sense and threw themselves at him. His face was so interesting and so . . . carnal. There was no other word for it. Raphael was all tightly controlled, virile sensuality, heat simmering just beneath the surface of his dusky skin.

And his body took my breath away. He was built lean, with crisp definition, proportionate and perfect with wide chest, narrow hips, and long limbs. My gaze drifted down to between his legs. And hung like a horse.

He had been kind to me, more kind than I probably

deserved. The first time, when my body betrayed me, he and his mother, Aunt B, saved my life by guiding me back into my shape. The second time, when my back was pierced by silver spikes, he held me and talked me through pushing them out of my body. When I thought back to those moments, I sensed tenderness in him and I wanted very badly to believe it was genuine.

Unfortunately, he was also a bouda. They had a saying about werehyenas: fourteen to eighty, blind, crippled, crazy. Boudas would screw anything. I had witnessed it firsthand. Monogamy wasn't in their vocabulary.

Raphael had seen the true me and he'd never come across anyone similar. To him I was the TWT-IHFB. *That Weird Thing I Haven't Fucked Before.*

The more I thought about it, the madder I got. He could speak in a warrior form just fine. Had he stayed awake, I would've gotten the whole explanation from him by now. Not to mention that if something attacked us, I'd be left to defend a limp man who outweighed me by about eighty pounds. What exactly was I supposed to do with him? Did he expect me to sigh heavily while admiring his naked body? Or perhaps I was supposed to take advantage of the situation?

I reached into the glove compartment and got out a Sharpie. Taking advantage of the situation didn't sound bad at all.

An hour later Raphael stretched and opened his eyes. His lips stretched in an easy smile. "Hey. Now that's a beautiful sight to wake up to."

I leveled my SIG-Sauer at him. "Tell me why the nice puppy was chasing you."

He wrinkled his nose and touched his mouth. "Is there something on my lips?"

Yes, there is. "Raphael, concentrate! I know it's hard for you but do try to stay on target. Explain the dog."

He licked his lips and my thoughts went south. *Andrea, concentrate! Try to stay on target.*

Raphael remembered to look cool and leaned back, presenting me with the view of a spectacular chest. "It's complicated."

"Try me. First, what are you even doing here? Aren't you supposed to dragging around giant rocks right now?" About six weeks ago, the lot of us had entered the Midnight Games, an illegal, to-the-death fighting tournament. We did it to prevent a war against the Pack. Both the Order and Curran, the Beast Lord, took a rather dim view of this occurrence. As a result, Kate was on medical leave, and the Beast Lord, who had actually ended up participating in the tournament with us, had sentenced himself and the rest of the involved shapeshifters to several weeks of hard labor building an addition to the Pack's citadel.

"Curran released me due to family hardship," Raphael said.

Not good. "What happened?"

"My mother's mate died."

My heart jumped. Aunt B was . . . she was kind. She saved my life once and she kept my secret to herself. I owed her everything. And even if I hadn't, I felt nothing but respect for her. Among boudas, as in nature among hyenas, the females ruled. They were more aggressive, more cruel, and more alpha. Aunt B was all that, but she was also fair and smart and she didn't tolerate any nonsense. When you're the alpha of a bouda clan, you have a lot of nonsense thrown at you.

Had I grown up under Aunt B instead of the bitches who ruled my childhood, perhaps I wouldn't be so messed up.

"I'm so sorry."

"Thank you," Raphael said and looked away.

"How is she holding up?"

"Not that well. He was a very nice man. I liked him."

"What happened?"

"Heart attack. It was quick."

Shapeshifters almost never died of heart complications. "He was a human?"

Raphael nodded. "They've been together for almost ten years. She met him shortly after my father died. The service was set for Friday. Someone stole his body from the funeral home." A low growl laced his words. "My mother didn't get to say good-bye. She didn't get to bury him."

Oh God. I gritted my teeth. "Who took the body?"

Raphael's face turned grim. "I don't know. But I'm going to find out."

"I want in on it. I owe your mother." Aunt B had a right to bury her mate. Or bury the thing that took her mate's body. Either way worked for me.

He grimaced. "Did you smell matches?"

I nodded. "It's the dog."

"Yeah. I picked up this scent at the funeral home and trailed it here. There was something else under it, but the dog stink is so damn acrid, it drowns everything else." Raphael gave me a hard look.

I motioned with my fingers. "Give."

"I thought I smelled a vampire."

A giant three-headed dog was bad news. A vampire was much, much worse. The *Immortuus* pathogen, the bacterial disease responsible for vampirism, killed its victim. Vampires had no ego, no self-awareness, no ability to reason. They had the mental capacity of a cockroach. Ruled by insatiable bloodlust, they killed anything that bled. If left to their own devices, they'd wipe out life on Earth and then cannibalize themselves. But their empty minds made a perfect vehicle for the will of a navigator, a necromancer, who piloted a vampire like a marionette, seeing through its eyes and hearing through its ears. Necromancers came in several varieties, the most adept of which were called Masters of the Dead. A vampire piloted by a Master of the Dead could destroy a platoon of trained military personnel in seconds.

And 99 percent of the Masters of the Dead were members of the People. The People were bad, bad news. Set up as a corporation, they were organized, wealthy, and expert in all things necromantic. And very powerful.

"Do you think the People stole the body?"

"I don't know." Raphael shrugged. "I thought I'd throw it out there, before you jump in with both feet."

"I don't care. Do you care?"

"Fuck no." Raphael's eyes glinted, making him look a bit deranged.

"Then we're in agreement."

We nodded to each other.

"So you tracked the sulfur scent here, then what?" I asked.

"I ran into Fido. He chased me into a crevice. I sat there for about an hour or so, and then he wandered off and I ran the other way. Apparently, he didn't wander off far enough. What kind of creature is Fido, incidentally?"

"I have no idea."

All of my training had been in contemporary applications of magic. I could recite the vampiric biocycle off the top of my head, I could diagnose loupism in early stages, I could correctly identify the type of pyromagic used from burn pattern, but give me an odd creature and I drew a complete blank.

"Who would know?" Raphael asked.

We looked at each other and said in unison, "Kate."

Kate had a mind like a steel trap, and she pulled absurdly obscure mythological trivia out of her hair. If she didn't know something, she would know who would.

I pulled a cell phone out of the glove compartment. There was only one functioning cellular network. It belonged to the military and as a knight of the Order and an officer of peace, I had access.

I stared at the phone.

"Forgot the number?" Raphael asked.

"No. Thinking how to phrase this. If I say the wrong thing, she'll be dashing down to the ley line in minutes." Kate had never met a person she didn't want to protect, preferably by hacking at the hostile parties with her sword. But Kate was also human and needed the rest.

Raphael gave me a dazzling smile. My heart skipped a beat. "Could it be that you want some alone time with me?"

I dropped the safety off my gun.

He raised his hands palms out, still grinning like an idiot.

I put the safety back on and dialed the number.

"Kate Daniels." My best friend's voice filled my ear.

"Hey, it's me. How's your stomach?"

"Stopped hurting. What's up?"

"I need to ID a twenty-foot-tall three-headed dog with blood-red fur and burning spit." *That's right, routine, casual, business as usual, I encounter giant three-headed dogs every day . . .*

A small silence filled the phone.

"Is everything okay?" she asked.

"Everything is fine," I assured her, smiling brightly at the phone, as if she could see me. "Just need an ID."

"Does the tail look like a snake?"

I considered the long, whip-thin tail with a barb on the end. "Sort of."

"Are you in the office?"

"No, I'm in our Jeep, out in the field."

"Look under the passenger seat in a black plastic bin. There should be a book."

Raphael hopped out, dug under the seat, and pulled out a dog-eared copy of *The Almanac of Mystical Creatures*.

"Got it," I said into the phone.

"Page seventy-six."

Raphael flipped the book open and held it up. On the left page a lithograph showed a three-headed dog with a serpent for a tail. The caption under the picture said CERBERUS.

"Is that your dog?" Kate asked.

"Could be. How the heck did you know the exact page?"

"I have perfect memory!"

I snorted.

She sighed into the phone. "I spilled coffee on that page

and had to leave the book open to dry it out. It always opens to that entry now."

I examined the dog. "It definitely looks similar. Ours was bigger."

"Ours? Who is there with you?"

"Raphael."

Kate's voice snapped. "I'll be in Atlanta in three hours. Where are you?"

"I said it's nothing major."

"Bullshit. You wouldn't work with Raphael unless the Apocalypse was imminent and that was the only way to prevent it."

Raphael put his hands over his face and shook, making choking sounds that suspiciously resembled laughter.

"Hardy har har," I growled. "We're completely fine on our own, thank you very much. If you want to help, tell me more about Cerberus."

"He belongs to Hades, god of the Greek underworld, where souls spend their afterlife. His primary function is to guard the front entrance. Also Hades occasionally sends him on an errand, according to myths. He's supposed to hate sunlight."

"This one had no trouble with the sun. Can you think of any possible reason he would manifest?"

"Well, a defilement of Hades' shrine might do it. But Hades didn't exactly have shrines. The ancient Greeks were scared to death of him. They averted their faces when sacrificing to Hades. They refused to even say his name. So I'm not sure."

"Thanks."

"You sure you don't need me to come?"

"Positive."

"Call me if anything."

I hung up and looked at Raphael. "Your mother's mate, what was his name?"

"Alex Doulos."

"Was he a Greek pagan?"

A frown twisted Raphael's face. "I have no idea. It didn't

come up. We had a careful relationship. He didn't try to be my dad and I didn't try to be his son. We met at holiday dinners and talked about sports mostly. It was a safe topic. What are you thinking?"

I shook my head. "I'm trying very hard not to think anything. I'm just collecting data at this point. Did you see the way Fido fell?"

"Like he was on a leash and it ran out." Raphael drummed a quick rhythm on the dashboard.

"It probably means he's somehow bound to a specific area. I think we should go and look at it."

"I'm game." Raphael shivered. "I don't suppose you have any spare clothes?"

"You should've thought of clothes before you decided to go human."

The sinful smile was back. "I always dreamt of being naked with you. Couldn't pass up the chance."

I started the Jeep. "Could you get any more full of yourself?"

"I'm mostly interested in getting you full of me."

The vision of being full of Raphael zinged through my brain, short-circuiting rational thought. "Come to think of it, there is something on your lips. Why don't you use that side mirror over there to check it out?"

He glanced into the side mirror and stared, slack-jawed. His lips were solid black. A thick black line of guy liner outlined his deep-set eyes and a little black tear dripped down his left cheekbone. He touched his cheek, stretching the skin to better examine the tear, his face a flat mask, glanced at me, and exploded with laughter.

I stood atop the Jeep's hood and slowly swept the vast network of ravines with binoculars. The Jeep itself sat on the edge of a shallow gap, just beyond the spot where Cerberus almost took a bite out of our backseat. Raphael, still gloriously naked, sat in the passenger seat and plucked random Hades-related trivia from the book.

"A fun guy, this Hades. Apparently he bridenapped his wife."

"Things were much simpler in ancient Greece if you were a god. I'm sure he got himself a harem of mistresses, too." The wind swirled with Raphael's scents: the light musk of his sweat, the delicious redolence of his skin . . . I was having trouble concentrating.

"No," Raphael said, flipping a page. "Actually, Hades didn't screw around. His wife was the daughter of Demeter, goddess of youth, fertility, and harvest. After Hades stole Persephone, Demeter refused to let the plants grow, starving everyone, and they had to reach a compromise: Persephone spends half of the year with him and half with her mother. The guy only had her for six months out of the year, and he still remained faithful. That must be some sweet sex right there."

I took the binoculars down so I could roll my eyes. "Do you ever think of anything but sex?"

"Yes, I do. Sometimes I think of waking up next to you. Or making you laugh."

I was beginning to regret this.

"Of course, I do occasionally get hungry . . ." he added. "And cold."

A white speck caught my eye. I adjusted the binoculars. A house. A two-story colonial, seemingly intact, sitting in the bottom of a ravine. I could only see the roof and a small slice of the upper story.

Interesting.

"Kate was right: the Greeks lived in fear of this guy. Instead of speaking his name, they called him the Rich One, the Notorious One, the Ruler of Many, and so on. Despite his sour disposition, he was considered to be a just god. The one sure way to piss Hades off was to steal one of the shades—souls—from his realm or to somehow avoid death. This dude Sisyphus apparently finagled a way out of death a couple of times, and Hades had it and made him drag an enormous boulder up a mountain. Every time Sisyphus almost gets to the top, the boulder rolls down and he has to do it all over.

Thus the term 'Sisyphean task.' Huh. I never knew that's where it came from."

He showed me a page. On it a man and a woman sat side by side on simple thrones. To one side of the pair stood Cerberus. To the other an angel with black wings and a flaming sword.

"Who is that?"

"Thanatos. Angel of death."

"Didn't know the Greeks had angels." I turned back to watching the house. And just in time, too. Cerberus trotted out of the ravine to the left of the house. I could barely see his back. He passed by the building and began to circle it.

"I see a house," I said.

Raphael landed next to me with inhuman agility. I passed the binoculars to him and he straightened, almost a foot taller than me. Standing next to him was a trial: his scents sang through me, the warmth of his body seeped through my clothes, and his skin practically glowed. Everything about him said "mate" to me. It wasn't rational. It was the animal me, and I had to be better than that.

"I'll be damned," he said softly. "Here is Fido. Going round and round. I wonder what's in that house?"

"I wonder why he doesn't just go in and get whatever it is."

"I think we should find out. Andrea?"

"Yes?" I wished he would stop saying my name.

"Why are your eyes closed?"

Because you're standing next to me. "It helps me think."

I felt the heat wash over me and knew he had leaned to me. His voice was a soft masculine rasp, entirely too intimate. "I thought you were trying not to think."

I opened my eyes and found the deep smoldering blue of his irises right next to me. I lifted my index finger and pushed his chest. He slid on the Jeep's hood, distorted by the charged-water engine underneath, and had to jump off, landing with the grace of a gymnast on the ground.

"Personal space," I told him. "I protect mine."

He simply smiled.

"How do we get to the house with the dog making shark circles around it?" I asked.

"Fido doesn't see that well," Raphael said. "It took him a while to find the crevice where I was hiding before, and he had to sniff me out. We fool his nose by masking our scent, we can probably get close enough."

"And how do you propose to do that?"

"The old-fashioned way."

I sighed. "Which would be?"

Raphael shook his head. "You really don't know?"

"No, I don't."

He trotted off to the side and dived into a ravine. I waited for a couple of minutes, and he emerged, carrying two dark objects, and tossed one of them to me. Reflexively I caught it even as the reek lashed my nostrils. A dead, half-decomposed cat.

"Are you out of your mind?"

"Some people roll in it." He grabbed the dog carcass and ripped it in a half. Maggots spilled. He shook them out. "I prefer to tear them and tie pieces on myself. But if you would prefer to rub it all over your skin, you can do that, too."

All my fantasies of touching him evaporated into thin air with a small pop.

"Hunting one-oh-one," he said. "Didn't your pack ever do the hunts in Texas?"

"No. I wasn't in that kind of pack." And I had fought my way out of shapeshifter society before it was too late.

My face must've showed my memories, because he paused. "That bad?"

"I don't want to talk about it."

Raphael reached to the backseat and pulled a roll of cord we kept there. He uncoiled a foot-long piece and tore the tough hemp rope like it was a hair. "You don't have to do it," he said. "I keep forgetting you're not—"

Not what? Not normal? Not like him?

"—properly trained. I'll be back shortly."

He wasn't better than me. Whatever he could handle, I could deal with as well.

I picked up the roll of twine. If I had been straight bouda, like my mother, I would've enjoyed all of the enhancements Lyc-V brought, but even though I wasn't as strong as a regular shapeshifter, I could handle the damn rope. I tore a piece, sighed, and pulled the cat apart.

"It's a good thing I'm part hyena," I murmured, moving along the bottom of the ravine. Bits of the cat corpse dangled from me, strategically positioned on my limbs and suspended from a cord off my neck. To a human nose, all decomposition odors were similar, but in reality each corpse gave off its own specific scent just as it did in life. And this particular carcass reeked of something nauseatingly sour. "If I were a cat, I'd probably die of the stink and the sheer indignity."

"You know who can't handle it?" Raphael scrambled up the slope like a gecko. "Doolittle."

"The Pack's doctor?" Even carrying my Weatherby, I made it out of the ravine faster than he did. What I couldn't match in strength, I made up in agility and speed.

"Yeah. Badgers are very clean. In the wild, foxes sometimes steal badger burrows by sneaking into them and crapping all over the place. The badger is so prissy, he'd rather dig a new burrow than clean his old one up. Doolittle will do open-heart surgery if he has to, but hand him a chunk of a putrid cadaver and he'll run for the hills."

An echo of a growl washed over us. He clamped his mouth shut. We'd reached the dog's hearing range.

A few minutes later we went aground on the edge. Several ravines converged here, forming a gap almost wide enough to enclose a football field. The house sat in the center of the gap. Two stories high, with a row of white columns supporting a triangular roof, it looked at us with twin rows of windows blocked by dark shutters. Its black front door stood closed and so did the doors of the cellar on the left side. A ten-foot-tall fence topped with coils of barbed wire guarded the house.

As we watched, Cerberus trotted out of the ravine. He whined softly, spit dripping in burning clumps of foam from between his fangs, and inched toward the fence. The left head stretched on his shaggy neck and sniffed at the mesh. A blue spark jumped from the metal to his nose. Cerberus yelped, clawed the ground in frustration, and trotted off.

Electrified fencing. Peculiar. No wires stretched to the house, so the power must have come from inside. I strained and heard the faint hum of a generator.

The doors to the cellar rose slowly. Something squirmed beneath them, something pale. The right half of the cellar door fell open and a creature leapt into the open. Its gaunt, vaguely humanoid body had lost every iota of its hair and fat long ego. Thick, bloodless skin sheathed the dry cords of its muscles, every rib distinct beneath its leathery hide. Its stomach was hard and ridged. Huge yellow claws tipped the fingers of its hands and its long toes.

A vampire. And where there was a vampire, there had to be a navigator. I raised the binoculars to my eyes.

The vampire's face was horrible, a death mask sculpted with human features devoid of emotion, intellect, and self-awareness. The creature paused, perched on the edge of the cellar entrance. It unhinged its maw, displaying twin sickles of yellow fangs, leapt straight up, and clutched on to the wall of the house like a fly. The vamp scuttled up the wall, ran along the dark roof to the white stub of the chimney, and hopped in like some nightmarish Santa.

We could possibly deal with the electric fence. But a vampire would prove problematic. We had no way of knowing how many of them were in that house. Two would present a challenge. Three would be suicide. Especially if magic hit.

"Andrea?" Raphael's voice was a soft cloud of warmth in my ear.

I glanced at him. *What?*

"Did you like the thing I left for you?"

The thing? Oh. The *thing*. Shapeshifters had an odd way of courtship. Mostly it involved proving to your prospective mate what a stealthy and sleek operator you were by prancing in and out of her territory. Because all of the land belonged to the Pack overall, "territory" came to be defined as the potential mate's house. Most shapeshifters broke in and left presents, but boudas had an odd sense of humor. They broke into the houses of their intended and played practical jokes.

Raphael's father glued Aunt B's furniture to the ceiling. Raphael's uncle lock picked his way into Raphael's aunt's house, flipped all the doors around, and hung them back on their hinges so the handles were inside. In fine bouda tradition, Raphael somehow snuck away during the Midnight Games, broke into my apartment, and left me the *thing*.

"You want to know that now?" I hissed in a fierce whisper.

"Just tell me yes or no?"

"Do you really think this is the best time?"

His eyes flashed with red. "There might not be any other time left."

I turned and saw Cerberus crouching in the ravine behind us. He stood there absolutely still, the three pairs of his eyes fixed on us with baleful fury.

I turned very slowly to Raphael.

"Did you like the thing?" he asked with quiet desperation.

"Yes. It was funny."

He grinned, his face made unbearably handsome by the flash of his smile.

With a deafening growl, Cerberus charged us. Fur sheathed the monstrous bloom of Raphael's jaws. I flipped on my back.

Cerberus's center head dove at me, his black maw gaping, ready to swallow me whole.

I fired.

The first shot punched the back of the dog's mouth. It yelped and I sank two more in the same spot. Flesh exploded and I saw sky through the hole where the back of the beast's throat used to be. The head drooped down. I rolled clear just as an enormous paw clawed the spot where I had dropped. The smallest claw grazed my side and leg, ripping the clothes in a hot flash of pain.

I leapt to my feet. The left head dove for me and missed as Raphael launched himself into the air, slicing Cerberus's nose with his claws. Cerberus jerked back and Raphael clutched on to his muzzle. The dog shook, but Raphael clung to it, flinging bloody chunks of dog flesh to the ground.

I backed up, reloading. Raphael carved huge clumps out of Cerberus's muzzle in a frenzied whirl of fur and claws. Blood spurted in dark streams.

The right head snapped at him, great fangs clamping together like a bear trap. Raphael hooked his claws into the dog's nose, dropped out of the way, swung his legs like a gymnast on a pommel horse, and smashed his clawed feet into Cerberus's right head.

I snapped the Weatherby up, anticipating Cerberus's recoil.

The huge head swung back, as if in slow motion, the ruby eye clear and bright.

Steady. Aim.

An ancient tie stretched between Cerberus and me, vibrating like a live wire. The bond between the hunter and her prey.

The head reared higher and higher.

I have time.

I fired.

Blood burst from the back of Cerberus's head. The head jerked straight up, its nose pointing to the sky. Fire leaked from its ruined orbit. The flames surged, engulfing the head. As it crashed down, bouncing once on the hard dirt, Raphael leapt to the ground. Behind him the last head shuddered and fell, catching the flames. Raphael straightened, a dark demonic figure silhouetted against the orange fire, his eyes two points of red light.

If I weren't a trained professional, I'd have fainted from the sheer overload of his badassness.

I pointed my rifle straight up, resting the butt against my hip, and put on my Order face. *Move along, nothing to see here, I do this every day.* I thought of blowing imaginary smoke from the rifle barrel, but the Weatherby was long and I'm barely five feet four, so I'd look pretty stupid.

Raphael strode to me. His voice was a ragged growl torn to tatters by his fangs. "Are you alright?"

I nodded. "A bit scratched up. Nothing major."

We walked away, slowly, trying to maintain our coolness. A greasy stench of charred flesh tainted the air currents.

"That was a hell of a shot," Raphael said.

"Thank you. That was a stunning display of hand-to-hand."

We killed a damn Cerberus. Kate would turn green with envy.

Then the magic wave drowned us, and we paused in unison as it penetrated our bodies, awakening the inner beasts.

A bright blue glow surged from the ground. It flashed and vanished—the ward, a strong magic barrier, going active. Approaching the house during magic would be problematic. We'd have to somehow break through the ward.

A ghostly white light ignited in the wall right in front of us. It struggled free of the house and approached us, moving in sharp jerks. Its fuzzy radiance halted just before reaching the boundary of the ward and solidified into a translucent older man with kind eyes and pale hair.

I jumped back and snapped my gun up on reflex. Not that it would do anything with magic up.

A grimace strained the ghost's face, as if he were pulling a great weight. "Raphael," he gasped. "Not safe . . ."

A spark of magic snapped from the house. It clutched the ghost and jerked him back into the wall. Raphael lunged at the ward. The defensive spell flashed with blue, twisting a snarl of pain from his lips. I grabbed him and pulled him back.

"Is that Doulos? Your mother's mate?"

He nodded, fury boiling in his eyes. "We must get him out!"

An odd sucking sound rolled behind us. I looked over my shoulder. Inside the ball of flames, Cerberus's skeleton rose upright. The fire flared once more and vanished, snuffed out like a candle. Flesh spiraled up the colossal bones. *Oh shit.*

"Run!" Raphael snarled. We dashed down the ravine.

We were halfway to the wall when the first growl announced the hellhound giving chase.

"And you're sure Doulos was dead?" I drove like a maniac through Atlanta's troubled streets. Next to me Raphael licked a burn on his arm.

"He was embalmed. Yeah, pretty sure."

"Then what was *that*?"

"I don't know. A shade? A soul on its way to Hades?"

"Is that even possible?"

"We've been almost eaten by a giant three-headed dog. There is not a hell of a lot that I consider not possible at this point. Watch out for that cart!"

I threw the wheel to the right and barely avoided a collision with a teamster, who flipped me off. "We need a bigger gun."

"We need a shower," Raphael said.

"Gun first. Shower later."

Ten minutes later I walked into the Order's office. A group of knights standing in the hallway turned at my approach: Mauro, the huge Samoan knight; Tobias, as usual dapper; and Gene, the seasoned former Georgia Bureau of Investigations detective. They looked at me. The conversation died.

My clothes were torn and bloody. Soot stained my skin. My hair stuck out in clumps caked with dirt and blood. The reek of a dead cat emanated from me in a foul cloud.

I walked past them into the armory, opened the glass

case, took Boom Baby out, grabbed a box of Silver Hawk cartridges, and walked out.

Nobody said a thing.

Raphael waited for me in the Jeep, a spotted monster smeared with blood and dirt. A fly apparently had fallen in love with a spot on his round ear, and he kept twitching it. I put Boom Baby in the backseat and hopped into the driver's seat. Raphael yawned, displaying a pink mouth bordered with thick conical fangs. "Big gun."

"Where do you want me to drop you off?"

The hyena man licked his lips. "Your apartment."

"Ha. Ha. Seriously, where?"

"Your face was exposed when we fought the dog and later when we spoke to Alex's shade. The bloodsucker saw you, which means the navigator would've seen you through its eyes. It's likely the navigator knows who you are. It's equally likely he's doing something he isn't supposed to in that ravine. Last I checked, stealing corpses was illegal."

Stealing corpses was very much illegal. With magic making new and interesting things possible, the lawmakers took theft of cadavers extremely seriously. In Texas, you got more time in a forced-labor camp for stealing a corpse than you got for armed robbery.

Considering the remote location and the electric fence, it was highly likely someone was up to no good. If it had been a legitimate operation of the People, we would've been approached by a human or vampiric sentry. Because of our law enforcement status, all navigators knew the knights of the Order by sight and recognized that we were an annoyingly persistent lot. The People would've made contact to convince me they weren't involved in anything illegal and get me to go away.

Since they didn't, either whatever was taking place in that house was too dirty for the People to admit their ownership of it, or it didn't involve the People at all. The second possibility meant greater danger. For all of their nauseating qualities, the People were tightly regulated and mostly law-abiding. For now, anyway. They wouldn't dare to attack a knight of the Order, knowing that the consequences would be public and painful. But a rogue navigator armed with a vampire had no such compunction.

Raphael's thoughts ran along the same lines. "The navigator will want to silence you before you create a paper trail he can't destroy. You might end up hosting a bloodsucking party tonight. So we go to your apartment, take what you need, and then go to my place. He didn't see me except in bouda form."

"Absolutely not."

Raphael twitched his nose. "Are you so scared to stay with me that you'd actually prefer to be ripped apart by a couple of vampires?"

"I'm not scared of you."

His lips stretched back in a nightmarish smile, exhibiting a wall of teeth capable of snapping a cow's femur in half like a toothpick. "I promise to keep my hands, tongue, and other body parts to myself. You risk your life by staying home. It's late and we're both too wiped out to go climbing into the People's lair tonight. What do you risk by coming with me?"

"A huge migraine from being in your company." Try as I might, I couldn't find any fault with his reasoning. It was logically sound. And I wanted to see his place. I practically itched with curiosity.

"I'll share my aspirin," he promised.

"And that's all you will share. I mean it, Raphael. Touch any part of me with any part of you without permission and I'll put bullets into you."

"I understand."

It took me almost ten minutes of chanting to start the Jeep. Equipped with an enchanted water engine in addition to its gasoline one, the Jeep managed to attain the speed of nearly forty miles per hour during the magic wave, which in itself was an enormous achievement of magic manipulation. Unfortunately, it suffered from the illness affecting every magic-capable vehicle: it made noise. Not the typical mechanical noise of an engine either. No, it snarled, coughed, roared, and belched thunder in its effort to attain sonic supremacy, so all conversation had to be carried out at a screaming level. I kept quiet and Raphael napped. When a tired shapeshifter wants his rest, you could fire cannons next to him. He won't care.

A few minutes later we pulled up before my apartment. Raphael followed me up the stairs, dimly lit by the pale blue glow of feylanterns, and sauntered into my living room. I opened the side door leading to one of the two bedrooms, which I used for storage, and heard Raphael suck in the air through his nostrils.

I glanced up and saw the *thing*. He had left it in the living room, but I kept bumping into it and eventually moved it here, to a corner by the barred window. A six-foot-tall metal chandelier-like contraption made of thin brass wire, the *thing* stretched from the ceiling to the floor, rotating slowly. Branches of wire stuck out from it and on the branches little glass ornaments shimmered, suspended on golden chains. The ornaments contained thongs.

"You kept it," he said softly.

I shrugged. I actually hadn't taken into account the effect it might have on him. A miscalculation on my part. "It beats digging for my underwear in the drawer."

His eyes widened. "Are you wearing one now?"

"Mind out of my pants!" I ordered. "One more infraction, and I'm staying home."

He said nothing. I grabbed a blue duffel bag and went about the bedroom collecting equipment. My travel kit: spare toothbrush, toothpaste, hairbrush, deodorant. Crossbow bolts in neat bundles, their broadheads safely wrapped in soft wool in a box. Sharpshooter IV, a nice light crossbow. I pulled open the dresser and plucked a few boxes of ammo from it. Silver point.

"You're the only woman I know who keeps bullets in her dresser," he said.

"I use this room for storage."

"There are bullets in the other dresser, too," he said.

I suppose it was inevitable. He was a man, a bouda, and he had access to my apartment. It would be impossible for him not to have examined the contents of my dresser. At least he didn't write on it in a big red marker, RAPHAEL WAS HERE.

"I like to be prepared. I don't want to wake up in the middle of the night, empty my clip into some crazed shape-shifter sneaking about my apartment, and then have to run around looking for more ammo when he doesn't stay down."

Raphael winced.

If he knew I had lied about the thing, he wouldn't be wincing. He'd be grinning ear to ear. I wasn't sure myself why I had kept it, except that it must've taken him hours to assemble it all, and it would've required nearly godlike ninja skills to slip away from the strict security of the Midnight Games to set it up. He went through all that trouble for me. I couldn't throw it away.

Having filled my duffel with weapons of destruction, I headed to my bedroom and shut the door in his face when he tried to follow. He didn't need to see me pack my spare underwear.

I packed a change of clothes and paused. I was incredibly filthy. Incredibly disgustingly filthy. I had to take a shower either here, where I had my shampoo and my soap, or in Raphael's apartment. I grabbed a change of clothes and a firearm and stepped out of the room. "I'm going to shower. Stay out of my bathroom."

"Okay."

I got into the bathroom, slid the tiny deadbolt closed, and heard him lean on the wall next to it. "I've seen you naked, you know," he said. "Twice."

"Near-death experiences don't count," I said, stripping off my clothes and trying not to think of Raphael holding me firmly and whispering soft encouragements in my ear, while Doolittle had cut silver out of my body. Some memories were too dangerous to carry around.

When I emerged, clean, dressed, and smelling mostly of coconut with only mere traces of dead cat, I found Raphael examining the photographs on my shelf. Short little me and my mother, a petite blonde, standing side by side.

"You're about eight?" he guessed.

"Eleven. I was always small for my age. Weaker than everyone else." I touched the photograph gently. "In the wild, hyena cubs are born with functioning eyes and teeth. They start fighting the moment they're born, and the stronger female tries to kill her sisters. Sometimes the weaker girls get too scared to nurse and die of starvation. The adults try to stop it, but hyena cubs will dig tunnels, too small for adults to enter, so they'll fight to death there."

"Boudas don't dig tunnels," Raphael said softly.

"You're right. They don't have to hide their violence from adults either." *They just try to beat you to death in the open. They do it right in front of your mother because they know she can't protect you.*

I reached into the frame and pulled out a small photograph resting behind it. The man on it hunched over oddly, nude, yet still dappled with faint outlines of hyena spots. His arms were too thickly muscled, his face too heavy on the jaws, its skin darkening at the nose. His round eyes were solid black.

Lyc-V, the virus that created shapeshifters, infected humans and animals alike. Very rarely it produced an animal-were, a creature who started his life as an animal and gained the ability to turn human. Most didn't survive the transformation. Of the rare few who did, the majority suffered from severe retardation. Mute and stupid, they were universally reviled. The human shapeshifters killed them on sight. But once in a while, an animal-were turned out to be intelligent, learned to speak, and could express his thoughts. And even more rarely, he could breed.

I was the product of a mating between a female bouda and a hyenawere. My father was an animal. The shapeshifters called people like me "beastkin." And they killed us. No trial, no questions, nothing but immediate death. That's why I hid my secret self deep inside and never let her out.

Raphael's clawed, furry hand rested on my shoulder gently.

I wanted him to hold me. It was a completely ridiculous feeling. I was an adult, more capable than most of protecting myself, yet as he stood there next to me, I had the heartbreaking longing to be held almost like a child, to draw strength from him. Instead I shrugged off his hand, slid the photograph back into the frame, and headed for the door.

"Home, sweet home," Raphael growled, pointing to a beautiful two-story brick townhome.

"Yours?"

He nodded. It was a lot of house and it looked quite dignified from the outside. Considering his Casanova tendencies, the inside was likely to feature heart-shaped vibrating beds and disco balls.

"What is it you do, Raphael?"

"This and that," he murmured.

I had run a background scan on him when he first came on to me, but aside from his first name and his status as the only child of Aunt B, the alpha of Clan Hyena, nothing came up. He belonged to the upper level of the Pack's command and his records were sealed. To dig deeper, I needed a warrant.

However, I had also made some inquiries with a couple of female boudas. His name was Raphael Medrano. The Pack owned a number of businesses, and Raphael ran one of them: Medrano Extractors. When magic brought down a structure, it ground concrete to useless powder, but it left the metal behind. The extractors went in and salvaged what could be saved and then sold it to the highest bidder or bought it themselves. The job carried a high level of danger, but with half of the world in ruins, Raphael wouldn't be out of a job anytime soon.

He took my duffel, unlocked the door, and held it open for me while I carried Boom Baby inside. The door opened into a spacious living room with a vaulted ceiling. The floor was wood, the rug plain and beige, matching an oversized soft sofa diligently guarded by a blocky dark wood coffee table. A flat screen hung on the wall, angled toward the couch. Massive cubes of wooden shelves lined the opposite wall, housing books and DVDs.

The walls were custom painted in a light-brown-and-gray pattern resembling stone. No pictures decorated them; instead, Raphael displayed weapons: swords and knives in every shape and size imaginable. The place was clean, neat, and uncluttered, free of knickknacks and throw pillows. A very masculine house. Like stepping into the lair of some medieval lord with a penchant for frequent dusting.

Raphael locked the door. "Make yourself comfortable. My fridge is your fridge. I'm off to shower."

I placed Boom Baby under the window for easy access in case of emergency and sat on the couch. Above me the soothing noise of the shower announced Raphael scrubbing himself clean. He'd napped on the way to the Order, so he would likely manage the transformation without passing out. The thought of naked human Raphael in the shower was terribly distracting.

Suddenly I was so tired.

I crawled off the couch and forced myself into the kitchen. Eating Raphael's food was out of the question. Shapeshifters attached a special significance to food. A shapeshifter approaching his or her mate would try to feed them. That's how Kate got burned once: the Beast Lord of Atlanta, the Pack's head alpha and the final authority, fed her some chicken soup. She ate it, having no clue what it meant, which, according to her, the Beast Lord found incredibly amusing. Curran had a peculiar sense of humor. Cats. Weird creatures.

I tried the phone. No dial tone. The magic was still up.

I went back to the sofa and closed my eyes just for a moment.

The enticing aroma of meat tickled my nostrils. My eyes snapped open. Raphael, clean and mind-numbingly gorgeous, stood in the kitchen, trimming a piece of steak.

My mouth watered, and I wasn't sure if it was the man or the steak that caused the reaction. Probably both. I was so hungry. And I so deeply wanted Raphael. I should've never come here.

Raphael glanced at me, his eyes like blue fire. My heart actually skipped a beat. "I'm cooking you dinner," he said. "Shocking."

"You know I can't take that from you," I said.

"Why not?"

I shook my head.

He casually flipped the knife in his fingers. His knife skills were uncanny. A flash of irritation flared in his eyes. He hesitated. "Look, I know you're starving. If you won't let me cook for you, will you at least cook for yourself?"

That was the first time I had ever seen him irritated. I pushed off the couch. "Sure."

He opened the fridge. A complicated web glistened in the back of it, gathering into a knot in the corner. An ice spider. It cost an arm and a leg. I, like most other normal people, had to buy friz-ice from the Water and Sewer Department to keep my fridge from getting warm when the tech failed and magic robbed it of electricity.

Raphael pulled another steak and slapped it on the cutting board next to his. "Here."

"Thank you."

"You're welcome."

We stared at each other for a second, and then I took the saltshaker and began to season my steak.

We glided in the small space of the kitchen, boxed in by the island and counters like two dancers, never touching each other, until we ended up next to each other searing our steaks on twin burners.

"I would just like to know if I have a chance," Raphael ground out. "I've been patient."

"And I owe you something because of that?"

He glared at me. "I just want an answer. Look, it's been half a year now. I call you every day—you don't take my calls. I try to meet you and you blow me off. But you look at me like you want me. Just tell me yes or no."

"No."

"Is that your answer or are you refusing to tell me?"

"My answer is no. I won't sleep with you. I've never led you on, Raphael. I told you from the beginning this wasn't going to happen."

Raphael's eyes went dark. "Fair enough. Why?"

"Why?"

"Yes, why? I know you want me. I see it in your face, I smell it in your body, I hear it in your voice. That's why I kept coming back after you like a fucking idiot. At least you can tell me why."

I unclenched my teeth. This talk was almost six months in coming. "Your mother is a good person, Raphael. Her clan is a good clan. But it's not like that everywhere. My mother was the weakest of six females in a small bouda clan. The others beat her every day. There were only two males and my mother didn't get to mate. Hell, if one of them looked at her, the others attacked her. In other places boudas don't stick that strictly to the Code. There's no Beast Lord to hold them to it and no punishment. They get to govern themselves, and the pack's only as good as the alpha. You know what my first memory is? I'm sitting in the dirt and our fucking alpha, Clarissa, is beating my mother in the face with a brick!"

He recoiled.

"My mother didn't want to mate with my father. They forced her to do it, because they got off on the perversity of it. He didn't know any better. He didn't understand the concept of rape. All he knew was that there was a female and she was made available to him. For three years my mother was raped by a man who had started his life as a hyena. He had the mental capacity of a five-year-old. And when I was born, they started beating me as soon as I could walk. I was beastkin. No rules applied to me. Under your precious

Code, I was an abomination. Every bone in my body was broken before I turned ten. As soon as I healed, they started on me again. And my mother couldn't stop it. She could do nothing. They would've killed me, Raphael. I was weaker and smaller than them and they would've kept beating me and beating me until there was nothing left, if my mother hadn't gotten together what little shreds of courage she had left. I live now because she grabbed me and ran across the country."

His face turned bloodless, but now it was too late to stop.

"When Kate drove me to the flare to your mother, I kept trying to get out of the cart, because I was sure Aunt B would kill me. That's what 'bouda' means to me, Raphael. It means hate and cruelty and disgust."

I shoved my pan off the fire to save the half-burned steak.

"So you refuse to be with me because of what I am," he said. "You can't be that shortsighted. What happened to you was awful. But I'm not them. I would never hurt you. My family, my clan, we would never hurt you. We protect our own."

"What you are is only a part of it. If you were a different man, maybe I could get over it. But you're a typical bouda male. I want love, Raphael. I might not deserve it, after some of the stuff I've done, but I want it. I want security and kindness and a home. I want monogamy and consideration for my feelings. What do you have to offer me? You've slept with every bouda woman who isn't related to you. Everybody had you, Raphael. They offered to give me pointers on what you like in bed. Hell, you didn't stop with boudas. You played with wolves, and with rats, with jackals . . . To you, I'm just another weird thing to hump. For God's sake, you got stuck inside a jackal girl while you were both in beast form and they had to call Doolittle out to separate you two. What were you thinking? You outweighed her by a hundred and fifty pounds and you aren't even of the same species!"

"I was fourteen," he snarled. "I didn't know any better. She wiggled her ass in front of me . . ."

"You're like a greedy kid in an ice cream store. You want everything and so you make this giant rainbow mess of a cone and gorge yourself on sweets until you can't even think anymore. You have no restraint and no discipline. Why would I want to get involved with you? So the next time someone wiggles her ass before you, you'll take off like a rocket? Please."

I grabbed a fork, stuck it into my steak, and marched out of the kitchen, carrying off my charred piece of meat. I got outside, climbed in my Jeep, and realized I had left my guns and my keys inside. There was nothing left to do but chew on my steak. I really wanted to cry.

I was so screwed up. I tried so hard to be a human, and he unhinged me. I just fell apart like a doll. The beatings, the humiliation, the fear—I had left those things in the past. I had interacted with other boudas and never once had been bothered by them. But with him all of it came flooding back in a choking painful wave.

Only Kate, the boudas, and the Beast Lord knew what I was. If the Pack found out that I was beastkin, the Beast Lord would protect me from physical harm. Curran had considered the issue of beastkin and come to the conclusion that he wouldn't tolerate genocide against us. But at least some of the shapeshifters would still despise me. If the Order found out what I was, they would expel me. The Order took a dim view of monsters in their ranks unless they were fully human.

Years of hiding, first in adolescence, then during the grueling training at the Order's Academy, stressed to my limit, tortured physically and mentally, hammered into shape, into a new me, then service in the name of the Order. I had rigidly maintained my humanity and composure through it all, and what undid me? Raphael, with his blue eyes and warm hands and voice that made me want to press against him and purr . . .

How could I have fallen for a damn bouda?

I slumped forward and rested my head on the steering wheel. Why did I tell him all that? What possessed me? I should've just laughed off his dinner invitation. But it had been eating at me for months now and I just couldn't help myself. There was this bitter emptiness inside me and it made me want to scream, *It's not fair!* and I didn't even know why.

It wasn't fair. It wasn't fair that I wanted to wake up next to Raphael. It wasn't fair that he was a bouda. It wasn't fair that for eleven years boudas tortured me and my mother.

Half an hour later Raphael emerged onto the porch and held open the door. Remaining in the Jeep was childish. Even storming out in the first place was childish. I took my fork, hopped out of the Jeep, and went inside with as much dignity as I could muster.

Raphael closed the door behind me. An odd light played in his eyes. He grabbed me by my shoulders and pulled me to him.

The breath jumped out of my lungs.

His stare was hard. "You will give us a chance."

"What?"

"Things happened before I met you and before you met me. Those things don't matter. You had no control over your past, but here, right now, you control the situation and you're voluntarily giving it up. You're punishing both of us because of something that happened half a lifetime ago. It makes no sense."

I tried to pull away, but he held me.

"There hasn't been anyone since I met you. I've been good, and don't think for a moment it was because of the lack of wiggling asses. Have you ever seen me with another woman since we met? Have you heard of me being with another woman? The same women who wanted to give you pointers will tell you that I haven't touched anyone since I saw you. Are you jealous of them? Is that it?"

My face went hot and I knew I had flushed. I was jealous of them. Of all of them.

"Andrea, you can't be jealous of someone I met before

I knew you. I didn't know you existed back then. I don't want anyone else now. Has there been anybody for you?"

I shook my head.

"I think of you a lot. Do you think of me, Andrea? Don't lie to me."

"Yes!" I snarled, my face burning. "Yes, I do! All the time. I can't get you out of my head. I wish I could!"

He hugged me so hard, my bones nearly crunched. "You've made yourself into a new person and so have I. We deserve a fucking chance. I want you and you want me. Why aren't we together? I'll deal with your hang-ups if you'll deal with mine, but if you're still too scared to even try, then you're not worth waiting for. I have some goddamn pride left and I won't wait forever."

He let me go.

I could either take control of it now or walk out. I clenched my teeth. This was *my* decision. I owned it, I took full responsibility for it, and no memories would make me cower and run away from him. I was worth it, damn it. He was worth it.

I did what I had wanted to do since I first saw him. I dropped my fork and kissed him.

We never made it upstairs to the bedroom.

The problem with falling asleep wrapped in a comfy blanket on the floor between the coffee table and the sofa is that in the morning, when the phone rings and wakes you up, you forget the coffee table is there. At least Raphael did. There was a solid thud as he sat up, smashing his head against the table, and then a string of foul curses as he staggered into the kitchen and picked up the phone.

"It's for you!"

I got up, wrapped the blanket about myself like a cape, and went to get the phone.

"Aha!" Kate's voice said on the other end.

"Aha what?"

Raphael must've recovered from his unfortunate connection with the table, because he set about trying to steal my blanket.

"Nothing. Nothing at all," Miss Innocence said.

"How did you get this number anyway?" I smacked Raphael's hand away.

"Jim gave it to me a long time ago. I tried your cell, the Order, and your house. This was the next logical number. I'm a trained detective, you know."

"You couldn't detect your way out of a shoe if someone lit the way with neon signs."

Raphael finally won the battle for the blanket and molded his body against mine, nipping gently at my neck. "Hold on a minute."

I covered the phone and turned to him. "About dealing with my hang-ups—this is one of them. I'm on the phone. Please let me be."

He sighed and went about the kitchen getting eggs out.

"I'm here," I said, pulling my blanket back up.

"How did it go with Cerberus?"

I briefly sketched it for her. "Even if destroyed, he continues to remanifest as soon as the magic is up. He's bound to that house. I'll be talking to the People today about the vampire. I doubt they'll tell me anything."

"How important is this?"

I explained about Aunt B.

"I'm so sorry."

"Me, too."

"Ghastek owes me a favor," Kate said. "I have it on paper, signed in the presence of witnesses. Call him on it."

"Thanks."

"It's the least I can do. Say, how did you even get into this mess?"

"Some man called Teddy Jo called it in."

Kate hesitated. "Be careful with Teddy Jo," she said softly.

"Why?"

"I don't have anything solid, but there is something that bothers me about Teddy. Just watch him carefully if he ever shows up."

I hung up. After Nataraja, the head of the People in Atlanta, Ghastek was the most talented of the Masters of the Dead. And also the most dangerous.

"Are you off the phone?" Raphael inquired mildly.

"Yes."

A hint of danger added edge to his smile. "Good."

When one says "pounce," most people typically think of a cat. Maybe a dog. But none of them can manage to pounce quite as well as a horny male werehyena.

It took us nearly forty-five minutes to get out of the house, partly because Raphael had jumped me and partly because I had lingered. I lay next to him, wrapped in his arms, and tried to sort it out, and all the while my brain feverishly pulled apart my emotions, the secret creature inside me purred and snuggled up to Raphael, blissful in her simple happiness.

Raphael went all out: black jeans, black T-shirt, black jacket, enough knives to fight off a gaggle of ninjas. At least he didn't wear leather, or we would've caused a slew of traffic accidents.

He had also called his mother. During his life, Alex Doulos was a Greek pagan, and he did worship Hades. Aunt B didn't know the particulars. Raphael didn't mention that her mate's shade was trapped behind a ward by some sort of necromancer. We both agreed that she could be spared that knowledge.

"What's bothering you?" Raphael asked, as I slid the Jeep into traffic. The magic had dropped again during the night. At least we could speak without yelling over the roar of the water engine. "Was the morning not good for you?"

He was worried. If he knew how completely he'd blown my socks off, his head would swell to twice its normal size. I tried my best not to laugh. "Sex, it's what for breakfast."

"Seriously?"

"It was great." The best I ever had, but he didn't need to know that. "Couldn't you tell?"

"You never know. Women are more complicated." He shook his head. "If not that, then what is it? You have that pinched look on your face."

"Aren't men supposed to be bad about reading women's faces?"

Raphael sighed. "Not when they are reading the face of a woman they've obsessed over for the last six months. Tell me."

I didn't say anything. He would think less of me if I did.

"This is one of my hang-ups," he said. "I'll keep asking you what's wrong until you tell me."

Fair enough. "I'm a professional," I said. "I went through the training, got knighted, the whole thing. I have decorations for meritorious service. But I have to rely on Kate to get the People to talk to me. It bothers me."

He waited for more.

"Back in Texas, my partner and I took out a group of loups. My partner caught Lyc-V and went loup. I killed her. The Order tested me, but I got the all clear."

"How did you manage that? The virus is in your blood."

"I had a silver ring implanted under my skin in my arm just below the armpit. It pinched off my blood supply and then I shot liquid silver into my veins. It killed the virus. I cut my wrist to bleed out the dead virus cells, and the ring kept Lyc-V from the rest of my body from entering my arm." The mere memory made me want to curl in pain.

"That was insanely dangerous. You could've lost your arm."

"I almost did. But the blood work came back clear, and the amulet in my skull, the one you pulled out during the flare, kept my magic from leaking into an m-scan. I was given a clean slate, but they still shipped me off to Atlanta. Ted Monahan, the knight-protector, put me on the back burner. Before coming here, I was on the way to becoming Master-at-Arms, Firearm."

Raphael nodded. "I take it that's a big deal."

"Very. I had all of my security briefings, passed all of the tests. All that remains is the formal nomination from my chapter's knight-protector. But Ted will never do it."

"Why not?"

"Because he senses there is something wrong with me. He isn't sure what, and until he figures it out, I'm the only knight without any active cases. I don't even have an office."

Raphael's jaw took on a stubborn set. I had seen it before a few times, and I knew what it meant. "I know that look."

He turned a dazzling smile at me. "What look?"

"Promise me that you'll cause no harm directly or indirectly to Ted by acting on my behalf. I'm dead serious, Raphael. Promise me."

"What he's doing to you—"

"Is exactly what I would do in his place. I knew the risks when I got into the Order. The Order has done absolutely nothing to renege on the terms of our bargain. All the fault lies with me. I deceived it, and if discovered, I'll pay the price. I accept that."

"What is the price?"

A spike of anxiety pinched me. My throat closed up for a moment. "They'll throw me out on my ass."

"Is that all?" he asked. "Are you sure they won't send someone after you to make sure you don't join the opposite side?"

"I'm sure," I said. "Their conditioning is very good. It would take a lot to break my devotion to the Order even if they put me out on the street. Promise me."

"Fine. I promise."

We drove in silence for a few minutes.

Raphael's eyes darkened. "Maybe we should be careful with public displays of affection."

I gave him my thousand-yard stare. "Oh no. I think you misunderstand the nature of our relationship. You are *mine*.

If there is an attractive female in speaking range, you *will* be publicly affectionate to me. Otherwise I'll end up pistol-whipping them off you, and I'm pretty sure injuring innocent civilian hussies would be considered 'conduct unbecoming a knight.'"

Raphael showed me the edge of his teeth in a slight smile. "And what will Ted think of you shacking up with a bouda?"

"Ted is welcome to show me a section in the Order's regulations that forbids me to do so. My knowledge of regulations is extremely extensive. I can quote entire passages from memory. I guarantee that I know the rules much better than Ted."

My brain took a second to process the words that had just left my mouth and realized how many things I had taken for granted. I said softly, "At least I hope you would be publicly affectionate."

Raphael laughed softly, like a bemused wolf. "You ruined a spectacular alpha snarl."

I had seen Raphael fight. He was devastatingly lethal. The way he tore up Cerberus's head took both skill and the berserk frenzy that made boudas feared in any fight. Physically he could overpower me. I was barely five feet four; he was six feet and change. He outweighed me by about eighty pounds of hard muscle, toughened by constant exercise. He was without a doubt the best fighter of the bouda clan. But he was also a male, and bouda males preferred the beta role. I had snapped into an alpha mode without even realizing it.

"I didn't mean . . ."

"I trust you to take the lead most of the time," he said. "With the understanding that when I really insist, you *will* listen."

I exhaled. "Agreed."

The Casino, the People's HQ in Atlanta, occupied the enormous lot that had once housed the Georgia Dome. The

People's architect had taken the Taj Mahal as a model and expanded the blueprint to twice its original size. Pure white in daylight, the Casino seemed to float above the asphalt, buoyed by the glittering streams of many fountains surrounding its walls. Its slender towers reached to a dizzying height, flanking the ornate central cupola. Elegant passageways united the towers, ethereal as if woven of spider's web or carved from a chunk of ivory by a patient sculptor. Its elaborate central gates always stood open, just as the guardhouses and engines of war on its thick walls were always manned.

I parked in a side lot and nudged Raphael to put Kate's book down.

A hundred yards from the gates, both of us paused in unison. The stench of undeath spread through the lot like a sickening miasma. No words could adequately describe it, but once you smelled it, you never forgot it. It was a sharp, leathery, dry stench, unmistakably of death but not of rot, the scent of sinew and bone wrapped in a foul, foul magic. I nearly gagged. Raphael slowed and I followed his example.

I've had the acclimatization training to accustom me to vampiric scent and presence, but it was one thing to watch a single vamp held tightly in check twenty yards away and completely another to be walking into the den of more than three hundred of them.

We made it through the doors past twin sentries dressed in black and armed with wickedly curved scimitars and stepped into the sea of slot machines. The air rang with a discordant cacophony of bells and chimes. Lights flashed. People screamed in manic glee, cursed, and laughed. More than half of the slots had been reworked to be completely independent of electricity. Even when the magic hit, the one-armed bandits would continue to quickly and mercilessly siphon cash out of the public's pockets and into the coffers of the People. Necromantic research wasn't cheap.

We halted before a service desk and I told a young man in a business suit who I was, flashed my Order ID, and explained I was here to see Ghastek. The young man, having introduced himself as Thomas, promptly affixed a smile on his face. "I'm sorry, ma'am, he's incredibly busy."

"Tell him I'm here on behalf of Kate Daniels."

Thomas's eyes went wide. He tapped the intercom, whispered into it, and nodded at us. "Unfortunately, he's in the stables and can't leave at the moment. He's most eager to see you, and someone will be here to guide you to him very shortly."

We walked over to the waiting area by the wall. A row of chairs waited for us, but I didn't feel like sitting down. I felt like someone had painted a giant bull's-eye on my chest and a dozen hidden snipers were ready to take a shot.

Raphael's lips bent in an odd little smile. If you didn't know him, you could mistake it for the dreamy absent-minded grin of a man quietly enjoying his private thoughts. This little smile meant Raphael was a single infraction away from whipping out his knives and slicing everything around him to pieces. He wouldn't do anything unless provoked, but once provoked, nobody could hold him back. The Pack and the People represented two sides of the same power coin: among all civilian factions in Atlanta, they were the most powerful. They had divided the city between them and stayed out of each other's territory, knowing that if open conflict broke out between the two of them, the fight would be long, bloody, and costly, and the victor would be so weakened, he wouldn't survive for long.

But as much as they avoided provoking each other, both found it prudent to show their opponent their teeth—and Raphael was all about proper etiquette.

A vampire dropped into the doorway. Female and probably black during life, now it had gained an odd purple tint. Hairless and emaciated, as if knitted together from twine and tough jerky, it stared at us with hungry eyes. Its mouth unhinged with mechanical precision, and the voice of a female navigator issued forth. "Good morning. My name is Jessica. Welcome to the Casino. Master Ghastek sends his deepest apologies. He's engaged in something he cannot postpone, but he instructed me to take you to him. With my sincere regrets for your inconvenience, I must ask you to please leave your firearms at the desk."

They wanted my guns. "Why?"

"The inner facilities house a lot of delicate and in some cases irreplaceable equipment. Occasionally our guests experience a heightened sense of anxiety and discomfort due to the presence of vampires, particularly when they visit the stables."

"I wonder why," Raphael said.

"We've had incidents of accidental discharge of firearms by our guests. We don't request that you surrender your bladed weapons, only your firearms. I'm afraid this rule can't be bent. My deepest apologies."

"That will be fine," I said, and deposited my P226s on the desk. Without my weapons, I felt naked.

"Thank you. Follow me, please."

We followed the creature down an opulent hallway to a stairway and then down, and down, and down, beyond the daylight to the artificial illumination of electric lamps. The vampire crept lower and lower, moving on all fours, making so little noise, it was uncanny. We wove our way through a maze of dim tunnels, interrupted only by the occasional bulb of electric light and dark, foot-wide gaps in the ceiling.

"Is there going to be a minotaur in this labyrinth?" Raphael growled.

"The maze is a security measure, necessary for proper containment," the navigator's voice answered through the vamp's mouth. "Unguided vampires are ruled by instinct. They don't possess the cognitive capacity to navigate the tunnels. In the event of a massive breakout, the tunnels will act as a buffer zone. The ceiling contains a number of heavy-duty metal grilles that will drop down, separating the vampires into easily manageable groups and minimizing damage resulting from bloodlust-induced infighting."

"How often do breakouts occur?" I asked. The stench of undeath had grown to a nearly unbearable level.

"Never. This way, please." The vampire scuttled to a brightly lit doorway. "Watch your step."

We entered a huge chamber and descended a dozen stairs to the floor. Harsh white light streamed from the high ceilings, illuminating every inch. A narrow hallway stretched to the center of the chamber, its walls formed by prison cells. Each six-by-six-foot cell housed a single vampire, chained by the neck to the wall. The chains were thicker than my thigh. The vampires' eyes burned with insatiable bloodlust. They didn't vocalize, didn't make any noise; they just stared at us, straining on the chains as we passed by them. Every hair rose on the back of my neck. Deep inside, my secret self gathered into a tight clump, watching them back, ready to leap out at the slightest opportunity.

The hallway terminated in a round platform, from which more corridors radiated like spokes from a wheel. On the platform stood Ghastek. He was a man of average height and thin build. His light brown hair receded from his forehead, focusing attention on his eyes: dark and sharp enough to draw blood. His attire was black, from tailored slacks to the long-sleeved shirt, collar unbuttoned and sleeves very carefully and precisely rolled up, but where Raphael's black was an aggressive, kick-ass darkness, Ghastek's black was the laid-back, business-casual shade, an absence of color rather than a statement of attitude.

He glanced at us, nodded briskly, and turned his attention to three young people standing to the side next to a console. They wore identical black slacks, gray dress shirts, and dark violet vests. Journeymen, the Masters of the Dead in training. One of the three, a tall young male with red hair, stood very rigid. His hands curled into fists. He stared straight ahead, at the cell where a single vampire sat at the end of its chain.

Ghastek nodded. "Are you ready, Danton?"

"Yes, Master," the redhead said through clenched teeth.

"Very well. Proceed."

The vampire jerked as if shocked with live wire.

"Easy," Ghastek said. "Remember: no fear."

Slowly the bloodsucker took two steps back. The hunger in its ruby eyes dimmed slightly. The chain sagged and clanged to the floor.

"Good," Ghastek said. "Maria, you may release the gate."

A female journeywoman with long dark hair tapped the console. The gate of the cell crept up. The vampire stood still.

"Disengage the collar," Ghastek ordered.

The vampire snapped the collar open.

"Bring him forward."

The vampire took a tentative step forward. Another . . .

Its eyes flared with bloodlust like two glowing coals. Danton screamed. The bloodsucker charged us, eyes shining, jaws unhinging, huge claws scratching the platform.

No gun.

I dashed forward, pulling a field knife, but Raphael beat me to it. He swung, slashing in a precise arc, and checked himself in midmove.

The vamp froze. It simply stopped, petrified, one clawed foot on the ground and the rest in the air. Raphael had stopped his knife blade a mere half an inch from the undead throat.

"You have excellent reflexes," Ghastek said. "A shapeshifter?"

Raphael simply nodded.

"I sincerely apologize," Ghastek said. "I'm piloting him at the moment, so he won't cause us any further concern."

The vampire leapt backward, landing at Ghastek's feet, and hugged the floor, his forehead pressed to stone. Ghastek's face showed no strain. None at all.

Raphael stepped back, the knife vanishing into the sheath at his waist.

On the platform, Danton slumped into a heap, moaning softly, white clumps of foamy spit sliding out of his mouth. A medical team with a stretcher emerged from the side corridor and loaded him up, strapping him in.

Both remaining journeymen stared at Danton in horrified silence.

"You may go," Ghastek said.

They fled.

"A shame, that," Ghastek said softly.

"What happened to him?" I asked.

"Fear. Done correctly, the contact with the undead mind, while repulsive to some, is completely harmless."

The vampire uncoiled and rose straight up. It had been quite tall during life, but its body had shifted to a quadruped locomotion. Yet it stood straight as an arrow, probably in pain but staring right into Ghastek's eyes. The Master of the Dead studied the twin points of furious red. "Fear of contact, however, can bring about horrible consequences, as you saw."

The vampire dropped on all fours. "Perhaps we had best continue this discussion in my office." Ghastek smiled drily. "Please."

I walked next to him, Raphael on my right, the vampire on Ghastek's left. "Navigating a vampire is similar to riding a large wave: you have to stay on top of it or it will crest and pull you under. Danton, unfortunately, permitted himself to drown. If he's lucky, he should be able to regain enough cognitive ability to feed himself and tend to his own personal hygiene. If he's unlucky, he'll spend the rest of his life as a human vegetable. Would you care for an espresso?"

The vampire sprinted ahead.

"No, thank you. Watching a man foam at the mouth tends to short-circuit my thirst and appetite." What happened to Danton deeply bothered me, but I knew the People's contracts, and everything that had transpired was completely within the law. The journeymen signed their lives away when they chose to work for the People.

"Again, my apologies. I could have postponed the test, but Danton had avoided it twice already after daring to brag about how well he would do. I don't tolerate displays of baseless egocentricity. The test had to proceed as scheduled.

He's a rare case. Most of our journeymen manage to fail without quite so much melodrama."

We climbed the stairs and headed through the maze of the hallways until Ghastek opened the door to one of the rooms. Spacious, it resembled a living room rather than an office: a semicircle of sectional sofa upholstered in a warm red shade, a plain desk in the corner, books lining the shelves. To the left, through the door, I saw a small kitchenette and a vampire mixing a drink. To the right, floor-to-ceiling windows offered a view of the stables from above.

"Please sit down."

I took a spot on the sofa. Raphael sat next to me, and Ghastek opposite. The vampire squirmed into the room and offered Ghastek an espresso. The Master of the Dead smiled quietly at his drink and sipped with obvious pleasure. The bloodsucker dropped to the floor and sat at his feet. It moved so naturally and Ghastek was so relaxed, I found it difficult to believe that the Master of the Dead controlled the vampire's every twitch.

"I believe we've met before," Ghastek said. "In Kate's office. You pointed guns at my vampire."

"You questioned my reflexes," I said.

"I was quite impressed by them. That's why I requested that you disarm."

"You expected the journeyman to fail?"

"Precisely. This particular vampire is appraised at $34,500. It would be bad business sense to put it into a situation where it would endure a dozen bullets shot through its skull."

What a cold, cold man.

Ghastek sipped his espresso. "I assume you're here to call in the favor I owe to Kate."

"Yes."

"How is she, by the way?"

Something in the perfectly neutral way he asked the question set my teeth on edge.

"She's recuperating," Raphael said. "And as a Friend of the Pack, she's enjoying the Pack's protection." He had been staying quiet so far and I knew why. Anything he said would be used by the People against the Pack. He minimized the amount of conversation, but he made the message crystal clear.

Ghastek chuckled. "I assure you, she's quite capable of protecting herself. She tends to kick people in the face when she finds them offensive. Is it true she broke a red sword during the Midnight Games by impaling herself on it?"

An alarm blared in my head. "I don't remember it quite that way," I lied. "As I recall, a member of the opposing team meant to strike with the sword. Kate interrupted his strike, and when he tried to free the blade, he cut himself on it. The blood from his hand shattered the sword."

"I see." Ghastek drank the last of his espresso and handed the cup to the vampire. "So what may I do for you?"

"I would like you to answer a series of questions." I had to phrase the questions very carefully. "This interview is conducted in confidence. I ask you to not discuss it with anyone unless required to do so by law."

"I'll happily do so, provided your questions are within the range defined by the conditions in the original agreement."

The agreement specified that he wouldn't do anything to directly harm himself, his team, or the People as a group.

"Are you familiar with the area known as Scratches, located west of Red Market?"

"Yes."

"Is it true that the People routinely patrol a large area of the city surrounding the Casino?"

"Yes."

"Do any patrol routes pass through Scratches?"

"No.

So the vampire wasn't the People's observer. "To your knowledge, are the People currently conducting any operations in the Scratches?"

"No."

"Are you familiar with Greek paganism?"

I watched him carefully, but he showed no signs of being surprised by the question. "I have a moderate knowledge of it, within the limits common to most educated individuals. I'm not, by any means, an expert."

"Keeping in mind the previous question, how would you define the term 'shade'?"

"An incorporeal entity representing the essence of a recently departed, a disembodied 'soul,' if you will. It's a purely philosophical concept."

"If confronted with a shade, how would you explain its existence?"

Ghastek leaned back, braiding his long fingers. "There are no such things as ghosts. All 'spirits,' 'lost souls,' and so forth are superstition. To exist in our reality, one requires a solid form. So, if confronted with a shade, I would surmise that it's either a hoax or a postmortem projection. For some magically capable individuals death comes slowly, in that even after their bodies cease their function and become clinically dead, their magic keeps their minds functioning for an extended period of time. In effect, they are mostly dead. In this state, some persons may project an image of themselves, especially if they are aided by the magic of a trained necromancer or a medium.

"Folklore is full of examples of such phenomena. For example, there's a tale in *Arabian Nights* that features a sage whose head was struck off his body after death and set upon a platter. It recognized people familiar to the sage and was able to speak. But I digress." He invited the next question with a nod.

"Are you aware of any necromancers unaffiliated with the People and capable of vampiric navigation who are currently active in the city?"

Ghastek's face registered distaste, as if he had smelled something unpleasant. He plainly didn't want to answer the question. "Yes."

"Please identify the individuals described."

"Lynn Morriss."

Oh wow. Spider Lynn was one the seven premier Masters of the Dead in Atlanta. All of the People's Masters of the Dead branded their vampires. Lynn's brand was a small stylized spider. "When did she leave the People?"

"She withdrew her membership three days ago."

According to Raphael, that was Alex Doulos's date of death. It could be a coincidence, but I highly doubted it.

"She also purchased several vampires out of her stable," Ghastek volunteered.

"How many can she pilot at once?" Raphael asked.

"Three," Ghastek said. "Up to four on a good day. Her control becomes shaky after that."

"Why did she leave?" I asked.

"She became disillusioned. We all seek to attain our goals. Some are willing to wait and others, like Lynn, lose their patience."

"How would you describe her?"

Ghastek sighed. "Precise, ruthless, single-minded. She was neither liked nor disliked. She did her job well and required little attention."

"What caused her to leave the People, in your opinion?"

"I don't know. But it was deeply profound. One doesn't walk away from fifteen years of hard work without a reason."

I rose. "Thank you very much for your time."

Ghastek nodded. "Thank you. When I made the agreement with Kate, I never imagined the restitution would be so easy. Let me see you out." The vampire moved by the door. "A word of caution: if Lynn Morriss has decided to make her new home in the Scratches, I would advise you to stay away from it. Lynn is a formidable opponent."

"Do the People plan to take any action against her?"

"No," Ghastek said with a small smile. "There is no need."

Outside I hopped into our vehicle, the taint of vampiric magic clinging to me like greasy smoke. "I feel soiled."

"Like walking into a room after a day of work, falling

into bed, and realizing the sheets are covered in cold K-Y jelly," Raphael said.

I just stared at him.

"With a funky smell," he added.

My Order conditioning failed me. "Ew."

Raphael grinned.

"I'm not even going to ask if that's happened to you." I started the vehicle. "Has that happened to you?"

"Yes."

Ew. "Where?"

"In the bouda house."

Ew!

"I was really tired and you've seen that place: everything smells like sex . . ."

"I don't want to know." I peeled out of the parking lot.

"So where are we going?"

"To Spider Lynn's house. We're going to dig through her trash, and if that doesn't work, we'll do some breaking and entering."

Raphael frowned. "Do you know where she lives?"

"Yes. I memorized the addresses of all the Masters of the Dead in the city. I have a lot of time on my hands."

He squinted at me, looking remarkably like a gentleman pirate from my favorite romance novels. "What else do you store in your head?"

"This and that. I remember the first thing you ever said to me. You know, when you carried me from the cart into the tub so your mother could fix me."

"I imagine it was something very romantic," he said. "Something along the lines of 'I've got you' or 'I won't let you die.'"

"I was bleeding in the bathtub, trying to realign my bones, and my hyena glands voided from the pain. You said, 'Don't worry, we have an excellent filtration system.'"

The look on his face was priceless.

"That can't be the first thing."

"It was."

We drove in silence. "About the K-Y," Raphael said.

"I don't want to know!"

"Once I washed it out of my hair—"

"Raphael, why are you doing this?"

"I want to make you go 'Ew' again."

"Why in the world would you want to do that?"

"It's an irrepressible male impulse. It just has to be done. As I was saying, once I washed it out—"

"Raphael!"

"No, wait, you'll like the next part."

By the time we reached Spider Lynn's house, my endurance had been tested to its limits.

Her place was a small ranch-style house, set way back from the road and hidden by a six-foot-tall wooden fence. I opened the trash can. A cloud of rancid stink hit me. Filthy but empty.

Raphael examined the fence, took a running start, and sailed over it, flipping in the air like a vault gymnast. I did it the old-fashioned way: I ran, jumped, gripping the edge, and pulled myself up and over. Raphael pulled out a couple of lock picks and inserted them into the lock. The door clicked and we entered a dark, empty garage. I blinked a couple of times, adjusting to the gloom, and then my night vision kicked in. Some people's garages resembled a yard sale postbombing. Spider Lynn's was orderly and precise, a collection of tools and cleaning utensils carefully hung on hooks. The floor was freshly swept. If I had a garage, mine would look just like it.

The door leading from the garage to the house was predictably locked and took ten seconds to be sprung by Raphael. Inside was an upscale suburban kitchen with stainless steel appliances and brand-new furniture. Perfectly clean sink. No odor of rot from the garbage disposal.

The scent signatures were old. She hadn't been in the house for two days, at least.

"Interesting," Raphael said.

I came to stand by him.

A large dent marred the living room wall just below a painting of some geometric shapes. A stain spread about it.

Below, shards of broken glass glinted, weakly catching the daylight from the windows, among shriveled green stems. Someone had thrown a vase against the wall.

"How tall is she?" Raphael asked.

"Two inches taller than me."

"It might have been her then. I'd hit a lot higher."

We look at the stain. "She was angry," I said.

"Very."

"Not a lover."

Raphael nodded. "White flowers."

I inhaled, sorting the pollen aroma: barely noticeable scent of white lilies, light perfume of carnations, sweet fragrance of snapdragons, dryness of baby's breath . . .

"Sympathy arrangement," we both said at the same time.

I crouched by the pile of stems and dug through it. My fingers slid against a damp rectangle. I pulled it free: a small card with a logo, a snake coiling around a wineglass. The letters under it said, "Bright Light Hospital, Thaumaturgy College of Atlanta."

I opened the card and read it out loud. "I am so sorry. Ben Rodney, MD, CMM." Doctor of Medicine and Certified Medical Mage.

Raphael bent down and tapped the card. "Alex was a patient there. I know what this is: when there is nothing more they can do, they send you the 'set your affairs in order' flowers."

"She was dying."

"Looks that way."

"At least we've established the connection between her and Alex." I looked at the card.

We searched the rest of the house. In the office we found a filing cabinet full of medical records. Spider Lynn was diagnosed with Niemann-Pick disease, type C. A progressive, incurable disease, it affected her spleen and liver and damaged her brain. Simple things like walking and swallowing had become increasingly difficult. She had trouble looking up and down. Her vision and hearing were fading.

Soon she would be a prisoner in her own body, and then she would die.

"Come see this," Raphael called.

I followed him to the library. Open books covered the floor. Raphael picked up one. "And so Hades seized Persephone and bore her away in his chariot to the depths of the bleak realm of the dead. In vain her mother, the generous Demeter, searched for her daughter. Alone the Goddess of Harvest wandered the world, clothed in rags, like a common woman, and in her sorrow she had forgotten to tend to the soil and cultivate plants. Denied her precious gifts, the flowers withered on their stalks, the trees shed their leaves in mourning, and everything that had been green and alive shriveled and died. Winter had come upon the world and the people wailed in hunger. Even the golden apples in Hera's orchard had fallen off the bare branches of the sacred tree."

"Cheery." I checked a couple of other books. "Same thing."

"This one is in Greek." Raphael held up a huge, dusty tome and pointed to the page. On it was a picture of an apple.

"So she is obsessed with Hades and apples. What do we know about these apples?" I looked through the book.

"Here's one," Raphael said. "'Eris, the Goddess of Discord, alone was not invited to attend the wedding. Quietly she sulked until, consumed by her need for revenge, she picked a golden apple, wrote "Kallistri," meaning "To the Fairest," upon its golden skin, and tossed it in the midst of the celebrating Olympians. And thus began the Trojan War . . .'"

"Well, that was slick, but it doesn't help us any." I searched through my book. "Here is the eleventh labor of Hercules. He needs to get the golden apples of immortality from Hera's orchard." I stopped and looked at Raphael.

"Immortality apples," he said. "How about that."

I tapped the book. "What do we know so far? Spider

Lynn is terminally ill. She's obsessed with apples of immortality, probably because she thinks they can cure her. She's holding the shade of Alex Doulos hostage for unknown purposes. Alex was the priest of Hades."

"Hades stole Persephone, who was the daughter of Demeter, Goddess of Harvest, who controlled the seasons, which affected Hera's apples of immortality. It's like playing six degrees of separation." Raphael flipped through his book. "It says here that apples are the food of the gods. They and ambrosia keep the gods young and immortal. What do you suppose happens if that bitch eats them?"

"Nothing good." We had both dealt with two wannabe gods during the flare. I still had nightmares. I could tell by Raphael's face that he didn't care to repeat the experience either.

"We're going to have to break into that house."

"Yes." Raphael's face was grim.

A house guarded by a giant hellhound, surrounded by an electric fence and a strong ward, and hiding at least three vampires, piloted by a woman overcome by anger and terrified of death.

It's good that I had Boom Baby.

We stood leaning against the Jeep, on the very edge of Cerberus's territory, waiting for the magic to drain from the world. Raphael leaned next to me, still engrossed in the book of Greek myths. He read, playing with a small knife, flipping it absentmindedly with his left hand, his fingers catching whichever end happened to point down. Tip, handle, tip, handle. The sun set, bleeding orange blood onto the pale sky. I sampled the evening breeze and petted my giant gun.

Being a professional meant you nurtured your fear. You struggled with your terror until you tamed it and made it serve you. It made you sharper and helped you stay alive. But no matter how tame your fear became, it still gnawed on your soul. I didn't want to go into the house full of vampires. I didn't want Raphael to be hurt.

I had fought so hard not to fall for him, but I had anyway, and now, having been with him, having woken up next to him, I knew we had something. It was a very small, fragile something, and I would rip through a hundred vampires to keep it safe.

"You're my Artemis," Raphael said.

I blinked.

"Fierce, prickly, beautiful huntress, forever pure and uncompromising."

Prickly? More like bitchy. "I'm not that pure."

He leaned over. His hand brushed the back of my neck and I felt the light press of teeth on skin. Every nerve in my body tingled. My nipples went tight, and a slow, hungry heat blossomed below my stomach.

Raphael's voice was a smooth, whispery seduction in my ear. "There is nobody to see us for miles and miles, but you're blushing. How is that not pure?"

His smile was pure sin. I shifted closer to him and leaned against his chest, resting my head on his shoulder. He stiffened, surprised, and I snuggled closer, soaking up the warmth of his body with my back. He raised his arm and put it around my shoulders. I concentrated and heard the steady beating of his heart, strong and a little too fast. He was anxious, too.

"If we get out of this mess alive and undamaged, would you like to spend the night in my apartment or do you want me to stay with you?"

"Either way will work," he said softly.

The six-month storming of my castle had put a definite dent in Raphael's body armor. It would take me a long time to convince him that he didn't have to be charming, witty, and sexy around me twenty-four-seven. Some part of me had hoped that once we had sex, everything would smooth itself out. But in the end, he was still insecure and I was still broken. Sex was simple. Being together was a lot more complicated.

We stood together and watched the sunset.

The magic crashed.

"Time to pry Doulos's shade from that bitch," Raphael said.

"You realize that if we're right and Cerberus is after his corpse, he will follow Doulos wherever we take him?"

"Yes. But my mother deserves to say her good-byes."

He took off his clothes, stood still for a moment, the breeze fanning his perfect form, and opened his mouth. A groan broke free, deepening into a hair-raising growl, as his body stretched and thickened, hard muscle encasing it. Fur sheathed him. He glanced at me and his eyes were completely wild.

I lifted Boom Baby. Raphael picked up a six-foot metal pole he'd wrenched from the slope on the way here. We headed down through the ravines to the house.

"Those bullets are the size of a dollar bill," Raphael said.

"They are Silver Hawks: armor-piercing, incendiary, explosive, silver-load cartridges. They slice through armor, set things on fire, and explode inside the target, delivering a load of extremely potent silver pellets. Boom Baby fires two hundred of these per minute."

An excited snarl rolled ahead of us. The ground trembled in sync with the beat of the giant paws.

"Can they handle the dog?" he asked.

"We're about to find out." I raised Boom Baby. "Here, Fido . . . Here, boy . . ."

Ahead, Cerberus rounded the curve and charged us.

I squeezed the trigger. A high-pitched whine of bullet flurry ripped through the air. Boom Baby bucked in my hands, the recoil hitting me hard. The bullets bit into Cerberus's chest, punching through the muscle to the heart. Blood flew. The great hellhound ran three more steps, not realizing the lethal swarm had already shredded his life, stumbled, and fell, paws over head. He rolled and slid to a stop five feet from me in a smoking ruin.

"Nice gun," Raphael said.

Five minutes later we reached the electric fence. Raphael braided the fingers of his hands together and offered them to me like a stepping stool. I stepped, pushing hard, and he threw me, adding his strength to my jump. I shot over the fence, flipped in the air, and landed in the dirt. Boom Baby came flying next. I caught it and gently lowered it to the ground. In the cramped quarters inside the house, it would restrict my movements too much. I pulled out my P226s, the familiar weight of the twin firearms reassuring in my hands. Raphael took a running start, pole in hand, and vaulted over the fence, landing gracefully next to me. There were times when Lyc-V came in handy.

We jogged to the house and I pressed against the side. Raphael hammered a single kick to the door and it flew off its hinges, crashing into the darkness. I cleared the doorway and stepped into the gloom. The door led to a narrow foyer. On the right, stairs led to the second floor. Straight ahead lay a hallway and past it, through a doorway, a sitting room waited steeped in the twilight, the dark bulky shapes of furniture like the spines of sleeping beasts.

The nauseating stench of undead flesh laced my nostrils. It clung to the floor, permeating the carpets. If smell had color, this reek would drip from the draft in oily, fat drops of black. It was impossible to tell where it came from.

A moment later I caught another scent entirely: the bitter, clinical scent of embalming fluid. A human body waited for us somewhere in the house.

My eyes adjusted to the low light. We padded through the foyer on silent feet, cleared the doorway, and emerged into the hallway.

Slow and steady, room by room. An undead waited at the end of this race, and I had a feeling it would find us before we found it.

Two small, musty rooms later, we stepped into the family room. The old furniture had been haphazardly piled at the walls. In the center of the room, on the filthy old rug, lay the corpse of Alex Doulos. A huge chain caught the body's ankle, binding it to a rod driven into the floor.

Two red-hot eyes sparked in the heap of furniture at the opposite wall.

I fired. The first two bullets punched the bloodsucker's head.

The vampire leapt.

My guns spat thunder and bullets in a lethal rhythm, trailing the bloodsucker as it hurtled through the air.

Raphael lunged from the left, and I raised the guns' barrels up a fraction of a second before he fell onto the vamp from behind. The bloodsucker went limp in his hands. My bullets had chewed its skull to mush. Raphael grasped the vamp's chin, exposing the neck; his knife flashed, and the head went flying across the room.

I reloaded. The bloodsucker had been unpiloted. Its eyes had been too crazed and it attacked me straight on, without any consideration for the fact that there were two of us. Spider Lynn was gone. She had left the vampire to us as a present.

It took us ten minutes to search the rest of the house. Empty as expected. I didn't think she would sacrifice another vampire. We did find the generator and I shut it off, cutting the power to the fence.

We returned to the body. Alex lay on his side, thrown on the floor like a dirty rag. Death had robbed him of warmth, but his features still kept hints of his personality: a network of laugh lines around the eyes; strong chin; wide, tall forehead. His hair was pure white and worn long enough to reach his shoulders. A small green object lay by him. I picked it up. A little toy car. How odd. I tucked the car into my pocket.

We had to take him out of this terrible place. Raphael touched the chain securing Alex's ankle and jerked his hand away. A silver-steel alloy.

The chain clasped Alex's ankle too tightly. Neither one of us could get it off without burning all the meat off our fingers. I ripped fabric off the nearest couch, wrapped it around the rod the body was chained to, and strained. It didn't even shiver.

"Let me."

Raphael grasped the rod. Veins on his face bulged and he ripped it free. He slung the body over his shoulder and let the chain trail behind him. It would have to do.

It took us three hours to cross the city. We drove through the dilapidated remnants of the industrial district and left Atlanta behind. Woods replaced ruins. The road grew bumpy. Neither of us said anything. The corpse wrapped in a blanket and resting in the backseat kept me from talking, and Raphael seemed immersed in thought.

Cold wind fanned us. The night was vast and filled with a flurry of scents. A sprinkling of stars shone high above, indifferent to us and our little problems.

Thirty minutes later we pulled onto the side road, dipping into the dense forest. The dirt road veered, we turned, and a large ranch-style house came into view. The bouda house. Usually it was full of life: sentries prowled the woods, and insane laughter floated on the wind currents, mixing with moaning and snarls of sexual release. But now it lay quiet. Raphael had said that everyone had left, letting Aunt B grieve in private, but it didn't hit home until I actually saw it.

A woman waited for us on the porch, her hands crossed under her breasts. Middle-aged and plump, she wore her hair atop her head in a bun. Careworn shadows distorted her usually happy face. She looked like a very young grandmother who had just realized her grandson's school bus was ten minutes late.

We parked. Raphael hopped out and gently picked up Alex's body. Alex's white hair spilled over Raphael's shaggy arm. Aunt B looked on without a word as the monster who was her son and my mate carried her lover's body to her and held it out. A single word escaped his monstrous mouth. "Mother . . ."

Aunt B's lips trembled. She slumped against the porch post. Her shoulders shook and she covered her mouth with her hand. Tears swelled in her eyes. No sobs escaped her lips. She simply stood there and cried, grief plain and raw on her face.

What do I do? She was the bouda alpha. Alphas didn't . . . they didn't show weakness. They didn't *cry*.

She was just a woman.

I walked up on the porch and hugged her. "Let's take him inside."

For a moment I thought she would snap my neck, and then she nodded wordlessly and I opened the door. We took him in and laid him to rest on a table in the back room. She sank into a chair next to him. Raphael sat on the floor next to her and she stroked his head.

I went into the kitchen, brewed herbal tea, and took it to her. Raphael was gone and Aunt B sat alone. Her face was wet with tears. Her eyes glanced at me. Still sharp and hard. She took the cup. "Thank you."

I nodded, not knowing what to do with myself.

"Are you and my son together?"

Everything inside me clenched, reminding me I was beastkin and she was the boudas' alpha. "Yes."

"That's good," she said softly. "I always liked you." She glanced at Alex. "Make the best of it. The way we did."

The magic surged, drowning us. The outline of Alex's body shimmered. A pale glow broke free of the corpse and congealed into Alex Doulos. He saw Aunt B. His voice was like the whisper of dry leaves underfoot. "Beatrice?"

"Yes," she said softly.

I tiptoed out of the room.

I found Raphael outside, on the porch. Too bulky to fit into a chair in his warrior form, he sat on the floor. Hard knotted muscle corded his back. His long arms lay folded on his knees and the claws of his right hand protruded, crisp in moonlight.

He truly looked monstrous. Just like the secret me.

I sat next to him.

"If I die, will you grieve for me?" he asked.

"Yes. But before I do that, I'll fight to save you."

"Why?"

I put my hand onto his furry forearm. "Because I feel good when you're near me. It's not just sex, and it isn't loneliness, it's more than that. It's kind of frightening. I think that's why I fought it for so long."

The lawn before us seemed to go on forever, each grass blade slick with reflected moonlight. Soon Cerberus would come running, his paws mashing big ugly holes in the perfect grass.

"Do you think we'll ever have what they had?" he asked.

"I don't know. I think what they had grew over many years. We still have a lot of things to work out. But I'd like to try, Raphael. When I said you're mine, I meant it. I don't do things halfway. For better or worse."

We heard light footsteps. The door opened. "He wants you," Aunt B said.

Alex Doulos had a soft, kind voice. "My time's short," he said. "Do you know the myth of Hades and Persephone?"

"Yes," Raphael answered.

"Good. That will make things simple then. I'm a priest of Hades. My family has served him for generations. One of our duties is to tend to secret shrines of Hades. They're scattered all over the world and kept hidden. During the flares, one of the shrines randomly grows an apple tree, which bears fruit."

"Hera's Apples," I said.

Alex motioned with his arm. "The Vikings call them Idun's Apples, the Russians call them Apples of Youth, and we call them Persephone's Apples. The name doesn't matter. The apples are supposed to grant youth and long life span to gods. When eaten by normal humans, who don't have Persephone's gift or immunity to it, the apples produce horrible consequences. That's why we guard the tree until the apples ripen and sacrifice the fruit to Hades. No part of the apples must remain in our world. It is my duty to make sure the apples are destroyed. It's the purpose of my service. But I've failed.

"My body was kidnapped by a woman who calls herself Spider Lynn. She's dying and she wants the apples for herself. She mustn't eat them. It's very, very important. She must not eat them."

"Where is Lynn now?" I asked.

"I imagine she's at the shrine. It's in the woods behind my summer house. Raphael, you remember, we had a cookout at that house last year."

I glanced at Raphael. "It's across the wood, bordering our territory. Not too far," he said. "How did she know the location of the shrine?"

Alex's shade shuddered. "I told her. She realized that she couldn't compel me to reveal it and she kidnapped my nephew. His parents are away and I was watching the boy. I couldn't let the vampires hurt the child."

I pulled the green toy car from my pocket. "The boy . . ."

"Yes," Alex confirmed. "It's his. Raphael, I know that you're not my son and you owe me nothing. But I beg you, please, don't let her get the apples. Save the boy. And whatever you do, don't eat them."

"I'll do it," Raphael said simply.

"The shrine's guarded by a serpent, but it won't last against Spider Lynn's vampires for long. Take the bracelet off my arm. It's keyed to the ward that's guarding the shrine. Lynn has enough magic to force herself past the defensive spell, but it will leave her weakened. She'll need time to recover. You won't."

A deafening roar shook the house. Cerberus had found us.

"He's come for me." Alex smiled. "It's time to go. Take the bracelet. It will unlock the ward and let you pick up the apples."

Raphael slipped the simple metal loop off the corpse's right wrist and placed it over his own. The bracelet barely enclosed two thirds of his wrist. "Are you really going to Hades?"

"I don't know," Alex said. "But the last of my power is fading. My body is dead, Raphael. I can no longer hold on to it. Earth is the home of the living, not the dead. Don't mourn me. My life was full and well lived. I was fortunate. Some might even say blessed. I only wish that I had lived a few days longer so I could destroy the apples myself instead of forcing this burden on you. That and your mother's tears are my only regrets."

Aunt B rose, picked up the corpse, and strode outside. We followed her. She walked onto the lawn. They said something to each other, too quiet to hear, and then she lowered him into the grass and stepped away.

The trees rustled. A giant shape muscled through the trunks and trotted into the open, its three heads close to the ground. The center head sniffed Alex's body and picked it up, clamping it in its great fangs.

"Take care of your mother, Raphael," a ghostly voice called out.

The body burst into flames. The great dog howled and vanished.

Raphael's eyes shone once, catching the moonlight. "Are you with me?"

"Who else will protect your furry butt?"

"I'm coming, too," Aunt B said.

Raphael shook his head. "We've got this."

Her eyes flashed with red, a precursor to an alpha stare.

"He didn't want you involved," Raphael said. "He asked me, not you. The clan needs you."

"We've got it." I nodded.

We turned our backs on her and headed to the Jeep. "Did we just defy your mother, who's also your alpha?" I murmured.

"Yes, we did."

I glanced over my shoulder and saw Aunt B standing there with a bewildered look on her face. "Let's go faster before she realizes that."

The magic was up and Boom Baby was useless. I took a crossbow and bolts from the Jeep and followed Raphael into the woods. He broke into a run, inhumanly fast in warrior form, and I struggled to keep up.

Half a mile later Raphael stopped. "The magic is up," he said softly.

"I know."

"You're slower in this form."

I had run as fast as I could. When we were both in human form, I was faster. But in warrior form, he beat me.

"You can't keep up."

I realized what he was saying. "No."

"Andrea . . ."

"No!"

"We're short on time," he said. "There's a little boy out there with at least two vampires. We don't even know if he's alive."

My heart hammered in my chest. "You don't understand. I lose control when I'm her."

"Andrea, please," he said. "We're losing time."

I closed my eyes. He was right. We had to save the boy. We had to get the apples away from Lynn. I had to . . .

I stripped off my clothes and reached to the beast living inside me. She smiled and leapt out, flowing over my arms, my legs, my back, giving me her strength. My bones stretched, my muscles swelled, and there I stood, revealed and naked.

The shapeshifters got a choice: human, warrior form, or animal. I had only two: the human me and the secret me.

Raphael's eyes shone with red. He ran.

I swiped up my crossbow and then dropped it. My claws were too long. I wouldn't be able to work it. I'd have to fight with my claws and teeth. I grabbed the little toy car and hid it in my fist.

Raphael was a mere shadow in the distance. I burst into a run. It felt like flying, light and easy. My muscles welcomed the exertion and I sprinted, catching him with ease. Together we dashed through the woods, two humanoid nightmares, fast and slick, our voices faint whispers on the draft.

"I can't see you."

"I don't want you to see me." I purposely picked my way so he caught only the mere flashes of me.

"Don't hide from me," he asked.

I ignored him.

Suddenly he burst through the brush. I had no chance to hide. He saw all of me: my limbs, my face that was neither animal nor beast, my breasts . . .

"You're lovely," he whispered as he passed me in a burst of speed.

"You're sick," I told him.

"You've a perfect union of human and animal: proportionate and elegant and strong. Your form is what we aspire to. How's that sick?"

"I'm a human!"

"So am I. You don't have to hide from me, Andrea. I think you are beautiful."

Nobody, not human, not shapeshifter, not even my mother had ever told me that the beast form was beautiful. Inside me, the human me put her hands on her face and cried.

Miles flashed by. We passed a house in a blur of speed. Trees parted, underbrush snapped, and we burst into a clearing. A ward ignited with gold, barring our way in a translucent wall.

Inside the ward, a dark-haired boy crouched on the ground, hugging his knees. Past him a dead vampire lay broken on the grass, its skull shattered. To the left, an unnaturally large snake was dying on the grass, a second vampire caught in its coils. The vamp's neck was broken, its vertebrae crushed. Blood drenched the snake's coils. With each new squeeze, more blood washed the scales.

Past them, a ring of colonnades carved of pure white stone guarded a narrow apple sapling. Four yellow apples hung from the branches. The fifth apple, with a small piece bitten off, lay on the grass, by the hand of a dark-haired woman. She slumped on the grass. Her horribly distended stomach had ripped through her tailored slacks.

Oh no. She ate it. We were too late.

"Now look what you did." A man walked up to us, his eyes fixed on Spider Lynn. "I done told you to leave the apples alone."

Raphael snarled. The fur on his back rose.

The man was tall and broad-shouldered, built with strength in mind. Dark stubble peppered his face. He wore a white T-shirt, a pair of old jeans, and yellow work boots. A flannel shirt hung from his blocky shoulders. He looked like a good old boy in search of a porch with a rocking chair and a glass of iced tea. He turned to us and said, "Hi."

This was surreal. "Who are you?" I asked.

"I'm Teddy Jo."

"You're the man who called me about Raphael running from Cerberus?"

"I called Kate," he said. "You answered the phone. Do you have the bracelet?"

"What?"

"Doulos's bracelet. You have it?" He saw the bracelet on Raphael's arm. "Oh good then. We're in business."

Lynn squirmed on the grass and began to cry. "What is happening to me?"

Teddy Jo glanced at her. "You've brought this on yourself."

Raphael lunged at him. His clawed fingers closed about Teddy Jo's throat, the bracelet glinting with steel on his forearm. "What are you doing here?"

"Well now, you might want to rethink that," Teddy Jo said, raising his arm. His sleeve fell back, revealing an identical bracelet, but made of gold. "Given as we're on the same side."

Magic slammed my senses. Teddy Jo's eyes turned solid black. The flannel shirt ripped on his back and two colossal black wings thrust into the night. Fire ran from his bracelet down into his hand and snapped into a flaming blade.

"Thanatos," Lynn squeaked.

The angel of death clamped Raphael's wrist and squeezed. Raphael bared his teeth and crushed Thanatos's throat.

Lynn's stomach twisted. She howled as if cut. Alex's nephew jerked.

"Stop!" I barked at the two men. "There's a kid in shock sitting behind that ward, locked with whatever is about to crawl out of Lynn's gut! Raphael, break the damn ward. Teddy Jo, I swear, you don't let go of him this instant, I'll rip your wings off!"

The two of them stared at me.

"Do it!"

Teddy Jo let go. Raphael thrust his arm into the ward and the wall of gold drained down, revealing the shrine.

I leapt inside and swept the boy up into my arms. "Listen to me."

He stared at me with empty eyes. To him I was a monster.

I opened my hand and showed him the car. He touched it gently and I handed it to him. "I won't hurt you. Uncle Alex's house, do you know where it is?"

He nodded.

"I want you to run to it and not look back. Okay?"

He clutched the car in his fist. I set him down and he ran.

Raphael snarled at Teddy Jo. "What the hell are you doing here?"

Teddy Jo shrugged his massive wings. "I'm here to set things right. I serve Hades just like Doulos, except that he was a priest and I'm something other."

"Where were you until now?"

"Look, fella, I follow the rules. I would have liked to come down earlier and start chopping people's heads off, but I have to sit on my hands and wait until someone bites the damn apple. I'm the emergency brake here. That's what makes me the good guy."

Lynn screamed.

"And there she goes," Teddy Jo said.

Lynn's stomach tore. A slithering green mass spilled forth, and as it boiled out, Lynn was sucked in, almost as if her body had turned inside out. The mass grew larger and larger, bigger than a house, bigger than Cerberus. Scales formed on its surface. Magic roiled inside it, whipping my senses into overdrive.

The mass flexed and uncoiled. An enormous reptilian body thrust across the clearing. Three dragon heads snapped at the air with wicked teeth, jerking on long necks.

The dragon tasted the night and roared.

Teddy Jo shot straight up and hovered, his sword a beacon of light. "I'll take the center head. You two do as you please."

Lynn the dragon whipped about and I saw her eyes: cold and green, devoid of any humanity or feeling. Something inside me snapped. Fury drowned the world, flushing the rational thought. I was very angry. She had stolen the body of a man, denying his mate her mourning. She had tortured that man. She had kidnapped and terrorized a child. She deserved to die.

Teddy Jo swept at the dragon. The flaming sword carved through her neck like it was butter. The head tumbled down in a whiff of scorched meat. Then the stump quivered and split in half, and two new heads sprouted in its place and lunged for Teddy Jo.

"A hydra! Gods damn it!" Teddy Jo veered out of the way.

I smelled her flesh, waiting for me just beneath her scales. My fingers flexed. My tongue licked my fangs. Rage warmed me from the inside, hot and sharp and so very welcome. Andrea, the knight of the Order, would have to sleep through tonight. Tonight I was beastkin, the daughter of a hyena.

The dragon's flesh beckoned, elastic and smooth, coiling before me, begging for a taste.

The world went red. I charged.

* * *

Blood. Rip, claw, rip, rip, more, dig, dig into flesh.

A huge, pulsating sac swelled before me. I sliced into it, laughed when blood drenched me, and kept ripping. All around me, wet, hot redness shuddered.

"Enough!" A force clamped me and tossed me aside. I flew through the air, landed on all fours, and charged my assailant. He tripped me and I fell. The air burst from my lungs in a rush. My head swam.

The reality came back with ponderous slowness. I lay on my back in the grass, my body slick with reptilian blood. Slowly the rage faded and I saw Raphael.

"Are you hurt?" I asked him.

"Nothing dire."

The dragon's corpse lay on its side, a dozen half-formed heads sprawling like the stalks of some disgusting flower. A big hole gaped in her gut. It looked like someone had tunneled through her. Teddy Jo stood bent over near her, breathing hard.

"Did I do that?"

Raphael nodded. "You ripped apart her heart. That's what finally killed her."

"The apples." I tried to get up, but my legs refused to obey.

Raphael scooped me up. "Are you okay?"

"Overdid it." Drowsiness swept over me. My muscles turned to cotton. I stuck my ugly head against his neck. I felt dirty and awful. My stomach clenched.

If he hadn't pulled me out, I would've cut and sliced until I passed out.

Slowly it sank in: we won.

"I'll take care of the apples," Teddy Jo said. "You take your lady home."

Raphael looked at him. "Good fight," he said.

"Yeah," Teddy Jo answered. "We didn't do too bad. I live down in the Warren. Look me up if you wanna have a beer sometime."

Raphael carried me off.

"Don't forget the boy," I whispered.

"I won't. We're going to get the boy and drop him off with my mother. Then I'll take you to my house. I have a garden tub. We'll get nice and clean and then crawl into our bed and sleep until noon. Would you like that?"

"Very much," I said and licked his neck. "Raphael . . ."

"Yes?"

"I killed them. The boudas who tortured me and my mother. I went back after Academy, and I challenged them and killed them all one by one."

He licked my cheek. "Come home with me," he said simply.

I held on to him and whispered, "You couldn't keep me away."

No matter what job a man has, he always ends up hating parts of it. Now, I loved my job, the sword, the wings, the chopping off the evildoers' heads and all, but I bloody hated flying down to Savannah. Every time I swung this way, I hit wet wind off the ocean flying through Low Country. It ate its way through me all the way to the bone. Enough to give a man the liking for one of those dumb-looking paratrooper jumpsuits.

It took me a bit of time to finally find the right house in the predawn light, a small place with white siding and green roof, nothing special except for the damn industrial-strength ward on it. I circled it once and felt the magic defenses go down: Kate had seen me. Nothing to do but land, which I did, right on the path before the porch.

Kate sat on the porch with a book on her lap. She was on the pretty side, tan, dark-eyed, dark-haired. Exotic, even. Didn't look like she was from around here, but then who did nowadays? Her sword lay next to her, a pale sliver. I paid attention to her eyes and the sword. She was a bit quick on the trigger with it.

"I always knew there was something odd about you, Teddy Jo," she said, nodding at my wings.

"Likewise."

I felt the magic coil about her. Too much power there. Way too much. She hid it well, though.

"How did it go?"

I shrugged. "Killed the snake responsible. Everybody's alive. Your friends are in one piece. I expect they'll celebrate in bed once they sleep it off."

She arched an eyebrow. "They were together? Like together-together?"

"Looked that way to me."

A grin bent her lips. Why now, she had a pretty smile. Who knew?

"I've got something for you here," I said, and showed her a sack of apples.

She closed the book and set it aside. The title read, *Lion, King of Cats: Exploring the Pride*. I handed her the sack.

"Couldn't find anybody else immune to Persephone's immortality?" She chuckled.

"You guys don't exactly grow on trees. I tried burning them, but fire does nothing to the damn things."

"That's because they are meant to be eaten or sacrificed." She picked up her sword, cut a small chunk, and popped it into her mouth. "Tart. Think they'll keep for a week? I've got company coming next Friday, and I'd like to make them into a pie."

"Can the company handle Persephone's Apples?"

"He can."

I made of note of that *he*. Didn't know there was anybody else in the area immune to Persephone's Gift. If I had to put money on it, I'd bet it was the Beast Lord. Magic was a funny thing. The older it was, the stronger it was. True, Hades' firepower was of an ancient variety, but the magic Kate threw around was so much older, it gave me a start the first time I felt it. Now, I'd seen the Beast Lord once. He'd passed by me and I about choked. The magic that rolled off him was even older than Kate's flavor. Primeval—not your regular shapeshifter. Enough to give a man a complex.

"I don't see why they wouldn't keep," I said aloud. "Damn things are near indestructible."

She lifted the sack. "Thanks!"

"Thank *you*."

I pushed from the grass and shot into the sky. The sun was rising. Its rays warmed my wings and I headed back toward Atlanta. I had had a hard night. It was time to get home, drink me some coffee, and feed my dogs. Cerberus made sweet puppies, but the damn things sure ate a lot.

Blind Spot

A GUARDIAN NOVELLA

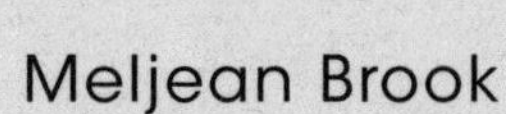

Meljean Brook

Chapter One

That morning, two hours after she received an anonymous e-mail that included an address and a short message, Maggie Wren boarded a flight from San Francisco to New York. Accompanied by the hellhound that Maggie's employer had demanded she bring with her, she arrived at JFK in midafternoon. The address led her to a brownstone in Brooklyn. Despite the busy streets and the glaring sun that exposed her movements, she picked the lock at the front door and dismantled the security system.

With a silent hand gesture, she instructed the hellhound to check the first level. Upstairs, the first two bedrooms stood open and empty, except for a shirt and jeans strewn over the floor of the second. Maggie kicked through a third door when she found it locked.

Her target—Geoffrey Blake—was sitting naked on the wooden floor, handcuffed to a radiator. He'd drawn his knees up and rested his back against the wall beneath a lace-curtained window. Although her foot slamming against the door could have woken the dead, his eyes remained closed.

Maggie swept the room with her gun before shoving the weapon into the holster beneath her blazer.

She crossed to Blake's side, retrieving her lock picks from her jacket's inside pocket. He wasn't completely naked, she noted. Her gaze skipped to his black briefs as she crouched and reached for the handcuffs. Yellow smiley faces grinned up at her from the elastic waistband.

"At least someone is happy to see me," Maggie said. Or maybe the smiley faces were just thrilled to be hugging his muscled abdomen. Smug little bastards.

"I would be," Blake replied in a deep, dry voice, "if I *could* see you."

He raised his head and opened his eyes, revealing irises of light blue—and no pupils. From rim to rim, the color was solid.

Maggie's fingers twitched. The metal pick slipped out of the keyhole and jabbed his wrist. Shit. She murmured an apology, her mind racing.

Blind. Yet nothing in Blake's dossier had indicated it. How had he kept the disability unlisted on his official records? *Why* keep it hidden?

And why hadn't Maggie's employer prepared her before she'd flown across the country to rescue him? More than that—what the hell had her employer been thinking by letting Blake come to New York alone? Had he actually expected his nephew—a man who couldn't see, for God's sake—to track down the woman who'd disappeared from a New York hotel room two days ago?

That the woman was Blake's sister was even more reason not to have sent him. Caring too much led to carelessness. Which, Maggie thought, was probably why Blake was handcuffed to a radiator.

But at least his blindness explained why her employer had insisted that she bring the dog.

"You didn't know," Blake said.

Maggie worked at the lock, pulling herself out of assignment mode and slipping back into the deferential courtesy required by her newest occupation: household management and personal security.

Which, she'd often thought, was just a nice way of saying that she was a butler with a gun.

She popped the first cuff, moved on to the second. "Mr. Ames-Beaumont must have considered your blindness irrelevant to my objective, sir."

"Is it relevant?"

"No, sir." She had to get Blake out of here, either way.

"Sir?" His faint smile didn't soften his strong features. The beginnings of a dark beard shadowed his jaw. His nose, Maggie thought, would have done a Stoic emperor proud. "If you are calling me 'sir,' then you must be the recently acquired—and, according to Uncle Colin, the already indispensable—Winters."

There was no point in correcting him. She'd been called more offensive names before. And she didn't know why Ames-Beaumont had taken to calling her "Winters," but considering the salary he paid her, she'd decided that he could address her however he wished.

The billionaire owner of Ramsdell Pharmaceuticals had high standards for his employees—and the closer to his family those employees were, the higher those standards were.

And he'd called her indispensable. Not easily disposed of and replaced. She'd never been that before.

But she couldn't afford to acknowledge the warm glow the secondhand praise brought, or the despair that it would change.

Yes, "Winters" was much better than what he'd soon be calling her.

"You are correct, sir." Despite the tightening of her throat, her voice remained even. "I am."

"Of course you are. And, of course, when we finally meet, I am like this." Blake gestured at himself with his free hand. "Do you know why you've found me half-naked? Do you know what this is?"

Finally meet? He'd said that as if they'd communicated before. Maggie was certain they hadn't. Blake had been in Britain since she'd begun working for his uncle three months ago. Before that, he'd traveled as often and as extensively as she had, but they'd never been in the same place at the same time—with one exception, four years ago. Maggie hadn't seen him then; she would have remembered. And he couldn't have seen her.

So whatever he meant by "finally," it had little to do with her. More likely, it referenced a conversation between him and his uncle—perhaps the one where she'd been described as indispensable. "I don't know, sir. What is this?"

"This is karma. This is every negative thing I've done, coming back to take a big bite of my ass."

The tightness in her throat eased. She strove to match the light tone his response invited. "That is unfortunate. Particularly as, in my professional opinion, the consequences of your actions are worse than you imagine."

"Why do you say that, Winters?"

"Because you are much more than *half*-naked, sir. And although I have many talents, protecting you from mystical karmic forces is not one of them."

He tilted his head, as if weighing that. "So chances are, I'll lose my shorts before we're done."

She ignored the little jolt in her stomach as his smile widened, carving crescents beside his mouth. In the humid air, his overlong hair had curled over his forehead and at his neck and ears. Combined with the smile, his dishevelment was unexpectedly appealing.

The job, Maggie. "We'll try to avoid that, sir." Though unlocking the cuffs required touch rather than sight, she focused on her fingers. "Your uncle sends his regrets that he wasn't able to come."

"I could hardly expect a vampire to catch an early-morning flight to New York."

Perhaps not a normal vampire, no. Even if one could rise from his daily sleep, he'd burst into flames at the touch of the sun. But Colin Ames-Beaumont wasn't a normal vampire, and so he could have come—but his fiancée couldn't travel during the day, and the vampire would never leave his partner unprotected.

"I was the most expedient option," Maggie explained.

"How fortunate for me."

Fortune had nothing to do with it. After reading the e-mail, she'd convinced Ames-Beaumont to send her, citing the same qualifications that had led him to hire her: a level head, weapons expertise, and a history of successful troubleshooting missions.

But Maggie hadn't mentioned the "You can stop me, Brunhilda" written in the e-mail beneath the brownstone's address, or that she had a very good idea who'd done this to Blake.

She grazed her fingers over Blake's inner wrist as she opened the second cuff. He was perspiring in the stifling room, and his skin was warm. Warm, but not hot—and so not belonging to a shape-shifted demon acting as a decoy.

Blake's large hand caught hers. It was difficult to remember that his eyes were sightless when he stared into hers with such intensity. "It's good to know that you're who you say, too."

Maggie didn't point out that she'd said her name was Winters. "There's a needle mark on the inside of your elbow."

Blake released her hand. "He took blood."

That was . . . strange. "How much?" She didn't think it had been *too* much; Blake's color was good beneath his tan. "Can you walk? Were you drugged?"

"Yes. Some sort of sedative." Blake lifted his jaw, exposing a swelling on his neck the size of a bee sting. "I was on the sidewalk outside my hotel. He pushed me into a taxi, told the driver I was drunk. I blacked out after that."

And his abductor hadn't tried to avoid being seen. Not a good sign. There were three primary reasons a criminal didn't hide his identity: he wanted to be caught, he assumed he'd never be punished . . . or he already knew he wouldn't get out alive.

"'He'? You're sure? And not a demon or a vampire?"

"Yes. Male. Human."

That's what she'd been afraid of. Demons were forbidden to physically harm humans, and so couldn't do anything except tempt and bargain. Vampires weren't bound by the same rules, but were helpless during the daylight hours.

But a human could be dangerous at any time—especially if it was the man Maggie suspected it was.

She prayed it wasn't James. If it wasn't, that meant she hadn't made the wrong decision three years ago when she'd let him go. But if James had sent her that e-mail, if he'd abducted Katherine . . . she might have to *really* kill him this time.

And then flee to save her own life. When Ames-Beaumont discovered her deception and her connection to the man who'd endangered his family, the vampire would kill her.

After she sent his nephew home in one piece, perhaps he'd make it quick. And if she found Katherine, maybe Ames-Beaumont would let Maggie go.

Or at least give her a head start.

"Your clothes are in one of the other bedrooms," she said, and stood. "Let's get you dressed and head out."

"Did someone come with you?" Blake asked.

Maggie glanced over her shoulder. Inside the bedroom, Blake was hitching his jeans up over a backside that, even chewed up by karma, still looked damn good. With his tall, leanly muscled build, *all* of him looked good.

But not flawless. A puckered scar marred his upper left shoulder. There hadn't been a scar in front, so the bullet hadn't punched through. Removing it would've required surgery, yet there were no gunshot wounds or hospital stays listed in his medical history.

According to his profile and the pile of write-ups from his supervisors, Blake did nothing at Ramsdell Pharmaceuticals but dick around behind his desks and research stations. According to his body, he did much more than that.

Maggie wasn't surprised by the evidence his body offered. Although she hadn't anticipated his blindness, she'd assumed there was more to Geoffrey Blake than his frequent transfers between Ramsdell's international subsidiaries suggested. Even if nepotism and family connections had played a part in Blake's employment history, Ames-Beaumont would never have relied on an incompetent man to lead the search for Katherine.

So Geoffrey Blake wouldn't be inept—and no stranger to dangerous situations.

"No," Maggie finally answered. "Except for a dog, I came alone."

Blake cocked his head before giving it a shake. To Maggie, his silence seemed to be of confusion rather than just caution.

Or was it disorientation? She continued, "We'll have your blood tested to make sure the drug—"

"No." Blake turned, pushing his dark hair back off his forehead. "The Ramsdell offices in New York don't have labs. We don't send my blood anywhere else. I'm fine."

She couldn't blame him for his paranoia, not after he'd already had his blood stolen. "Very well. Are you ready?"

As an answer, Blake walked unerringly toward her. Guided by the direction of her voice, Maggie guessed. When he drew close and stopped, she had to look up at him. That didn't happen often, whether she was in boots or bare feet.

Her gaze skipped from his knees to his ribs to his throat. A single blow would eliminate her height disadvantage.

But taking him out wasn't necessary; getting him out was. "Have you trained with guide dogs?"

His expression tightened, but she couldn't read anything in his face. "Yes. Uncle Colin sent one with you?"

"In a manner of speaking." Maggie backed into the hallway and called out, "Sir Pup!"

The hellhound trotted into view and clambered up the

stairs, his tongues lolling from each of his three enormous heads.

"We need the harness," Maggie said as he reached the landing. "You'll escort Mr. Blake downstairs and to our vehicle."

Sir Pup brushed past her hip and padded into the bedroom, his black fur gleaming over heavy muscle. His middle head looked Blake up and down. His right examined the room, and with his left, he turned to glance over his shoulder at Maggie.

She had no doubt that the expression pulling at his lips and exposing razor-edged teeth was a grin.

Her eyes narrowed. "You won't take him anywhere but to the vehicle and through the airport," she ordered. "And you won't *leave* him anywhere, either."

The hellhound's grin lengthened. Oh, damn. Most likely, she'd just added another idea to whatever mischief had already been percolating in his heads.

She returned her gaze to Blake and frowned. His skin had paled to a sickly gray. When he weaved on his feet, she stepped forward and caught his elbow.

"Mr. Blake?"

He visibly gathered himself. His chest rose on a long breath before he echoed, "Sir Pup?"

Maggie began to nod, then realized Blake wouldn't see it. "Yes."

"The *hellhound*? The one that my uncle watches from time to time?"

Actually, it was the other way around. Sir Pup was the companion to Ames-Beaumont's closest friend, and it was true that the vampire sometimes let the hellhound stay in his mansion. But it was the hellhound who watched over Ames-Beaumont; Sir Pup helped Maggie protect the house on those days the vampire succumbed to his sleep.

Demons were the only real threat to Ames-Beaumont while he slept, and they had nothing to fear from Maggie's gun—but Sir Pup's venom could paralyze a demon, and his massive jaws could easily rip one apart.

Maggie was not willing to reveal the details of Ames-Beaumont's security, however—even to his nephew. She said only, "Yes."

"In his demon form?"

He wasn't, thank goodness. But if Blake knew that Sir Pup *had* a demon form, then it was no wonder he'd been so pale a moment ago. Maggie was used to the three heads, but she didn't think she'd ever be comfortable with the giant, terrifying hound he could become.

"No. Right now he looks like a three-headed black Labrador." A very large black Lab. When Maggie knelt beside the hellhound, her eyes were level with his shoulder. "Once we're outside, he'll shape-shift back to one head. Sir Pup, the harness?"

The guide apparatus appeared in her hand. Sir Pup's invisible, formless hammerspace allowed him to store almost any object, but even a hellhound couldn't make a retriever-sized harness fit over a bear-sized torso.

"And shrink, please," Maggie said, rolling her eyes. The hellhound was being a pain in the ass by forcing her to ask him to shift into a smaller form.

Probably, she thought, so that Blake wondered exactly how big the hellhound *had* been. Though Sir Pup was friendly enough to be considered a bad hellhound by Hell's standards, he still enjoyed making people uneasy. He just had a better sense of humor than most hellhounds—and was less likely to tear out throats first, and eat the rest later.

Or so Maggie had heard. She'd never been to Hell, and so she'd never met any other hellhounds. If her luck was good—and if every negative thing she'd done in her life didn't land her in the Pit as soon as she bit the big one—she never would.

And if her luck was very good, she'd never run into another demon, either. After discovering that her previous employer was one, she'd had enough of them to last her a lifetime.

She adjusted the last harness strap and gave Sir Pup a scratch behind the ears of his left head. His dark eyes glowed faintly crimson before rolling back in ecstasy. A freakishly powerful and terrifying hellhound, sure—but pettings and food were two things guaranteed to make him more biddable.

"Don't leave him anywhere," Maggie murmured, "and I'll see that Ames-Beaumont buys out a butcher shop for you."

Apparently satisfied with that bribe, Sir Pup pranced to Blake's side. Blake curled his fingers around the harness handle.

"Why would it be a problem if he *does* lead me out to the middle of nowhere? You'll be there."

Blake had heard her? There was obviously nothing wrong with his ears. "I won't be," Maggie said, moving into the hall and gesturing for Sir Pup to follow her down the stairs. "I'm taking you to the airport. He'll accompany you on the plane."

"What plane?"

Maggie stopped beside the front door and glanced through the window. Her gaze skipped from vehicle to vehicle, from person to person. She didn't recognize anyone, and no one tripped the instinctual alarm in her gut that, over the years, she'd learned to trust.

Of course, it had let her down a few times, so she kept her hand on her gun.

"Sir Pup, you have too many heads," she reminded the hellhound before answering Blake. "I'll charter a plane to take you back to San Francisco. Mr. Ames-Beaumont can look after you while I—"

"Not a chance," Blake said.

"—find your sister," Maggie finished over him.

"Find her where? Do you have information about where he's taken her that I don't?"

She opened the door. "No."

Not yet, anyway.

Chapter Two

Once they hit the sidewalk, Geoff got his first look at Maggie Wren in four years. His first look in person, anyway. A little over three months ago, he'd seen her picture in the file his uncle had sent along with the rest of her history. He'd recognized the woman immediately, her pale eyes. They'd been impossible to forget, considering the last time he'd seen them it had been over the barrel of her gun just before she'd squeezed the trigger. She'd been a CIA operative carrying out a mission in Darfur—both of them a long way from home.

Where her home had been, exactly, he wasn't sure. Abandoned as a child, she'd been moved around the foster system until she'd found a steady home at the age of twelve. From there, she'd gone into the military and had been recruited early into the CIA. For years, she'd been based in D.C., but had been away on assignments most of the time.

Her transition back to civilian life hadn't been smooth. She'd lived in with her last employer, a congressman—and a demon. After she'd learned what the congressman was, she'd left his employ and taken a position with his uncle Colin.

Geoff hadn't known her name until his uncle had sent over her file for his records.

And he didn't know if she called the house she'd recently bought in San Francisco, not far from his uncle's mansion, home. And whether buying it was defense against his uncle, or a signal that she was settling in for the ride. After all, she'd taken the job with his uncle, knowing what *he* was.

And so Geoff held out hope it wasn't just another job to her.

Just going by appearances, the job suited her. Even Bilsworth, the majordomo who'd lorded over the family's British estate since Geoff had been in short pants, couldn't have faulted the precise roll of pale blond hair at her nape, the starched white shirt, or the black waistcoat and jacket. The knife-edge crease in her black trousers had withstood travel and the New York humidity.

There was something inhuman about that sort of rigid neatness, but Geoff couldn't call it demonic.

Calling her a Valkyrie might have fit, though. She was taller than he'd thought. Between her height and the hair, he understood why her fellow operatives had nicknamed her Bullet-Eating Brunhilda.

Rather, he understood the Brunhilda part. He assumed the bullets were another story, buried in a classified file that he hadn't yet seen.

A man on the sidewalk glanced at Maggie's face as he walked past them. Geoff couldn't read her expression. Not once since they'd come outside had she shown any emotion.

She had been surprised by his blindness, but by now she'd covered it. He could imagine what she'd been thinking: *What the hell is a blind man doing here?*

There were two answers to that. The short explanation went: He wasn't blind. He just couldn't see through his own eyes.

The explanation for that was the long one, about Lucifer and the demons who'd waged a second war upon Heaven, and the man who'd brought an end to the battle by killing a Chaos dragon with his sword. The man had become a Guardian, an angelic protector. There were more Guardians, but it was the sword that had shaped the Ames-Beaumont and Ramsdell—and eventually the Blake—families.

That sword, changed by the dragon's blood and imbued with the dragon's power, had ended up in the home of Geoff's ancestor. Two hundred years before, Uncle Colin and Geoff's many-times-over great-grandfather, Anthony Ramsdell, had performed a blood brother ritual with it, and the sword had tainted their blood. Later, Geoff's many-times-over great-grandmother—Uncle Colin's sister—had also been cut by the sword. Both his great-grandparents had been slightly altered by the taint in their blood—and so had their children. Now and then, one of his relations was born with a bit of the uncanny in them, possessing empathic abilities, flashes of telepathy, telemetry, or foresight.

Geoff's parents had been distant cousins; both could trace their bloodlines back to the many-times-over great-grandparents. So the taint had combined, multiplied, and he and Katherine had ended up the uncanniest of the uncanny.

Geoff had been born without pupils and with the ability to see through the eyes of anyone near him—but his connection to his sister was stronger. He could link to Katherine's eyes whenever he wanted, no matter how distant she was.

But her eyes hadn't been open since the evening before. That likely meant she wasn't awake.

That likely meant she'd been drugged. Whether just to keep her quiet or because her abductor was aware of their connection, Geoff wasn't certain. But considering that only their parents and Uncle Colin knew about the link between them, Geoff thought it must be to keep her quiet.

When Katherine woke up, she'd find a way to let him know where she'd been taken. In the meantime, Maggie Wren's expertise would be useful.

If she hadn't been involved in Katherine's disappearance.

Since receiving the picture, he had been hoping to see her again, just to *see*. He'd been fascinated by her. Had barely resisted the impulse to pepper his uncle with questions about her like an infatuated schoolboy.

Not that it would have surprised anyone if he'd shouted his interest. The men in his family had a history of obsessing over women from afar.

Geoff was the first who hadn't even met the woman yet.

And he hadn't imagined their meeting would be like this. But it was probably best that he found out now if she'd betray the family.

He watched her through the hellhound's eyes before he was forced to move on to someone else's. Now that Sir Pup only had one head, the sensation wasn't as bloody room-spinning as when Geoff had first connected with the hellhound's mind. His vision was so clear and sharp, however, that it made Geoff's brain ache.

Then there were Maggie's eyes.

Geoff couldn't keep up with them. He was used to taking in as much detail as he could in a quick glance, but this was beyond his scope. She constantly changed her focus; her gaze was continually moving. Everyone they passed was given a speedy head-to-toe examination, and she used every available reflective surface to keep watch behind them.

He had her eyes, but without her brain behind it, looking through them was almost as dizzying as seeing through the hellhound's. And he could usually navigate busy sidewalks and streets by knowing his position relative to the people he looked through, but he couldn't do that with Maggie. For the first time, he was grateful for the harness and the dog at his side. Uncle Colin had sent Sir Pup to protect him, but Geoff was just glad he wasn't tripping over curbs trying to follow her.

He slipped into the eyes of the man walking behind them, instead.

The bloke was staring at her ass. Jesus, Geoff couldn't

blame the man. From the top of her head to her endless legs, Maggie Wren was worth a second look—then a third and fourth. But still, there were lines. You looked, then looked away. You didn't stare down even the finest ass like a wolfhound at a dinner table.

Geoff stopped, turned. The man's attention lifted to his own forbidding expression. Geoff waited until the pervert zeroed in on his solidly blue eyes before grinning. The pervert's gaze snapped to the left, and he walked hurriedly on.

"Is something wrong, Mr. Blake?"

"No." He used her eyes again. Her field of vision had narrowed slightly, and was shadowed at the upper edge, as if her brows had lowered.

She looked at Geoff's eyes, then his mouth. Then she was away again, taking sharp, quick glances over his shoulder at the people walking behind them, focusing hard on their faces. She went back to him, then made a lingering—for Maggie—perusal of a man passing her.

The pervert, Geoff realized. She studied the back of the man's neck, his knee.

Geoff jumped into another person, then another, until he found someone looking at her face. He saw her eyes, the gray cold and dangerous, before she slipped a pair of rimless dark glasses from her inside pocket. A hard smile touched her lips as the pervert looked back at her, met her eyes, and hastily glanced away.

And there she was. Geoff recognized that expression. There was the woman who could slip a knife into a man or put a bullet in his head. The woman Geoff had watched do both.

He pushed into her mind again as they resumed walking. Her shielded gaze ran over everyone she saw—and hesitated very briefly on their knees, their hands, their stomachs, and their necks.

Not just looking for threats, he realized. She was searching for their vulnerable points. Every person they passed, she lined up as a target.

But she'd been out of the CIA for three years now. Not enough time to unlearn what a lifetime had taught her?

Maybe it could never go.

The SUV she'd rented was black and boxy, and the backseats had been removed. The harness disappeared from under Geoff's hand when Maggie opened the rear door. Sir Pup hopped in, lay down, and then grew to the same size he'd been when Geoff had first seen him—through Maggie's eyes—on the stairs. When the hellhound stretched out, his body took up most of the cargo area.

Maggie swung open the passenger door and took Geoff's arm. He let her help him in. She was smart, she was observant, and she knew there were more things in heaven and earth than fit in the average human's philosophy. If Geoff proved too capable, she might suspect that he wasn't as blind as he appeared.

He waited until she'd climbed into her seat. "We need to return to my hotel—"

"It was on our route from the airport, so we've already stopped. Sir Pup has your things in his hammerspace." Through her eyes, he saw his own puzzled expression. She continued, "It's like a psychic storage space."

Geoff nodded. He'd heard demons and Guardians had something similar. "Is my computer in there?"

He immediately felt a familiar weight on his lap. Geoff searched for his headset, his fingers moving along the edge of the laptop. "There was a microphone and—Ah, thank you," he finished when the headset landed in his palm. A convenient thing, that hammerspace.

Maggie's gaze left him as she pulled onto the street, but he didn't need her eyes for this. With a combination of touch and voice commands, he searched the computer for the files he wanted . . . and was mildly surprised when he found them.

"Did they toss my hotel room, take anything?"

"If they did, they weren't messy about it." The car slowed. A look through her eyes showed a yellow traffic light before her gaze moved to his profile. "Did the one who drugged you say anything about Miss Blake? Anything about why he'd taken her, or who he was?"

"No. But a few hours before he grabbed me, hotel security e-mailed this to me. It was from the day that Katherine disappeared from her room." He angled his laptop, showed her the photo he'd pulled up.

Maggie briefly glanced at the screen. Then she looked at the picture again and didn't take her eyes away.

Through them, Geoff saw the same face a taxi driver had seen just before Geoff had blacked out. The same face someone outside the brownstone had seen, only moments after he'd taken Geoff's blood and left him handcuffed to a radiator.

He saw the face Maggie did, but he had no idea what she *saw* when she looked at the picture. A friend, a former lover—an enemy? Or just a man she happened to have worked with in the past?

"This is the hotel elevator. He got off on Katherine's floor," Geoff said.

Maggie blinked once, slowly. Her voice was flat. "That's a good lead. I'll follow up on it."

"While I'm flying out of here to safety? You might want to reconsider. When I didn't check in last night, what do you suppose was the first thing Uncle Colin asked his fiancée to do?" When Maggie didn't answer, he continued, "I'd bet he asked Savi to pull my phone records, then hack my e-mail accounts. She'd find out what I'd received in the past couple of hours, who contacted me, where I might have gone. And she would have found this picture."

Maggie's eyes closed, then opened. She stared ahead at a green light.

"And with Savi's photographic memory, it wouldn't take much for her to connect that face with the one in *this* picture."

The second photograph was from a political rally in Washington, D.C., only a few months before Maggie had resigned from the CIA. The original photo had been enlarged to show Maggie—slightly blurry but recognizable—

standing in the far background, wearing a dark suit and a military-straight bearing. Beside her was the same man from the first photo.

A horn blared behind them. Maggie tore her gaze from the computer screen and drove through the intersection.

Geoff pushed into the hellhound's mind. Pain spiked through his head, but he was in luck: Sir Pup was watching her, and so Geoff could, too. He could see her indecision, the rapid beat of her pulse, the tension in the faint lines at the corners of her mouth.

But she wasn't denying a connection to the man. And, thank God, she wasn't trying to lie to him.

He asked quietly, "How did you know where to find me?"

She hesitated, then said, "I got a tip."

"From . . . ?"

Her gaze flew to the picture.

Had she forgotten he couldn't see that silent admission? He wouldn't remind her. "Do you think he'll contact you again?"

"Yes."

"Then you want me with you, Winters. Right now, I'm the only person standing between you and my uncle."

Her lips firmed, as if in frustration, before curving into a reluctant smile. "Then let's go find your sister, Mr. Blake."

Chapter Three

According to the ISP, the e-mail she'd received that morning had been sent from southern New Jersey. Maggie doubted James was still in the same place, but it gave her a direction to go until she had more information.

A direction, but no solid destination—and reaching the same area he'd been in when he'd contacted her meant spending hours on the road. It had been years since Maggie had tried to leave the city on a Friday afternoon, but she doubted they'd be driving faster than a crawl. So there was business to take care of first: food and clothes.

She asked Sir Pup for jeans and one of the shirts they'd taken from Blake's hotel room. They fell, still neatly folded, into her lap.

She glanced over at Blake. He'd called Ames-Beaumont and spoken briefly with the vampire, and was now carrying out the rest of their conversation via instant messaging—Blake typing, and then listening to the response through his headset.

Anxiety tightened her stomach. Blake had said he'd stand between her and Ames-Beaumont, but it wouldn't be for Maggie's sake. Blake wanted to find his sister, and Maggie was their one connection to James. Blake's offer of protection wouldn't last any longer than it took to find Katherine.

But even up to that point, his offer meant very little. Ames-Beaumont was family, and the most powerful vampire in the world—and Blake didn't owe anything to Maggie. If his uncle came after her, Blake would be an idiot to stand between them.

So her goals hadn't changed, even if Blake was now coming with her; she'd keep him safe and find Katherine. And if she managed to do both—and if the vampire didn't hold her as responsible for James's actions as she did herself—maybe Ames-Beaumont would let her go.

It had become her mantra: maybe he'd let her go.

Her fingers clenched on the steering wheel. God, she didn't want this mess. She wanted her job. Before that e-mail, everything had been good. Her new life was insane, full of vampires and Guardians, and her employer was an eccentric, to say the least—but she had been, for the first time she could remember, happy. The world had become strange and new, but she'd understood the people around her, what motivated them, and she'd finally felt as if she fit somewhere. And that feeling had been bone-deep.

And one decision from her past had shattered it.

Blake clicked his laptop shut and slid off the headset. When the computer disappeared, Maggie tossed the clothes onto his lap.

His palms swept over the material, as if identifying it. His brows lifted. "Is this a hint? A shower would be better."

"You don't have an odor, sir," Maggie said.

Sir Pup made a doubtful noise in the back. Relieved to have a distraction from the bleak thoughts circling in her head, Maggie glanced into the rearview mirror. The hellhound had covered the end of his nose with his massive forepaw.

Maggie didn't fight to hold her straight expression.

Blake couldn't see her reaction, so she could relax, just a little. She'd keep her responses appropriately formal, but *she* didn't have to be.

"*I* cannot detect any odor, Sir Pup," she said, before looking at Blake again. "It's to ward against any bugs—tracking or listening devices—that he might have inserted into your clothing."

Blake fingered the collar of his shirt. "You think he'd do that?"

"I would."

That must have convinced him. As she pulled into a fast-food lot, Blake shucked his jeans and shirt. When he reached for the folded jeans, Maggie shook her head. "Your shorts, too, Mr. Blake. And quickly, or the girl at the drive-thru window is going to get a good look."

Sir Pup rolled over onto his back, chuffing great bursts of air. The hellhound version of a laugh.

It apparently amused Blake, too. He wore a smile as he hooked his fingers under the waistband. "Is this really about bugs? Or are *you* planning to take a peek?"

She didn't need to. She assumed it hadn't been a pair of socks filling out his oh-so-happy undershorts. She averted her gaze when he lifted his ass from the seat and worked them off. "We're on the trail of your abducted sister, Mr. Blake. What kind of woman would I be if I did that?"

"One I'd like to get to know better."

Maggie's fingers flew to her lips to hold in her laugh. Oh, he was dangerous. She could end up liking him. And liking led to caring, caring to carelessness. She couldn't afford that.

And he already knew enough about her. More than he should.

She wadded up his clothes and shoved them into the trash can sitting beside the drive-thru menu. The smiley faces didn't seem so smug crowded in with the discarded coffee cups. Poor little guys.

The menu was loaded with junk. Not a problem, except that she would be motionless for the next several hours. She'd never liked feeling weighted down when she couldn't move enough to work it off. "How hungry are you, Mr. Blake? We won't stop again until later tonight, so order as much as you think you'll need."

Blake paused with his boxer-briefs on and his jeans halfway up one leg. Though he was bent over at the waist, there wasn't a crease or a bulge anywhere that wasn't muscle. "I could easily eat three hamburgers."

Of course he could. Maggie tripled that for the hellhound and ordered coffee and a fruit-and-yogurt for herself.

She paid cash. James might be trying to track their movements, and she wouldn't make it easy for him. Hopefully, though, he'd make it easy for her.

You can stop me.

It wasn't a question or a challenge. It wasn't a plea. Just a statement.

But how would she stop him? And why *her*?

She tapped her fingers against the steering wheel, pondering it. By mutual agreement, she and James had decided not to contact one another again—and, despite the circumstances, they had parted on good terms. Her gut said this wasn't about revenge.

What, then? Was it just coincidence that his path had crossed with hers?

Maggie couldn't make herself believe that.

Was it about Ames-Beaumont? Was James acting on his own, or had he been hired? And if someone was paying him, had James told them of his connection to her . . . and to Ames-Beaumont?

But why go after his family and not make any demands?

Frowning, she glanced at Blake. Where had he gotten that picture of her and James? And who had told Blake that the faces in the two photos matched? Not Savi, Ames-Beaumont's fiancée. If she'd hacked Blake's e-mail, she wouldn't have seen the picture from hotel security until after Blake had been taken—so they hadn't had an opportunity to compare notes.

So Maggie was missing a step, not seeing a connection

somewhere. And since the hellhound was watching, she couldn't use the interrogation method she was most familiar with: aiming her gun at him. That meant digging. Finagling.

Which also meant dropping a little more of the formality. Butlers did not initiate conversations, yet Maggie needed to. "You're not what I expected, Mr. Blake."

"I gathered that."

"Not your blindness. Not *just* that," she admitted. "I've looked at your dossier."

"Have you?" Both his voice and his expression were neutral.

"Yes." She had to look away from him to take the bags at the window. She passed the first to him, then set the others on the console between them. "It's full of reprimands, complaints, transfers. You've been shuttled around Ramsdell for almost fifteen years."

"I'm not very good at my job."

She recognized a practiced answer when she heard it—a cover story. "Except that, every time you've been transferred to a new branch, a problem has quietly gone away. In London, it was embezzlement by a senior executive. Someone in the Paris labs selling research to a competitor. Using Ramsdell warehouses to smuggle cocaine in Florida. A problem with Ramsdell shipments getting to Doctors Without Borders in Darfur." Those were only a few, but she didn't need to go on. And if she wasn't mistaken, there was a hint of surprise—and relief—in his face now. "You go in, act the doofus who yanks out the disability card at every opportunity and lets everyone think you're getting by on the family name. And while whoever you're after is feeling secure, because they don't think they'll need to pull the wool over the eyes of a blind man, you're finding what you need to get rid of them. The pattern speaks for itself. Enough that when we heard about your sister, and Mr. Ames-Beaumont said that you were flying in to look for her, I thought it was a good move."

"But you don't think that now?"

"Now I'm wondering how you manage it."

"You don't want to know, Winters."

"I'd tell you, but then I'd have to kill you?" She let her amusement bleed into her voice, so that he would know she was smiling.

"Something like that." He didn't return the smile. "At least, my uncle would seriously consider it."

A shiver raced down her spine. Whatever he was hiding, it was different from the knowledge that Ames-Beaumont was a vampire. And there were only two reasons Ames-Beaumont would kill without a thought: either his fiancée was endangered, or his family was. He would kill to protect the community of vampires he led, but only after deliberation. With his heart and his family, however, there were no questions asked, no shades of gray.

Since Savi was safe back in San Francisco, chances were that whatever Blake wasn't revealing could threaten the family.

How incredible it must be to be a part of a family like that. And how terrifying to be considered their enemy.

She held herself steady, pulled back onto the street, and began to make her way to the Manhattan Bridge. As she'd expected, traffic was crawling.

And she was no good at finagling. "Where did the second picture come from?"

"Your previous employer's files."

Maggie shook her head. "The agency would have no reason—"

"Not the CIA. Congressman Stafford."

A knot of dread tightened in her chest. Stafford knew she'd had national security and intelligence experience. But her references wouldn't have given him that photo. He must have gotten it from another Washington connection . . . but *who*? "Where'd he get it?"

"We don't know."

And they couldn't ask him. Stafford had been slain by the Guardians three months ago.

Blake unwrapped one of his burgers and bit in. When Sir Pup whined in the back, Maggie remembered to do the same for him. She twisted her arm back between the seats. Hot breath brushed her fingers before Sir Pup gently lifted the hamburger; even as she heard him gulp it down, two more whines came from the right and left. A hellhound's appetite, in stereo.

She was in the middle of unwrapping the fourth when Blake said, "Tell me about him, Winters."

"Stafford?"

There wasn't much to tell. Thomas Stafford had been a charming politician and the perfect employer until he'd tried to pin a murder on her. But it could have been worse. Even if he'd successfully framed her, a life in prison would have been better than if he'd maneuvered her into a bargain that bound her in service to him. A bargain that, if not fulfilled, would have trapped her soul in a freezing wasteland between Hell and the Chaos realm.

Yes, she'd take prison over eternal torment any day. Luckily, the Guardians had saved her from either fate.

"Not Stafford. The man in the photo."

So Blake wasn't going to finagle, either. But Maggie could deflect just as well as he had.

"If I tell you, then I have to—"

"His name is Trevor James," Blake said. "He served with you in the CIA from the date of your recruitment and training until three years ago—when, under orders, you assassinated him. It was your last assignment; you retired after that."

Her hands, her brain felt limp. Her voice was hollow. "How do you know this?"

"You were investigated by the Guardians and vetted by my uncle. He passed the information to me, for my records. Do you think he would allow you anywhere near his home if he wasn't certain of you? To have any access to his family?"

One of Sir Pup's heads nudged her shoulder, knocking her out of her stupor. She fed him another burger, and forced her mind to work again.

The deep vetting wasn't a surprise. *How* deep they'd

managed to get shocked her, but she couldn't focus on that yet. She was still trying to figure out why Ames-Beaumont would have sent her file to Blake for *his* records. She wasn't a Ramsdell employee.

But maybe, to Ames-Beaumont and to Blake, there wasn't a difference.

Sir Pup whined again. Maggie ignored him, trying to read as much as she could in Blake's face each time she took her gaze off the road. There wasn't much to go on. For a man who had never seen another face—or his own—he had a highly developed sense of how much an expression could give away.

"Vampire communities have an enforcer," she said, feeling her way through it. "Someone who protects the community from outside threats and enforces the rules within the community. In San Francisco, Mr. Ames-Beaumont fulfills that function. And that's what you are—the Ramsdell enforcer. You protect Ramsdell Pharmaceuticals."

Maggie realized that wasn't *quite* right as soon as she'd finished. He wasn't protecting the business itself, and that was why Ames-Beaumont had sent Blake her file. It was about protecting the family—every aspect of it—and Ramsdell Pharmaceuticals just happened to be the family's primary financial resource. Blake probably had files on every employee working at any of the family's estates.

Blake didn't confirm or deny it. He wiped his mouth with a paper napkin and asked, "Which direction are we going?"

"South. Eventually." Slowly.

He nodded. "I received information last evening. Katherine was headed south. She's in a large caravan."

"An RV?" His British accent, which she'd barely been able to discern until now, had become stronger. Did that mean he was suppressing an emotion, or loosening up? "A motor home in August isn't going to be easy to pin down."

"No, it isn't."

Sir Pup whined, and she gave him a quelling glance in

the rearview mirror. All six of his eyes were focused on the bag sitting on the console. Three one-track minds, but it was all greed. A hellhound didn't need food; he just liked to eat.

"Just a minute, Sir Pup." She didn't want to be distracted. "Where did you get this info?"

"Would you believe your friend talked in front of me?"

Would she? James was inviting her to come find him—stop him. But to blab in front of someone like a cartoon villain? "No. How do you know where she's headed?"

"Why did you pretend to kill him? Why didn't you carry out your assignment?"

She clenched her teeth. "You have my file, Mr. Blake. Why don't you tell me?"

"I've seen the kill order. I've seen the report you filed, saying the mission was completed. I've seen the forensic report, which stated that the charred chunk of flesh they'd found—which was all they'd been able to recover after you'd blown his house to hell—was a DNA match to James. But none of those forms tell me anything that happened between."

Her mouth fell open. A kill order *and* the follow-up reports? Those weren't kept electronically, weren't something Savi could have hacked. Someone had physically gone into CIA headquarters and copied records that she—or even her direct supervisor—wouldn't have had clearance to access. A Guardian, maybe—teleporting, or slipping through shadows.

"You've obviously no intention of giving me an answer," Blake said, but he didn't sound frustrated. He sounded relieved.

And his accent was still audible.

"Are you going to give one to me?"

"No." He smiled, and his eyes met hers, eerily direct. "But it's for your own protection."

"I could say the same." But more than that, she just couldn't—wouldn't—divulge classified information. Blake could poke around all he wanted. She wouldn't spill sensitive details about her job now, or fifty years from now. She pointed out, "And knowing what happened then doesn't change anything. We still have to stop him."

"Knowing how I discovered where Katherine was last night doesn't change anything, either. We still have to get her."

All right, she couldn't argue with that. Yet there must be another way. "Sir Pup, would you let me shoot him? Torture him for answers?"

Blake had a deep, rumbling laugh. The hellhound pushed one of his heads between the seats, his expression curious.

She sweetened the offer. "For a steak?"

Though she could barely see him behind Sir Pup's big head, she heard Blake say, "What did my uncle ask you to do if she threatened me?"

Instantly, Sir Pup's head shifted four times larger, his teeth serrated like knives. Scales rippled over his fur; barbed spikes ripped through, tipped with blood.

His eyes glowed with crimson hellfire and fixed on Maggie's hand, clenching the steering wheel. Cold sweat broke out over her skin. His mouth was gentle when his enormous jaws closed over her forearm, but she got the message.

She was trembling when he let her go. She hoped she didn't sound as terrified as she felt. "Thanks, Sir Pup. That's good to know."

The hellhound shifted back to his former size and snagged the fast-food bag from the console. He retreated into the back, giving her a clear view of Blake again.

His face was gray, his hands shaking as he pushed them through his hair.

"Christ, Maggie," he said. "I didn't know that he would—I shouldn't have asked him that. I'm sorry."

She nodded. She hadn't expected it, either. But she was glad Sir Pup's demon form hadn't just scared the shit out of her. Blake had obviously been just as—

Wait.

How the hell had Blake known what happened?

"You saw that. You saw him change." Her heart knocked

against her ribs. She stared at his solid-blue eyes, stunned—but couldn't deny the evidence. "You can *see*."

"I—" His eyes widened. His mouth closed. His jaw tightened. "You don't know that," he said flatly.

"I don't? Because I sure as hell—"

"No, Maggie. You don't. If *anyone* asks, you don't know. Not until we find Katherine. Not until the problem with James is settled."

"All right." She understood that. Her knowing was something that didn't go farther than this vehicle. Not even to Ames-Beaumont. Because if Ames-Beaumont learned of it while he was uncertain about her role in Katherine's kidnapping . . .

Maggie smiled grimly. It wouldn't be the first time someone had been killed for knowing too much. She stole a glance at Blake. His eyes were closed, and he was pressing his clenched fist to his forehead. If she had to guess, he was giving himself a heated telling-off.

But maybe, she thought, maybe he'd meant it when he'd offered to stand between her and Ames-Beaumont. *If* it came to that.

Not, of course, that she would let him. But it was still a good feeling.

Chapter Four

"She's awake," Blake said quietly.

Maggie blinked away her highway stare and glanced over at him. A few minutes ago, he'd been asleep. His eyes were still closed, but he'd raised his seat from its reclined position.

"She's moving slowly," he continued. "In the bedroom at the back of the caravan. She's not tied, but the door won't open. They've left her a basket of food, bottles of water. There are windows, and they've been darkened with some kind of film. She's waving. No one in the other cars is noticing. The setting sun is on the left."

"Heading south," Maggie said hoarsely. A shiver kept running up and down her spine.

He was seeing, she realized. He was looking through his sister's eyes.

Blake nodded. "On a divided highway. Two lanes each direction. The car behind them has South Carolina license plates. So does the one passing it."

And she and Blake were only halfway through New Jersey. The RV had at least twelve or thirteen hours on them.

But not as many hours as it could have had. Whoever had taken Katherine would have been farther if they'd driven straight through. They'd pulled over either to rest or to wait for someone.

"There's a water closet. The window doesn't open. She looks all right in the mirror. No bruises." The monotone recitation broke for an instant, and he laughed. "That's right, Kate, flip me the bird. She's got an injection site in her neck, the same as mine. They took blood, too. And she's looking at the toilet, so that's my cue to head out for a bit."

Maggie's heart pounded. She couldn't think of a thing to say.

Blake was silent for a few seconds. Then he told her, "She can't see through mine."

"Whose are you seeing through now?"

"Yours."

Maggie stared out the windshield. Sickness clawed at her stomach—she wasn't sure why. Revelations like these were one of the reasons why she'd taken a job with a vampire. She couldn't have gone back to normal life after finding out about dragons, or Guardians. She'd have always been looking, and wondering.

She drove and waited for the sick feeling to resolve. It finally did.

Her reaction wasn't in response to his ability, but the implications of it. Blake possessed a form of remote viewing. What nation wouldn't want to use that for intelligence gathering—or take steps to prevent it from being used *against* them?

Jesus. No wonder Ames-Beaumont was so obsessed with protecting his family. If he hadn't been, every government in the world would have been trying to exploit them—or destroy them.

"And this is the reason Miss Blake was taken," Maggie realized. "And it's why they haven't asked for a ransom. What can *she* do?"

She hadn't really expected an answer. And she didn't anticipate the ease with which Blake delivered it.

"She locates things," he said. "Items, not people."

That took a second to sink in. Once it did, Maggie frowned. "Then it could be anyone, looking for anything."

"No. It has to be someone with resources, access to information, and organized. To begin, they knew she was on holiday in America."

Maggie nodded. Yes, she'd have used the same opportunity—the target was alone and on foreign soil. "But not military. They wouldn't be heading down the interstate in an RV. Probably not a vampire, because he wouldn't need James to take Miss Blake, and he can't drive during the day."

"And there are at least two of them. Katherine was on the road when James was in New York last night." His long fingers tapped against his knees, and a thoughtful expression creased his brow. "It could be a demon driving, if James was the one who drugged her."

"You think it was a demon? We've got to call in the Guardians, then."

Blake turned his head, met her eyes. Using *her* vision, she realized, to know where to focus his.

"No," he said.

"We can't go up against—"

"A demon has to follow the Rules—no hurting humans, no denying their free will—so he can't do anything to us. If he's got vampires with him, we only move in to find Katherine during the day. James is our biggest concern, and Guardians wouldn't be able to do anything to *him*, because they've got to follow the Rules, too." Blake paused. "And we've got Sir Pup."

Which meant, Maggie guessed, that even though Ames-Beaumont worked closely with the Guardians, he hadn't told them about his family . . . and he didn't want to risk them finding out.

"Does anyone else know what you can do? What others in your family can do?"

"No one except Savi. A few others who've married into

the family. Uncle Colin has kept it that way for two hundred years."

Successfully? Maggie doubted that. Human nature was human nature; even someone like Ames-Beaumont couldn't squash it. "No one has put it to use? Either for money, or for the government?"

"Some of us have put it to use. We just don't tell anyone we're doing it. As for the money, no one in the family needs it." Blake leaned his head back, closed his eyes. "They've stopped. It's dark. She can't see much. Trees. A few small fires."

"A campground?" When he nodded, Maggie said, "We can catch up while they're stopped. Or at least get closer."

"That's—" Blake cut himself off, sat up straight. "They opened the door. There's James. And another man, standing behind him. Tall, dark hair. The wanker looks right out of *GQ*."

Blake flinched, once.

"The bloody bastard James drugged her. She's out again."

Around midnight, Maggie began alternating between a fixed stare at the highway and skipping her gaze around the interior of the car and searching the sides of the dark highway, all the while blinking rapidly. Her vision hadn't been in such a hyperactive mode since they'd left the Brooklyn street.

She was keeping herself awake, Geoff realized.

"We'll stop," he said. "You're knackered." And so was he, despite the nap he'd taken earlier.

"I'm on West Coast time. I can go longer."

"How early this morning did you get the e-mail?" Her silence told him it was very early. "We'll get a hotel room."

"Mr. Blake, I thought you'd never ask."

Geoff smiled, but damn if he didn't wish that he could see her face at that moment. She'd been overruled, yet was responding with humor. She'd held firm when he'd pressed for classified details about her orders to kill James. She was a woman he desperately wanted to know better.

And he might as well throw his cards on the table. "You only joke because you assume I don't think about you that way, Maggie. You're wrong."

That apparently surprised her, because she didn't reply—but he watched where her focus went: to his hands. She was a hands woman. And, remembering how her gaze had lingered on his bare stomach when he'd been handcuffed, and later, when he'd changed his clothing, he amended it to *a hands and abs woman.*

Her silence extended. She was looking at the road again, mostly. She glanced at the rearview mirror, once; Sir Pup lifted one of his heads and returned her gaze. The hellhound might appear lazy, Geoff thought, but was completely alert. Then her gaze returned to his hands, darted up to his mouth, and remained there until Geoff began to smile. Her attention flew back to the road.

He'd given her something to think about. And—thank God—she seemed to be thinking about it.

Unfortunately, he also had to push the issue in a direction that, if taken the wrong way, might spark her resistance. "And we are to share a room tonight."

But, no—Maggie didn't mistake him. "You don't trust me," she said.

"I don't trust you to not try resolving this on your own. If we're in separate rooms, you'll likely run off in the middle of the night and attempt to find Katherine alone."

"If we are in the same room, what's to stop me from handcuffing you to the bed and leaving?"

Sir Pup pushed one of his heads between the seats again, his ears pricked forward. Unease crawled over Geoff's skin until he heard the jingle of metal.

Maggie looked down and gave a short laugh when she spotted the handcuffs that had landed in her lap. "He thinks it's funny," she said. "And maybe even a good idea."

In Geoff's opinion, every good idea that involved Maggie and handcuffs wouldn't include Sir Pup. "Would he let you handcuff me and leave?"

"I don't know. He follows directions, but interprets them how he likes. If Mr. Ames-Beaumont told him to protect you—and Sir Pup agreed that you were safer handcuffed to a bed and away from James—he might not bite off my head for it."

Geoff tried to see Maggie through the hellhound again, but had to pull out when the three perspectives pushed his vision into a nauseating spin. She was scratching Sir Pup's ears, and his eyes were glowing with a soft red light.

Would the hellhound really hurt her? Or had the threat earlier been for show? Geoff had no doubt that his uncle had given Sir Pup orders to protect him—but the hellhound also apparently had a mind of his own. Like Maggie.

Suddenly, he liked the hellhound much better.

"Can you see through animals, Mr. Blake?"

"No." It wasn't a lie. Sir Pup couldn't be included among normal animals, and Geoff had never seen through any dog, horse, or cat.

"Just through people?"

"Yes. And no more 'Mr. Blake.' *I* am not your employer."

"Yes, sir." She was smiling; he caught the edge of her reflection in the rearview mirror. "I plan to shower with my eyes closed, Mr. Geoffrey."

"Right." Geoff sighed. "And now I wish doubly that you hadn't found out the truth."

Blake took the first shower while Maggie set up her computer and called San Francisco on her encrypted line.

To her relief, Savi was the one who answered it. Though Maggie liked Ames-Beaumont, she loved the young vampire he intended to marry. Maggie had never met anyone like Savi—who was as *genuine* as Savi. In her profession, that quality had been hard to come by, and Maggie adored her for it.

Not that she would ever be so unprofessional as to admit it.

After a few friendly inquiries about Maggie's and Blake's status, Savi got to work. Within minutes, all of the files Maggie had requested were being downloaded to her computer. She engaged the speakerphone so that she could use both hands to type; in the background, she could hear Savi's fingers flying at super-speed over her own keyboard.

After a few seconds, Savi gave a short "Woot!"

Maggie blinked. "What did you find?"

"Campground reservations. The entire state system is online. I'm in, so I'll start running the registered plates."

"*All* of them?"

"Why not?" She could easily imagine Savi's shrug. She'd seen it a million times, on both the young vampire and the brilliant geeks who made up the CIA's tech support. "Something might pop. A plate that doesn't match the vehicle make, or is listed as stolen." Savi snorted out a little laugh. "Stealing a motor home. That takes some balls."

"More brains than balls," Maggie said. "If it had been kept in storage, weeks might go by before the owner reports it missing."

"Good point." The clacking stopped. "Hey, Maggie . . . Colin's not here, but I can speak for both of us."

Her chest seemed to freeze. "Yes?"

"Katherine's still alive. Chances are, they'll keep her that way because they want something."

"Yes," Maggie agreed quietly. Her tongue felt numb. If she looked in the mirror, she was sure her face would be pale, her lips bloodless.

"So we're still cool now. And it's not that we don't trust—" Savi stopped. Started again with, "Geoff is good at what he does. And you were good at what you did."

"Killing people?"

"Getting them out of bad situations," Savi said. "Troubleshooting."

Usually by shooting whoever was causing the trouble. But Maggie wasn't going to argue. "All right."

"You know we've got the pictures."

She closed her eyes. "Yes."

"We wouldn't have hired you if we didn't trust you, and it helps that James led you to Geoff." The deep breath Savi took was audible over the speaker. "But if you betray that trust without good reason, I can't—*I won't*—protect you from Colin."

What was a good reason? But she only said, "I know. Thank you, Miss Murray."

"Jesus, Maggie, don't thank me. Just make it back, okay?" She sighed when Maggie didn't answer. "All right. I'm going to finish up here, and I'll shoot you everything I find when I've finished. Give Sir Pup a kiss good night for me."

Maggie disconnected and looked over at the hellhound, taking up one of the two king-sized beds. He lifted his middle head and licked his chops.

Maggie shook her head. "Not going to happen, pup."

The bathroom door opened. Blake came out, rubbing his hair with a towel and wearing a pair of pajama pants. The muscles in his chest and stomach flexed with each vigorous rub.

Maggie glanced away. Dammit. She hadn't even realized how often she'd looked him over until she tried to avoid doing it.

"Why 'thank you'?"

She turned, stared at him blankly. "What?"

"Savi said she wouldn't protect you. You said 'thank you.' How does that work?"

"I appreciate knowing where I stand."

Blake nodded and tossed the towel onto the bureau. "She was lying, though."

"She doesn't trust me?"

"She *would* stop him. Talk him out of it, if she could. And if she couldn't, she'd help you get a head start, complete with a new identity." The shrug of his shoulders did gorgeous things to his chest again. "But, of course, she can't tell you that."

"And you can?"

Small lines fanned from the corners of his eyes when he smiled. "I just did."

"Why?"

He didn't answer immediately. From her seat by the desk, she watched him settle on the bed with his long legs stretched out, his ankles crossed, and his shoulders propped by the pillows. He laced his fingers over his stomach.

She dragged her gaze away again. "Do you need a shirt, Mr. Blake? I believe Sir Pup has several more in his hammerspace."

"I'm comfortable, Winters." He grinned, and she was suddenly looking at his mouth.

Dammit. She stood and stripped out of her jacket and weapon harness. "*Why*, Mr. Blake?"

"I was in Darfur four years ago."

Though her back was turned to him, she could see him in the mirror. He was no longer smiling. "I know you were. And?"

"And there are times when I'm looking through other people, I see things I don't want to."

Maggie closed her eyes, suddenly unsure she wanted to hear this. "Yes, I suppose your parents kept their bedroom dark."

"Unfortunately, no." She heard the smile in his voice before it left again. "Four years ago, I slipped into the head of a man with a young girl. She was maybe ten or eleven. Tied up on a bed. She'd already been . . . He wasn't done."

Maggie faced him. "I get it. Go on."

"He must have been nearby, but I didn't know where the hell he was, so I started looking. And I knew by his surroundings that it was one of the government houses, because everyone else lived in shacks."

The same way he was looking for Katherine now, she guessed. Recognizing surroundings, narrowing down a location.

"What were you going to do when you found him?"

"Get her out of there. Kill him."

Probably not in that order. "*Did* you find him?"

"No. Someone else did. I don't know what she was doing there, what trouble she'd been sent to fix—but she opened the door, and she looked at him. She looked at the girl. And she shot him. Just raised her gun and fired."

Realization struck, made breathing suddenly painful. "You were in my head then?"

"No. His."

Jesus. "You weren't . . . hurt . . . by being in him when he died?"

"No. I just lost contact. So I moved into the girl, stayed with her after you helped her to the exit. She limped down the street right past me, and I made sure she got where she was going. I tried to find you again, but . . ." He shook his head. "I didn't."

"He wasn't my target," she admitted. Not her target, never reported, and not classified.

"He should have been."

Maggie toed off her boots and tucked them beneath the desk. "If the girl had screamed, it might have compromised my mission."

"Yet you did it anyway."

"Yes." She hadn't even had to think about it.

"With a reaction like that, you were in the wrong line of work."

Yes, I was. But she only asked, "Why tell me this?"

"I never got a chance to thank you."

"I didn't do it for you."

"What does that matter? You did what I couldn't, and I'm grateful for it. Just as it doesn't matter now whether you're helping me find Katherine because she needs to be found, or if it's because you feel responsible for James after letting him go alive. Either way, I'll be grateful for the help when we find her."

Who *was* this man? Was he for real? Her fingers were clumsy as she unbuttoned the cuffs of her sleeves. What kind of person offered trust like this? Acceptance? She wasn't family. Their only connection was one of the few impulsive acts Maggie had performed in her lifetime. She shouldn't even matter to him.

And yet . . . his acceptance and trust had begun to matter to her, too. It must have, because her throat was aching, and she wanted to say "Thank you" in return.

But as she moved toward the bathroom, she only said, "You aren't at all what I expected, Mr. Blake."

Chapter Five

She looked too soft with her hair blown dry and loose around her shoulders. She *felt* too soft, and so Maggie braided it into a rope before leaving the bathroom. Her only clothes were a tank and underwear, but she had no intention of looking down at herself.

Sir Pup hadn't abandoned his sprawl across the second bed. She studied him, wondering how to maneuver through this. Sleeping had never been an issue before.

"It seems an easy choice, Winters. There's hardly enough room over there for a child."

She narrowed her eyes at the hellhound. "He could get up. He doesn't *need* to sleep. Or eat. So I don't *need* to buy him a bag of sausage biscuits tomorrow morning."

Sir Pup yawned, exposing three sets of gigantic teeth, and rolled onto his back.

Maggie sighed and crawled onto the bed next to Blake.

"You caved?"

She reached for the light and clicked it off. "He probably wouldn't let me eat tomorrow, either. It's a practical decision."

"And this marks the first time a woman has come to my bed for practical reasons. Usually, they say it's a mistake."

"I don't make mistakes." She turned on her side, facing away from him. "Not many."

"You trusted James."

She stared into the darkness. "Yes, I did."

"Was that a mistake?"

She hadn't thought so. But she *had* wondered, even back then, if caring about James as a person—and as a friend—had given her a blind spot, prevented her from seeing some terrible truth. But, in the end, she'd made her decision and lied about following through on the kill order.

The reasons behind the kill order hadn't been given—reasons were rarely given—but the kill order itself hadn't made sense. Operatives didn't assassinate other operatives. Even if James had been a traitor to the country, if he'd sold government secrets, or come across sensitive information that an operative couldn't be allowed to possess, the first step would have been to convict him. Perhaps the public would never hear of it—or even most agency employees—but there would have been hearings. And if James fled custody and posed a security risk—which he hadn't—Maggie shouldn't have been the one to take him out. Someone higher up would have done it, *very* quietly.

And so from the moment her superior had given her the order, her gut had told her something was off. Way off. She'd have bet her life that James hadn't committed a breach of national security, but had witnessed someone else's. Someone within the CIA. Someone higher up the chain of command, who could distance himself from the kill by pushing it down through the ranks.

When she'd spoken with James on that final night, he hadn't verified her suspicions. He'd kept his secrets as well as she did. But she'd worked with him too long, known him too long. And although she wouldn't stay with the agency and try to discover who *had* betrayed them—that would have been signing her own death warrant—she wasn't going to murder James for that person, either. So she'd told him to run.

Behind her, Blake turned heavily over, and she heard the thump of his fist against the pillow as he punched it into a comfortable shape. She could visualize him, on his stomach and his head turned to one side. And though he could be facing either way, she was certain that if she rolled over, she'd find that he'd turned his face toward her.

"No," she said quietly. "I don't think it was a mistake."

As soon as he replied, her instincts were confirmed: Blake *was* facing her . . . and was closer than she'd thought. Not invading her personal space, but not across the bed, either. "James knew how to contact you. Do you know where he was before this?"

"I wasn't in hiding. It'd have been easy for him to find me." She paused, weighed the rest, and decided she could reveal it. "I didn't want to know where he was. We'd agreed: no contact, ever."

"Because the agency keeps tabs on you."

"Yes." Maybe not deep surveillance, but some. "Not enough that Ames-Beaumont considers my employment a security threat to *him*."

"Savi would take care of that, anyway."

Maggie nodded, the pillowcase cool and soft against her cheek. Then she remembered to say, "Yes." She heard him thump his pillow again. "Is your sister awake?"

"No."

"Tell me about her."

"You don't already know?"

Maggie thought of the files she'd had a chance to look over on the flight to New York. "I know she's a police inspector in London. Her cases-solved rate is high." Extraordinarily high. "She buys her groceries on Wednesdays and Saturdays, usually rents romantic comedies or horror movies—"

"The two genres have more in common than you'd think."

She smiled and thought about turning over. If she explored him with her hands, her mouth, he'd be warm and solid. He'd kiss her, slide deeply inside her, and she'd wrap herself around him.

And they wouldn't get much sleep. They'd be tired, and perhaps careless, when they started out again tomorrow. Katherine needed better from both of them.

Silently, Maggie clamped her hand between her thighs, and used the pressure to soothe the burn her imagination had sparked. "It helps to hear from someone who knows her well; memorizing data isn't the same."

"No," he agreed. "It isn't. Ask away, Winters."

"She lived with a man for eight years. He moved out a month ago. Did he know about her ability? About you?"

"No."

"You're certain?"

"Yes."

Katherine had been in a long-term relationship—and she'd kept it hidden from her partner? But more than that, she hadn't even revealed that she was concealing something. How would that affect a relationship? Would that be more difficult than revealing to the other person that there was something she just couldn't share with him?

It probably depended on the other person.

"What has her emotional state been like?"

"It was a blow when Gavin left her. But this, she'll look at as she would a job. She'll keep her head. And she'll be searching for a way out."

Maggie closed her eyes. "Hopefully by tomorrow, we'll give her one."

Maggie's multipurpose phone beeped at four a.m. She fumbled for it on the nightstand and squinted at the soft white glow. The text message had come from Savi: "Check your e-mail and finish sleeping on the plane."

The plane? What plane?

She scrubbed at her face before engaging the encrypted

mode on her phone and logging in. God, she hadn't run on this kind of schedule in years. But back then, she also hadn't opened her e-mail from bed, warm and comfortable, ensconced in blankets and with Blake's back and shoulders against her own.

She had to resist the urge to press back tighter against him. Somehow, their position felt more intimate than spooning. And strangely familiar, like going through a door with an operative that she trusted by her side.

She read the message, then stumbled into the bathroom and blasted a hot, two-minute shower. Geoff was using her phone when she came out in her bra and panties, with Sir Pup—sporting only one head—peering over his shoulder.

Sir Pup turned to look at her. Blake's hands went slack, the phone tilting in his grip.

She glanced at the screen as she walked by the bed, then did a double take. Blake was accessing his own mail, reading a message identical to the one Savi had sent to her . . . but he shouldn't have been able to get that far. Using it for anything other than a phone call required Maggie's password.

She lifted her arms and began coiling her hair into a roll at her nape. "Did Savi give you a password for my equipment?"

"You did, a few minutes ago," he said. A slight frown had formed at the corners of his mouth, and his voice was still rough with sleep. "You look at your fingers when you use the keypad."

That explained how he'd discovered the embezzlers at Ramsdell Pharmaceuticals. He'd just watched them input their fraudulent numbers, and they'd never known they were being watched.

But *she* had known what he could do and hadn't guarded against it. If Blake hadn't already been Ramsdell security, she could have just compromised Ames-Beaumont's.

The potential mistake didn't piss her off as much as knowing that she hadn't even *thought* about guarding against it. Taking a risk with her eyes wide open was acceptable. Acting blindly and stupidly was not.

And why hadn't she thought? Because she'd been cozy.

She jabbed in the pins that secured her hair, then stepped into her trousers and yanked them up. "Why didn't you read my e-mail when I did, too?"

"That would be an invasion of privacy, Winters." His brows lowered, darkening his expression. "I have limits. For instance, when you're in there"—he tilted his head toward the bathroom—"I'll not look without permission. But if you come out here dressed as you are now, I'll take whatever eyeful I can."

"But whose—" No, she didn't need to ask.

Sir Pup had begun chuffing. His other two heads sprouted from his shoulders and joined in.

Blake weaved on the bed and pressed his hand to his forehead, swallowing hard. Obviously, looking through the three heads didn't agree with him.

"If I may be so bold, Mr. Blake—you just got what you deserved." Maggie pulled on her shirt. "You said you couldn't see through animals."

"I can't. And don't bloody call me Mr. Blake." He stood abruptly and came toward her. "Are those why you were called 'Bullet-Eating Brunhilda'?"

"No." She didn't look down at the scars scattered over her stomach as she buttoned her shirt. "It's because I'm blond, and I'm tall, and men don't use much imagination when they are nicknaming women. Your uncle, of course, is the exception—'Winters' is preferable to 'the Ice Queen' or 'the Frost Giant.'"

"'Winters' has nothing to do with your hair, Maggie." His gaze was steady on hers. "Will you turn around?"

Nothing he'd just said was what she'd expected. "Why?"

"Because there's a mirror behind you. And because you've retreated behind that damnable butler's tone, and so I'm not able to tell if you're angry. I want to see your face, not mine."

That was just too bad. "We have a plane to catch, sir." She shouldered her weapon harness and deliberately swept her gaze down his bare chest, his ridged stomach. "You have five minutes to get ready. I suggest you get started."

He stepped in closer. Maggie drew in a breath, waited for him to do more. To say something, to argue . . . to touch her.

God, she was looking at his hands again.

Her jacket hung on the chair behind her. She grabbed it, put distance between them. He stared at the spot where she'd been for a moment longer before turning his back to her and moving toward his own clothes. The bullet scar on his shoulder was pale against his tan.

"For the record, Maggie," he said, "it wasn't my intention to upset you. I'm simply not in the habit of asking first."

No, he wouldn't be. He couldn't keep his ability a secret if he sought permission to use it.

The tension that had been stiffening her muscles slowly eased away. "For the record, sir—I am very easy to upset when I find myself awake at four in the morning."

He was facing the other way, so she didn't know if he smiled. She didn't mind. He couldn't see hers, either.

"Now that you've forgiven me, I ought not to admit this," Blake said as soon as they were both settled into the SUV. "But I've no idea why we are to catch a plane. I only read half of Savi's e-mail."

Because he'd been distracted when she'd come out of the bathroom in her underwear, Maggie realized, and four fifteen in the morning suddenly felt a little brighter.

"The Ramsdell corporate jet is waiting at the Richmond airport," Maggie told him. "It'll take us to Charleston."

"Savi located the RV, then?"

"No. But it'll get us to the right state faster than we can drive, and we don't lose the time sleeping."

Blake's smile was wry. "Sensible. And very kind of her not to point out that if I *could* drive, we wouldn't have needed to stop."

Yes. Last night, she would've slept while Blake drove, and they'd have been in South Carolina by now.

Maggie frowned, her fingers tapping against the steering wheel. "They stopped, too. James and the other one. And not to switch off—they could have done that in a parking lot or beside the road."

But at a campground, Maggie realized, they could pay for the site and leave the RV. It would be a while before anyone listed it as abandoned.

And they'd drugged Katherine again rather than asking her to locate something. So that it'd be easier to carry her out of the RV, take her to another vehicle?

Blake must have been thinking along similar lines. "So they've left the caravan, changed their mode of transportation."

"With a nearby destination, probably. If she's drugged, even a hired plane is too risky—and so is taking the chance that she'll wake up when she's in a car. She'd get someone's attention."

"A local destination," he repeated, his voice grim. "Where they can start questioning her."

"Yes." She glanced over at him. "We'll be at the airport in ten minutes. You call Savi, fill her in. It'll be somewhere isolated. Probably a house, rented or leased in the past six months." The date Katherine had bought her plane ticket to New York. "Have her cross-reference names with the campground registrations and the real estate agent who was selling the brownstone in Brooklyn."

"She won't find anything."

"No," Maggie agreed. "But it's better than doing nothing."

He nodded, and she listened to the one-sided conversation with her mind hundreds of miles south. *You can stop me, Brunhilda.* But she couldn't anticipate James, because she couldn't see why he was doing this.

She lowered her window to let the wind rush past her face and finish waking her up. Even this early, the August air was warm. From the cargo area, Sir Pup whined. She rolled the rear window down, and a moment later one of his heads was blocking the view in her side mirror. His tongue and ears flapped like wet flags.

His eyes were also glowing crimson, but there wasn't enough traffic to worry about his being seen.

"Demon," Blake said quietly. "I'll ring you again in a moment, Savi."

Startled, Maggie glanced over at him. Was he worried about the red eyes? But she didn't think he'd been looking at Sir Pup.

"She's awake, in a bedroom, and there's a man sitting in the corner who looks like Gavin."

His sister's ex. But it couldn't be him; Maggie knew Ames-Beaumont had put men on Gavin's tail the moment Katherine had disappeared.

And a demon could shape-shift to resemble anyone.

"Oh, she's right pissed. Her hands are waving around in that way she has. He's attempting to calm her. Good luck with that, you bastard." A moment passed. "And there he goes, out the door. He's locked it. Come on, Kate, give me something I can work with."

Maggie's phone beeped. Seeing that it was Savi, she simply engaged the speakerphone.

"There she goes to the window," Blake said. "She's upstairs. It's dark outside, but there's a light . . . a lighthouse, I think it is. It must be to the north of her. The water's on the right."

Faintly, she heard the clacking of Savi's keyboard. Already narrowing the search.

"The house is white. There's a dock, and a boathouse. A good-sized sailboat tied up."

That meant money, Maggie thought. But with a demon involved, that wasn't a surprise. "Do you see a name on it?"

"No. She's searching through the room now. The drawers are empty. No phone. No television. No periodicals."

"Nothing that gives away their location." Savi stopped typing. "Do you think they know what Geoff can do?"

"If they did, they'd have blindfolded her." Maggie took the airport exit. "They probably just don't want her to feel comfortable, so that leaving the room will be a reward—"

Blake gave a short laugh. "Clever girl, Kate. She's turned over a lamp on the nightstand. On the base, there's a label: 'Laura's Antiques and Design, Hilton Head, South Carolina.'"

"Which is . . . " There was a moment of furious clacking. "Right on the water. It's an island."

"And a tourist trap," Maggie said. "Probably not isolated enough."

"True. I'll concentrate fifty miles up and down the coast. I'll also find pictures of local lighthouses for you to look at, Geoff. Once the sun rises, maybe Katherine will be able to see enough that you'll recognize one. And I'll have the pilot file a new flight plan that will take you closer to Hilton Head than Charleston is. And, Maggie—I'm monitoring your e-mail, so that if James tries to contact you again, I can get you a location ASAP."

"Thank you, Miss Murray."

"Oh my god, I wish you'd stop calling me that. Does she do that to you, Geoff?"

He aimed a grin at Maggie. "Yes, Aunt Savi."

"And *that* is a million times worse. You're six years older than I am." The vampire sighed. "Okay, I can't put this off anymore. I'm on my way to tell Colin that a demon has Katherine. And that the demon probably knows what she can do."

"In other words," Blake said, "we shouldn't be surprised if, by the time the sun sets tonight, you and Uncle Colin have arrived in Hilton Head."

"Yeah, that about covers it," Savi said. "Be safe until then."

Silence fell between them after she'd disconnected, until Maggie said, "How much do you want to bet she chartered a plane within a minute of you first saying 'demon'?"

His agreeing laugh faded too quickly, and he scrubbed his hands over his face. "Katherine hasn't found anything else. Nothing to write with, either. She's sitting, waiting."

Maggie nodded. Unfortunately, that was what she and Blake would be doing, too.

Chapter Six

"Why did he choose 'Winters,' Mr. Blake?"

Maggie's gaze was focused on the lighthouse filling the laptop screen in front of her, but Geoff immediately felt the shift of her mood. Her eyes had been in hyperactive mode from the time they'd arrived at the airport, so that Geoff's reliance on Sir Pup's guide harness was, once again, not completely faked.

And she hadn't let up on the drive to Hilton Head, or after they'd entered the open-air café where they'd decided to have breakfast and look through the lighthouse photos Savi had compiled.

After Geoff mentioned his difficulty using her eyes, Maggie had made an effort to let her gaze rest on each photo. But she'd still managed to give a once-over to every customer, almost every pedestrian on the sidewalk, and many of the drivers passing by in their cars.

As she asked about the nickname, however, Maggie became *too* focused. Though Geoff had heard the hostess seating at least two newcomers, Maggie's gaze hadn't yet darted to them—which told Geoff that the answer was as important to her as their security.

And he wasn't above using that knowledge to his own ends. "I'll tell you, but only if there's no more of this 'Mr. Blake.'"

Her gaze lifted to his face. Christ, he hadn't intended for his expression to appear that tense, that dark. "Mr. Blake" didn't anger him. It just . . . frustrated him.

"All right. Just Blake."

No "mister," and so no longer something she'd use with a superior, or an employer. He watched the line between his eyebrows vanish, saw how he eased back in his chair. Watched through *her* eyes.

And so Maggie knew, too, how much that had mattered to him. He began to push his hand through his hair, then realized how relieved the gesture seemed—as if he'd just fought a battle and won.

He was in the process of becoming completely wrecked by this woman. And seeing himself like this wasn't helping his confidence.

He searched for someone who was looking at her, instead. He found one, two tables away, who was either staring blankly into space or fascinated by the platinum of Maggie's hair in the bright sun. The focus wasn't on her face, but Geoff could see her profile well enough to know her expression wasn't giving much away.

And that she had a beautiful, incredible mouth.

With both hands, she brought her coffee cup to her lips. From any other angle, the ceramic rim would have hidden her smile, and he couldn't hear it in her voice when she prompted, "Winters?"

"Winters," Geoff said, "was the name of my uncle's valet. His first valet, his second, his third, and his fourth."

The corners of her mouth tightened. "I see."

No, she likely didn't. Not yet. She assumed that Colin, the son of a wealthy British earl, had lazily taken to calling all of his valets "Winters" so that he wouldn't have to remember their names.

"They all *were* of the Winters family. Sons and grandsons. One a nephew. But it was the first who was in my uncle's employ when he became a vampire. Whenever he traveled away from Beaumont Court, he took Winters. And it was the first Winters who was with him when he was cursed."

He had no doubt Maggie knew of the curse. She would have noticed how few mirrors were in his uncle's mansion. Every other vampire could see his reflection, but the taint of the dragon's blood had erased his uncle's. To a man as vain as Colin Ames-Beaumont, the inability to confirm his beauty truly was a curse.

"Oh," Maggie said quietly. "Not just a valet. A gentleman's gentleman. A man he trusted to do what he couldn't—maintain his appearance, and protect him during his daysleep."

"And, according to Uncle Colin, who remained one of his few links to sanity during those early years." The family, of course, being the other. "There hasn't been a Winters since the Second World War—not, at least, one who has served my uncle. His support of the Winters family allowed them to rise in class enough so that when my grandmother married a Blake, it didn't raise any eyebrows. And Uncle Colin didn't think it was appropriate for family members to serve as his valets, so he began to dress himself."

With great care, she set her coffee cup on its saucer. "Your grandmother was a Winters?"

"Yes. And she hadn't any more blond hairs on her head than I do." He reached for his juice and raised it in a tiny salute. "And that, Maggie, is the story of the Winters name. You can infer what you wish from it."

If she did infer anything, she didn't share her conclusions. Instead, she slowly ate a piece of toast.

Geoff assumed her silence meant she'd been affected by it. Good, he thought. Very good.

Even if it meant that he was a bastard for telling her. He knew what she was looking for, what her psychological profile had laid out, describing a chain of events that had started when a young woman had given Maggie her last name, and nothing else. Then bandied about the foster system until she was twelve. She'd found stability, after that, with foster parents who hadn't been able to have children of their own—and who'd taken in children not out of love, but to fulfill a sense of duty. The father had been a military man through and through, with a schedule for every aspect of the children's lives. It had been constancy Maggie had desperately needed, but the sense of belonging she'd craved hadn't been fulfilled until the service.

The CIA had known that, had used that when they'd brought her in. They'd depended on her loyalty—not just to her country, but to her fellow operatives. Whatever the CIA had given her, though, it hadn't been enough after they'd told her to assassinate James.

And Geoff was a bastard for using that knowledge, too—but he was also determined to see that his family would be enough.

He lost sight of her a moment later. *Damn, and double damn.* The person he'd been looking through had come out of his reverie and glanced away from her.

When he slipped into Maggie again, she was studying his face. "Given how protective he is, I'm surprised that Ames-Beaumont hasn't tried to force you out of the field."

"You can be sure he's tried. The first time I was shot, he threatened to break my legs every four weeks to keep me in bed."

"The *first* time?"

"The scar you've seen was from the last—the latest one. That was eight months ago, in Colombia. And it was the first time I was too far from a Ramsdell facility. So I wasn't patched up with vampire blood."

By the movement of her head, Maggie was nodding. "Sir Pup carries blood in his hammerspace for emergencies. I haven't had to use it yet—and I didn't realize it healed *that* well."

"It's not completely miraculous. The others did leave a bit of scarring." He wondered if his easy posture and the hint of his smile looked as casual to her as he hoped it did.

"And it's because of the blood that Uncle Colin will soon have his wish."

Her vision darkened at the edges, as if her eyes had narrowed. "How so?"

"Ramsdell is building a new facility in San Francisco. The research will focus on the blood, which Uncle Colin has never allowed before—and so my focus will change, as well. I'll head up security and operations, and only go out in the field when it's necessary. And I'll take a more direct approach when I do."

"No more playing the doofus."

He suppressed his wince. Even knowing "doofus" was true—hell, it had been deliberate—it wasn't an easy thing to hear her say. "Yes."

"And you'll be living in San Francisco."

"Yes."

"Why the change?"

"It's time. I've been protecting the family so long, I haven't had time to start one for myself." Whatever form that family took. "And I came out of Colombia; Trixie didn't."

Her gaze returned to his face. "She was . . . your guide dog?"

"For ten years." He felt the familiar twinge in his chest and pushed through it. "She spoiled me. And traveling doesn't have the same appeal without her. So when Uncle Colin told me about the plans for the San Francisco facility, I told him I would help him out."

Her gaze settled on his mouth before moving to the photo of the lighthouse on her laptop. "There's no interesting story behind my scars," she said. "I wish I *had* eaten bullets, because that would mean that I'd taken a calculated risk. But it was just a mistake. I went left when I should have gone right. And I can't tell you who carried me out."

She couldn't, but she didn't need to; her implication was clear. James had.

"In other words," Geoff said. "You want to save him from the demon, too."

He thought she shrugged, but he found someone looking at her too late to be sure.

"I don't know if he needs to be saved. But I'm not sure I could kill him. Not if the only reason is that he knows too much."

Is that what she thought her role here was? That they expected her to perform a cold-blooded assassination?

"We're just here to get Kate out, Maggie."

"And then?"

"Uncle Colin will step in." Which wasn't, Geoff reflected, the best way to put it. He shook his head, and tried again. "When Katherine was eight, we were visiting a neighboring estate, and the lady of the house mentioned a locket that had gone missing twenty or thirty years earlier. My sister told her where to find it. The locket was of some historical significance, so the story was written up in the local paper. Just a minor little piece. But within a fortnight, two government men arrived at Beaumont Court to talk with her. When they left, they said they'd be calling on us again. My mother rang Uncle Colin. We didn't hear from them again . . . but they *are* still alive."

From across the café, he caught the edge of her smile. "He scared them."

Terrorized them, because their deaths would only raise more questions. But fear created an ally of sorts; those two men would forever deny finding out anything unusual about Katherine or seeing the need for further investigation.

"And so if James can be persuaded to remain silent," Geoff said, "we have no problem. The demon, however—"

"Needs to be slain."

"Yes. But we'll not likely be handling that, either." From beside his chair, he heard an eager chuff. He shook off the memory of the giant demon dog, its teeth closing over Maggie's arm. "And, so. No murder required. Just a rescue."

Maggie was studying his face again. Specifically, his mouth.

"Maggie," he warned. "Don't look at me like that."

Her gaze dropped to his hands.

"Not there, either."

She met his eyes. He'd known few people who could hold his sightless gaze for more than a couple of seconds.

"I look everywhere," she said.

"Yes. But not for as long as you look at me."

She closed her eyes; he saw darkness. He heard the scrape of her chair. Warm lips pressed hard against his. Her fingers raked through his hair. His shocked inhalation brought her into him. Christ, she smelled incredible. Tasted like heaven. He wanted more, wanted to see her, too. But the idea of finding another pair of eyes to look through had barely begun to form when every sensation that was Maggie left.

Then she was back in her chair, and he was staring at his own astonished expression.

She looked down at her toast, picked up another slice. She must have noticed that her fingers were unsteady at the same moment that he did—her gaze snapped to the street, to the sidewalk, and began its familiar skip from face to face.

"I shouldn't have—"

His temper flared. "You'll not apologize for it."

"Your sister is still missing."

Yes, she was. Bloody hell. Katherine wouldn't begrudge either of them that kiss, but dammit—there were priorities.

He nodded, pushed his hand through his hair. It'd felt better when Maggie's fingers had done it. "More lighthouses, then."

Blake found the lighthouse half an hour later. The photo had been taken from a position nearer to it than Katherine was, but it gave them a direction: about thirty miles north.

They'd only been on the road for a few minutes when the demon came to see Katherine again. In the passenger seat, Blake's shoulders straightened, his eyes squinting slightly. As if, Maggie thought, he were trying to urge Katherine to look at something more closely.

"He's GQ again. And he's speaking to her, but Katherine isn't . . . " Blake tilted his head, frowning. "She's not looking at him, so I've no idea what he's saying."

She shouldn't have been surprised, but she was. "Can you read lips?"

"Not perfectly. Enough to catch a word here and there, put it together. Come on, Kate, you know I need to see his face."

Oh, no, Maggie thought. She glanced in the rearview mirror, saw Sir Pup gazing steadily back at her. A hellhound wouldn't know, and a man might not realize what that meant—but Maggie could guess.

Katherine was attracted to the demon. Probably trying not to be . . . but still attracted.

Demons, unfortunately, could be charming, so that their lies dripped like honey. And the shapes they took were usually as gorgeous as sin.

"He's holding out his hand to her. She's not taking it, but she is following him down the stairs. The curtains are drawn at the front windows."

"So that no one can see in," Maggie said. "Or so that she can't signal to anyone."

"There's James, standing near the doorway of a dining room. He's decked out in black, wearing a shoulder holster." Blake frowned. "There's food. It's a nice setup. GQ is smiling, pulling out a chair for her. What the hell is he doing?"

"Playing good cop, bad cop," Maggie said. "In a few minutes, James will get pissed, start yelling, pull out the gun. The demon will be the voice of reason and put himself between Katherine and the weapon."

And then there was the food, she thought. How hungry was Katherine by now? Even if she didn't want to feel gratitude, she would be thankful for the chance to eat. It was human nature.

Blake frowned. "So he's creating an express version of Stockholm syndrome? He'll make her trust him, so she'll give up the location faster?"

"I think so." Katherine knew the Rules, and what the demon couldn't do to her. She wouldn't worry about him, but look for ways to get around James. "They'll want to keep her afraid of James, but they'll also give her a friend." A handsome, sympathetic friend. "One who can convince her that as soon as she helps him, he'll let her go."

Blake was silent for a few minutes, then said, "You were spot on, Maggie."

"The fight?"

"Yes. The demon is taking her back upstairs now." He pounded his fist against his knee. "And she's still not looking at him, though he's speaking with her. Still not . . . Oh, but she's taken a scone with her and heaped it with jam."

Jam? Maggie glanced over, saw his wide grin. "What?"

He shook his head. "We've only to wait now, and we'll know what it is he wants."

As soon as the demon left her alone, Katherine used the jam to write "dragon blood" on the bathroom mirror.

Which, Maggie thought, was not as helpful as it might have been.

"Dragon blood?" Blake scrubbed his hands over his face. "How would she find that? There's only been one on Earth, and it was killed thousands of years ago."

By the sword that had tainted his uncle's blood. And—

Maggie's stomach sank. "Is that what happened to you? And Katherine? You were changed by the sword?"

"Not directly."

Born different, not changed. "Someone else. Your parents or your grandparents were tainted by it."

"No. But go back two centuries, and you'll land on them. What are you thinking, Maggie?"

"The reason your uncle hired me was that a few demons found out he was different from other vampires, so he needed that extra protection from them. And that if your family has been different for two hundred years, there will be a pattern that shows up. No matter how hard he tries to hide it. If a demon looked at him first, then looked at his family . . ." Maybe Blake's pattern wasn't as easy to establish. But his sister— "Katherine's cases-solved rate is incredibly high."

"And they took blood from us both." His grim tone matched the lines of tension beside his mouth and nose. "So that's how they knew. But that still doesn't tell us where she'll find dragon blood now."

Her stomach seemed to sink lower. Maybe Katherine didn't have to *find* dragon blood. Maybe the demon thought she already had it. "Do you know about the grigori?"

"No."

That was no surprise. Ames-Beaumont, she knew, had only learned of them recently, too. "Demons can't have children. But before the war with the angels—when the dragon was killed on Earth—Lucifer made some demons drink dragon blood. They were changed by it, and they mated with humans. The offspring are the grigori."

She watched his face, and saw the horrified realization that *his* family had been changed by dragon blood. His voice was low and furious. "Is he trying to experiment with her? To see if he can impregnate her?"

"If he is, there is one silver lining: it has to be of her free will." As in everything else, the demons' Rules had to be followed.

"And so he does the nice-guy routine before he tries to—" He bit the rest off. Anger and horror battled for equal play in his expression.

"Yes." She focused on the road again. "But maybe we're wrong. It just might be . . . Oh, Jesus."

The SUV sped past them, heading the opposite way, but she was certain she hadn't mistaken the driver. James. Her heart began pounding, but she fought the impulse to slam the brakes, to whip the vehicle around and follow him.

She pressed the button that lowered the rear passenger window. "Sir Pup. It's the black Land Rover that just passed us. Do you have your locator?"

"Is it James?" The fury hadn't left Blake's voice.

"Yes." A tracking device landed in her lap. "All right, Sir Pup. Just lead us to him. If you can do it where no one can see it, detain him. But don't shape-shift."

The hellhound gave a disappointed whine.

Maggie slowed as soon as James's vehicle was out of sight, then pulled off onto the shoulder. Sir Pup jumped out the window.

"Can he catch up at highway speeds?"

"Yes." She watched the dark blur streak across the road. "If he'd run from San Francisco instead taking the plane with me to New York, he would have arrived before I did."

"He'd have . . . Bollocks."

Maggie met her own flat stare in the rearview mirror. "Do I look like I'm joking?"

"I don't know. I'm with him. And he's running . . . very fast." Blake reached forward, braced his hand on the dash. "It's a bad amusement park ride. Oh, hell. He's purposefully running in front of oncoming vehicles."

He probably was. Maggie pulled back onto the road and headed after the hellhound. And hoped that whatever chaos Sir Pup left in his path didn't delay them too long.

And that he didn't interpret "detaining James" as "eating his legs."

At least, not yet.

Chapter Seven

James is a lucky man, Maggie thought. He'd stopped at a beachfront park, a location too public for Sir Pup to do anything more than lie in the sand a hundred yards away and stare at him.

Maggie parked and turned to Blake. "You can see him?"

"At one of the tables. He looks to be on the phone." He held up his hands, moved his thumbs. "Not talking. Texting."

And she would have to cross an open expanse to reach him. After a quick check of her gun, she said, "You'll stay with Sir Pup while I talk to him."

"Not a chance."

She knew he'd say that. "He won't talk with you there."

"We don't need him to talk. Just to point out the house."

"Geoff, I need you to trust me." And to be out of James's line of fire. She couldn't trust James, not until she knew what his role was.

And even then, it would be difficult.

A muscle in his jaw twitched. "This isn't about trusting you, Maggie."

"No. You're angry on behalf of your sister, so it's about you wanting to break your fist on his face." She touched his hand, the tight, white-knuckled clench. "We can't charge blindly into the house. We can't take that risk."

The fingers beneath hers loosened slightly.

"You can start punching *after* we get her out."

He released a heavy breath and nodded. "All right, then."

The relief that swept through her was too strong, she thought as she spotted James at the table. Relief like that came from caring.

And she wasn't going to be careless with Geoff.

She knew the moment James spotted her. The expression on his boy-next-door face didn't change, but beneath the table, his booted feet shifted slightly wider. Getting ready to dive to one side or the other.

She didn't sit on the bench and offer an easy gut shot below the table. She leaned her hip against the tabletop instead, her arms casually folded beneath her breasts, her right hand on her weapon and concealed by her jacket.

"This *can* be easy," she said. "But it's up to you."

He laid the phone down and placed both hands flat on the table. "I'll make it easy." With his chin, he gestured at the phone. "I sent you another message. You found me faster than I thought you would."

And she'd never tell him how. "My employer has interesting friends." Let him wonder about that. Wonder and worry. "And yours is a demon."

"He used to be yours, too, Maggie." He leaned back slightly, looking up at her face. "The demon is Langan."

Their handler—her superior—at the CIA. The one who'd given her James's kill order. She didn't allow her surprise to show. And wondered if he was lying, just to make her stumble.

But it was possible. If Langan had been a demon, he *couldn't* have killed James; giving Maggie the kill order would've been the only way to get rid of him without breaking the Rules. And Maggie didn't know Langan's current status . . . but she would have Savi check into it the moment the vampire came out of her daysleep.

"Langan," she repeated flatly. "And what does he have on you?"

"A bargain. I help him find what he needs, and he doesn't tell the agency that I'm alive . . . and that you faked the kill."

A demon or vampire could have heard the pounding of her heart, might have sensed the fear that spiked through her. A human couldn't. Her smile was thin. "I could make it real now." She waited a beat. "That kill order was bogus. You know it, and if the agency looked close enough, they'd know it, too. Even if they dragged us back, we'd get the equivalent of a slap before they started hunting for Langan. So what else does he have that would make you stupid enough to bargain with him?"

Sweat beaded above his upper lip. "I took an assignment. A leadership change."

A political assassination. "So?"

"I couldn't complete it. I took the shot, but couldn't complete the assignment. So I disengaged and reported to Langan. Reported everything."

Maggie frowned. Failure wasn't reason to—

Ice slid through her veins. "*Couldn't?* Because he healed? Because bullets couldn't kill him?"

"Maggie . . ."

"A vampire or a demon?"

He blinked. Was going to lie. But she knew, didn't she?

A political assassination.

"Stafford," she breathed. And James hadn't known Stafford was a demon. An American citizen, on American soil. Oh, God. She *had* made a mistake. She should have followed through on that order. "What was in it for you?"

"A promotion, and a desk."

Disgust poured through her. She didn't attempt to conceal her reaction.

James sat back. "Goddammit, Maggie. I was tired of seeing my—our—friends shot in the field. Tired of seeing them killed. And it was a *demon*."

One that Maggie would have killed herself, if she could have. But James hadn't known Stafford had been a demon until after he'd tried to kill him.

Not that it mattered now. Katherine did.

Maggie swallowed, forced herself to relax.

"A demon, yes. Okay. And another demon has you in this bargain now." And if James didn't fulfill it, his soul would be trapped in Hell. Which was, she thought grimly, enough incentive to make James do almost anything. "You just have to *help* him, is that right? You don't have to actually give him whatever it is he's looking for?"

"Right." Almost tiredly, James nodded. "Just help. But he decides what 'helping' is."

"Then we'll make it simple. I'll go after Katherine when you aren't there, so that you don't have to help him stop me. Like now."

His lashes flickered. "I'm due back in a few minutes. If I stay much longer, he'll be suspicious, and ready for you. This evening, I'm supposed to pretend to argue with him, leave the house angry and stay away for several hours. I'll contact you then, and give you the address."

Maggie straightened. "All right. Tonight."

She waited at the picnic table until she saw the Land Rover pull out of the parking lot. The ocean seemed louder than it should have, filling her head with noise. The sand was deep and soft. Her feet were hot inside her boots and her body bathed in a light film of sweat by the time she made it to Geoff's side.

Geoff was cold, pale with anger, his voice ice. "What the bloody hell was that?"

A small directional microphone lay in his lap—no doubt

from Sir Pup and the supply of equipment in his hammer-space.

Well, that made everything easier. She wouldn't have to repeat her entire conversation with James; she'd just have to explain it.

Geoff stood. "You let James go. Might as well have told him to tell the demon we were coming."

No, he wasn't cold. He was close, and he was pissed, and she could feel the heat coming off him as well as she could the sun. Sweat trickled down her back, between her breasts.

Maggie glanced at Sir Pup. "Follow him. Detain him *gently*. But don't let the demon see you."

White still edged Geoff's mouth, but color was returning to the rest of his face. A breeze pushed at his dark hair and cooled the back of her neck. "What was that, Maggie?"

"He's bound to help the demon. *I* won't force him to break his bargain and damn him to Hell." She had a feeling James was doing a good job of getting there on his own. "But if he's heading back to tell the demon—to help the demon—and Sir Pup prevents him from getting there . . ."

"He doesn't break it."

"Exactly."

She turned toward the parking lot. Geoff caught her arm. "And the rest?"

Langan, Stafford. Kill orders that Langan must have known would never be completed. And the certainty that she had narrowly escaped the trap James was ensnarled in now.

"I . . . can't," she said. "I can't think of it now. It's too much, it's too big. Maybe after we get Katherine." She closed her eyes. "And for just one moment I need to . . . this."

She leaned in, buried her face in his throat. Tension held Geoff stiff for a second before his arms slid around her.

"I'm tired," she admitted, and let herself rest against him. Not physical exhaustion. Emotional. As if she'd been slowly wrung out since receiving that e-mail. "I haven't been this tired since I left the agency."

His voice was a soothing rumble against her cheek. "We'll be finished soon."

"Yes." She stepped back. Her hand drifted down his arm until her fingers linked with his. Then she let her hand drop back to her side. "We need to go."

Chapter Eight

Maggie drove just above the speed limit, her gaze constantly returning to the device tracking Sir Pup's location. He and James weren't too far ahead—but not, Maggie had said, so close that James would spot their vehicle.

Geoff nodded, casting ahead in an attempt to find Sir Pup, and was surprised when she admitted, "It's almost a relief. To know I was wrong about him."

She'd said that she couldn't talk about it yet, that it was too much. But maybe, Geoff thought, too much *not* to. At least a bit. "Wrong, how? The kill order was a setup."

"Yes. That's not what I—Not exactly." She checked Sir Pup's position, still on a steady course north. "I was afraid I'd have to choose."

"Choose what?"

"I didn't know." He heard the long, shaky breath she drew. Saw her hand make an open gesture, grasping at air. "Choose *something*. Something that would turn out to be karma coming back to bite me on the ass. Something that meant I wouldn't be going back home."

Home. She glanced over at him, and he wondered if she

saw his face. If she knew what she was looking at when she did.

"But now," she continued, "I feel I've done what I could for him. And the rest isn't my choice, or my responsibility."

Geoff didn't point out that it never had been. Saying it wouldn't mean she hadn't felt it hanging over her head.

"Anyway." She took another of those long breaths, but this was deep, steady. "I don't feel so tired now. Thank you."

Surprise shot through him again. "What for?"

"For caring." She searched his features, and this time he was certain she saw. "Don't get careless, though. Or do anything stupid. And I won't, either."

She was in an emotionally weak moment. It was probably unfair to press her now. "After we retrieve Katherine, I want a week with you. Or two. Time set aside every evening. Even if we'll do nothing more than sit in your garden."

"I killed all of my flowers trying to discover if I had a green thumb."

"I'll not look at them if you don't."

The mirror caught the corner of her smile. "All right."

He should have asked for a month. Geoff pushed ahead, found a driver, went farther—slipping into more than thirty people before the world exploded around him in sharp, brilliant detail. Each flap of a bumblebee's iridescent wings as it flew past Sir Pup. Minute particles swirling from mufflers, the pits in the pavement rushing beneath his feet.

His head began to throb, but he didn't want to lose the connection. Narrowing his own focus on the Land Rover helped.

"I have him," he told Maggie, and that was all that was said between them until, ten minutes later, Sir Pup began to slow.

"James is turning right. It looks to be a shared drive, marked with a stack of yellow stone blocks. I—" He clutched his head, fighting nausea as everything blurred.

A house rushed by, a second. Then a glimpse of the boathouse Katherine had seen from her window before Sir

Pup was standing, peering through green-leafed shrubbery at the driveway.

Low, Geoff thought. Lying or crouching.

"I believe . . ." He swallowed hard. "I believe he looked over the layout of the area. There are three houses, but they are a good distance apart and separated by trees and plantings of some sort." His thumb was no greener than Maggie's. "The driveway is lined with the same. He's waiting there now, on a bend. He's past the lanes for the other two houses."

"We'll be at the turnoff in about a minute."

Geoff nodded. Good timing. "And there's James," he told her.

The vehicle moved along the driveway at a good clip. Sir Pup seemed to rise from the ground—then darted forward.

Tendrils of smoke rose from the tires as they skidded over the pavement. Geoff didn't hear the crunch of the metal hitting flesh, but he saw the bumper dent from the impact, the drops of blood that splattered the black paint.

The world spun once, twice. Sir Pup rolled to a stop twelve feet from the vehicle, his unfocused gaze directed under the Land Rover.

Playing dead, Geoff thought.

His own body had clenched, he realized, as if braced for impact. He drew in a deep breath, then another. "Does he heal quickly?"

"Sir Pup?" Her voice had a sharp edge. "Why?"

"He jumped in front of the SUV."

"Oh." Her short laugh was high, relieved. "Yes."

James's booted feet appeared beside the Land Rover and jogged over to Sir Pup. The hellhound lay still until James knelt beside him.

To Geoff, it only appeared as if Sir Pup batted James with a forepaw. Then Geoff lost sight of him until the hellhound rose to his feet and looked over at the Land Rover. The windshield had shattered. James slid down the hood and crumpled to a heap on the driveway.

Geoff's heart pounded and echoed in the suddenly hollow space between his ears. "And you say that while my uncle sleeps you're alone with that dog?"

"I've never said that. Is James still alive?"

Sir Pup was sniffing at the man's legs, his arms. At James's throat, his pulse beat faintly beneath his skin.

"Yes," Geoff said, then slipped back into Maggie's eyes when she next spoke.

"There they are."

Maggie rolled James over and stripped him of his weapons. Nylon cable-tie handcuffs bound his wrists behind his back, his legs at the ankles. With Geoff's help, she loaded him into the back of the Land Rover.

She pulled off her jacket and tossed it on the front seat. "Can you shoot a gun?" When Geoff's brows lifted, she said, "If the demon looks at you, you'll be able to aim and shoot him. The bullets won't kill him, but they'll hurt him a little."

And with luck, provide enough distraction that Sir Pup would be able to do his thing.

At Geoff's nod, she fitted him with a 9-mm from Sir Pup's hammerspace and screwed on a sound suppressor. Sleek and effective.

"We'll drive up in the Land Rover," she told him. "Sir Pup—you go on around."

The driveway bent to the right and down a small rise. Maggie studied the house longer than she might have if Geoff weren't looking through her eyes. A columned veranda wrapped around the front of the house. It rose three stories, topped by a widow's walk. Exits in the front, she noted, and likely in the back.

For a demon, though, any window could serve as an exit.

"I walk ahead of you," Geoff said. And before she could protest, he added, "So I can see where the hell I'm going."

And when he could see where he was going, Maggie

realized, he moved as smoothly and as confidently as any of the operatives she'd worked with. He took the front steps and moved to the side of the door. He held up his hand before she could kick through.

Geoff pointed to his eyes, then the door. It took her a moment to understand.

The demon was waiting for them—and looking at the door from the other side.

On the stairs, he mouthed clearly.

Her pulse raced, and she couldn't stop her grin. The British and American governments had no *idea* what they were missing.

He reached down and depressed the door handle. It opened easily.

Maggie swept through low, aimed—and froze. Katherine stood on the stair landing. Tall and dark, just like Geoff. Her eyes widened, and she raced down the stairs.

Geoff came in beside Maggie and raised his arms. His gun.

Oh, Jesus.

"No!" Maggie launched herself at him—too late.

He fired. Katherine's cheek opened up; blood spit across the wall beside her. She staggered, fell.

Maggie's weight knocked him to the side. He caught his footing, caught her with his free hand.

"Maggie! What the bloody . . ." He stopped, and his brow furrowed. "What are you seeing?"

She looked back at the stairs. Katherine stared at them, her gaze clouded with death. Crimson soaked into the cream-carpeted stair pillowing her head.

Coldly, Geoff aimed again. "My sister's eyesight isn't that good, Maggie."

And the wound on her cheek was healing.

The tricking, lying bastard. Maggie clenched her teeth and opened fire.

The demon lifted his head, the ragged wound opening with his grin. But he didn't stay Katherine and let them shoot him full of holes.

And knowing that a demon couldn't hurt them didn't make him any less terrifying when he shape-shifted.

The change was instantaneous.

If Geoff was looking through the demon's eyes, he wouldn't see the scales that covered the massive body, the glistening fangs, the ebony horns that curled back over his head. Hands became claws.

But it was the knees that made Maggie want to sink whimpering to the floor and curl into a ball. They were just *the wrong way*. Like a goat's hind legs, but she couldn't look at them without imagining her own knees snapping backward.

Maggie instinctively stepped back as the leathery wings snapped open and air gusted over her face. Her heart jumped into her throat as the taloned wing tips slammed into the stairwell walls, forming a barrier.

The message was clear: The demon couldn't harm them. But it didn't have to let them pass, either.

Where the hell was Sir Pup?

Geoff's gun clicked. Out of ammunition. And Maggie almost screamed as something brushed by her leg.

A dog. Golden retriever. Wearing a guide harness.

Oh, thank God.

"Yours, Mr. Blake?" The demon's grin spread wide over his fangs. A sword appeared in his hands. "Foolish. The Rules do not apply to animals—"

Sir Pup shifted as he leapt. Maggie grabbed Geoff's arm and swung him around, dropping them both to the ground.

She looked, but couldn't follow what happened. The demon crashed through a wall. A painting thumped to the floor beside Geoff's head, then tipped over them. The house shook. Sir Pup yelped, once, and the echoing growl that followed it turned her blood to ice.

Geoff squeezed her hand. Maggie pushed at the heavy frame. Beside them, a ripped piece of wing bled onto the floor.

"If Sir Pup uses his teeth," Maggie began, then shrank

back as something huge rushed by them—demon or hellhound, she couldn't be sure. The floor trembled.

Geoff pushed her tighter against the wall, shielding her with his body as she finished, "If Sir Pup bites him, his venom gets into the demon. Paralyzes him."

Paralyzes him was said into sudden, deathly silence.

Maggie sat up, and her hand flew to her mouth.

The once beautifully decorated house was destroyed. Plaster and drywall gaped open, exposing the walls' support posts like wooden bones. Carpeting had been shredded. There was blood . . . everywhere. On the furniture, the floors, the walls. Her stomach roiled.

"Bugger me," Geoff whispered beside her.

A shadow darkened the dining room wall. A shadow, Maggie realized, with three heads.

With his left head, Sir Pup dragged the demon beside him, knocking chairs out of his blooded path. He was limping, Maggie saw. Limping and bleeding.

The demon had the stump of a right arm and a bite taken out of his torso. And he was still alive.

She swallowed down the bile that rose and held back her shudder. "Hold him here, Sir Pup," she said. "We're going to get Katherine."

Geoff went up the stairs ahead of her. The door was locked. He slammed his shoulder against it, and it splintered open.

Katherine stood on the other side, holding the heavy antique lamp like a baseball bat. Uninjured, but obviously scared out of her wits.

Maggie reloaded her gun through their hasty reunion.

They weren't yet done.

Geoff dragged James inside while Maggie brought their rented vehicle to the house. Sir Pup could vanish the blood. They'd leave the broken mess.

Katherine found food in the kitchen and brought it out to the living room while they waited for James to wake up.

Geoff's sister didn't kick the mutilated and paralyzed demon when she walked by him, stretched out motionlessly on the floor beside James. Which meant, Maggie thought, that Katherine was a better woman than she would have been.

Geoff spent twenty minutes on the phone with Ames-Beaumont. "Uncle Colin has canceled his and Savi's flight," he told them. "And has scheduled ours for this evening."

Maggie nodded. It'd be enough time. James was already stirring.

"And he wants to know what they were looking for," Geoff said.

Katherine frowned. "I told you. Dragon blood." She looked at Maggie. "They said it was something that your congressman had. That he'd kept it since the war of the heavens, intending it for a time when it could be used. Now that your demon is dead, *he* wanted it." She pointed at the demon. "It's not much to speak of. A few drops trapped in a crystal rock."

Maggie forced herself to look again at the demon's missing arm, the wound in his side. How much power did a few drops have that the demon had gone through this?

"Do you know where it is, Kate?"

"Yes." She flipped over a blood-spattered cushion on a sofa and sat. "And I'll tell you where you can find it once we've reached San Francisco. You can hand it over to Uncle Colin, and he can give it over to the Guardians. If I don't, I suppose I'll soon be repeating this experience."

Geoff's face was grim. "And someone else will be forced into a demon's service."

It could have been me, Maggie thought. She sank into a shredded armchair and brought her legs up.

Langan would've known when he'd given James the assignment to kill Thomas Stafford that it couldn't be completed. It might have even been plotted by both demons, so that they would have—if they needed one—a hold over a human who could carry out assassinations, who didn't have to follow the Rules. It wouldn't have been the first time Stafford had used a human to kill for him.

And knowing her psychological profile, they'd probably even predicted that she'd fake James's death. But even if her resignation had surprised Langan, she had no doubt that her placement in Stafford's house had been his idea. He'd probably been the one to give Stafford that picture of her and James.

If the Guardians hadn't slain Stafford, what might have happened? Would she, too, have found herself trapped in a bargain—forced to kidnap or kill to save her soul?

She laid her cheek against her knees and closed her eyes. But it hadn't happened. Karma, luck, or maybe something else . . . She had escaped that fate, and ended up with Ames-Beaumont instead.

And Geoff.

Opening her eyes, she looked up and met his. They were slightly unfocused; they were never like that when he was looking through her. Her gaze moved to Katherine. His sister's stare was as intense as Geoff's could be.

She heard him say quietly, "Just a few more seconds, Kate."

How wonderful to have family, Maggie thought.

Especially this one.

Chapter Nine

They made it simple for James. They sat him on the sofa and explained what would happen if he ever spoke a word about Ames-Beaumont's family, or about what Geoff and Katherine could do.

They waited on the veranda while Sir Pup killed the demon in front of him.

When the hellhound was finished, Maggie cut through James's handcuffs and let him go.

Maggie awoke in a familiar bed that wasn't hers, with the most powerful vampire in the world glowering down at her.

She sat up, clutching royal blue satin to her chest. A chest that was, thank God, covered by the tank she wore beneath her uniform.

"Sir," she said, and in the course of the word, tried desperately to remember how she'd ended up sleeping in his mansion.

She *hadn't* fallen asleep on the plane. She *did* remember

disembarking, and that her employer and Savi had met them at the airport. She'd said, "Sir." He'd said, "Good God, Winters. You're bloody exhausted."

That was the last she could recall. Which probably meant that Ames-Beaumont had given her a psychic shove and *put* her to sleep.

He sat on the edge of the bed, avoiding the sunlight streaming in through the eastern windows. When she'd first met him, she would have sworn the sun rose every morning purely out of hope it might shine on his face. There was beautiful, and then there was Colin Ames-Beaumont. He . . . glowed. Not physically, she knew, but psychically. The first weeks of her employment had been filled with humiliating leaps of her heart every time he'd entered the room she was in. Then she'd adjusted, the psychic effect had worn off, and she'd finally been able to look at him without catching her breath.

His deep frown could still affect her heart rate, though. She waited, holding her breath.

"I am disturbed, Winters." His gaze, when it met hers, was slightly accusing. "I believe my nephew plans to steal you away from me."

Her fingers clutched the sheet more tightly. God, she wished whoever had put her to bed had left her uniform on. "I have no intention of giving up my position here, sir."

He tilted his head, and the sun hit the wild disarray of his hair, lighting the burnished gold. Mirrors were of no use to him, and Maggie knew he didn't possess a single comb. "I can hear them plotting downstairs. My own family. She tells him where the dragon blood is, and he says he will persuade me to allow you to accompany him while he retrieves it."

Maggie's expression was a perfect blank. "It would be prudent, sir, for someone to accompany him—and to protect him."

His gaze narrowed. "He also intends to spend a good fortnight flying about the world, so that if he were to be followed by some unknown party, they would lose track of him."

"That also seems a well-conceived plan, sir."

"A bloody expensive one, if you ask me. And what will I do, Winters? You cannot serve me if you are family."

"I do not *serve* you, Mr. Ames-Beaumont. I am employed by you. I do not see any reason for that relationship to alter, whatever my relationship with Mr. Blake may become."

He stood and slid his hands into the pockets of his tailored trousers. A pleased expression lit his features. "If you do become family, Winters—I suppose that means I will be able to pay you less?"

"I think, sir, you would have to pay me more."

The vampire heaved a melodramatic sigh and turned toward the sitting room. "Do not break his heart, Winters, or we will have words."

Maggie began to breathe again. She must have been breathing his entire visit—she only just now realized she was able to.

"And if he breaks mine, sir?"

He looked back and flashed a grin that seemed to be all fangs. "I would have to thrash him quite soundly. I have many nephews, but there is only one Winters."

She was still clutching the sheet to her chest when Geoff came through the sitting room doors.

And she couldn't allow this to happen again. Geoff in *her* bedroom? Yes. In her employer's house? In his *bed?*

Far too awkward.

Geoff stopped at the foot of the bed. His hair was still damp from a shower, his jeans and T-shirt new. His gaze locked with hers.

And he couldn't see her at all.

Her heart slipped into a heavy, steady beat.

"Uncle Colin said he spoke with you."

"He did." She threw back the covers and held his gaze as she walked on her knees to the end of the mattress. "And apparently, we will be spending the next two weeks in each other's company."

He reached out, his fingers brushing the sides of her waist. Her skin tightened and prickled with delicious sensation. "I'll be happy with a fortnight in your garden, Maggie."

She touched his jaw. "I wouldn't be."

"And I lied." His laugh rumbled over her fingers. "I wouldn't be, either. Ah, Maggie. I'm pushing you into this too fast."

"What makes you think I can be pushed anywhere I don't want to go?"

"No, I don't suppose you could be." He drew a deep breath. "Look, I ought to tell you—I crossed lines, Maggie. I had reason to go over your files, but I went over them again and again, and I went deeper than I should have. I was desperate to know you. If James hadn't taken Katherine, if we'd met later, after I'd moved here, I'd have pushed you then. And if you'd said no, I'd likely have followed you everywhere in hope that someone would look at you, so that I could, too."

Did he expect her to back away because of that? Not a chance. She didn't know what they had now or what it would be, but she was going to grab on to it—on to him—and hold tight.

"So, stalking and surveillance." She shook her head, smiling. "To someone like me, that's either a precursor to killing someone . . . or to sleeping with them. So I think we'll work out fine."

He was still laughing when she bent forward and eased her mouth over his. Last time, she'd surprised him. It had been just a press of lips, her hands through his hair. Now she took her time, explored his taste, sought more of him to touch.

His hands at her hips pulled her closer, and he was warm, hot, would burn her alive.

Her pulse raced when she pulled away. "Not here," she panted. "I can't here."

His large hand cupped her cheek. He kissed her again, then nodded. And she felt his disappointment when he let her go.

She walked past him, into the bathroom, and closed the door. A wall panel, when she slid it aside, revealed the one mirror in the house. He would see her there. She would lean back against the door, and he would lift her, and watch her face as she welcomed him in.

And it would be hard the first time, and rough, because she cared so much she knew that she'd be a little careless.

But it wouldn't be her employer's bed. She cracked the door open again and called out softly, "Mr. Blake?"